# On the Spot

## AW Gardner

Pen Press

46 406 044 9

First published in Great Britain by Pen Press

All paper used in the printing of this book has been made from
wood grown in managed, sustainable forests.

ISBN 978-1-78003-424-9

Printed and bound in the UK
Pen Press is an imprint of
Indepenpress Publishing Limited
25 Eastern Place
Brighton
BN2 1GJ

A catalogue record of this book is available from
the British Library

Cover design by Jacqueline Abromeit

*To Richard Walduck OBE JP DL MA*

# About the Author

Alf Gardner was born in Islington, London, 27th April 1918. He left school at 14 years of age (no choice, as this was the school leaving age then). He served with the Royal Engineers in Norway, Africa, India and Burma; at one time was Company Sergeant Major with the 4th Field Company Engineers (the same company mentioned in this book); and served with the Royal West African Frontier Force for 5 years ('Royal' granted to the WAFF in 1920 for loyal service to the Crown).

He was married for 53 years to the girl who waited those long war years, settled in Hertfordshire. When his wife died in 1998, he remained in Herts. with memories that never die.

Other titles by AW Gardner:
*Na Godé*
*Take a Coffin*
*No Coffins*
*The Golden Stool*

# PROLOGUE

The outskirts of Manchester, 1918.

'It's on the other side, yes?'

'Yes, sir.'

'Well, if you think I'm going to climb over that, you can think again. Catch my "tonsils" straddled astride the top, my wife will not be a happy one.'

Detective Sergeant Ted Warren was referring to a six-foot-high chain link fence, stretched taunt between concrete posts, which seemed to go on for miles. His 'sidekick' Detective Constable James Greaves, knowing the sergeant's wife, hid a smile.

The DS peered through a gap in the unkempt hawthorn that bordered the fence. His eyes searched the rough ground, covered by weed-topped knee high grass that encroached almost to the sleepers of a railway track.

'I can't see it.'

'Not from here you won't, sir; it's covered by the long grass,' the sergeant from the local nick said.

'So who did?'

'A railway worker, a wheel tapper, walks the track periodically to inspect the lines, went for a slash, nearly pissed on it, spotted a foot.'

'And did he?'

'Did he what?'

'Piss on it.'

'You will have to ask him.'

'Where is he?'

'At the railway station. I told him to wait there.'

'How far, the station?'

'Half a mile or more.'

'What's "or more"?'

'More like a mile.'

'Christ! So why bring me here? I ain't a bloody monkey, you know; did you expect me to climb over the fence? Get some stepladders.'

'I think this is where the body was put over the fence, and whoever did it climbed over to hide it in the long grass.'

'You do, do you?'

'Twigs have been forced down, some partly broken at the top of the hedge; thought you would want to see for yourself. That's why I brought you here.'

The DS looked around. 'This footpath, used much?'

'It's a short cut to the station for some who live alongside here; some have a door in the garden fence, come out the back way. Not after dark; a bit dodgy as there are no lights.'

'Those fences that run along that side, you mean.'

'Yes. The path is railway land; get to it from an alley between the houses back a bit, ends at the railway station.'

'I take it we can walk along the track.'

'Yes, via the station platform, I have a constable on duty there, making sure no one ventures near.'

'Good, you did well. Forget the stepladders. Hope it's not more than a mile; let's do a "shanks's".'


'About time you lot got here; I've been hanging about for more than two hours. I shall want paying for that.'

They were greeted by an irate grizzled railway worker, who rose from a platform bench at the railway station to meet them.

2

'Have you now?' the DS exclaimed. 'The constable has also been waiting, and we have been traipsing more than a mile to get here, and faced with the same to get to where the body is and back again. I take it you are the one that found the body, found more then you bargained for; that'll teach you to piddle on Mother Nature. Could be charged with exposing yourself.'

'What? Who to? Nobody out there.'

'If there was a train passing and folk looking out of the windows there would be; 's right, DC?'

'Yes sir, very serious offence.'

The wheel-tapper looked at the DS, the DC, then the sergeant and finally to the constable, who pursed his lips and nodded.

'You're taking me on.'

'More like taking you to the nick as a suspect.'

'What for? I ain't done anything.'

'But you can do. Uphold the law by answering a few questions.'

'Oh, I see! Pleased to help; I was joking when I said I wanted paying.'

'Yeah, I guess you was. So. What time did you – ah – spot the body?'

'Now let me see, yes, it was 9.35.'

'You railway workers always know the time?'

'Yeah, part of our job; we don't have to ask a policeman.'

'Oh, very funny. Did you finish?'

'Finish? What? Oh, yeah. Pissed myself and scooted back to the station, told the station master who sent for the police.'

'Did you touch anything?'

'Not bloody likely. Showed the sergeant where the body was, or rather pointed it out, from the track; didn't want to look.'

3

'See anybody when you was inspecting the track?'

'No, not a soul.'

'Right, that's all for now; may want to speak to you again. What's your name?'

'Jimmy Walters.'

'Is that "Jimmy" as in "James"?'

'Dunno, always been called Jimmy.'

'Well, Jimmy, don't go mouthing to the press; I don't want it known yet that we've found a body. Mum's the word. Understand? Otherwise…'

He left the sentence unfinished. Jimmy nodded.

'Right, you can clock off now.'

The constable led them to the scene of the crime, marked by a stake driven into the ground.

'Don't they ever cut the grass?' the DS asked. 'It's like looking for a needle in a haystack. Or would have been if Jimmy boy hadn't gone for a "Jimmy". Cockneys, eh! Jimmy riddle-piddle.' He laughed. The DC raised his face to the heavens and rolled his eyes.

The DS knelt alongside the body. Naked – face down, the head skewed to one side, the jaw tight against the right shoulder. The legs slightly apart, the grass growing between, likewise between the arms and body, and around the perimeter, ruffled by a gentle breeze, entwining, forming nature's shroud to respect the dead.

'Neck broken,' the DS began. 'Take note, James. And not by accident. Not sunburnt, so not been here long; not thrown from a passing train; killed close to where he was put over the fence, as you said, Sergeant; smudge marks on the back, The body used as a stepping stone?' He turned the body over. 'Abrasions across the stomach. Yeah, from the top of the fence and hedge, possibly? Circumcised. That does not necessarily make him Jewish; certainly not a German.' He examined the hands. 'Not a labouring type, more sedentary. Know what it means, James?' Turning to his DC.

'Yeah, sitting on his arse behind a desk mostly.'

'Right – you've got the picture. Can't see any distinguishing marks; leave that to the Path boys. Why stripped naked?' He stood. 'Any ideas?'

'Didn't want the body identified by the clobber he was wearing. Maker's name or tabs we could check on? Dunno really, don't add up.'

'How about you, Sergeant?' the DS asked, addressing the local sergeant. 'What's your name, by the way?'

'Wayne, Robert Wayne, sir. Could've been a deserter from the army: had enough of the trenches, wanted civilian clothes, couldn't go home, knew the redcaps would be waiting.'

'A possibility. Drilled in unarmed combat, arm around the neck from behind, one hand on the chin, click-clunk: dead duck. Myself, I think this was premeditated: knew what he was doing, stalked his victim, picked his time. Revenge.'

'But why strip the bloke?' the DC asked.

'Some form of ritual, payback time, leave him with nothing, naked to the world. The first thing is to find out who he is – or rather who he was. I'll shove off, arrange for the body to be collected. You stay here, James: search the area; the sergeant and constable will help; see if anything was dropped by the killer to give us a clue, though I very much doubt it. Make a list of the names and addresses of all that work at the station; I'll deal with them later. Then—' He turned to the sergeant. 'You can help out here, Robert. That's a good name for a bobby; are you called "Bob"?'

'Off duty at times.'

'Well, it will have to be Sergeant Robert, I guess. Being local, when the DC has finished here, visit the occupiers of the houses behind the footpath with him, ask if anyone heard or saw anything unusual, be diplomatic, don't give too much away. My guv will let your chief know you are doing a bit of detective work for us. That all right with you?'

'Yes, sir. Only too pleased to.'

'Good. You could also enquire on the side; if any person's reported missing, pass the message to me at our HQ. You know where?'

'Yes, sir.'

'Right, I'll get going; see you back at HQ, James, when you've finished here.'

'We can give you a bunk over the fence, save you a walk.'

The DS looked at the top wire strung along the top of the fence, the barbs of the straggly hawthorn. 'No, I don't think so.'

'We can lift you, the three of us, cock your legs over the top; you can sit and slide down the other side.'

He hesitated, nodded. 'All right.' Held one hand under his crotch for protection. 'Let's do it.'

Looked down where he had landed, swore. 'Sod it.'

'What's the matter?' the DC asked as he peered through the fence.

'Dogs crap, that's what's the matter; you bloody idiots dropped me in it.'

Late that evening Sergeant Robert Wayne wiped his boots on the doormat, heard the voice call out, 'Take 'em off.' Ignored it and entered the kitchen. Took off his tunic, hung it on the back of a chair, sat down and placed his elbows on the table in front. His wife, standing at the sink, turned, looked at the tunic, said, 'And the boots, take 'em off.'

'No, they're clean, unlike those of the DS covered with you know what. Step in it, brings good luck.' He chuckled. 'We dropped him in it.'

6

'That's funny, is it? For heaven's sake, grow up. And who is this DS?'

'A detective sergeant. We had to laugh.'

'I suppose you are going to tell me, otherwise you will sulk all night.'

'Well, if you don't want to know, it's about a murder.'

'A murder? Oh, my God.'

'Thought you might be interested. Yes?'

So his wife sat and listened while Bob Wayne related the events, finishing with, 'The DS asked me to help with the enquiries as I am local. So you could say I'm working under cover.'

'Under cover! You've been reading too many tuppenny "who done it" novels. Under cover in bed, more likely.'

'Well, I'm good at that under the covers; you ought to know.'

*Two weeks later*

Inspector Wainwright, sitting behind his desk in an office of a division of CID, looked up as DS Warren entered.

'You wanted to see me, sir?'

'Yes, sit down, Ted. What's the latest on the naked body case?'

The DS spread his fingers. 'Nil – not a sausage – who is he, where did he come from, where was he going: not a clue. Assume he was on the way to the railway station when he was killed; there again, he could have been arriving. Did he reside here, know the footpath was a short cut to the station? All enquiries have drawn blank. Missing persons? Nobody wants to know; the public have had enough of the war, lists of missing persons in the press, assumed killed in action. What they mean is blown to smithereens. What's one more dead? We are stumped at the moment, chief; until we discover who he is – or should it be "who he was"? – we are not going anywhere.'

'All right, I get the picture. Keep probing; with a bit of luck, something might turn up.'

'The sergeant from the local nick called to the scene: seems a bright spark, knows the neighbourhood. I used him to help with enquiries, told him to keep his nose to the ground, let me know if he hears anything; that all right with you, chief?'

'Yes, I'll let his chief know, don't want him to think we are overriding his authority. Do the best you can, don't lose too much sleep over it. You realise we can't keep the body too long in the morgue; if no one claims the body, say another couple of weeks, if will have to be a lime pit.'

Sergeant Robert Wayne, sheltering from a cloud burst in the doorway of the tobacconist and newsagent-cum-sweet shop, watched the raindrops bounce off the pavement. *Rain, rain, go away, come again on washing day, or was it 'another day'? We sang that when we were kids.* He was at a loss, having questioned shopkeepers – the butcher, the baker, the candlestick maker – narks, spivs, the tarts that frequented the dives, sitting with backs to the wall, skirts above crossed knees, the price chalked on the underside of a shoe sole that could be elevated to be visible to a would-be punter. All to no avail; now he was down in the dumps, cheesed off with jibes from his wife about his undercover work, although said with a smile as she appreciated his exploration undercover in bed, nevertheless wearing a bit thin.

He was contemplating what other avenue he could explore when the rain ceased as suddenly as it had started. The sun shone; the paving slabs steamed; he brightened, decided to visit the crime scene again for maybe an inspiration, arrived at the junction of Station Road and the alley leading to the railway footpath and stopped for a moment. Two soldiers marching in step passed him by, then it hit him, like a bolt of lightning. Transfixed he croaked, 'The uniform. He wanted the uniform.' His voice dry with the excitement that he may have found the inspiration he was looking for. The spittle came; he called out, 'You two – wait – wait.'

The two soldiers halted, turned. 'You calling out to us?' one asked.

'Yes, I want to ask a few questions.'

'You're not a redcap and we have a train to catch.'

'Yeah, I know, but I *am* a police sergeant.' He paused, not wanting to get off on the wrong foot. 'Sorry, I won't keep you long, just some information; it is important,'

'Yeah, all right, but don't take too long about it.'

'You come from here?'

'Yeah, both of us, been on leave, now on the way back to our unit.'

'By train, I take it?'

'And by ferry, across the moat as the froggies call it.'

'What other army personnel would use the train?'

'That's a stupid question, any of 'em would.'

'Of course, I'm not thinking straight. From here, I mean, not on leave.'

'There is the old TA quarters and drill hall near Wythenshawe. They could, some of the staff.'

'Do you have to report there when you arrive and leave?'

'No. We gets our pass and travel warrant from our own unit, and the redcaps come looking for us if we don't get back on time. If anything happens, like an accident, or something "beyond our control" as in army jargon, we reports to the nearest army depot or a police station to cover ourselves, as we don't want to get shot for desertion.'

'So, if someone went missing, the army would know?'

'Of course.'

9

'This depot at the old TA quarters: you know anything about it?'

'Not much: a holding unit, shuffles men about; you'd better ask them. A retired colonel is in charge, promotes war savings.'

'Thanks. I'd buy you a pint if you had time.'

'We will have when we gets to Dover.'

Wayne laughed, dug in his pocket for a shilling. 'That'll buy you a pint each and five Woodbines.'

The one who took it spat on it before pocketing it. 'Say cheers, Jack,' he said. 'Let's go.'

They turned and marched away. Jack called over his shoulder, 'Thanks, Sarge.'

Wayne couldn't report to DS Warren quick enough. He set off at a fast pace unbecoming of a police sergeant. 'Has to be a soldier – has to be a soldier,' he muttered in time with his step. He halted at the entrance to the police station that housed the offices of the division of the CID, straightened his tunic, steadied his breathing and entered. The desk sergeant looked up.

'Well, I'll be damned if it isn't old Bob Wayne; bit out of bounds, aren't we?'

'Hullo, Randy; not so much of the "old". Long time no see.'

'Yeah, last time I danced with your wife, very nice.'

'You did?'

'Police ball, before the war. A tango, real sexy, wow.'

'I don't remember.'

'You were too pissed at the time. Ask your wife; tell her I look forward to the next time if they ever start again. So, what are you doing in this neck of the woods?'

'Come to have a word with DS Warren.'

'Anything I should know?'

'You had better ask him.'

'Don't get shirty, Bob, it was only a dance.'

'Have some information on an ongoing murder case that happened on my patch; I was involved.'

'You didn't do it? All right, all right, only joking.' Holding his hands up. 'Second floor, the name's on his door, knock loud as he's probably taking a nap.'

The DS wasn't asleep, was standing looking out of a window when Wayne walked in after knocking. Wayne took a quick glance around the room. Two desks with chairs, a typewriter on each, vying for space amongst the clutter of open files, bottles of ink, pens, ash trays and half opened packets of cigarettes. A filing cabinet against one wall, a map of the area pinned to a board, a calendar hanging alongside. *Not very impressive.*

DS Warren turned. 'Ah, Sergeant Wayne. Hope you have brought something for us to grasp at, as at present we haven't a straw.'

'I think maybe, sir? It struck me, on seeing a couple of soldiers on the way to the railway station, that it could have been a soldier that was killed.'

'A soldier? But why strip the body?'

'The killer wanted the uniform.'

'Never gave that a thought. Who would want a uniform? Plenty of them going spare.'

'Sorry, just a thought. There is an old TA depot near Wythenshawe; they would know if anyone from there is missing, and we've had no joy from our enquiries as to missing persons, and the weeks are passing...'

'Robert, you have brought us a straw; you're looking at a drowning man, so let's grab it.' He scribbled on a sheet of paper and placed it on one of the desks. 'A note for the DC,' he said. 'Let's go.'

The RSM. A row of medals in a neat strip was pinned to his left breast; he sported a moustache, the ends waxed to fine points – two rapiers ready for the thrust. He eyed the two of them up. 'You in charge, sergeant?

The two in question, DS Warren and Sergeant Wayne, had been questioned at the guardroom and finally led to the office of this 'patriarch' they were now facing, a defender of the British Empire of days past.

'No, sir, Detective Sergeant Warren CID is.'

'Plain clothes, eh! Don't like it.'

'Goes with the job, Sergeant Major,' the DS responded, taking some form of control.

'Still don't like it; should wear a uniform. So, what do you want?'

'To enquire if anyone is missing from your establishment.'

'Missing? No, and if there was it would be down to the military police to sort it.'

'Sorry, Sergeant Major, I should have mentioned it at the beginning: we are investigating a murder, no identity as to the victim, all our enquiries to date have proved fruitless. No persons reported missing, going back some weeks. We understand the army would know if any serving went missing, AWOL, and we gave it a thought that the victim could have been a soldier.'

'You would know if it was, surely?'

'No, sir, the body was stripped naked.'

'Oh, I see. Well, not from here, I can assure you. We are a small unit made up of time expired reservists, our colonel brought back from retirement to promote war savings, acts as CO. Captain Richards acts as Adjutant and as movement officer. A sergeant – was colour sergeant on recruitment until 1916 when conscription came into force, now twiddles his thumbs – a corporal and eight privates; that's about it. I know them all.'

'You mention Captain Richards as movement officer. So you have other army personnel passing through?'

12

'Yes. Better have a word with him; he'll put you in the picture.'

The two moved up an echelon, to Captain Richards's office.

'Yes, we do.' Captain Richards answered the DS's question. 'Only officers and warrant officers from overseas – the Far East. They report here on arrival. I issue leave and travel warrants. Some return to their units abroad after leave, others to "home" units – theirs not to reason why; I will not go into detail. All postings of officers and warrant officers come through the War Office.'

'How about anyone leaving here between four and six weeks ago?' the DS asked.

'That's no trouble; not many, mainly in dribs and drabs. Two if I remember right.' He reached for a file. 'Yes, one officer, one warrant officer. Here it is. The WO went back to his own unit abroad, the officer to the Essex Regiment.'

'Would you know if one went missing?'

'Missing, why would they go missing? I wouldn't know; once they leave here it is not my concern. Oh, I see, you think your victim could be one of ours?'

'Well, if you would be prepared to look at the corpse, identify if it is one of the two, it would help our enquiry.'

'Yes, of course.' He looked at his watch. 'A bit late now, say 0900 hours tomorrow?'

'Fine, sir; meet you at the morgue.'

'That body? You will have to dig it up, but I doubt whether you would be able to identify anyone after it's been lying in lime.' An apparition in a smirched, soiled smock and skullcap answered DS Warren's question through a square of gauze strapped across his nose and mouth.

'Christ!' said Warren. 'Who authorised the burial of the corpse?'

13

'Christ, you said? No, he doesn't pay the rent. There's a limit to the time we can keep the dead. If no one claims the body, it's the lime pit.'

Captain Richards looked at the other two. 'Sorry I can't help, then; I'll have to be away.' He paused. 'Was there any identification at all on the body?'

'No, none, only that he had been circumcised.'

'Well, it could not have been the warrant officer, as he had a tattoo on his right forearm.'

'Could you find out if the other officer did arrive at his destination?'

'Now you are asking for the moon. I'll try my damnedest, will take some time.'

'Thanks. By the way, what is the name of the officer?'

'Blankensy. A Major Blankensy.'


## The CID offices

DS Warren knocked on the inspector's door and waited for the 'Come in' before entering.

'You sent for me, sir?'

'Yes. I wanted you to know I have heard from Captain Richards about the officer we thought might be missing, Well, he isn't. He arrived at the regiment he was posted to. The "Essex", at present somewhere in France. So we are back where we started.'

'Blast, and I thought we were getting somewhere, and we haven't even a body since it was dumped in a lime pit.'

'It would appear the theory that the killer was a deserter on the run wanting a full kit of civvy clobber is the best bet, but I doubt if the army would give us a list of deserters. They look after their own. Keep probing, Ted; we need a bit of luck with this one. Concentrate on missing persons. It could well be that the victim wasn't going to the station, just unlucky, about the right size for the killer.'

'Yes, sir.'

# PART ONE

*9 November 1918*

The German government accepted the armistice conditions. The stage was set to end the bloodiest war man had ever known.

*11 November 1918*

At 5 am in a railway carriage stationed in the forest of Compiègne the armistice was signed, giving six hours to the moment it would come in force.

*Whom the gods would destroy, they first send mad.*

Euripides

## 10 January 1919, Shepton Mallet, Somerset

Snow had fallen during the night, spreading a white blanket to enfold the discarded human matter, dog-ends and dogs turds. A prisoner in full marching order, minus arms, a kitbag balanced across his backpack squared to box shape by cut cardboard, marched in the gutter with an escort in front and one behind, their boots crunching the snow underfoot. The NCO in charge, on the pavement alongside, matched the pace. They halted at the massive iron clad door let in the outer walls to the 'glasshouse', the military prison.[1]

'Escort stand aside – stand easy,' the NCO ordered.

Eyes observed them from behind an iron grill let in a small side portal. They waited. The prisoner stood at attention, and in spite of the cold, beads of sweat appeared on his forehead. Finally they heard bolts being withdrawn, locks undone, the jangle of keys as the door was opened and a voice yelled, 'On the spot – double mark time.'

Immediately the NCO countermanded the order with 'Escort and prisoner stand firm.' He then turned to the figure that had appeared. 'Not yet; I'm in charge out here until you sign for the body.' He held out a clipboard. 'Here.'

---

[1] The first building used as a military prison was at Aldershot in 1894 and had a glazed roof. To 'Tommy Atkinses' it was 'the Glasshouse'. The name stuck, and was used to refer to all military prisons that followed.

The guard, red in face, blustered, 'You been here before, have you, you jumped up two striper; know it all, eh?'

The NCO nodded. 'Yeah, I have, and don't try to take it out on the prisoner.'

'It's regulations; prisoners double march everywhere, and on the spot.'

'Not out here he don't. Just sign and we'll be off.' He looked at the signature. 'I'll remember the name.'

The portal closed behind the prisoner and they heard the command shouted: 'On the spot – double mark time.'

The NCO let his breath out. 'All right, you two, let's get back to the station.'

'Blimey, Corp, I fought that guard was gonner explode; you 'aven't done ti—'

The corporal cut him short. 'Just thank your lucky star it wasn't you going in there.'

'Did yer know the prisoner, Corp, sticking yer neck out for 'im back there, as 'e's not from our mob?' Sapper Harry Parker, one of the escorts, inquisitive by name and nature, being a Cockney, asked on the way to the railway station.

'Yeah, I think so, but he wouldn't know me.' *My mum wouldn't have recognised me then, the state of me clock.*

Harry looked at the ugly wound running from under the corporal's peaked cap to a deformed cheekbone. 'Was it to do wiv—'

'Something the matter with your nose, sapper?'

'No, Corp.'

'There will be, any more questions. So put a sock in it.'

'Sorry, Corp.' Harry had to get the last word in.

'We can relax now the prisoner is off our hands. Get some shut eye,' said the corporal. They were entrained, escort duty *finito*. The NCO sitting on one seat, back against the corner near the window, the other two on the seat opposite,

19

one to each corner, in an otherwise empty carriage compartment.

'Good,' said Sapper Parker. 'I'll kip in the luggage rack.'

'No you bloody well won't. Pull the blinds down; if anyone tries to enter, tell 'em we have a dangerous prisoner likely to go berserk at any time, and no more chit-chat.'

Corporal Clive Jones stretched out across the seat and closed his eyes.

*There was a time when Clive would have not been noticed: nondescript, average height, average build, clothes off the peg, pass in a crowd unnoticed. At school in Wales he was taught English and Welsh. At home his father insisted Welsh only be spoken. Jones senior did not care much for those living the other side of Monmouth, the only benefit being that English pubs opened on Sundays: midday until two, and six to ten in the evening. So, hardly scraping a living, he admitted defeat. Upped stakes and with family moved to London Town to make his fortune. (The streets are paved with gold, aren't they? Those the other side of the Irish sea said so.) With his meagre savings rented a small shop with rooms above, situated in a side street off Camden Town high street, and became 'Jones the baker' and spoke English. Made and sold pastry, squeezed a table and chairs alongside the counter; for the princely sum of tuppence, a cup of tea with a crusty cheese roll was available for the local office workers during their break. Other pastries enticingly for sale under glass on the counter.*

*Clive grew up to master the London dialect and Cockney rhyming slang and became of age, no longer to share a room with his two younger sisters. Two years managing on a 'put you up' in the small sitting room, work scarce. Not wanting to be a burden on his parents, decided it was time to fly the nest, landed in Brompton barracks at Chatham and became a sapper in the Royal Engineers. He answered to the name Jones on roll call; if he had enlisted in a Welsh regiment it would have been 'Jones 213' or '214' or '215', or whatever the last three digits of his army number were, as there could have been a dozen with the same name in the regiment. A Celtic lilt to his voice, and the name; his mates in the army had him pinned down as 'Taffy'. An assassination in Sarajevo triggered a world war – be all over by Christmas – it lasted four years. A stripe added to the chevron on Clive's sleeves, and it was Corporal Jones RE.*

Clickity clack – clickity clack – the wheels rhymed, the carriage swayed. Corporal Jones turned over, murmured, 'Yeah it must be him. The nose. I could see the nose, he was carrying me. Sod you, Parker, lifting the shades.' Lulled as in a crib, he drifted into hell.

*The Somme, 1916. 'Over the top, lads, through our wire; spread out in line, don't run, it will be a walkover.' Yeah, a cakewalk, I don't think. Silence, the barrage lifted, the big guns silenced too soon, not half way across, the fireworks start, 'O God our help in ages past.' Skittles – no, not skittles, men – fall. 'Has the bonfire gone out, Mum?' I can't see, pain pain go away come again another day, no – rain rain go away come again on washing day, that's it, rain rain wash the blood away. I can see a nose, one eye – am I a cyclops? Where's me other one, where am I? What'd you say? Can't hear... 'Casualty, you're lucky, would have bled to death if the sergeant hadn't brought you in.' Sergeant? What sergeant? Dunno.*

Clive Jones no longer 'nondescript'. No two scars are the same. A fingerprint of the war had left him identifiable.

Back at the glasshouse, the prisoner, stripped naked, was standing rigid to attention, knuckles clenched, thumbs pointing down in line with where the seams of his trousers would be when they were worn. His nose and big toes touching the dank bare brick wall he was facing. He could hear the sound of boots pounding the quadrangle to the command, 'On the spot, double mark time,' the smell of carbolic in his nostrils.

Bill Cox, late of the Palestine police (time expired), well versed in the use of the billy club – the steel tip of a boot – the butt of a rifle, and with no compunction as to who was on the receiving end, had the necessary credentials to apply and was accepted as staff to the notorious glasshouse. This suited him to the ground: to inflict mental and physical pain, without any comebacks, on the inmates. Although most of them were the toughest lowlifes in the British Army, none wanted to come back or boast 'done it on my eyebrows' after finishing their sentence.

Sadistic bastard that he was, he felt a pang of compassion as he gazed at the back of the latest admission. Raised his swagger cane, which was a permanent feature of his daily life (it was said it lay alongside him in bed). Changed his mind from the usual tickling the kidneys (prodding the small of the back) and lightly touched with the brass ferrule tip of his cane the puckered scar tissue under the right shoulder blade, standing out in relief against the skin pallor and goose pimples.

'Went right through, Roberts?'

'Took a piece of sternum with 'em, Staff.'

'High velocity?'

'So they said, Staff.'

'I heard you were likened to the proverbial cat with nine lives; used them all up now, eh? Hit your spine on the way in, or an inch or two to the left, it would have been your ticker gone for a Burton, and you would have been knocking at the pearly gates, or most likely stoking up down below, instead of spending the next six months here.'

Roberts never answered.

Bill Cox inspected the army issue kit laid out on the floor. All items in the right order as per regulations. He noticed the darker shade of khaki where a sergeant's chevrons had been removed from the sleeves of the tunic, the faintest marks of stitching, an MM ribbon on the breast. Resisted the usual procedure to use the boot to send the articles flying, and the remark, 'Call that laid out correct? Do it again.' Nodded.

'You don't give orders any more, Roberts. You get the same treatment as the rest of the prisoners. Ask permission to speak, otherwise you don't speak unless spoken to. Scrub your webbing, no blanco. Double everywhere, and on the spot at times. You know the drill, probably brought a few here in charge of the escort yourself. I know what you did, Roberts. Broke his jaw. You should have killed the bastard; I would have done.' Without warning Cox bellowed, 'ABOUT TURN.'

Ex-sergeant Roberts swivelled on his bare right heel; the left followed and he came to attention facing the warden.

'Christ Almighty,' Bill Cox exclaimed as he gazed at the numerous frontal scars. 'That wasn't smallpox.'

'Potato masher, Staff, the Somme.' A German stick grenade.

'That's what you get for being a bloody hero. Were you passed A1 on discharge from the hospital?'

'I guess so, Staff.'

'Short arm inspection, was it? Cough, they lifted your knackers – fit' He laughed. 'Don't want you to die on us in here; we'll see.' His voice rose. 'On the spot, double mark time. Knees up – up – up.'

Roberts's knees rose and fell, his bare feet pounding the deck, genitalia swinging in time.

'Sod it,' Bill Cox murmured. Shouted, 'Halt.' He glanced down; a vestige of a smile creased his lips. 'Everything seems to be working fine. You don't deserve this, Roberts. First ablution, get dressed in fatigues, barber's to get cropped, then I'll find you a cell for you to sit and ponder.'

The train stopped with a jerk and a hiss of steam. Corporal Clive Jones woke with a start – back to reality – took a deep breath and sat up.

'Sod you, Parker.'

'That's twice you said that, Corp, once in yer sleep.'

'Well, sod you again; that makes it three times. Where are we?'

'Slough, I fink.' He pulled up the blinds and looked out. 'Yeah, gotta change.'

## Chatham

The sentry didn't give them a second glance as the trio passed the guardroom.

After a change of trains, a march from the station, they were back in Brompton Barracks, where Clive's first day as a soldier had begun almost seven years ago.

'You two, back to the platoon; I'll report in at the coy office.' Corporal Jones gave the order.

'Any trouble, Corporal?' the CSM asked as Jones entered and closed the door behind him.

'No, sir; all delivered in one piece and signed for,' Clive answered as he handed the signed document to the sergeant major.

24

'Right, then it's back to routine playing at soldiers now.' He grimaced. 'Barrack half empty, no recruits; where they gonner come from, eh? Heaven knows. All those poor sods that volunteered, and the conscripts, wiped off the face of the earth, not one to replace them. How comes we're still here, Jones, can you answer that? No, lucky ain't we, but you nearly bought it. As for me, not a scratch; well, a gouge out of my right forearm parrying a bayonet before mine went in. I didn't know him; he didn't know me; if I hadn't killed him, he would have killed me. Funny old world, ain't it? Kill or be killed, us regulars were taught that, God forgive us, but some deserved to die young. Think of it that way if your conscience troubles you. What am I going on about? Change the subject. You staying on?'

'What?'

'Signing on again; your seven years is nearly up.'

'Hadn't thought about it.'

'Well, think of it before it expires. The CRE will be asking.'

'Yeah, will do, Sergeant Major. Can I ask you something?'

'Depends.'

'That prisoner, do you know anything of him?'

'Why?'

'I think he was the sergeant who saved my life in '16.'

'Why didn't you ask him?'

'Regulations. Not allowed to converse with a prisoner on escort duty.'

'For Chissakes, you could have asked him that.'

'I never thought about it until on the way back, when Parker started asking questions.'

'Forget it, Corporal. The war's over; let it drop; better that way.'

'I thought I had, but it's back to haunt me now. I have to know if it was him.'

'All I know is that he was court martialled for striking a superior officer, reduced to the ranks, and got six months in the glasshouse.'

'Why did we get the job as escort, and not some from his own mob?'

'You fathom it out.'

'You don't think because—'

'No.' The CSM cut him short. 'No, I don't. Ours is not to reason why, remember?'

'But it seems such a coincidence, me getting picked to be in charge of the escort.'

The CSM cast his eyes to the ceiling, shook his head. 'Look, Corporal, finish this right now. You've had a long day, the past caught up with you, made you think of it; forget it, let sleeping dogs lie. Get yourself smartened up, get down to town, have a few drinks to drown it, get pissed. If the Marines are dusting up the navy as usual, don't get involved.[2] Be on parade in the morning. No black eyes. That's it, now go.'

'One more question, Sergeant Major, What regiment was he from?'

'Persistent sod, aren't you, Jones? The Essex. Now shove off, not another word.'

As the door closed behind the corporal, the C.S.M. muttered, 'Coincidence, who was it said that? Coincidence, no such thing; it's fate, kismet.'

---

[2] Marines were originally stationed aboard naval ships to quell a rioting strike by naval ratings. Henceforth they were not on good terms with those who had to be subdued, and for many years to come with serving sailors. Other than the REs both had barracks at Chatham, and after a 'few' drinks at the same bar, and a snide remark passed, they were at each other's throats.

*9 November 1918, the Lys front, France*

Dark clouds, heavily laden, bursting at the seams, hung low in a grey sky. Matinee over, the fire curtain lowered on the stage, the big guns silent, the light fading fast as Major Blankensy climbed the wooden ladder that led from the communicating trenches to the firing step. The sentry leant his chest against the revetments, steel helmet tilted low over his forehead so as to offer the smallest target possible to any sniper seeking prey. He peered over the sandbagged parapet, his eyes searching the once fertile land between the lines of barbed wire, anchored to rusting pig-tailed iron pickets between the German and British trenches. A dead man's land, no man's land, devoid of all living matter, no bird song, pockmarked with craters filled with stagnant water once fresh from the heavens, now polluted by putrid flesh torn from limbs and excreta. Spent cartridge cases lay spewed from magazines that had been emptied and reloaded countless times; unexploded shells lay buried, harbouring death, waiting to blow future tillers of the soil to smithereens or, if lucky, kingdom come.

'Any movement out there?'

The sentry swivelled, straightened and saluted, surprised to see the OC alone, stepping on to the firing step.

'No, sir. All quiet, nobody wants to get killed now. Jerry sitting it out, all safe and snug deep down in their dugout. It's all over, ain't it, sir?'

'No, it's bloody well not all over, not until I say so.'

'Yes sir, of course sir.'

The major looked left and right to discern shadowy figures of other sentries on the firing steps. 'Has the duty officer put in an appearance?'

'Yes, sir, with the duty sergeant; said they will be back at stand to.'

The major grunted, lifted the binoculars that hung from his neck and focussed on the German lines, grunted again, 'Bloody winter, can't see,' let the binoculars hang. 'What's your name, sentry?'

'Reynolds, sir.

'That redoubt over there.' Nodding towards the German lines. 'Sitting in there laughing at us; what say we capture that tomorrow? Then it will be all over. What say you, Reynolds?'

'Yes sir, of course sir.'

'Stout fellow, carry on.' He turned and left.

'Stark raving bonkers,' Reynolds muttered to himself after the major's head had disappeared below the firing step. 'How the hell we ever got lumbered with him, God knows. He should have been here when we captured these heights after that first suicidal attempt, wiped out most of the regiment; mostly all newcomers now, the reinforcements. Take the redoubt my arse.' He turned and leant against the revetments, taking up the same position as before.

The blast curtain dropped into place after the major entered his own dugout. Private Tomkins looked up.

'Brewing, sir, the char.'

'Has to be at four o'clock.'

'Of course sir, will be sir, on the dot as usual, your orders sir.' *There isn't any war when the clock strikes four; everyone stops for tea. You silly bastard.*

'Make sure it is, and smarten yourself up – your buttons are tarnished – and after you've served tea, find the duty officer, ask him to report to me here.'

'Yes sir.' *Three bags full, sir, and I'll just pop along to the corner shop and buy some Brasso.*

'You wanted to see me, sir I believe?' Lieutenant Satchwell asked as he saluted and entered the dugout.

'Yes-yes-yes, I have a plan.' His thin lips formed an ambiguous smile. 'The Diehards end the war. What do you think, yes?'

Satchwell gave a sickly smile. 'I'm not quite sure what you mean, sir.'

'Capture that redoubt the Germans have been sitting in, laughing at us for too long. A great finale to end the war by the regiment. *My* company.'

'Do you think that wise, sir, such an attempt as that? An armistice has been agreed; no need to lose any more lives.'

'Think of the honour and glory for the regiment.'

'The men will not want any more honour, they want to go home. They took these heights with a great loss of lives, and have held them since; surely that is enough—'

'Enough, Lieutenant; this will be different, a covert attack, surprise the Hun. They will not be expecting an attack now, an armistice signed, sitting snug down in their dugouts. Take one platoon with fixed bayonets, after stand to in the morning. There will be just enough light to sneak across, cut the wire, climb the wall, silence the sentries, drop a few grenades down to seal them down below before they can scramble up the ladders; they won't even get a chance to open up...'

The lieutenant looked on with amazement as the OC prattled on.

'Sir, the men won't take too kindly to this, they know the war is over—'

'No, it bloody well is not over, not until I say it is,' the major, red in the face, spittle spluttering from his lips, shouted to cut the lieutenant off. 'They will do as ordered;

29

they are still on active service or face a firing squad, you understand?' He leant back and folded his arms across his chest, an emperor giving orders. 'They may get a medal, we all may. Reynolds is all for it, told me so himself.'

'Reynolds, sir?'

'Yes, the sentry on duty; now brief the men.'

Lieutenant Satchwell saluted and left. Outside he stood a while, could not believe what he had heard. *So that's what it is all about, he wants a medal. The man's obsessed. Dare I have a word with the colonel? Say what? The OC is raving mad?*

Private Tomkins watched the lieutenant shake his head and walk away. *Poor sod, I heard all that; that bastard Blankensy is sending men to their deaths. He wants putting down.*

Sergeant Roberts was thinking, *A couple more stand-tos and it will all be over. I can't believe it, all for what?*

'Lieutenant Satchwell wants to see you, Sergeant.' The voice of Harry Watts, the lieutenant's batman, shattered the sergeant's musing. 'And 'e ain't a happy man, back with orders from the OC.'

'We go over the top early tomorrow morning, Sergeant.' No preamble, the lieutenant came out with it as soon as Roberts entered the dugout and saluted. He noticed the amazement that appeared on the sergeant's face, glanced down at the faded MM ribbon on the breast of his tunic. 'Please don't question it, Sergeant; I've done that to no effect. I've had my orders: take that redoubt with one platoon. I'm sorry, that's it. Sit down, I'll explain, and we can discuss it.'

'I can't believe it, sir, on whose orders?' He paused. 'Of course, the OC's. Can't you query this with headquarters? The colonel?'

'You know I can't do that, go over his head, also no time, all the red tape to cut. The OC believes this can be done.'

'He believes he is God.' Roberts raised his voice.

'Sergeant!' The lieutenant shook his head, placed a finger across his lips. 'Keep your voice down.'

'Sorry, sir, he is sending men to their death for some crazy half-baked scheme that is doomed from the start. I want it recorded that I query this order as being unlawful, considering an armistice has been agreed,'

'Remember we are still on active service. If you want to make a statement, be careful of the wording.'

The sergeant wrote:

> *I, 150985 Sergeant Roberts, will do my utmost to achieve the object of the orders issued by Major Blankensy on November 9 1918 to capture a German redoubt with one platoon under the command of Lieutenant Satchwell on the 10 November 1918. As an armistice has been agreed, and I fear an ultimate loss of lives, I write to record my belief that the action called for is unnecessary and will do nothing to hasten the end of hostilities.*

He signed and sealed it, and duly passed it to the orderly room sergeant for safe keeping with his army records.

No. 1 platoon stood stunned after listening to Sergeant Roberts's orders, voices raised in protest until the sergeant reminded them they were still on active service. To refuse would be to face a court martial and a firing squad.

'We have a thousand to one chance that we may pull it off, and have a few medals handed out.' *A forlorn encouragement to ease the load.*

31

'Sod the medals, Sarge. You know, we all know we ain't got a snowball's chance in hell. Someone got a pencil? I've gotta write home.'

Corporal Tony Kearn found Sergeant Roberts after he had walked away, standing alone.

'I want my lad out of this one, Chas; he's only seventeen, been over the top before, but this one is suicide. It will break his mother's heart. You can do this for me; we've known each other long enough, soldiered through thick and thin together.'

'You know I can't do that, Tony.'

'Sod it, Chas, I'll break his bloody arms so he can't go.'

'You know he'll want to go with you; that's what he joined up for. He won't stay put.'

'I'll do it, Chas, so help me God; better a broken arm than—'

'All right, all right, I'll order him to stay, sentry duty or something to make it official, and get Wilkie, that sergeant in 2 platoon, to get a couple of his men to hold him down, tie him up if necessary.'

'Thanks, Chas, I owe you one. I'll do your stint stoking the boilers down below, yeah, how about that?' He laughed.


## 10 November 1918

A foggy day in London; on the Lys front in France the air was heavy with moisture. It dripped from steel helmets and noses, everything damp to the touch.

No. 1 platoon of Company C could not spit a sixpenny piece between them, their throats as dry as sandpaper with the fear before action. Nerves taunt, tense, waiting for the order to go and the adrenaline to kick in. Then, it's shit or bust.

Lieutenant Satchwell nodded; Sergeant Roberts gave the order. Knife rests were dragged back, leaving a gap in the barbed wire for them to pass through. *Though I walk through the valley of – shut up.* The rest of C Company watched them go.

Their faces blackened, crouching low they spread out in line, a few paces apart after clearing the apron of barbed wire. The lieutenant leading in the centre, Sergeant Roberts in the middle of one half of the platoon on the right flank, Corporal Kearn acting the same on the left flank. *Cut the German wire; at the wall of the redoubt, in pairs hold a rifle between as a step and lift for the next in line to reach and scramble over the parapet. You know the drill.*

An anguished cry followed them. 'DAD – DAD!'

'Quiet, Tom, for Chrissake.'

Corporal Kearn's son struggled to break free from the arms that held him tight.

A German sentry pricked up his ears, strained his eyes to pierce the gloom, called out a warning and at the same time reached for a 'fairy pistol'. The flare bust high to shed a light on a Dantesque scene. Shapeless figures, caught and transfixed as in Hades.

'Lie still, men, wait for the light to die out, hope we haven't been spotted, then run, make for the wall, our only chance,' the lieutenant called out. *A forlorn chance, no way.*

'The Tommies are coming, Conrad,' Hans shouted.

'Are they mad?'

The German machine gunners doubled up the ladders to their posts to give cross-fire on fixed positions, loaders at their sides; controlled staccato bursts began their song of death.

'What bloody imbecile started this?' a German officer called out.

No way back, no way forward for No. 1 platoon. In a shambling run, stumbling to keep on their feet, they were cut down. *Corn before the reaper's scythe.*

Lieutenant Satchwell went down mortally wounded, blood gurgling at the back of his throat, silencing the order to retreat.

'Don't leave me to die out here, Sarge.'

Sergeant Roberts heard the plaintive plea faintly, hesitated, glanced left and right. *Where's the platoon, am I the last one standing?* Looked down to see Private Cooper's fingers trying to stem the blood from a stomach wound.

'Please, Sarge.'

Another flare burst. Sergeant Roberts laid his rifle down, put his arms under Townsend's knees and back and lifted him. Cooper's head dropped and his steel helmet fell and rolled forward. The sergeant took two steps; a sledgehammer blow in the back caused him to drop Cooper, who lay still. It took two seconds before he had realised he had been shot. He fell; his forehead hit the rim of the upturned steel helmet; a blinding flash of light registered the pain before the comfort of oblivion.

'You see that, Hans, that sergeant shot in the back carrying a wounded comrade? Remember that officer doing the same here in April when we were holding the heights?'

'Yes, God in heaven, we are all raving mad; an armistice has been agreed and we are still killing. Don't ask me to feed that gun any more, Conrad. I wonder if he survived, that officer; we dragged him back to our lines when the British retreated, handed him to our medics. What made us do that?'

'To salve our conscience for all the killing we had done, I guess.'

It became quiet; a faint glimmer of light in the east took over from the last sparks of the flare.

'I'll get the bastard that ordered this.' A raised voice came from No. 2 platoon, watching from the British trenches.

'Who said that?' the CSM asked.

'Jesus effing Christ, that's who.'

## *11 November 1918*

Lips silently counted the strokes as Big Ben sounded the eleventh hour. Many knelt and prayed, others wept. A day never to be forgotten, history in the making. The church bells pealed, people poured into the streets of towns and cities, the centres, Piccadilly Circus, Trafalgar Square and the like became 'chock-a-block'. Mass hysteria, morbid? No, pent up emotions freed. Complete strangers hugging and kissing each other. Telegraph boys no longer shunned as messengers of death, but welcomed, bearing glad tidings of loved ones coming home. Many others sat quiet behind curtained windows mourning loved ones that would never come home.

## *12 November 1918, Military Hospital Shorncliffe*

Sergeant Roberts's mind stirred; his eyelids were glued tight; he tried to blink; they slowly opened; he could see nothing but white, realised he was lying on his back. His right arm would not respond, would not function. He tried the left; it moved; gingerly felt with his fingers; it was soft to touch. *What did Corporal Tony Kearns say? 'I'll do your stint at the boilers down below, Chas; I owe you one. No need to, Tony; I'm in heaven floating on a cloud.* His eyes closed; slowly it came back to him.

*The pain, a voice, you're alive sergeant, the jab of a needle, slipping back and forth into consciousness – the journey – by train, boat, and the bone-shaking ride by ambulance on a stretcher alongside others.*

He woke with a start. 'God, what am I saying?' He shouted, 'Tony!'

'You're awake then, Sergeant.'

He saw a nurse standing at the end of the bed.

'Where am I?'

'Hospital, Shorncliffe.'

'I thought I was in heaven.' He forced a smile. 'Now I know I am: a bed and clean white sheets, an angel and bells ringing.'

'That was yesterday, the bells. The armistice signed; it's all over, the war finished, thank the Lord, and who is Tony?'

'Oh my God, Tony, the platoon, where are they?' He tried to move.

'Steady, Sergeant, don't try to move yet; you've had a narrow escape, lucky to be alive.'

'I must know, please, who else was brought in with me from my platoon?'

'I don't know; you will have to ask the matron when she does her rounds. Now drink this.'

'What is it?'

'A sedative, and don't get on the wrong side of the matron when you speak to her; she is three RSMs rolled into one.'

He swallowed the draught; his eyes drooped. Comfort in oblivion.

Sergeant Roberts came awake from an induced troubled sleep, lay with eyes shut collecting his thoughts, no idea of the time of the day or if it was night. He felt across his front with his left hand, found the fingers of the right, explored further. The right arm was in some form of sling and bound tight to his bandaged chest. *So that's why I couldn't move it.* He worked on his legs, tried to draw back his feet; the bed covers were tucked in tight sides and bottom, like being in a straitjacket, so no pyramid. He slowly opened his eyes, back to the real world. No angel at the bottom of the bed, but a formidable figure dressed in dark blue, a short cloak covering her shoulders.

'Back in the land of living, Sergeant?'

'Yes, Matron. I want to—' He saw the nurse standing behind the matron, finger across her lips, and stopped short.

'I know what you want, Sergeant. Listen to what I have to say, don't interrupt, then you can ask. You are a lucky man. Two bullets close together in your back, went right through, a few inches to the left would have shattered your spine. The field hospital at the front cauterised the wounds, a red hot poker I assume, albeit a thin one.' (A ghost of a smile lit her face.) 'Very effective to ward off infection from the filth you could have lain in; again lucky, you weren't there very long, as the Germans allowed the dead and wounded to be picked up as soon as the assault failed, so I was told. Bone splinters from your sternum and scapula were removed here; you may find some surfacing in years to come; not to worry about that. The fact remains that if an armistice had not been agreed, you would still have been lying at the side of a road waiting for a train with hundreds more. Tell me, Sergeant, why this action when an armistice was agreed?'

'You had better ask my OC that, Matron.'

'You mean you were ordered, not some bravado act?' She shook her head. 'Unbelievable. Now, Sergeant, what is it that you want to know?'

'My platoon: were any brought here, and if so how many?'

'One other, a Private Cooper, stomach wound, serious, touch and go; not so lucky as you, Sergeant.'

'What about the rest of the platoon? The lieutenant – Corporal Kearns?'

'I wouldn't know, could be still at the field hospital if not seriously wounded, otherwise – I'm sorry.'

'Could you find out for me, Matron? Please, I must know.'

'I do what I can, meanwhile you rest; will be able to get on your feet in a few days, but it will take some time before you can use that shoulder. Behave yourself, think how lucky you are.'

'Yes, Matron.'

'None of your platoon were taken to the field hospital, Sergeant; I'm sorry.'

It was three days later, three days of torment and restless nights for Sergeant Roberts, when Matron answered his question.

'You say sorry, Matron; does that mean—?'

'No, no, Sergeant.' The matron cut him short. 'I'm sorry that's all the information I could get via the ambulance crews.' *Leave him a glimmer of hope.*

## *17 November 1918*

Private Tomkins came to a halt, stood and gazed at the front of the hospital, dragged a piece of cloth from his pocket and wiped the drips from his nose. *Bloody taters, enough to freeze the nuts off a brass monkey; they gonner let me in?* Stuffed the rag back in his pocket, strode to the main entrance and entered.

A bare-headed uniform behind a counter, his back to a wall covered with shelved boxes, a tag hanging from each, looked up, called out. 'What d'you want, soldier?

'I've come to see Sergeant Roberts.'

'No visitors.'

'What? Why not?'

'Orders.'

'Sod the orders, the war's over. I've come from the front. I know 'e's in 'ere, from my unit, and Cooper.'

'You on leave?'

'Yeah; now can I see 'em?'

'I doubt it. There are many serious and disturbing cases here. You know, no limbs.'

'Yeah, I know, seen 'em in the trenches; better be blown to pieces then have to be spoon fed and your arse wiped by someone, I fink. Could yer ask who is in charge, if they are fit enough? I'll be as quiet as a mouse.'

'From the front, you said?'

'Yeah, Lys. Essex Regiment.'

He looked at the threadbare tunic hanging slack on a skimpy frame. *I wonder how many weeks that's been slept in.* The ashen skin drawn tight across high cheekbones, but something different, the eyes, a glint, alive, not like the dull given up hope of the many that were brought into the hospital.

'I'll see what I can do; depends on which ward and the matron. Roberts and Cooper, right?'

'Yeah, ta.'

'One thing, don't get me wrong, as I don't want a right hander. Have you been deloused? The matron'll kill me if you bring any in.'

'Yeah, and scrubbed with carbolic. The sappers, bless 'em, 'ave been laying on cauldrons of 'ot water, talk about washing day, clothes lines galore, and strip tease acts.'

'Wait here until I get back, here mind you; don't think of trying to sneak to the wards.'

'You can see the sergeant,' the uniform said on his return. 'Roberts, not Cooper; he is in a different ward, in a bad way. Go to Ward 4, the rest room. Not the ward itself, get it?

'Got it.'

'Tomkins, well I'll be damned.' Roberts looked up from a comfortable chair, one arm in a sling, his chest bandaged. Laid down a paperback novel he had been reading. 'How did you manage it, get leave?'

'Yeah.'

'What's the news, the platoon? I've been asking, no joy from the matron.'

'Not good, Sarge.'

'Out with it, I must know.'

Tomkins hesitated. 'Sorry, Sarge, they all bought it; only you and Cooper left.'

'Christ! All of them?' Roberts shut his eyes, clenched his teeth. *I'll sort you out, you bastard, when I get out of here; call yourself an officer?* 'Corporal Kearn's lad, how's he taking it?'

'Went raving mad wiv 'is bayonet fixed, shouting blue murder that 'e'd kill the major. Took three to 'old 'im down. When it got light, Jerry called out for us to collect the dead and wounded. Saved you and Cooper; left there, yer'd 'ave bled to death. The next day when we knew armistice had been signed, a Jerry officer stood on the parapet of the redoubt, called out so we could hear, "What a waste of lives," then 'e saluted. It was so quiet, nobody knew wot to do; some sat down and cried. The colonel sent for the major; we don't know wot 'e said, but 'e came back wiv 'is tail between 'is legs. "Four o'clock, Tomkins, must be four

40

o'clock." Yeah, I don't fink. I told 'im 'e can make 'is own tea, and bat 'is own wicket. Yer know wot? 'e didn't say a word. 'e's no gentleman officer; dunno 'ow 'e got a commission; bought it, I suppose. No one in the company stands to attention or salutes 'im now, and 'e can't do anyfing about it. Sorry, Sarge, me ranting on; should 'ave asked 'ow yer making out. See yer on yer feet, so that must be good news, ain't it?'

'Yeah, I'll be all right if I can get over losing the platoon.'

'Don't say that, Sarge, you didn't lose the platoon, nor did the lieutenant; yer was ordered to do some mad-brained plan that was doomed. 'e must 'ave a nut loose, Blanky, but 'e'll pay for it one day, mark my words. There's plenty in the company wouldn't think twice about sticking a bayonet up 'is arse, and 'e knows it; 'e keeps out of the limelight now.'

'You're a hard sod, Tomkins.'

'It's an 'ard world, Sarge, least-ways the one I was born into. Don't fink too much, get on wiv it, and yer'll get by, like those when I served in Indi; born to be a shit wallah, and yer die being a shit wallah, right?'

'Down to earth, your philosophy, Tomkins.'

'Dunno about that mumbo jumbo, yer jest 'ave to get on wiv life. Don't blame yerself, Sarge; the war's over, some of us survived. Kismet, 'oratio said. I'll down a pint for those that didn't.'

The door opened. The matron entered. Tomkins stood to attention. 'All right, Matron, I'll be on me way.'

'Have you told the sergeant what he wanted to know?'

'Yes, Matron.'

'And?'

'All the rest of the platoon killed, Matron. Only the sergeant and Cooper left.'

41

Her eyes darted from Tomkins to the sergeant; she was momentarily lost for words.

'I-I'm so sorry, Sergeant.' She glanced at Tomkins. 'You stay awhile. Ten minutes.'

And left as abruptly as she had arrived

'Matron,' a nurse called as she saw the matron hurrying along the corridor.

'Not now, nurse.'

On reaching her office, the matron closed the door, sat with elbows on the desk in front and head between her hands. *When will they ever learn?* Four years of pent up emotions overflowed, the stiff upper lip quivered and the tears came.

The days passed. Private Cooper, on the slow road to recovery, became aware that life would never be the same again, living on gruel. Sergeant Roberts was allowed to visit him in the ward for short periods to converse a while. Finally was passed fit to return to his unit.

_18 December 1918, the standing barracks of the Essex Regiment_

The sergeant major of C Company was trying to come with terms with the fact that he had not got much of a company left. Three depleted platoons other than the motley shower that made up HQ, the surviving volunteers and conscripts discharged, and what was left was not worth a monkey's fart. Ever since that fateful day in November, when No. 1 platoon had been wiped off the face of the earth, the remainder of the company had been left disgruntled, discipline gone to the wall; applications for transfer to one of the other companies of the regiment lay waiting on his desk. All down to that useless excuse of an officer now skulking in his office. _The sooner he goes the better, to find a stone to hide under, a big one, and they get turned over sooner rather than later. Someone will find him._

He leant back in his chair and gazed at the parade ground through the window and pondered.

_44 years of age, 26 years of service, 30 counting boys' service; less than a year to go before being catapulted out into civvy street. Better to have stopped one going over the top than to be a nonentity as a civilian: out in a blaze of glory, a name engraved in stone on a memorial alongside others I fought with. 'No, not you, Sergeant Major, you stay put; besides you're too old, done your bit, the Boer war or was it the North-West Frontier?' (That got a laugh.) At least an army pension will help to cope._

The door crashed open, ended his musing. Roberts entered, calling out, 'In his office, is he?'

Before the CSM could answer, Roberts had by-passed him and forced his way into the OC's office. The major rose to his feet, 'What the hell—?'

A clenched fist caught him on the point of the jaw, sent him crashing onto the chair behind, which splintered, leaving him on his back dazed. He heard the words faintly: 'You murdered my platoon.'

The sergeant major rushed in and grabbed Roberts from behind, pinning his arms to the sides of his body. Roberts forced them apart. 'I'll kill the bastard,' he yelled.

'Enough, Roberts, enough. Back up, outside. Listen to me, that's an order.'

The orderly room sergeant came running in. 'What's going on?'

'Nothing to do with you, get out,' the sergeant major ordered. 'Come on, Roberts, calm down, don't make it any worse.'

The OC pushed himself to his feet. Holding his jaw, mumbled, 'Put that man on a charge, Sergeant Major, under close arrest.'

## The Court Martial. 8 January

Number 150985, Sergeant Roberts MM, sat stony faced between an escort, two of equal rank, facing the panel of three who would sit in judgement.

The court convened, presided over by Lt Col. Stoney MC of the Corps of Royal Engineers, who sat flanked on both sides by a captain. The RSM of the regiment sat to one side, ready to answer any questions relating to the King's Regulations. The prosecuting and defence officers sat behind their respective tables.

The charge was read. A nod from the colonel; the prosecuting officer stood. 'I call on Major Blankensy to give evidence.'

The major rose and began.

'On the day in question, I was sitting behind my desk when the office door burst open and Sergeant Roberts charged in. I rose to my feet; before I could question him as to why this abrupt entrance, his fist struck my chin with such force I was knocked back and fell across the chair behind, which shattered. I lay stunned momentarily and recall the CSM entering and endeavouring to restrain the sergeant. I called out – ordered the CSM to charge and place Roberts under close arrest.'

'Thank you, Major.' The PO sat; the DO stood and began.

'What did Sergeant Roberts say, Major? Did he give any reason for his action?'

'No. I heard him shout "I'll kill the bastard".'

'Then he never threatened you.'

'He meant me.'

'Why do you think Roberts did what you stated?'

'I have no idea.'

'No? Then I will read a statement, written by Sergeant Roberts and handed to the orderly sergeant for safe keeping on the ninth of November.'

It was read out loud for all to hear, and passed to the colonel, who read it, grim faced, before passing it to the other two officers on either side.

The DO sat and waited until the colonel gave the signal to continue.

'Do you still say you have no idea why the sergeant did what you allege? Roberts was seriously wounded; only one other survived the slaughter of his platoon, including Lieutenant Satchwell. Did he question your order?'

The PO stood. 'I must remind the DO that it is Sergeant Roberts that is facing a charge here. What the lieutenant may have said, or not said, is irrelevant.'

'I do not need reminding that I am defending a brave, an honourable soldier, the holder of a Military Medal for his actions. Lieutenant Satchwell was killed, so cannot give evidence as to whether he agreed with Roberts's statement that the order given by Major Blankensy, knowing an armistice had been agreed, was unnecessary, bordering on unlawful, leading to the loss of many lives. Perhaps the major would wish to enlighten the court.'

The major stood. Swivelled his head, sniffed twice; a slight sneer turned his lips down. 'Enlighten the court, you said? Then perhaps Sergeant Roberts can answer. How comes he was shot in the back? He stated he would do all he could to carry out my orders. How? Turning his back on the enemy?'

The DO jumped to his feet. 'That's outrageous; are you implying that the sergeant turned tail?' The DO turned to the panel. 'Colonel. Sir. May I call Sergeant Roberts to answer this slur?'

'Sergeant Roberts is facing a charge of striking a superior officer, nothing else. But yes, you may.'

Sergeant Roberts stood and began.

'Sir. A German flare lit the scene as we were stealthily advancing on the day in question. We were caught in the open, exposed; the men dropped to seek cover. Lieutenant Satchwell shouted, "Lie still, hope we are not spotted. When the light fades run for the redoubt wall, our only chance." There was no chance; as soon as we moved, the heavy machine guns opened up with cross-fire, another flare burst. The lieutenant went down, he waved an arm, I understood the meaning: get back. I looked left and right, could not see anyone left standing of the platoon, heard a voice, Private Cooper calling, "Don't leave me to die out here, Sarge." He'd taken a shot in the stomach and was bleeding real bad. I thought I could save his life if I got him back to be treated in time; nothing else I could do. I bent over and lifted him; that is when I was hit. I don't remember any more. I must have hit my head on falling. Sir.'

'All right, Sergeant, you may sit,' the DO said. He turned to face the major. 'You heard Sergeant Roberts. I will remind you that the rest of your company was watching from the trenches on that day. Now will you answer my question, and I repeat: did the lieutenant question your order?'

'Major Blankensy,' the colonel intervened. 'You do not have to answer, but a negative response tends to lead to confusion, if you get what I mean.' *The lieutenant sure as hell did ask. I'll do some probing of my own later.*

The major hesitated. 'I, I can't remember, he may have.'

'Let's leave it at that,' the colonel snapped. 'I want this finished. Sergeant Roberts, step forward.'

Roberts stood, took two paces forward and came to attention.

'Sergeant, I am truly sorry for the loss of your platoon. I've read your service records. Military conduct exemplary. The MM Mons, yes?" He nodded. "I want a straight answer, yes or no. Did you strike Major Blankensy?'

'Yes, sir.'

'Thank you, Sergeant; remain where you are.' He leant forward and whispered to the captains who sat either side, looked up to face Roberts.

'You are guilty as charged, Sergeant; I have no alternative. You will be reduced to the ranks, and serve a lesser six months rather than 12 in military prison due to exemplary military conduct.'

A nod to the RSM who stood and marched rather than walked to Roberts, produced a blade and carefully cut the stitches binding the chevrons to his tunic. Whispered, 'Sorry, Roberts.'

## The Glasshouse

Roberts, dressed in fatigues, head shaven, stood back from the barber's chair. The 'barber' an inmate himself, well versed in the use of clippers and a cut-throat, performing on his mates in the trenches at a penny a go for an 'all over' and a shave to thwart the lice. Now serving a year – a brawl in a pub, using the cut-throat as in the Gorbals, Glasgow, leaving his calling card, a cut from cheekbone to chin. 'Did the bloke a favour; saved him going over the top for a few weeks.'

An order from Bill Cox, and Roberts stepped outside the barber's cell and stood to attention. For the benefit of the barber's ears, Cox shouted, 'Double mark time,' followed by, 'Forward.' Cox followed, the usual routine, a slow walk whilst the prisoner doubled ahead a distance until the command 'On the spot', which the prisoner followed until the warden caught up, and so on until they reached their destination, usually the parade ground for more square bashing. The only exceptions were those on the top level in solitary, for murder. Given a rifle and bayonet, and taught how to use them – to kill – many times, '*Good for you, Tommy Atkins, a medal to wear on your breast. Come home on leave to find your missus having it off with a conchie. Lose your rag, strangle her, now it's the chop – no, that's old fashioned – the drop, and waiting for Thomas Pierrepoint with a noose to arrive. Won't have to wait long;*

*no more than a couple of days; the army don't hang about. Sorry, mate, hard luck.'*

Bill Cox shouted, 'Halt.' Closed with Roberts and in lowered voice, 'I can't be seen or heard treating you any different to the others in here, you understand, Roberts, but I'll do what I can do to make it a bit easier for you while you are here. Now, I'll find you a cell as promised.'

Michael O'Leary stood to attention and faced the inside of the cell door on hearing the command 'Halt' and boots hitting the floor. They stood facing each other through the bars. Roberts gazed at a giant of a man, three or four inches taller than his own six feet one inch, wide as a barn, six feet between eyes in a face with a complexion not the pallor of confinement but of sun and wind, the colour of burnished copper.

'Your new cellmate O'Leary,' said Bill Cox. 'Has one up on you, broke an officer's jaw; lost his stripes, same as you. You may speak.'

'Thank you, Staff. I've had my fun o' the corp'ral's guard; I've made the cinders fly. I'm here in the clink for a thundering drink and blacking the corporal's eye.'

'You know your Rudyard Kipling, Roberts?' Cox asked.

'Some, Staff.'

'You'll know most of it before you leave here. O'Leary was born in India. His father served there, North-West Frontier. Don't ask him who his mother was, and I'm sure you'll get on fine.'

'That's not a bone crusher, is it?' Roberts exclaimed, looking at the huge hand outstretched as the cell door closed behind him.

O'Leary chuckled. 'Only if I want it to be.'

'Well, don't want it to be, otherwise I'll return the favour with a kick in the knackers.'

Thunder rumbled in O'Leary's chest and laughter erupted. 'Cox could be right, the bastard. Call me Michael, never Mick; put it there.'

'Chas, not Charlie,' Roberts responded as he slid his hand into Michael's big mitt (*a bunch of boa constrictors if ever there was one*), taking a firm grip, aware of the strength there, this time as comforting as the boa around a lady's neck. In the weeks that followed, a bond was cemented, never to be found wanting.

### *Camden Town, London*

Clive Jones, greatcoat collar turned up against a biting north-east wind 'from Russia with love', head not up, as on parade, but down, looked where he placed his feet, not wanting to land on his arse. The snow that had fallen virgin white a week ago, now a dirty grey, lay in misshapen heaps on kerbs and filled the gutters, gathering discarded cigarette butts, empty Woodbine packets and the odd frozen dog turd to add a bit of colour, swept there by some shopkeepers not wanting it walked into their premises. Others left it where it had fallen, the snow, to freeze and be trampled into a myriad of patterns, a hazard to the unwary.

The warmth circulating from the oven in the back room welcomed him as he entered 'Jones the Baker's'. His parents and sisters added to the warmth as they hugged him in turn, and asked the question that was asked to all given leave. 'When you got to go back?'

'I now know the man that saved my life at the Somme in 1916.'

It was late evening, the shop door closed, the blind pulled down. Flames dancing merrily behind the grate in the living room. The family sitting comfortably after eating,

51

Gwyneth, the younger of the two sisters, cushioned on the floor with her back against Clive's shins. All at peace with the world when Clive startled them with the news.

'Oh, Clive, you must bring him home,' Colin senior said. 'We all want to thank him.'

'Yes, yes,' his mother added. 'We can never repay him enough.'

'I can't. At least, not yet. He is in prison. A Sergeant Roberts, or was a sergeant before being reduced to the ranks, and I had to be the one to escort him there.'

'How? Why?' they asked in chorus, then they sat agog as Clive related the events leading to the prison. He finished with, 'I wasn't sure if it was him then, but now I am sure as our CRE presided at Roberts's court martial. I got all the information from the officers' mess sergeant, who has his ears to the ground.'

'I can't believe it,' said Clive's father. 'Sending a platoon, sentencing more like it, to their death, knowing an armistice had been agreed, and the last day of the war. That officer should be the one in prison, better still in front of a firing squad.'

'I would imagine there would be plenty of volunteers in Roberts's company for that squad; seems they watched from the trenches that platoon walk to their death, wiped out in minutes for some whim of a useless officer.'

'So what are you going to do, son?'

'One thing for sure, Da: meet up with Roberts, be there when he gets released, shake his hand and see if there is any way I can repay him. I have to make up my mind if I am going to stay in the army.' He fingered his facial scars. 'Not much chance of a job in civvy street looking like this, unless it's sweeping the streets or the likes; at least in the army I get fed and clothed, no more trenches, and scars go with medal ribbons. I'll think on it, meanwhile enjoy my leave.'

## Headquarters of the Essex Regiment

Lt Col. Stoney CRE, flanked by two officers, was on the warpath. The path being the perimeter of the parade ground. (Sacred ground, not allowed to walk across it.)

The RSM saw them coming from his office. Stood, straightened his tunic, grabbed his peaked cap, planted it firmly on his head, called out to the adjutant in the adjoining office: 'The sappers are here, sir.' Went out to meet them.

The colonel acknowledged the salute given by the RSM as he halted, his boots hitting the ground with a resounding slap and a 'Good morning, sirs.'

'Has the brigade major arrived, Sergeant Major?'

'Yes sir, with the regiment's colonel, in his office.'

'Where is Major Blankensy?'

'Off duty, in the officers' mess, sir. We thought it best.'

'Good.' A smile. *I like the 'we'.* 'Lead on, Sergeant Major.'

Chairs were drawn up around a table. The brigade major, the colonel and the prosecuting and defending officers from Roberts's court martial sat down after introductions. The brigade major began.

'I am here on behalf of the brigadier to chair this meeting, requested by Colonel Stoney to discuss a certain order given by Major Blankensy. I am aware of the events that followed that order, as you all are, so no need for them to be repeated. I first ask Colonel Stoney to justify his request.'

'Gentlemen,' the colonel began. 'Knowing the circumstances and the date of this order to take place, I ask you: would you have given such an order? It wasn't necessary, no point, a sheer waste of lives. Sergeant Roberts, known for his courage, queried it, made a written statement to the fact. When Major Blankensy was asked if

Lieutenant Satchwell had queried it, he hesitated, replied, "I can't remember, he may have." He may have! I ask you, you can draw your own conclusion from an answer such as that. I say that it did most probably happen, as I made some questioning of my own after the trial and discovered that the major's batman, Private Tomkins, had overheard the lieutenant questioning the order with Blankensy. The major shouted at one point, "The men will obey the order," as Tomkins described it. Which makes it appear that the men themselves possibly queried the order. I must add here that not one man refused. When I asked Tomkins why he had not come forward before, he replied that no one had asked him, and he had not known it would be brought up at the court martial. The lieutenant tragically killed with his platoon cannot confirm this. Only two survived. Sergeant Roberts, his career as a professional soldier finished. Private Cooper, in hospital, seriously wounded, will never be the same man again. I say the order should never have been given.'

'You've made your point, Colonel. Many orders are given during hostilities that lead to a great loss of lives, but in this instance I must agree with you.' The brigade major looked at the other three. 'How say you, gentlemen, to Colonel Stoney's question?'

Silence for some minutes, then three affirmatives made it unanimous.

'Anyone wish to add a rider?' the brigade major asked.

'Yes,' the regiment's colonel answered. 'I want this man removed from my regiment as soon as possible. I have no hesitation in saying that his life is not worth a tinker's curse. So be it, but I don't want to see anyone serving under my command to be strung up through an ill-conceived irrational act.' He paused. 'Better if one of us draw the short straw.' The others looked up, startled. 'Only joking, gentlemen.' *Far be it.* 'At least he must resign his commission.'

The brigade major pursed his lips. 'Anyone anything to add?'

The officer who had acted for Roberts's defence spoke.

'Yes, I would like to say that I feel I let Sergeant Roberts down, as I never gave it a thought that someone could have overheard the lieutenant questioning the major.'

'No,' Colonel Stoney intervened. 'It would not have made any difference to the outcome. Roberts was charged with striking an officer; I had no alternative but to pass sentence.'

'If that's all, gentlemen, we will leave it at that. You realise this is unofficial, no word of this to the outside; if the press got hold of it, there would be hell to pay.' The brigade major finished with, 'I will report to the brigadier.'

After they had left, the regiment colonel sent for the RSM.

'The brigade major was not here, there was no meeting. Understand, Sergeant Major?'

A week later Major Blankensy resigned his commission.

## Folkestone

Spring had sprung early this year of grace, 1919. A cloudless sky, with a tang in the air wafted inland by the benevolence of a line of seaweed deposited on the shingle from the hand of Neptune. Golden forsythia fluttered its corolla, enticing the early bee to sip nectar of the gods; daffodils showing a glimpse of colour, bursting to compete, nodded as Private Tomkins passed on foot uphill on way to the military hospital.

'Ne'er cast a clout till May be out, yeah, I know, could snow next week,' Tomkins murmured as he pulled his greatcoat tighter around his waist. On reaching the grounds of the hospital, no hesitation this time, bold as brass he marched straight to the main entrance and entered. A uniform looked up from behind a counter.

'I've come to see Cooper,' said Tomkins.

'Have you now?'

'Yeah, the matron knows me, wouldn't let me see 'im last time I was 'ere. I fink 'e should be on the mend by now.'

'Oh, I see, the matron knows you, does she?'

'Yeah, ask 'er, tell 'er I was the one that came to see Sergeant Roberts, 'im an' Cooper the only ones left out of a platoon that was wiped out.'

'What's your name?'

'Tomkins.'

'Wait here, I'll find out.'

'That's wot the ovver bloke said.'

'What other bloke?'

'The one that was wearing your uniform last time I came.'

'Oh, very funny.'


'Yes, the matron remembers you,' a surprised uniform said on return. 'She wants to speak to you. Her office, first floor, the name on the door.'

'I'll find it.'

Tomkins knocked and waited for the 'Come in' before entering.

'Good morning,' the matron greeted him. *A bearer of bad news*. 'I didn't get your name when you came before.'

'Morning, Matron; it's Tomkins.'

'Right, Tomkins, I wanted to ask you how Sergeant Roberts is faring.'

'Dunno about faring, Matron; 'e's in the glasshouse. Got six months for whacking that officer who sent 'is platoon to their death.'

'Sorry to hear that. Sorry for the sergeant.' She smiled. 'Not the officer.'

''im the bas— sorry, Matron, nearly swore then. 'e resigned 'is commission. Resigned me arse – sorry, done it agin – been booted out, more likely.'

'I forgive you, Tomkins, I understand how you feel, but don't make a habit of it while you are here.'

'Yes, Matron. I mean no, Matron.'

'I believe you came to see Cooper, yes?'

'Yes, Matron.'

'I'm pleased to tell you he is on his feet. Lost a kidney, his intestine snipped and stitched; he is tough, will take some time, he'll survive with care. He is in the rest room, allowed up for short spells. You know where it is; cheer him up; don't stay too long.'

'Fanks, Matron.'

'Well, strike a light, look what the cat's brought in,' exclaimed Harry Cooper, sitting propped up, cushioned in an armchair.'

'That's a ruddy good welcome, I must say. I'll go out and come back agin, shall I?'

'Sit yourself down, you silly sod; pleased to see that ugly dial of yours. Did you bring a drink in? I'm on gruel for Chrissake, drinking through a straw when I was on my back for days, like a kid.'

'Sorry, 'arry. Good job I didn't, as the matron wanted to see me first; she's got eyes like a hawk, and she'd smell yer breff, know I'd brought it in, I'd be for the 'igh jump then real proper. Did she tell yer about the platoon?'

'No, Roberts did, came and sat with me when it was allowed. I had to know. Took a couple of slugs himself; another one of his cat's lives gone, he said. Is he back with the unit?'

'No, in the glasshouse. Got six months; broke Blankensy's jaw when he got out of 'ere.'

'You still making tea for that bastard? I'll do more than that when I get out. I'll kill him, so help me God.'

'You'll 'ave to find 'im first, 'e's been booted out.'

'That's not good enough. I mean it, Bill, get his address.'

'No, 'arry, 'e's not worth swinging for.'

'Look at me, Bill. I can't have a drink, can't smoke, can't have a bit of the other, not much to look forward to. The rozzers would have to catch me. If they do, I'll be happy watching him stoking the boilers down below. Find out where he lives; it'll be in the company office, the address. Don't ask, go through the files on the QT.'

''arry, it'll be weeks before you get out of here. Forget it.'

'Yeah, I know, meanwhile I'll be dreaming of that day when I meet him face to face. You can do it for me; that's all I ask.'

'I might not be 'ere. The British Army – wot's left of 'em – 'ave got to go to Germany, occupy the Rhine or somefink like that. I'll see wot I can do; don't get worked up about it, jest get yerself fit. Now let's talk about somefink else. Yer remember Smudger Smiffy in No. 1 platoon? 'e told me 'is missus shaves 'er legs when 'e's away; 'e gits the bristles when 'e gits 'ome.'

Harry Cooper suppressed a laugh; it came out as a chuckle. 'Jesus, Bill, turn it in.'

'Well, the matron told me to cheer yer up. Listen, anovver time me and Smudger was out on pass, whiling the time away waiting for the boozers to open, looking at the bikes on display outside that shop in Kentish Town Road. I said "That's the one I'd git" and a geezer passing gave me a black eye.'

'I don't get it.'

'No. I did: 'e must 'ave come from Liverpool. The "one eyed git".'

'Enough, Bill, I'm already in stitches.'

'That's clever, 'arry, in stitches. I'd better shove orf now; matron told me not to stay too long. I'll come agin, all being well.'

'What about lolly, the train fare?'

'No bovver, I don't pay; the CSM gives me a travel warrant. 'e knows I was coming 'ere, said give yer a kiss.'

'Get out, you sod, and don't forget that address. That drink you're gonner have, mine's a Guinness.'

The landlord carefully poured the Guinness, drew a pint of bitter, placed both glasses and the change on the counter. Watched as Tomkins drank from the glass of Guinness. Asked, 'Is your mate coming?' nodding at the bitter.

'No. That's mine; I'm drinking 'is.'

'I'm with you. The hospital, your mate, yes?'

'Yeah, you've got it.'

'I take my hat off to you blokes, the trenches, bloody heroes; don't think I could have taken that. I was RNR but too old to be called back. Lucky, I suppose.'

'You the ancient mariner, then?'

The landlord smiled. 'Dunno about ancient; "old salt", perhaps.'

'Well, I'm no bloody 'ero. Brown nosed it, wheedled me way into being a batman; saved me going over the top many times. Looked after some captains those last three years. Gentlemen, real toffs; watched 'em going over the top, one by one, each wiv a revolver in 'is 'and, leading a platoon. Packed their belongings up ready to be sent 'ome after they bought it. Not for the one that followed 'em, the last bastard, never seed 'im go over the top. No gentleman 'im, a shit of a major, 'ow 'e got to be an officer I don't know. Bit of a mystery, somefink don't add up wiv 'im'

'I take it you didn't care for him?'

'Care for 'im, I could 'ave strangled 'im.' Tomkins drained the Guinness. Stood looking up with the glass in hand for some moments.

'You all right, mate?' the landlord asked.

'Yeah, just finking.' *Cheers, Cooper. Couldn't do it then; nuffink to stop me now.*

Roberts paced the cell, back and forth like a caged leopard. Mike watched him from his bunk.

'Won't do any good, Chas,' said Michael. '"Use your loaf"; that's what you Londoners say, "ain't it"?' – mimicking a Cockney accent – 'so sit down; you're making me giddy.'

Roberts took no notice, kept pacing, one two three turn, one two three turn. Michael slid his legs over the edge of his bunk, stood, and in one quick movement his huge arms encircled Roberts from behind and pinioned him. Roberts was lifted clear of the floor.

'You're not listening, are you, Chas? You are not in solitary, there's two of us in here, so talk. If you're thinking of taking a swing at me when I loosen you, you're welcome, but that won't do any good either.'

Roberts, his feet on the floor, free of the bear hug, turned to face Michael. 'What the hell do you think you—'

'Don't say anything, Chas. Listen. Close your eyes. Do it, Chas. You're standing on top of a hill, the breeze caressing your cheek; you take a deep breath and look at the valley below, the lush grass—'

'All I can see is your Adam's apple, you big bear. You nearly squeezed the life from me; what the hell was that for?'

'Because you're all het up, like when you came out of hospital – a bad-tempered kid kicking his mother's ankles in a tantrum – rushing and punching your OC. Where did that get you – eh?'

'It was bad enough getting shot – losing the platoon – the last straw getting six months banged up in a cell.'

'All right, Chas. Do your time, scrub your webbing, the floors, the walls, the ceiling, wash the coal, whitewash the coal bucket, square bashing, press ups, anything you're told to do as when you was a raw recruit; do it and you win. Six months is no time at all. Treat it like a holiday camp; no more pacing up and down, then you will walk out of here free. I'll be waiting outside as I finish my time before you, then you can deal with that bloke – what's his name, Blankensy that got you in here. After, if you are with me, we'll do what I've had in mind for some time, sod the army. Go and seek gold.'

'Mike, you're talking in riddles. First I'm on top of a hill looking at lush grass, now it's prospecting for gold. What about our army service?'

'I'm time expired. Had to carry on due to the war, whether I liked it or not, but I finish when I get out of here, and that was my fault being here. But you: the army turned its back on you, stripped you down to private, a prison sentence on your records – for what? For obeying an order that sent men to their death for no reason at all; the bloody war was finished, for God's sake. I'll come with you when you face this excuse for an officer, get a few answers. Now, you don't want to sign on again, surely? And it's not prospecting for gold; it's buried, waiting to be found.'

'I don't understand, Michael.'

'All in good time, which we have plenty of whilst being banged up in here.'

## Headquarters of the Essex Regiment

20 June. The usual topic on greetings of the day – the weather. This day more so than ever, as the temperature for three days had been in the mid-eighties.

*Another scorcher – yeah, a heatwave – too bloody 'ot – could do wiv some rain – don't say that, it never stopped last week…*

Private Tomkins undid the two brass clips that linked his tunic collar tight under his chin, ran a thumb under it to ease it away from his sweating neck as he made his way to the company office.

The orderly room sergeant was engrossed in reading and trying to fathom the list of amendments received from the War Office. Each one needed to be cut carefully to size and pasted over those to be deleted in the army's red bound bible, the King's Regulations. He heard the outer door open, looked up to see Tomkins enter.

'You're improperly dressed, Tomkins. The collar.'

'It's bloody 'ot, Sarge.'

'No excuse, do it up.'

'Peace time bullshit now, is it?'

The sergeant looked down at what he had been reading. 'You can say that again.'

'Well, it won't worry me soon, as I'm time expired.'

'You may regret that when you are broke and hungry, can't get a job. It's tough going in civvy street.'

'I don't see any sash on yer, Sarge.'

'No, I'm not acting as a colour sergeant, not recruiting, but you get fed, clothed and paid in the army, nothing to be sneezed at.'

'Yeah, but it'll be the same as before the war, like Rudyard said. "*It's Tommy this and Tommy that, Tommy go away. But it's 'Thank you, Mr Atkins' when the band begins to play.*"'

'Blimey, come all over lyrical, Tomkins, have we? Now what do you want? I'm busy.'

'Blankensy's address.'

'What do you want it for?'

'I promised Cooper I'd git it for 'im.'

'You going to see him?'

'Who, Cooper? I've already seen 'im at the 'ospital.'

'Blankensy, you know who I mean.'

'Why would I want to see 'im?'

'Because you've asked for his address, and you certainly are not going to write to him, so stop stalling, Tomkins. What's going on?'

'Nuffink.'

'I can't give it to you. Regulations.'

'Sod the regulations; I'm time expired, ain't I? Well, in a few days. Write it down on a piece of paper, put it on the desk and look away; yer ain't given it to me then, if anyone asks.'

'Hope you know what you are doing, Tomkins, but *I* don't want to know.'

Tomkins picked the paper up, folded it and tucked it into his pocket. 'Ta, Sarge.'

'Tear that paper up after you've read it.'

'Yeah, will do after I've wiped me arse on it.'

'Tomorrow I'm out of here,' said Michael, sitting alongside Roberts on the bottom bunk. 'Plenty of time to get back to my unit, pick up my discharge papers and back here to see you walk out in twelve days' time. After you get your discharge, we pay a visit to this Blankensy fellow. You have your say, make him grovel, shooting him in the kneecap would be a good idea, very painful, he'll remember that all his life. Unless, of course, you want to finish him off and have done with it. Then we go for gold.'

'You've got it all worked out, Michael. I don't need anyone to hold my hand; I'm a big boy, you know.'

'Not so big as me,' said Michael, with a laugh. 'I taught you how to control your mind when you first arrived here. To will yourself to be someone else, live another's life. Charge with the Light Brigade. Be a frontiersman crossing the wild west, fighting the Apache, feel the breeze, see the lush grass. Your choice when you couldn't sleep through those hours of darkness. It worked, didn't it? No more pacing the cell. Your time is almost up; we will be both free as the air, fit as fiddles, and I'll be there to hold your hand if need be.'

'Strads, you mean?'

'Yeah, but not that old, mellowed.'

'So, this digging for gold mystery: you gonner tell me now?'

'Yeah. You listen, don't interrupt.' And Michael began.

'1900. I was seven years old, on the way back to Blighty with my mother on a Bibby Line trooper. My father a regular with the British Army in India – the regiment going home after serving on the North-West Frontier. The ship was diverted to the Gold Coast, West Africa. The troops were taken off as reinforcements to take part in what would be the last of the Ashanti wars. He became friendly with a white sergeant that served with the WAFF – you know, the West African Frontier Force – who was going on leave after the Ashanti warriors were defeated, and was on the same trooper as my father's regiment, or what was left of them. It appeared this sergeant had been six years with the WAFF so far, and granted leave every two years. They had plenty of time to talk on the voyage, and this is what he told my father.'

*It all began, by all accounts, with Okomfo Anokye, factotum to Osei Tutu, one of the Ashanti kings who reigned from 1692 to 1731. Okomfo was a wily bird, not only a factotum: a wizard – a manipulator – a Svengali all rolled into one, but most of all a visionary, whose eyes were on the lucrative riches and gains that could be had on the Cape Coast of the Gold Coast. He realised that a great army would be needed to overcome any opposition, well trained and commanded as one, not separate armies under lesser kings and chiefs, as was the situation at that time.*

*How to unite them into one mighty nation, that was the question he needed to find the answer to. An inspiration came to him one night as he lay awake thinking. A seat of power like the English had, one that must be revered, sacred, not to be defiled. A golden stool.*

*In secret he 'materialised' a carved stool, covered in gold and golden artefacts.*

*At a special meeting with all the lesser kings, chiefs and officials present, Okomfo held the golden stool high and addressed the gathering. 'This is the spirit of all Ashanti, descended from the heavens, to be touched by the hand of King Osei, chosen to be the first guardian of the golden stool and king of all Ashanti until such time as a successor shall be appointed in his stead.' Such was the mystic power of Okomfo, all swore allegiance to the golden stool.*

So, inspired and united, the army grew in strength and numbers, strictly trained and disciplined. Their object: the coast.

1806. The Ashanti armies reached the coast and the killing began. The population was more than decimated. It was estimated that six thousand of the Fante tribes perished before the Ashanti warriors returned triumphant to Kumasi.

1816. Osei Bonsu was appointed the next guardian of the golden stool and sat supreme king of all Ashanti. His armies were soon on the march again, causing havoc to trade on the coast. A committee of the African Company decided something had to be done.

It wasn't until 1822 that Sir MacCarthy landed on the coast determined to sort out this king of the Ashanti once and for all. He organised companies of the African Corps and enrolled native militia. On 24 January 1824 10,000 Ashanti warriors advanced and halted on the north of the river Prah to face MacCarthy's forces. MacCarthy was slain, his forces slaughtered, a cast made of his skull in gold and paraded every year at the festival of the yams.

1867. Kofi Karikari was appointed guardian of the golden stool, His reign of terror continued, sweeping all opposition aside, drinking a toast to victories from the golden skull.

1874 saw the first British troops under the command of Sir Garnet Wolseley land on the coast. On crossing the Prah into Ashanti territory they were met by King Kofi's forces; a bloody battle ensued, and for the first time the Ashanti warriors were driven back. On reaching Kumasi, Wolseley found the town deserted. The golden stool had been spirited away with other treasures. The town was sacked. Wolseley returned to the coast empty handed, but with his skull still intact.

The destruction of Kumasi dealt a severe blow to Kofi's prestige, so much so that many chiefs opposed his authority.

*The cost of the war had left him in dire straits. Not used to living frugally, he resorted to raiding the royal mausoleum, taking jewellery from dead ancestors. When this was discovered, the chiefs were furious and gathered to confront him. On hearing they were coming, he ordered his servants to surround him, and waited alongside a barrel of gunpowder and the golden stool, threatening to blow himself and the golden stool to kingdom come if anyone tried to take him. He had virtually signed his own death warrant by threatening to destroy the golden stool. The chiefs, fearful for its safety, bargained, promising him his liberty together with his treasures if he handed over the golden stool. When the stool was safe in their hands, they blew him up with his own gunpowder. His buried cache of treasures and the gold skull were never found.*

*Mensa Bonsu was the next guardian, and set about restoring power to the court. Kumasi was rebuilt. He sent a golden axe to the governor, begging that the queen of England accept it as a peace offering. The more warlike chiefs did not want peace, and Bonsu was booted out.*

*1888. Prempeh was enstooled at the age of sixteen as heir apparent, and made guardian in 1894. The British government decided the Gold Coast and Ashanti should be part of the protectorate. Prempeh was having none of this, saying Ashanti would remain independent. Hearing the British were preparing for war, he decided to send an embassy to London, hoping this might bring peace. Too late. The smell of blood was once again in the air.*

*1900. The last battle at Kumasi ended with the defeat of the Ashanti armies. King Prempeh exiled.*

Michael paused. 'The sergeant told my father, if you ever get to Ashanti to seek buried treasure and the golden skull, don't ever mention or ask about the golden stool. If it was thought that you were seeking that, it would be another war started, and you would be the first to die. The golden skull itself must be worth a small fortune – think what descendants of the MacCarthys would pay – without what other treasure Kofi Karikari stashed away.'

Roberts stood abruptly and hit his head on the upper bunk. 'Sod it,' he said. And he sat back with a thump.

'What did you do that for?' Michael asked.

'To make sure I was awake; I thought I must have been dreaming listening to all that tosh. You kiss the Blarney stone, Mike? Must have done to cajole me into trying to believe that lot of codswallop, and waiting six months to tell me. You're glib, I give you that. Tell me, when were the battles of Hastings and Waterloo?'

Michael smiled. 'Ah, you are wondering how I could remember those dates, a doubt creeping into your mind if it could be true. I have a memory like an elephant. 1066, 1815. I remember what I was taught at school, but not those dates about the golden stool and skull. I looked that up. The sergeant told my dad the sequence of the events; I don't think he would have known all the dates himself. Nevertheless it is true. It's history, Chas; as I said, I looked it up. You look it up yourself when you get out of here.'

'No-no-no-NO – Michael, it's crazy to give it a thought; even if it was true, there would be more chance of finding a snowball in hell.'

Michael looked at Roberts with a bland expression on his face, a smile hidden behind his eyes. A Mona Lisa.

Roberts was the first to break the silence that ensued. 'No, Michael, don't count me in on this mad scheme. I'm going to catch some shut eye.'

He scrambled on to the top bunk, called out, 'Night, Michael.' Lay on his back and closed his eyes, but sleep would not come.

Michael stretched out on the lower bunk and listened to Roberts twisting and turning. Smiled and murmured, 'When the time is right, and it will be.'

Michael O'Leary stood still for a moment, his kitbag alongside, as the clang of the iron gate closing behind him resonated. 'Don't come back.' The words came faintly to his ears. He looked up at a clear blue sky above and took a deep breath, held it a while before letting it escape through pursed lips – *phew*.

He was in full marching order, minus arms. The webbing, having been scrubbed for many weeks, designated him as 'ex-glasshouse'. Buttons and other brass gleamed in the sunlight. Boot-caps, polished, shone akin to black snooker balls.

He had shaken hands with Roberts, saying, 'See you in twelve days' time; I'll be there outside waiting.' Collected his kit and doubled across to the outer gate as ordered, and there 'on the spot' until Bill Cox caught him up and gave a nod to the guard to open the gate, saying, 'Good luck, O'Leary.'

With ease Michael slung the kitbag over his backpack and stepped off at a steady pace towards the railway station, a travel pass safely in his pocket.

Back in the cell that evening, Bill Cox addressed Roberts.

'You're on your own now, Roberts; pick which bunk you want.'

He decided on Michael's, the lower one, to save clambering. That night he dreamt. A figure dressed in a flowing gown from neck to feet appeared, holding a gold skull high.

The first thing Tomkins did on leaving the company office after cajoling the orderly room sergeant into divulging

Blankensy's address was to undo the brass collar clips to ease his neck. The second to take from his tunic pocket the piece of paper to read the address, then – he walked smack into Tom Kearns, who had stood still watching Tomkins approach. He was brought up with a jerk, the paper fluttering to the ground.

'Bloody good job I wasn't the sergeant major, sauntering along reading, and yer collar undone,' Tom said, bending low to pick the paper up 'Wot's this? Is it—'

Tomkins grabbed the paper and stuffed in his pocket before Tom could get another word out. 'Nuffink, an old mate, used to be wiv the regiment, lost touch, fought I'd write, got the address from the orderly room sarge. How's yer mum?' Tomkins asked, changing the subject quickly.

'Bearing up; got to, ain't she, like all the ovver war widders.'

'Sorry, Tommy; yer dad was a good bloke even though 'e was a corporal.'

'Yeah, I'll git that bastard Blankensy, if it's the last fing I'll do.'

'No, Tommy. Forget it, yer young, got yer life to live. Git a good gal and git spliced, then yer can keep an eye on yer mum, not git yer neck stretched for the likes of 'im; it ain't worf it.'

'They'll 'ave to catch me first.'

Tomkins shook his head and walked away. Tom watched him go. *Old mate's address me arse, Blankensy's, I bet.*

Back in barracks Tomkins sat on the edge of his cot, and read the address. 86 Arlington Road, NW1.

*Gotcha, Camden bloody Town. I'll 'ave a nose around, git to know the lay of the land.*

He closed his eyes and visualised the route to take. The back-doubles through the maze of streets that only a

Londoner would know. That evening he set off. Tom Kearns watched him go, and followed at a discreet distance.

At the same time, Corporal Clive Jones was being greeted by his parents and sisters once again on arriving on a carefully connived leave, timed to allow him to visit the glasshouse at Shepton Mallet to meet Roberts on his release.

'Last time I was here, snow was on the ground, freezing, now the sun shining,' he remarked. 'Brilliant; a walk in the park would be nice, see the girls in their lunch break lolling on the grass, skirts above their knees, seeking a tan.'

'Clive!' his mother exclaimed, her voice rising, the Welsh lilt conspicuous in mock severity.

'I should be so lucky,' Clive said, fingering the facial scar.

'No, don't say that,' Gwyneth, his eldest sister, butted in. 'I know two who ask, "When is your brother coming home on leave?" I'll tell them, then watch the fur fly.'

Tomkins walked the Camden Town high street, asked a passer-by, 'D'yer know Arlington Road, mate?'

'Yeah, crosses the top of Delancey Street, next turning on the right.'

The bookie's lookout on the corner eyed Tomkins up as he turned into Delancey Street, a slight shake of the head; the street bookie at the junction to Arlington Road carried on passing a betting slip, the money slipping into his pocket. Tomkins sniffed the aroma as he passed Jones the baker's shop. *Lovely grub.* Halted at the junction, shook his head at the bookie's 'Do yer want to lay a bet?'

'Left or right?' Tomkins asked himself. He peered round the corner; no sign of Blankensy. Took a chance, turned right to check the house numbers

Number 51 was the first house Tomkins looked at, followed by number 53 on this length of Arlington Road bisected by Delancey Street. 'I was right,' he murmured. Odd numbers one side, evens on the other side: three-storey stock brick built Victorian houses with basements facing each other. Stone sills under sash window frames, spear headed iron railings at pavement level guarding open basement areas (*One, two, three O'Leary, my ball is down the airey, don't forget to give it to Mary*) over which a flight of stone steps led to buildings that once housed single families. Now converted to flats. Gates in the railings, with stone steps giving access to individual living space.

Tomkins walked on the odd-numbered side of the road, quickened his pace with head averted, felt isolated, not wanting to be seen by Blankensy if he suddenly appeared. He counted the houses, passed 86, taking notice with a quick glance across the road, and like Felix kept walking until he reached the junction to Parkway. The last two houses, 123 and 125, were now offices. Brass plates inscribed with names and professions indicated which floor they occupied.

He stood head down and pondered what to do next, *Can't just go and knock at number 86 and ask if a Mr Blankensy lived here, no, I'll 'ave to keep watch, try and catch him going out, but from where? Fink about it.* He looked at the basement of number 123. An arm reached up and drew the blind down on the basement window; a door opened and closed; a figure appeared and climbed the steps two at a time, pushed the iron gate closed behind him.

'Thinking of writing your memoirs, soldier?'

'Wot?' Tomkins's head jerked up.

'I saw you looking; seemed as if you was contemplating what to do. I am, or rather we, my partner and I, are book publishing agents.'

'Yer must be joking, I was finking. But writing? I can't spell for toffees, and writing? Just about me name. Can tell a few yarns, that's about it.'

'There you are then, you just said it: tell a few yarns. If you've something good and spicy, a ghost writer does it for you; could make you a fortune.'

'I don't fink so, mister.'

'Well, you never know.'

As he walked away, Tomkins called out, 'What time does yer office open?'

'Ten in the morning until five o'clock. Why, you thinking about it?' The answer and question came in one, over his shoulder.

Tomkins looked at the basement. *A good shell 'ole to 'ide in wiv 'ead just above the parapet.*

Tom Kearns peered around the corner from Camden Town High Street.

'Wot's this, a ruddy invasion?' the bookie's lookout said, watching Tom. 'Or on manoeuvres?'

'No, playing silly buggers. My mate, which way did he go? I'm supposed to be tagging him.'

'Right at the junction, Arlington Road.' He laughed. 'Wanner put a bet on that yer catch 'im, ten to one, yeah? Or do yer get a medal if yer does?'

'A black eye, more than likely. No, nuffink like that; 'e's looking for someone, and so am I, but I don't want 'im to know I'm looking for the one 'e's looking for.'

'For Chrissake, git out of 'ere.'

'All, right, all right, only kidding. Tell me, where does that Arlington Road come out?'

'The way yer mate's gone, Parkway. If yer wants to git in at that end, back to the Old Mother Red Cap in the high street, turn left.'

'Ta, 'e may spot me if I follows into Arlington: all 'ouses, nowhere to hide.'

Tom set off back along the high street at a double. 'Where's the fire, mister?' an urchin shouted as Tom dodged the passers-by. He turned into Parkway, slowed to a walk, cautiously approached the junction to Arlington Road and came face to face with Tomkins, who had decided to return to barracks via Parkway, it being a shorter distance.

'Wot the bloody 'ell yer doing 'ere?' Tomkins said, his voice raised to a volume that challenged that of a sergeant major on a parade ground. 'Yer followed me, yer sod.'

'No need to shout, Bill, I'm not deaf. I knew you wouldn't tell me Blankensy's address, but I guessed that was what was on that paper you dropped back in barracks. Yeah, so I followed yer. So, this is where 'e 'angs out, is it, Arlington Road? Wot's the number?'

'All right – all right – all right, Tommy, I'll calm down, but I told yer to leave it, didn't I? Wot d'yer fink yer gonner do if yer meet 'im: walk up, bang-bang, shoot 'im in the 'ead, or stick 'im wiv yer bayonet? Then wot? Yer mum's wept enough. Yer dad told Roberts that 'e'd break yer arm if Roberts didn't git yer off that attack, knowing 'e wouldn't git back. Did yer know that? 'ow d'yer fink yer mum would feel if ycr was strung up? It'll break 'er 'eart. Blankensy will git 'is comeuppance, but not by Tommy bloody Kearns. Yer copy? I know this bloke better than anyone in the company; I was 'is batman, wevver I liked it or no. 'e's a nut case, but not stupid; speaks well, but not like a toff. 'ow 'e got commissioned, buggered if I know, unless frough the ranks, but a major, no, I don't buy it.' Tomkins shook his head. 'Don't add up. I've brought water for 'im when 'e's been stripped to the waist to wash in 'is dugout, 'ard muscles, and 'is 'ands, working man's 'ands I tell yer.' Tomkin stopped. 'I've 'ad my say. I'm not gonner tell yer the number; in any case they are big 'ouses, made into flats or rooms; I gotter find out which one 'e's got. Now I want yer word that yer're gonner stay out of this.' He placed both hands on Tom's shoulders and looked straight into his eyes.

A woman passing by stopped, looked at the two staring at each other, hesitated, about to speak, saw Tomkins slowly shake his head, passed on.

'Well, Tommy, yer gonner promise?' Tomkins broke the silence.

'Yeah, all right.' Tom finally gave the answer.

'See it wet, see it dry. Finish it, Tommy,' Tomkins said.

'Cut me froat if I tells a lie.'

'Good. We'd better git moving, we've a route march across 'alf of the smoke to cover before lights out.'

They marched off in step, heads held high. The woman passer-by turned to see them go. She shrugged her shoulders. *Wonder what that was all about.*

The sentry at the gate stopped them as they marched in.

'You're in the shit, you two. The CSM wants to see both of you in his office as soon as you turn up.'

'You 'aven't seen us,' said Tomkins.

'Oh yes I have,' said the sentry. 'I don't want to be in it up to my neck as well.'

'Where have you two been?' barked the CSM, his voice high in decibels. 'You may be waiting for your discharge papers, but you are still in the army, can't just wander off without leave. I've given you some license; don't take it for granted.'

'Sorry, Sergeant Major, it was a lovely day, went for a walk in the park, fell asleep.'

'What park?'

'Regent's Park, sir.'

'Regent's Park!' His voice rose a couple of decibels. 'And you, Kearns?'

. 'I went to find 'im sir.'

'Jesus Christ. You know what you are, the pair of you?'

76

'Yes, sir. Lying sods.' Tomkins answered for both of them.

'You got it right that time, Tomkins. Now in future you get permission to leave barracks, and book out and in at the guardhouse, satisfy the commander you are properly dressed. Now dismissed. Not you, Tomkins, you stay put.'

'I've an inkling of what you are up to, Tomkins, but I do not want young Kearns involved,' the CSM stated forcibly as he stood, his face inches away from Tomkins, after Kearns had left. 'Do I make myself quite clear?'

'Absolutely, Sergeant Major, sir.

'Right, dismissed.'


'Wot did the CSM want?' Tom Kearns asked outside, when Tomkins appeared.

'Nuffink much: if I'd changed me mind about signing on again. Said it wasn't too late.'

'I don't believe yer. 'e's sniffing, ain't 'e? 'e could 'ave asked yer when I was in there.'

'Yer can believe wot yer like. Now leave it, Tommy.'

'Yer going back to Arlington Road?'

'I said leave it, Tommy, fer Chrissake; yer promised.'

'I only asked.'

'Well, don't ask any more; git off my back,' Tomkins shouted. 'I don't want yer wiv me any more. Go and git yer 'ead down before lights out.'

That night Tomkins twisted and turned in his cot. *He was standing in a shell hole, water up to his waist, his head just above the parapet; a girl was kneeling on the edge pleading, 'Giss me ball back, mister, I'm Mary.' He tried to move, his feet stuck firm in the mud. Go 'ome, go 'ome yer'll git killed, not until yer gimme my ball, yer can reach it, I'll drown, cowardly custard, bricks and stones will*

*break me bones, words will never 'urt me. 'I'll git it,'*
*Tommy said. NO Tommy NO, go away, I'll do it.*

A boot landed on his head, woke him with a start; he heard the voice, 'Shut up, fer Chrissake, you'll wake the dead.'

'That bloody well hurt. Ta just the same, I was 'aving a nightmare.' He slung the boot onto the floor, turned over and finally dozed off.

*Get out of bed, get out of bed you lazy buggers.* The sentry mouthed the words as the bugle sounded reveille.

Tomkins groaned, rubbed his head where the boot had landed, slung back the blanket, swung his legs onto the floor and stood. Pushed the bottom half of the iron bedframe back under the top half, folded the blankets and laid them on the bed, three biscuits, then joined the scramble at the ablutions. Dressed, boots and buttons polished expertly by one doing jankers for a penny the night before.[3] Double to the mess room for breakfast in time for parade.

Parade finished. Tomkins sought Tom Kearns.

'Sorry I shouted at you last night, Tommy; we're still mates, ain't we?'

'Yeah, guess so. 'e got at yer, didn't 'e, the CSM?'

'No, not really; 'e was finking of you, Tommy, didn't want yer to git into any trouble, fought I was leading yer astray. That's all.'

'I can look after meself, don't want anyone to 'old me 'and.'

'If yer say so. Now. Wot yer doing today?'

'Nuffink much, waiting for mail call, expecting a letter from me mum. So wot are yer gonner do, off to Arlington Road?'

---

[3] A soldier punished with 'jankers' is confined to barracks and must report to the guardroom every hour on the hour.

'Sod it, Tommy, I told yer not to ask any more.' He strode away in a huff. *That'll be the day when I get a letter.* He had taken a dozen or two strides and suddenly stopped in his tracks. Hit his forehead with the knuckles of his clenched right hand. *Why didn't I think of it before? Want to know the time, ask a copper; want to know where someone lives, ask a postman.* He turned. 'I could kiss yer, Tommy,' he shouted.

'Wot?'

'I'm gonner see a postman. Never mind, tell yer later.'

*No. 585. Guilty until sufficient evidence provided to prove innocent.*

The orderly room sergeant read it again. 'Blimey, that's a new one. Bit much, ain't it?' he murmured. It was two hours after Tomkins had been let out, having been inspected and logged. He picked up the scissors, carefully cut the addition to the amendments, pasted it in position, wiped the page and closed the red bound book of the King's Regulations, ready for the RSM to digest. 'Thank Christ that's the last of 'em.' Three days on and off it had taken. He leant back in his chair, hands behind his neck, and stretched his legs under the desk.

He sat up with a jerk as the door opened, to see a silhouette framed against the sunlight pouring in. He screwed up his eyes to see whoever it might be spoiling his moments of relaxation

'Don't yer recognise me, Sarge? It's me, Cooper, back from the dead.'

The ORS stood to gaze at a pair of unnaturally bright eyes sunk in a tanned face, contrasting with the pallid skin under a uniform that hung loose on a sparse frame.

'Yeah, yeah, of course, Cooper, just surprised to see you; caught me unaware. Sit down,' the ORS said, indicating a chair as he sat himself.

Cooper swivelled his head and nodded at the inner door.

'It's all right, the CSM will understand; sit down. He'll be pleased to see you've recovered. You've lost some weight, but got a bit of a tan.'

'Yeah, they let me sit outside in the grounds at the 'ospital when I was well enough, but yer right, lost some weight: a kidney, 'alf of me guts, and Gawd knows wot else. On liquids, gruel they said; couldn't fart, let alone crap. I've 'ad it, Sarge, on the scrap 'eap, no longer fit to serve, sent back to git me discharge papers, join the queue in civvy street. I can't cope wiv that, Sarge. The army's been my family since boys' service, don't know anyfing else. 'ow to kill, yeah, four years of that; now fit for sod all, because of that bastard Blankensy. Better I'd bought it, same as the rest of the platoon.'

'Don't say that, Cooper, you're alive.'

'Yeah, that's wot they all say: "lucky to be alive." Well, I suppose so, I guess, all those times going over the top, and a suicidal mission by that bastard. Wot's 'e do that for, when there was an armistice? Seems 'e wanted us killed. 'e'll pay for it, if it's the last fing I do.'

'Careful what you say, Cooper, don't shout the odds for all to hear.'

'Don't matter, Sarge, got nuffink to lose. Is Tomkins about? 'e came to see me in 'ospital, yer know.'

'Yeah, left a couple of hours ago, he'll be back.'

'Did yer give 'im anyfink?'

'What d'you mean?'

'You know wot I mean, an address.'

'You had better ask, Tomkins. I don't want to know what you're up to.'

'I git it, mum's the word.'

'Good, then I'll book you in, get you on the ration strength. You go and see the quartermaster sergeant, get a couple of blankets, not that you'll need them this weather;

you could fry an egg on the parade ground. Get a bed space, there is plenty there, the company down to nearly half strength. Do you want me to come with you?

'No, don't you start fussing, Sarge. I may 'ave one leg in the grave, but the other one is dandy. I'll git me 'ead down for a bit, wait for Tomkins to git back.'


## Camden Town

'You again?' the bookie's runner exclaimed as Tomkins approached. 'Did yer mate catch yer yesterday? 'e went back up Parkway, playing 'ide and seek.'

'Yeah, 'ead on.'

'So, wot's so special about Arlington Road? Yer mate said yer was looking for somebody, but didn't want 'im to know.'

'Did 'e now? 'e wants to learn 'ow to keep 'is mouf shut. I'm looking for a postman.'

'A postman? Yer not ginger, are yer?'[4]

'Looks that way, dunnit? I fink I must be, wot I'm up to, as if I didn't 'ave enough during the war.'

'We were all barmy then, mate. Yer wouldn't fink it, but 'im up at the corner, there's not tuppence worth of 'im, got the MM and they don't come up wiv the rations. Now 'e's taking bets at a tanner a time.'[5]

'And you?'

'Me! I've got flat feet. Lucky, yer might say, as they don't 'ave yer in the army in peace time, but I 'ad to go; take yer if yer 'ad two left feet in the war. Shoved into the Labour Corps, dug trenches, buried more bodies in one day than a grave digger would in two lifetimes. 'appy days, eh?'

---

[4] Urchins would call 'Ginger, you're barmy' to redheads.

[5] A 'tanner' was a sixpenny piece.

'Yer can say that agin.'

'Yer really wanner see a postman?'

'Yeah, a local one.'

'Yer Essex Regiment.' Looking at Tomkins's cap badge. 'Right? And yer traipsed over 'ere to see a local postman, Oh yeah, I git it, it's to do wiv Arlington Road; well, yer've missed the first post, the next's at four o'clock. Plenty of time to 'ave a kip in the park, or better still 'ave a cuppa and a cheese roll in Jones the Baker's, very good, 'e's got two lovely daughters, Welsh rarebit. Watch yer step, mind, as their brother is back 'ome, a real tough squaddie. Christ!' he suddenly shouted. 'A rozzer coming, nearly missed 'im, talking to you' He put two fingers in his lips and blew a shrill whistle, then took off as his namesake, 'a runner'.

The bookie at the far corner took off and turned left; a punter did the same, turned right, and both disappeared. Tomkins was left alone in an empty street. The policeman arrived at a run, panting, a finger pointing at Tomkins.

'You, was you going to place a bet? I saw you talking to the runner.'

'No. Certainly not.'

'What was you doing here, then?'

'Looking for a postman.'

'You taking the piss? I'll run you in as soon as look at you, soldier or not.'

Tomkins thought quick. 'Wanted to know where the post office was.'


'Home to roost, then,' Tomkins said as he shoved Cooper's legs off the cot and perched himself on the edge. He was back in barracks after a weary tramp back from Camden Town. He had been logged by the guard room sergeant and told that Cooper was back from hospital and waiting for him. He had found him lying on a cot in the barrack room, legs crossed and hands behind his head, stripped to the waist, rib cage standing out in relief against taut pale skin. An operation scar across a concave stomach peeped above the trouser belt, two rows of stitch marks showing pink.

'Not for long, I'm being booted out,' Cooper replied, struggling to sit up. ''ow are yer, me old cock? Bloody 'ot, ain't it?'

'Yeah, why don't yer take yer trousers and boots off and 'ave done wiv it?'

'Nuffink to be proud of down below, and I've got 'oles in me socks. While I fink of it, the matron sends 'er love, said give yer a kiss. I fink she fancies yer. I told 'er the jokes yer told me, cracked 'er face it did.'

'Ha-ha-ha, I'm rolling in the aisles. I'll dream of 'er tonight. Now yer back, join the queue, a few of us waiting for discharge.'

'Young Tommy Kearn, 'ow's 'e standing up, losing 'is dad?' Cooper asked.

'Same as you, and 'alf the company, wanting to 'ave a bash at Blankensy.'

'They'll 'ave to git behind me. 'ave yer got it, the address?'

'Take it easy, 'arry, yer not fit.'

'I've been taking it easy on me back for weeks in 'ospital, so don't mess me about, Bill, 'ave yer got it?'

'Yeah, but—'

'No buts,' Cooper cut him short. 'I'm gonner kill that bastard Blankensy, end of story.'

'I'm not gonner argue wiv yer any more. I've 'ad enough; let's go, right now, get dressed, right now, don't 'ang about, it's a five mile route march. I'll show yer where 'e lives. Yer go in, break 'is neck, better still shoot 'im in the 'ead. Then I'll see yer hang. 'ows that suit yer?'

'Don't git silly, Bill, losing yer temper.'

'Who's being silly? If yer want to give 'im 'is deserts, fink about it. We'll go over there, watch for 'im to come out, follow 'im, wait for the right time. Meanwhile git yerself fit. Can you walk five miles there and back?'

'All right, Bill, I'm listening. We can git a tram, can't we?'

'Git yer 'ead down, I'll see yer in the morning, yer crazy sod.'


## Shepton Mallet

The area surrounding the prison walls was bare. Not a tree allowed to flourish in the vicinity, denying any branch the right to hang over, let alone reach any wall.

Michael O'Leary stood in the shade of one such wall, and leant his back against it some feet from the double iron gates, a pleasant sight only to a prisoner seeing one opening on his release. Clive Jones adopted a similar stance a few feet on the other side of the gates. He had arrived half an hour after Michael, nodded at him, wondered, *Who is he waiting for? He's a big'un. Wouldn't like to mix it with him.*

Michael had nodded back, thought the same, but not concerned by how big Clive was.

The sun was rising fast, taking the temperature with it. The past few days it had been in the eighties, and this day promised the same.

Michael, not good at geometry, wondered how a shadow could be longer then the height of the object that had cast it. Something to do with angles; what did the teacher at school say? *The hypotenuse is…* No, he could not remember, didn't know, forget it. He did know, from the time he had spent there, that a prisoner's sentence ended at midnight of the last day, not a minute later. Never any added for a misdemeanour, as that was dealt with 'on the spot'. Never any less for good behaviour, as all inmates were on good behaviour at all times, or heaven help them. Nevertheless, a few hours might be conceded to release a prisoner in time to report back to his unit before lights out.

As the sun soared higher in a cloudless sky, Michael watched the shade shrink. 'If they don't let Roberts out soon,' he muttered, 'I'll fry standing here.' He gazed at a tree that flourished outside the nominated 'bare area' at some 15 yards' distance. Its leafy arms outstretched to pray, the shade beneath spreading like ink spilt on blotting paper to one side.

*My back to that trunk, my arse on the ground, an oasis methinks.*

He straightened, about to move when he heard boots pounding the parade ground the other side of the wall, then the command 'Halt'. Clive also heard, and stepped away from the wall, hung back, waiting for Michael to move first, not sure if more than one prisoner was being released. A few strides and Michael faced the gates to see the warden Bill Cox alongside Roberts grinning through the iron bars.

'Thought I might see you, O'Leary. He's all in one piece and fit as a fiddle, tuned to play,' Cox said. 'Fifty press-ups, no trouble. Right, Roberts?'

'Good to see you, Michael,' said Roberts, ignoring Cox's remarks.

'I said I would be here, and here I be. You going to open up, Staff? Been waiting long enough,' Michael said, turning to face Cox.

'All in good time; don't get too cocky, O'Leary.' He nodded to the duty guard, who produced a bunch of keys and unlocked the small portal to allow Roberts his freedom.

Michael grabbed Roberts's kitbag with one massive hand and shook hands with Roberts with the other. 'Any trouble, Chas?'

'No, was given VIP treatment. Well, some of the time.'

Michael laughed. 'VIP treatment my arse, that's good. Let's get on the way, first things first, to the nearest pub; I couldn't spit a tanner, this heat.'

Roberts turned to look at Cox through the bars of the gates, touched a finger to his forehead and nodded. Cox nodded back, called out, 'Watch your back, Roberts, and a kick in the goolies to you-know-who from me.'

Michael slung the kitbag over one shoulder, asked, 'What was all that about?' as they walked away.

'Cox saw me all right,' Roberts answered. 'I had the cell to myself. He sat and played chess with me at times.'

'So, not all wardens are bastards, then?'

'He could be at times, but as I said, I got VIP treatment.'

Clive bided his time, and stepped in behind the two as they walked away.

'Excuse me,' he called out. They stopped and turned. 'You may not remember me; I was the NCO in charge, escorting you – Sergeant Roberts – when the snow lay on the ground.'

Roberts looked hard at Clive, slowly nodded. 'Yes, as a matter of fact I do, because you had an altercation with the warden signing for me; he wanted me to double on the spot whilst outside the gates. That didn't do me a favour, as that one had it in for me at the least chance. So what do you want? And it isn't sergeant now, as you well know.'

'You're still sergeant as far as I am concerned. My name is Clive Jones. I want to thank you for saving my life, the Somme '16, as I believe it was you; in fact I am sure now.'

'The Somme? Who were you with?'

'The sappers.'

'You can talk as you walk,' Michael butted in. 'Let's get moving; it's too hot to stand about. You can chat about history after we've slaked our thirst.'

'That's Michael O'Leary giving orders,' said Roberts. 'We have something in common, but I'm one up on him: I whacked an officer, his one was only a sergeant. Did you two talk whilst waiting?'

'Don't tell me, let me guess, you boarded together.' Clive chuckled. 'No, we didn't converse. Strangers waiting outside a prison? One doesn't ask questions in that situation.'

'Well, Clive Jones, meet Michael O'Leary,' said Roberts. 'A warning: don't ever call him Mick; it's Michael once you've shook hands.'

'Jones, that sounds Welsh,' Michael said as he offered Clive a hand.

'Indeed to goodness,' Clive responded, mimicking a Welsh accent, followed by 'Not 'alf it ain't,' as in Cockney. 'Fair enough, yes, I was born in Wales, school in London after my parents moved: have a baker's shop in Camden Town, do a bit of baking themselves. They would love to meet you... what shall I call you?' Clive hesitated, flummoxed for a moment as he looked at Roberts.

'Chas, same as Michael does. Join us for a drink.'

'Wild horses wouldn't keep me back. Can we shake hands? Been waiting a long time. Never thought I'd ever meet up with you.'

They shook hands.

'Now all the shaking of hands has been done, let's get moving,' Michael said.


'So, what made you think it was me that saved your life?' Roberts asked, after a pint of ale had been downed by three parched throats and three empty glasses refilled. Clive had insisted on paying.

'Your nose,' Clive answered.

'My nose?' Roberts felt his nose. 'What's the matter with my nose?'

'You ain't gonner whack me if I say?'

'Depends.'

The glasses had been replenished, the barman was waiting. Clive placed a shilling on the counter for the second time.

'Must be Thanksgiving day,' Michael said. 'Let's sit down.'

Three pints were carried carefully, after 'collars' had been supped, to an empty table, and they sat down.

'Well?' asked Roberts. 'My nose, you said.'

'It's rather big, misshapen and a scar across the bridge. Although that doesn't show much now, looked as if it had been hit with a sledgehammer. That's what stabbed at me as you bent over to lift me and carry me to a first aid post. They told me there that I would have bled to death if a sergeant hadn't brought me in. Sorry, but you asked; you ain't gonner make mine look the same?' Clive paused.

Roberts smiled. 'No, but it wasn't a sledgehammer; that's another story, so carry on.'

'I tried to find you after I was finally discharged from hospital. I did not have any name, only that it was a sergeant that saved me. The war moved on, and I was carried along with it. Then six months ago, I was detailed as NCO to escort you to the glasshouse. I wasn't sure if you were that sergeant. I found out what regiment you belonged to, the Essex. And they were at the Somme in 1916, then I was sure. Am I right?'

Roberts nodded. 'Yes, I was there. You were lying out there bleeding like a stuck pig. That first assault had failed, the remnants of an army straggling back. The plaintive call of stretcher bearers heard. I nearly stumbled over you. What were the sappers doing out there?'

'Having a go at cutting the German wire that was not supposed to be there after a week's solid bombardment.'

'Yeah, like we were told there would be no enemy left. That was the Somme that July the first. Tell me, where did you come from?'

'Today, you mean? London, I'm on leave, time expired pending whether to sign on again, staying at my parents' place. They want to meet you, make you a slap up meal and thank you. Perhaps you could make that when in London.'

'Sounds good, a slap up meal, I'll go for that. Tell me, did you come all this way to thank me?'

'Yes, been waiting a long time to do that. I would have walked to Timbuktu to shake your hand. Such a coincidence after two years or more, us meeting.'

Michael, listening, said, 'Kismet, same as you being put in the same cell as me, Chas.'

There were a few moments of silence before Michael rose from his seat. 'I'll leave you two to think about it. I'm going to drain off.' The pub door swung to with a thud behind Michael as he exited to find the outside toilet.

Clive looked at Chas, questioned, 'What's he going on about – kismet?'

Chas shrugged his shoulders. 'That's Michael, he's fey. Forget it. You going back to London?'

'Yes.'

'You could join us. I have to report to my HQ in London, then I have a little business to attend to.'

'Is Michael stringing along?'

'I guess so.'

'Yes, pleased to join you both. That "little business" you have to attend to, is it to do with that officer that landed you in the glasshouse?'

Michael's return saved Chas having to answer; instead Chas said to Michael, 'Clive is coming with us to London.'

'Yes, that's right, destined to. Thinking of that, let me have a look at your travel warrant, Chas.'

'What d'you want that for?'

'To see what the railway stations are to and from.' He produced an envelope from his pocket, withdrew two blank forms and replaced the rest. Called out to the barman, 'Can I borrow a pen and ink?'

'You are the limit, Michael, where did you get them?'

'Where do you think? My old orderly room clerk was a wearer of the green. I never paid to travel on the railways. They are all franked, just want filling in. King's Cross, is it, we get off? Right. One for you also, Clive.'

The forms were duly filled in and signed. The signature, like most, was illegible.

'One more pint, then we'll be off. My turn,' said Chas.

'No, it's on me today,' said Clive, jumping and making for the bar.

'Let him,' said Michael, as Chas stated to rise. 'That's what he wants.

Twenty minutes later, three squaddies side by side stepped out in time to the railway station, Michael with the kitbag slung over one shoulder.


## Wythenshaw holding unit

Captain Richards leant back in his chair, tunic hung on the back, legs outstretched, ankles crossed, hands clasped behind his neck, eyes closed. He was not asleep, was contemplating the future. The war over, this cushy job was going to end. He had been lucky: no mud and trenches in Flanders for him, being a reservist, a bit long in the tooth and downgraded to 'B' medical-wise. *Not a word from the War Office, forgotten we exist; as long as the pay and rations arrive, why worry? Four years to be added to my service will help bump up the pension, I hope. Then what, kicked out into civvy street again? What will be will be.*

A rap on the door brought him back to earth. He sat up with a jerk. The RSM was standing at the open door, a look of disapproval on his face as he glared at the captain's state of undress. Richards hurriedly slipped into his tunic and buttoned up.

'Caught me improperly dressed, Sergeant Major; blame it on the heat.'

Sweat showing on the RSM's brow, tunic clipped tight, cutting into his neck, face as red a beetroot. *Yeah, I'll have my tunic off as soon as I get alone in my office, but the door will be locked.* 'Yes, I did, sir; lucky it wasn't the colonel. I've come to report two new arrivals, on leave from West Africa. Captain Reid and a Warrant Officer Mansfield.'

'Show them in, Sergeant Major.'

Captain Reid's peaked cap brushed the top of the door frame as he entered. WO Mansfield, five inches less in height than Reid's 6ft 4ins, made up for it by the width of his shoulders, almost brushing the sides of the same door frame as he followed, a formidable figure, a ribbon of the Military Medal showing on his breast.

Captain Richards introduced himself: 'Richards, adjutant and acting CO.' He shook hands with Reid. Mansfield saluted. 'Take a seat; you must feel at home, this heat.'

'It is a little warm,' Reid answered with a smile.

'Are you both from the same regiment?' Richards asked.

'Yes, 2$^{nd}$ Gold Coast,' Reid responded. 'WO Mansfield was my platoon sergeant when I was a two pipper. He is now the CSM of the same company I'm in. He saved my life in the Cameroons, we served together for some years. Now, he look for me.'

'Look for you?' a puzzled Richards asked. 'I don't understand.'

'No, I don't suppose you do. It's West Africa lingo. A guardian angel, you might say. Save a life, and you fend for him forever after. We now be "*Dan wanna*". Blood brothers. I suppose you do know that the WAFF won the first two battles of the war. Took Togoland, then the German Cameroons.'

'Yes, some news did filter through. Congratulations, and congratulations on your MM as well, Sergeant Major. I suggest we move to the RSM's office, and he can prepare your travel warrants.'

'I want to ask you something, if I may?' Reid asked.

'Fire away.'

'A friend of mine, we soldiered together as regulars. He was posted to an English regiment some nine months ago. He promised to write to me. I know mail takes for ever to reach WA, but not hearing a dicky I fear the worst. He must have reported here. I wonder if you could help me?'

'What was the officer's name and rank?'

'Major Blankensy. I have a photo.'

'Yes, I do remember the major; there was a warrant officer with him. It just happened that an incident occurred at that time. Both had been issued with travel warrants. A body had been found alongside the main railway line, naked, no distinguishing marks. The police, pursuing their enquiries as to missing persons, called to ask if any were missing from this depot, or any that had passed through. Don't worry, Captain, it wasn't your Major Blankensy,' he added, seeing the concern showing on Reid's face. 'We knew it couldn't be the warrant officer, as he had a tattoo on one forearm. I was asked to check if Major Blankensy had arrived at his destination. This took some time, but eventually I had the answer back from the Essex Regiment's headquarters. Yes, he had arrived, and been sent to France to take over as OC of one of their companies.'

'Thank you. Have you the address of the Essex headquarters? I will enquire there whilst I am on leave, hoping that he is still with us, if you know what I mean, as I'm still concerned, not having heard from him.'

'The headquarters are in London; that's all I know. Ask a soldier when you are in the smoke; that's what they call it.

Now let's get your travel warrants signed and I'll see you when you've finished leave. Get you passage back to WA.'

## Camden Town

'Look out for the 'orse shit, 'arry,' Bill Tomkins said as the two alighted from a tramcar at the busy junction of Camden High Street, Chalkfarm Road and the Parkway.

'It's lucky if yer steps in it, and it's good on rhubarb,' said Cooper.

'Not if yer slide arse over tit on it, and don't come out wiv that old un, I know wot yer want me to say, "we 'ave custard on ours".'

They negotiated a passage to the pavement, dodging horse-drawn carts and the solid-tyred wheels of Thornycrofts trundling by. A fresh trail of dung lay waiting for the 'scoop' used with dexterity by a lad with brush and pan in hand, performing acrobatic feats under horses' bellies to reach it before it turned to mash. They were on their way to Arlington Road. Tomkins had conceded to Harry Cooper's plea to take a tramcar, which meant three, each on different routes, the last being from the Archway Tavern at Highgate via Tufnell Park, to enable them to cross London's maze of streets.

The heatwave continued, softening the surface tar on roads, which stuck to horseshoes and soles of boots alike. *On the sunny side of the street.* The words of a song in vogue were being ignored. The shady side sought by pedestrians. Not so for one.

A pavement artist. He sat with back to railings, convenient for a pair of crutches to hang from, one leg outstretched, the trouser leg on the other pinned back above the knee covering a stump. 'Pip, Squeak and Wilfred'[6] clung to his left breast. A galleon lay at anchor in a chalky sea on one paving stone; an upturned cap held a mixture of coloured chalks and a similar cap with mouth agape waited to enfold pennies from heaven, flanking the galleon.

Tomkins leant forward and fed the cap, then dug Cooper in the ribs; Cooper did likewise. ''ow yer doing, mate?' Tomkins asked. 'Bit 'ot this side of the road for yer, ain't it?'

'Not bad, not enough room on the ovver side, and there's the shops. Better 'ere, good people pass on this side on the way to the park. One time a toff gave me a bit of silver – a bob – a real gent, had a patch over one eye and a scar down the side of 'is face. And I don't mind the 'eat; the stump likes it, aches when it's cold and wet. Yer didn't 'ave to do that, yer know.' Nodding at the cap with the coins in.

'No, of course we didn't. I'll take it back. So, 'nuff of that talk; who were yer wiv?'

'The Middlesex.'

'Good mob, the Diehards.'

'Yeah, and they did. Die hard.'

'Was it worf it?'

'You tell me, ask the muvvers and widders.'

'Me, I can't talk. Lucky, I guess. My mate 'ere, Cooper, just out of 'ospital, 'alf 'is guts taken out, right, 'arry? I take it yer live local?'

'Yeah, not far, jest orf Chalkfarm Road.'

'Anyone at 'ome?'

'The missus. Got a job in the laundry, so we git by.'

'Well, good luck; we'd best be orf.'

---

[6] 'Pip, Squeak and Wilfred' were medals: the Mons Star, the War Medal and the Victory Medal respectively.

'Wot now?' Cooper asked as they stopped at the junction of Arlington Road.

'Dunno, let me fink a bit,' said Tomkins. He looked around, idly watched an urchin kicking a ball along in the gutter. 'Got an idea.' Called out, ''ey, son. Wanner earn a copper?'

The kid stopped, picked the ball up and turned round. 'Who, me?'

'Yeah.'

He came and joined them, looked at their uniforms, said, 'Who've I gotta kill?'

'Oh, very funny,' said Tomkins. 'Wot's yer name?'

'Jimmy.'

'Well, Jimmy, all yer 'ave to do is knock on a door to see if the bloke that lives there is in, that's all.'

'Yer could do that yerself. Wot's 'e got as a pet, a lion or somefink?'

'Bloody comedian, eh? Do yer want the penny or not?'

''e ain't gonner whack me, this bloke, is 'e?

'No. If 'e answers the door, just say, "Sorry, guv, must 'ave the wrong 'ouse." Somefink like that.'

'Wot road and number?'

'86 Arlington Road, the basement.'

'Giss us the penny, then.'

'When yer git back, we'll be waiting.'

Blankensy heard the knocker drop. He peered through the corner of the window, the curtain pulled back enough to allow him to see at an angle to the outside of the door.

Whoever was there must have been standing close to the wall on the left of the door. He knew threats had been made against his life; he was not going to open the door to anyone from the Essex Regiment, so he waited, not knowing who it was.

Streetwise Jimmy knew there was times when his mother, and many others, did not open the door to the rent collector, when they didn't have the 'readies' to hand, so he knocked again, this time with more force, striking the knocker hard onto the iron stud. And waited likewise. *Stalemate.*

Finally, Blankensy watched Jimmy climb the basement steps; waited until Jimmy had reached pavement level (Jimmy, out of the corner of his eye, saw the corner of the curtain twitch and drop. *Fought so, 'e's 'iding, so wot's going on, not wanting to open the door?*), passed along the outside of the railings. He wondered what he wanted – a kid: who was he? Curiosity killed the cat; should he follow? He came out and mounted the stone steps until his head was just above pavement level in time to see Jimmy disappear around the junction at the Parkway, decided to follow.

'Yeah, 'e's in,' Jimmy said as he joined the two of them again at the corner. 'Wouldn't open the door though.'

''ow d'yer know 'e was in, then?'

'All this mystery, worf anovver penny, ain't it?'

'Not only a comedian. Yer a bloody extortionist.'

'Wot's that?'

'Someone asking for a thump; now, 'ow did yer know?'

'Saw the curtain twitch; 'e was 'iding. Is 'e a spy, or owing yer some money?'

'Never you mind. I ask the questions,' said Tomkins. 'Now, yer sure 'e was in?'

'Well, someone was. Now can I 'ave me penny?'

Jimmy got his penny, spat on it and put it in his pocket. 'If yer want any more doors knocked on, I'll do it, penny a time. Six at 'alf price.' He glanced back. 'Whoever it was, 'e's on the move.'

'Get back, don't let 'im see yer, Jimmy,' Tomkins said as he grabbed Jimmy's arm.

97

'That was quick, Bill,' said Cooper. 'D'yer fink 'e smelt a rat?'

'Could be. Which way, Jimmy? 'ave a gander. No, don't look round like that; on yer belly like a sniper, Jimmy. Not too near the corner, keep back a bit.'

''e's coming this way,' Jimmy reported, lying prone.

''e's following yer, Jimmy, the crafty bastard, wants to know if yer on yer own. Lead 'im on a wild goose chase, then lose yerself. We'll follow 'im.'

'That's worf anovver penny.'

'Yeah, all right, Jimmy. Where d'yer live, in case we want to git in touch wiv yer?'

'10 Osnaburgh Street. Not far.'

Another penny changed hands and disappeared into Jimmy's pocket.

'Keep forking out like this and we'll 'ave to walk back to barracks, 'arry,' Tomkins remarked. 'Git going, Jimmy; don't look round once yer know 'e's tailing yer. Saunter along innocent like, no trouble for you with your talent. Take yer time, look in a couple of shop windows, don't 'ave to tell *you* 'ow to use yer loaf. We know where to git 'old of yer next time if we want a sniper; 'ave to be after we've been paid.

The two crossed the road after Jimmy had left, and dodged into a pet shop. Rabbits in hutches; goldfish circled in glass bowls. A parrot gave them a malevolent look from its perch fixed across a pole. A slim chain attached to one scrawny leg and to the pole denied any flight to freedom. A tramcar rattled by; the parrot did a hop and squawked, 'Fares please.'

'Where the 'ell did it learn that?' Tomkins asked, seeing the proprietor appear from behind a rack of birdcages, wherein budgerigars and canaries twittered to each other.

'A conductor on the trams started it, calling out, and others took it up as they passed. Now it does it every time a tram passes.'

'Yer ain't got a crocodile as well, 'ave yer?'

'Yeah, under the counter, can't yer 'ear the clock ticking? Captain 'ook, 'e's upstairs, 'iding.'

''e's one up on yer, 'arry,' said Tomkins. They all laughed.

'So! Is this an evasion?' the proprietor asked. 'Or are yer wanting to flog a tiger yer brought back from the Indies?'

'No, never got out there; the trenches for us. We're keeping tabs on geezer that'll be passing by in a few minutes, then we'll be gorn. That's all.'

'I won't ask. Army business, I guess. Can I sell yer a boa constrictor while yer wait? They make good pets, hug well.'

''e's gone by, Bill.' Harry Cooper interrupted the banter, peering through the window.

'Best be orf, then. Fanks for the use of the shop, mister; might take yer up on the offer of the boa, or maybe a rattlesnake would be better.' A parting shot came from Tomkins over his shoulder as they both sidled out.

'Any time,' the proprietor answered. 'Bring the rest of the regiment next time, and you shut up,' to the parrot as a tramcar rattled by.

'You go a'ead, 'arry,' Tomkins said when they were outside. 'Blanksy knows me, being 'is doormat when I was batman, not you, I shouldn't fink; 'e didn't mix wiv the troops, or the officers, come to that. I'll 'ang back, on the opposite side of the road. Pity we didn't wear civvies.'

'I ain't got any.'

'Yer'll 'ave to git some soon.'

Blankensy watched Jimmy enter a sweet shop, come out sucking a liquorice stick and walk away along Chalkfarm

Road. Satisfied the kid was no danger, he crossed the busy junction at Camden High Street, turned south and took the first turning on the left.

'Where's 'e orf to now? Seems to know 'is way about,' Harry Cooper muttered to himself as he quickened his pace, not wanting to lose sight of the quarry. Bill Tomkins, watching from a distance, followed.

It so happened that at this time, Clive Jones was being greeted by his parents in Delancey Street on arriving back from Shepton Mallet.

'Did you meet the sergeant? Where is he?' his father asked.

'Steady on, Da, give me time to get in. Yes, I did meet him, and it was the sergeant that saved my life; he's had to report to his regiment headquarters. That answers your first question. And to save you asking more at rapid fire, I'll tell you. He has a friend with him, Irish and big enough to step across the Giant's Causeway. He was waiting to meet Roberts outside the prison as I was. We had a drink – let's say two or three – at the nearest pub to the glasshouse, the three of us, after Roberts was released, then travelled back to London together. When I left them, as far as I could tell, Roberts – Charles, "Chas" for short – is not going to sign on again, will wait for his discharge papers. He will come to meet you. Michael O'Leary, his Irish friend, no doubt will be with him; don't refer to him as "Mick"; call him Michael; just thought I'd mention that. He is Roberts's shadow. Against all regulations, because of the welcome Roberts received on returning from prison, O'Leary was given a bed space. The CSM doing a Nelson, "but not on the rations strength",' he quoted. 'That will be no trouble for the mess sergeant. Now how about a nice cup of tea? Any questions can come later.'

Blankensy passed one other turning and entered Bayham Street. Stood still, with his back to a wall to the rear of a block of two-storey tenements. His eyes roved the length of the street. He watched one pedestrian, no jacket, shirt sleeves rolled back, wearing a Panama which seemed out of place, as he walked away and disappeared at the far end of the street corner. A dog with back legs spread wide lay with belly flattered on the pavement, tongue a-loll in the shade. His eyes stopped at three shops, sandwiched between a builder's yard and a row of terraced slate-roofed houses, the front doors opening directly on to the pavement. The windows of the middle shop were nailed and boarded.

Cooper peered around the corner and quickly drew back as he caught sight of Blankensy standing motionless. He waved to Tomkins, who was entering from the high street, for him to cross over to the right, indicating by signals that Blankensy was around the next corner. Tomkins edged forward until he was directly opposite Cooper. They both waited.

''ave to take a gander, ovverwise we'll be 'ere all day,' Cooper murmured. He sidled forward enough to see the back of Blankensy as he walked away. He watched as Blankensy stopped opposite the shops and leant back against the brick wall.

*Wot the 'ell is the madman up to?* Cooper shook his head. *Can't make any sense of this.* Tomkins, on the other side of the road, wondered what was going on, couldn't contain himself, whistled and beckoned Cooper to cross over to where he was.

'Wot's 'appening?' he asked when Cooper joined him.

'Buggered if I know, nuffink makes sense.'

''e won't recognise yer like 'e would me, 'arry, if 'e looks this way; you watch, and tell me what 'appens.' Tomkins drew back to let Harry take his place.

The minutes ticked by. Tomkins nudged Cooper. 'Well?'

'Nuffink, I'll tell yer when.'

'I always fought 'e was bonkers. "Tea at four, Tomkins" lark. Now I know 'e must be.'

'I don't fink so Bill, 'e seems to know wot's wot, knew 'is way 'ere; 'ang on a mo, a bloke's just come out of a shop and walked away. Yeah, I git it, a customer, Blanksy was waiting for 'im to go. 'e's on the move now crossing the road; 'e's gone in that shop, Bill.'

Tomkins stepped forward so he could see. 'It's a mystery; 'e didn't come all this way to buy somefink, that's for sure.'

'Keep back, Bill, I'll tell yer wot's 'appening. Don't want to blow it now.'

They waited. Minutes passed.

''e's coming out now, two of 'em, the other geezer must be the bloke that runs the shop. Blanksy's tried the 'andle on the middle shop, it's boarded up; 'e's kicking the door now, peering through the cracks in the boarding over the shop window, banging 'is fist on 'em, shaking 'is 'ead. The geezer's puts 'is 'and on Blanksy's shoulder, looks as if 'e's trying to calm 'im down. Blanksy shakes it off. Wish I could 'ear wot they're talking about. Blanksy keeps nodding, 'is 'ead'll fall off if 'e keeps on like that; now 'e's stabbing the geezer in the chest wiv 'is finger, the bloke 'e's nodding now. Well, I'll be blowed, they're shaking 'ands; looks as if Blanksy 'as got wot 'e came for. The geezer's gone back in the shop. We'd better scarper, Bill, Blanksy's coming back this way.'

The two drew back to the high street. 'Separate, 'arry; I'll 'ide, you follow 'im, and I'll tag along as before,' said Tomkins. He then stepped into a 'sixpenny bazaar' shop and watched through the front window. Harry lost himself in the crowd and waited for Blankensy to appear, watched him cross the high street and turn into Delancey Street.

Clive had finished his tea and answered his sisters' enquiries as to what Sergeant Roberts was like, handsome, how old and so on, with, 'You'll have to wait and see.' Remembered it would be the sofa for him, and he wanted some shaving soap; decided to pop out and buy some. Stepped out of the shop door, and almost knocked over Blankensy, who was passing at that very moment. He apologised. 'Sorry, my fault.' Frowned as the two of them faced each other. 'Do I know you from somewhere?' he asked.

'No.' A quick retort from Blankensy, who pushed Clive aside and hurried away, head down.

'Not again?' the bookie's runner greeted Cooper as he entered Delancey Street. 'Who's following who this time?'

Harry Cooper tapped the side of his nose with one finger, and then placed it over his lips, and carried on.

Clive noticed Cooper's cap badge as they drew level. 'You're with the Essex. Right?'

'Yeah, that's right. Why?'

'Your Sergeant Roberts is back in barracks; thought you'd like to know. I travelled back with him from Shepton Mallet.'

'Oh, that's great news, I've been waiting to see 'im, to fank 'im. 'e saved me life, yer know; I ain't been out of 'ospital all that long. Yer wasn't inside wiv 'im?'

'No, went to meet him. Snap.' They shook hands. 'Jones, Clive Jones. I'm with the sappers, or was. He saved my life also, the Somme 1916.'

'Well, it's a small world, ain't it? Sorry I can't stop, see yer anovver time, call in the barracks when yer can. Name's Cooper, 'arry Cooper.' Harry pushed on, not wanting to lose the quarry.

'Jones the Baker's, my da's shop.' Clive pointed and called out, 'Pop in any time.' The words floated on air as Cooper disappeared round the corner to Arlington Road.

'Yer a non-runner,' the bookie's runner greeted Tomkins as he arrived at the corner of Delancey Street. 'Yer mate's well past the post by now, I reckon. He went that way.' He jerked a thumb, indicating a right into Arlington Road.

'Ta, mate,' Tomkins said over his shoulder as he hurried to catch Cooper up.

The runner shook his head. *I wonder what the two of 'em are up to? Something dodgy, I bet; ten to one on that.*

''e's gone back into 'is funk 'ole,' Cooper told Tomkins as they met. 'Wot are we gonner do now? Don't wanner be too long getting back to barracks. Roberts, he's back. I want to fank 'im.'

''ow d'yer know that?'

'A sapper told me.'

''arry, yer all right? Got a touch of the currant bun?'

''e's back. I'm telling yer. Now wot are we gonner do?'

'Well, now we are 'ere, 'ave a word wiv that shopkeeper bloke that Blanksy chatted wiv, see if we can find out wot's going on.'

'Softly softly catchee monkey, Bill,' said Cooper as they approached the shops on Bayham Street. 'I don't want the bloke to clam up on us.'

'Yeah, as yer say.' Tomkins peered through the boarding. 'The window's been smashed, can't see inside, too much muck on the glass.' He stepped back to look at the facia. The name had been daubed over. Small lettering read 'Leatherwork, boots repaired'. The shop to the right had a sign written board reading 'Furniture repairs, French polishing'. A handwritten note pinned to the door read 'Back in one hour'.

'Gives 'im some leeway, no time as to when it was written; clever, eh, 'arry?'

The shop on the left read 'Ironmongery. Paraffin sold here.'

'That's to tell yer 'e don't give it away, 'arry.'

Cooper looked through the window of the ironmonger's. 'Couple of customers inside, 'arry.' They waited until both had left, and then went inside.

Bill Tomkins started the ball rolling, asked, 'Sorry to trouble yer, mister, me and me mate 'ere was 'aving a look at the empty shop next door. D'yer 'appen to know if it's up to let?'

'Why?'

'We're being forked out of the army soon, got to make a living, fought we'd go in business for ourselves, selling army surplus gear.'

'No, it ain't.'

'Yer know who owns it, then? Perhaps we could 'ave a word wiv 'im, might change 'is mind.'

'No, I don't know 'im.'

''ow d'yer know it ain't − never mind, the estate agent, landlord then?'

'Wot's this, the third degree? I ain't answering any more questions, so shove off.'

'Don't git on yer 'igh 'orse, we only wanted to know if we could rent it.'

'No yer can't, so buzz off.'

'Eh, 'ang on a mo mister, who the 'ell d'yer—' He was cut short by Harry, taking his arm and leading him away.

'Wot'd yer do that for, pulling me away? I ain't taking any lip from the likes of 'im.'

'Yer ain't gonner git anywhere losing yer temper, Bill. If there is somefink going on between 'im and Blanksy, 'e's just as likely tell 'im two squaddies were asking questions. We can ask about anovver day, maybe the French polisher bloke; someone must know why that shop is boarded up. Let's git back to barracks, I wanner fank Roberts.'

'Blimey, 'arry, come up for breaf. Yer right, let's go, but we've gotta walk, I'm broke.'

'I've got enuff.'

'Yer crafty sod, 'arry.'

'Always put a bit aside for a rainy day, me mum told me, and I know wot yer gonner say, it ain't raining, but me boots are cracking for want of blacking.'

'Star, News and Standard. Read all about it,' the news vendor was shouting to all and sundry as they arrived at the Old Mother Red Cap at the junction of the high street.

Bill Cooper leant over to read the headlines of one of the papers atop a pile stacked on an upturned orange box against the pub wall; the partition halfway along the wall, acting as a shelf, held more. A small square of tarpaulin was folded alongside, ready for a cover against rain.

*The man they couldn't hang. Flint beats the hangman.*

'If yer wants to read all about it, yer pays yer penny,' the vendor said.

'Can't read, only look at the pictures,' Cooper joked.

The vendor looked at the medal ribbons. Laughed. 'All right, take one; I've been where you've been. That lot'll be gone soon, anovver delivery on the way, they're selling like 'ot cakes. The news will fill the papers for days, weeks probably.'

'Wot's it all about, Bill?' Harry asked when the two of them were sitting on the tram, on the first leg of the journey back to barracks.

'Yer can read it yerself after I've 'ad a dekho.'

## The Essex barracks

'I'm so sorry, Sarge, it was all my fault yer 'aving to do six months in the glasshouse, and losing yer stripes. Yer should 'ave left me.'

Cooper was thanking Roberts after he and Tomkins had arrived back.

'It was worth it, wasn't it? So forget it; you're all in one piece, that's what counts.'

'I'll make it up to yer, Sarge. Me and Tomkins 'ave been tagging Blanksy, the bastard; I'll git 'im if it's the last fing I'll do.'

'No, oh no you don't. You leave that to me, and don't keep calling me sarge; I'm a ranker, same as you.'

'Yer'll always be Sarge to me. More than that, yer saved me life; I would 'ave bled to deaf out there. I ain't got much, wot I 'ave is yours, so if there is anyfing I can do for yer, yer'd tell me, wouldn't yer?'

'Yeah, of course. You can tell me where Blankensy hangs out for a start.'

''e's got a basement at 86 Arlington Road, Camden Town, we tagged 'im going to a shop—'

'I'm not concerned about him going shopping, just his address. If anyone asks questions later, you know nothing. Understand?'

'Yeah, all right, Sarge, but Blanksy wasn't going shopping; the shop 'e looked at was boarded up, been empty for years by the looks of it.'

'Perhaps he wanted to buy it. Look, leave Blankensy to me. All right?'

'If yer sez so, Sarge.'

'Wot's 'e 'ave to say, 'arry?' Tomkins asked when Cooper rejoined him.

'Nuffink much. As long I'm all in one piece, that's all that matters.'

'Did yer tell 'im about Blanksy, wot we've been up to?'

'Yeah, told me to leave it to 'im.'

'So, we gonner leave it now?'

'No. You can if yer likes. I don't want the sarge to git into any more trouble if 'e does wot I fink 'e's finking of doing. It's down to me. I'll do it, got nuffink to lose. Yer don't have to git involved, Bill.'

'I'm wiv yer, 'arry, all the way, I told yer before. We'll ferret Blanksy out, see wot 'e's up to, then decide. 'ave yer got 'nuff for the tram fare?'

'Just about.'

'That's settled. Let's git some shut eye.'


## The baker's shop, Delancey Street

'Penny for your thoughts, Clive,' Colin Jones said, seeing his son leaning back on the sofa, hand behind his neck, gazing at the ceiling.

The shop was closed for the day, the family resting after the evening meal. Gwyneth in her usual seat, a cushion on the floor, her back resting against her brother's knees. Grace, her elder sister, alongside Clive on the sofa.

'Trying to put a name to a face,' Clive answered. 'Someone I bumped into when I popped out earlier. He pushed past me; didn't want to know me, it appeared. I'm sure I know him from somewhere.'

'Forget it, the more you rack your brains the more it will elude you. It will come when you're not thinking of it. That's how it works,' his father said.

108

'Think about when you are going to bring Sergeant Roberts and his friend to see us. That's more like it,' Grace butted in.

'Yes, Clive.' Gwyneth added her voice. 'We're all agog to see how handsome they are.'

'Oooh, like that, is it?' Clive came back at them. 'I'll go to the barracks first thing in the morning, bring them back for tea. How's that?'

'I'll shut the shop early; more time to have a chat, get them something to eat and drink,' his father said.

'Don't fuss too much, Da, they won't want that.'

'Your mother and I want to thank the sergeant; not a question of making a fuss, Clive.'

'We all do,' both sisters called out. 'Leave it to us.'

Evening shadows lengthened, the sun losing its grip as it slid down behind chimney pots; the pavements cooled as Blankensy sat, his eyes focussed on the basement window. The inner image a shard of glass, red with blood, behind the haze that was his eyes. The lamp lighter halted at the lamp post outside, his 'wand', a long slim pole, held aloft. He inserted the end with a hook through the small aperture of the lantern atop the post: a chain pulled, the hiss of gas escaping, a click, a flint sparked, the mantle lit.

Magic. A pool of light shed a shadow of the railings across the basement window, seeming now as that of a barred cell.

Blankensy blinked. The madness that had been with him was ending; he knew also that time was running out for him. He went to a drawer and took out a service revolver, spun the cylinder, shook his head, replaced it. Found a sharp-pointed paring knife amongst the cutlery in what acted as a kitchen, wrapped it in a duster and pocketed it. It was time.

He went out, climbed the basement steps, hesitated at the top, turned left, not wanting another encounter at Delancey Street, and made his way to Bayham Street via Parkway.

Last orders had been called at the Old Mother Red Cap. Towels spread over the pump handles on the bar, he noticed through the open door as he passed. Ignored the newspaper vendor, wrinkled his nose as he passed the urinal.

'It stinks in 'ere, wants some more pitch on the wall.'

'Well, you're not 'elping; point it downwards in the gutter, not up the bloody wall.'

He heard the voices from the other side of the wall, and hurried on.

Bayham Street boasted two lamp posts, sited on opposite sides of the street at the regulation distance apart, which gave sufficient yellow glow at night to see one's way.

At day, out of school hours, enterprising young girls tied their skipping ropes together and slung them over the ladder bar to swing on. '57 varieties' mongrels cocked legs at the base.

He took up position, near enough equidistant between the lamp posts with his back to the wall as before, enough light in the sky even at this late hour. He watched two figures enter from one end of the street, cross to the row of terraced houses.

'Yeah, all right, got it, Ernie, mum's the word.'

'Don't be late.'

'Missus'll see to that; kicks me out of bed when the alarm goes off, then turns over.'

The voices came faintly to his ears. He waited until they had entered their respective abodes, and with no other body in sight he crossed the street to the boarded shop, bent down and felt for the key hidden under a brick. A new lock had been fitted to the door, the key turned smoothly, he opened the door, the hinges protested, the door creaked, he entered, closed the door behind him and stood still and was taken back four years. There was adequate light filtering through the cracks of the boarding to see the debris and broken glass on the floor, the jagged edges of what was left of the large shop window. He stretched an arm for support against the wall; a momentary loss of control overwhelmed him, four years of pent-up emotions about to explode. He steadied himself and made for the workshop area at the rear.

A three different foot size iron cobblers last lay on a bench among scattered hobnails, metal blakies and strips of leather. A stool rested on its side on the floor. He bent and lifted it, placed it on its legs and sat down; the disturbed dust assaulted his nose; he sneezed and squeezed his eyes tight to stem the tears. The shutters of his mind opened. He lived it again.

It was 1914. War had been declared. No hands wringing in anguish. 'It will be over by Christmas.' Thousands rushing to enlist to join the fray before it finished. Groups of friends, factory workers, lordships' estates, public schools queued *en bloc*, wanting to stand back to back, with sword in hand, defending the colours on the battlefield, returning home heroes with medals. No sir, three bags full sir. Blown to pieces by huge guns never seen, for rats to eat the remains and gnaw the bones. That's what, sir.

Christmas came and went. Not many could say they enjoyed the festive season. Curtains drawn across the parlour windows of the 'heroes' not coming home. Telegraph boys on red bicycles were dreaded – messengers of death. Seeing them drew intakes of breath from passers-by. *Oh my God, not another.*

It began to dawn on the populace that this was turning into a world war. A slaughter about to take place. Unfounded rumours began to circulate of atrocities taking place in Belgium by German soldiers, babies bayoneted and the mothers raped. Those of German descent domiciled in

Great Britain feared for their lives as mobs ranged the street shouting 'Kill the Hun'.

In Bayham Street, the 'French polisher' saw them coming. He hurried out, locked the door behind him and took off as fast as his legs could carry him. The ironmonger took refuge behind the counter, peeped over the top to watch.

His mother was arranging a small display of leather goods on the counter adjoining the shop window, handmade purses and bags, when the brick smashed the window.

He was engrossed at the workbench, cutting the pattern of a boot sole from a new section of leather, when the crash came. He jumped up, the stool crashed to the floor, he turned and within a few quick paces was there. She had fallen across the counter, blood pouring from her neck, a jagged shard of glass embedded in the jugular vein.

He tried to stem the flow of blood by pressing the palm of his hand tight over the wound; it was not circulating, the heart pumping it out between his fingers. A second brick hurtled through the smashed window, and struck his forehead with such force as to stun him. He fell back, losing his grip. He never heard the police whistle, or was conscious of following events.

He opened his eyes. Try as he might, only flickering images came to mind.

*Blood in his eyes – kicking and shouting – arms restraining him – handcuffed and ankles bound – the 'Black Maria' – standing in the dock charged with assaulting an officer – six months' penal servitude and interned for the duration – Mother? – Sorry – could not be saved, too much loss of blood – burial – no other next of kin – will be as the law dictates.*

He knew now. The blanks filled in by the ironmonger who had stood by and watched, unable to help. He had gone berserk, trying to get at the mob in the street. The police restraining him, he had broken one of the constable's arms. He knew now who threw the bricks. His mother buried in a pauper's grave unknown.

Blame the war that made heroes, cowards, and sent others mad.

He found the knife he had been using those years ago, the curved pointed blade, sharp as a razor, that could cut leather as easy as slicing cheese; exchanged it for the paring knife in his coat pocket. Searched carefully among the shattered glass, found what he wanted, wrapped and pocketed it. One last look around before he left. Locked the door behind him. Looked at the key, undecided what to do with it, shrugged his shoulders, slid it into his trouser pocket.

The ironmonger who had waited patiently, seated low behind the counter in the dark in his own shop, watched him walk away. *I knew he would come, and I know where he is going. God forgive me.*

He wearily climbed the staircase to his rooms above, knowing he would not sleep this night, or peacefully in the future.

### *Landsdown Buildings, Camden Town*

The locals never knew where the name 'Landsdown' came from. A councillor perhaps. The tenants were quite happy with it, quite posh actually. One end led into Pratt Street; it could have been named 'Pratt Buildings'. Dread the thought. It had three arched entrances in its length that gave access to the ground floor rooms and a stone staircase to the upper floor, which even on the brightest of days was in semi darkness.

Ernie Betts had rooms on the ground floor. He worked for the LNER out of a depot adjacent to King's Cross station, had done so since leaving school, now at the age of 31 years was a ganger, oversaw a gang of platelayers that no longer laid plates. (That was a name given to workers before the introduction of the edge-rail in place of the plate rail.) Now they walked the sleepers, to check all was in order: the nuts, the bolts, the spikes, the gauge, if the granite chippings needed ramming under the sleepers, and any maintenance work to make safe the section they were responsible for. Betts had had no fear of having to serve in the trenches during the war, maintenance of the railways being a reserved occupation. He was also a trade union shop steward, dreaming of being a leader, having a posh office and secretary, if he could master the rhetoric: the florid oratory needed.

A knock came on the door. *Wonder who that could be this late in the evening? One of the gang, wanting to skive off work tomorrow?* He opened the door, could not see who was standing in the shadows, heard the voice.

'Betts, isn't it?'

'Yeah; wot d'yer want? Who are yer?'

'You don't remember me, Betts, no?'

Betts screwed his eyes, peered closer. Fear came with recognition, his mouth dried – parched. At that moment he knew he was damned, doomed. He could only croak.

'Yer, yer—'

'Yes, Betts, yes, you do recognise me then?'

''ow'd yer—'

'How did I know it was you, or how did I find you; is that what you want to know? There was a witness, kept quiet all those years, fear of reprisal, it was wartime, what was done was done, After all, did it matter? I was led away, no, not led away, carried away, put in a straitjacket at times.

You killed my mother, Betts. Get inside. Don't want to disturb your neighbours.'

Betts tried to close the door, it was slammed back, Betts stumbled, he was grabbed from behind, the door closed behind by a heel. The knife came to hand, gripped tight by the short wooden handle, the curved blade pointing down alongside his thigh, as he followed close. Two steps into the room, the arm circled, the point of the blade went into the side of Betts's neck, the blade cut deep. He stepped back. Betts, his mouth agape, his eyes wide open with shock, stood immobile for a brief moment; his knees gave way, he knelt and fell forward, the blood spouted as a fountain from the jugular vein.

He stood and waited whilst the blood drained from Betts, staining the linoleum. He carefully drew the cloth from his pocket, unwrapped the shard of glass, leant down and withdrew the knife from Betts's neck and inserted the shard of glass in its place. Stood and listened. All was quiet. He wrapped the knife in the cloth that had held the shard of glass and pocketed it. Opened the door a crack to peer through. The coast clear, went out, quietly closed the door behind him and walked away.

The moggies were on the prowl as he walked. The shadow of death in his face, a ginger astride a garden wall arched its back with unsheathed claws and hissed as he passed.

It was finished, the last piece of the jigsaw in place, the picture complete in his mind. One last act, to leave the pieces for others to fit together.

He crossed Camden High Street, and decided. There was no longer need for anonymity, so Delancey Street rather than the Mother Red Cap's stinking urinal.

He stopped opposite Jones the baker's shop. The light shone from the window above the shop. The top half of the

115

sash open seeking air, the curtain drawn back. He heard their voices, the laughter.

*You asked, 'Do I know you?' Yes, you do know me, Clive, but you would not want to know me now; that's why I pushed past. I remember when you enlisted, your parents and sisters. Grace always brought me a fresh pastry when she came to collect the boots I had repaired – her smile – I held her hand on one occasion – if events had turned out differently, who knows? God bless you all; I doubt if He will me.*

He walked away, laughter ringing in his ears.

The shadow of the railings showing as bars to a cell on the basement window were there when he walked in, leaving the door ajar. They would still be there until the lamplighter came with his magic wand at dawn.

He removed his jacket, washed the leather cutting knife and placed it with the cutlery, took the service revolver from the drawer, inserted one shell into the cylinder, lined it up with the firing pin, closed it, sat down, and waited. It would not be Russian roulette.

He recalled his first time in an English school. All classes at the morning assembly in the big hall. The Lord's Prayer recited. *Forgive us our trespasses.*

The hours passed.

The lamplighter stopped at the lamp post outside number 86 as an officer emerged from the basement steps, walked away with head down.

'And good morning to you, thanks very much,' the lamplighter said. 'Got out of bed the wrong side, did we?'

He raised his magic wand. 'Plop,' the mantle said. 'That's me finished for the day.'

The bars across the basement window faded as the first streaks of light appeared.

The sun heralded the dawn, warning of another scorcher. The lamplighter was on his way. Jones the baker slid out of bed, quiet as a mouse so as not to disturb his wife and the rest of the household, and crept downstairs to light the oven. The ironmonger gave up trying to sleep after tossing and turning all night, dressed and made a cup of tea. The bugler at the Essex Regiment sounded reveille.

'We gonner go, Bill?' It was two hours later, ablutions and breakfast over when Harry Cooper put the question to him. 'See if we can git anyfink out of that French polisher geezer?'

'Could be wasting our time, 'e may not be there. That note about "be back in an hour" I reckon is a lot of whitewash.'

'We've nuffink else to do except twiddle our fumbs waiting for our discharge papers; 'sides, I wanner know wot Blankensy is up to.'

'Got 'nuff for the tram fares, or we gotter walk?'

''nuff for one way.'

'All right, but don't expect me to carry yer on the way back.'

'We can always 'ave a kip in the park, rest up a bit before we starts back. Tell yer wot, talking about the park, take some chalk, do what that pavement artist we spoke to does. Might pick up a copper or two.'

'Yer a real bleedin comic, ain't yer, 'arry? Git off yer arse, let's go.'

## Highbury Station

'Nice of you to come, Sergeant Major; any trouble getting here? Been enjoying your leave?' Captain Reid shook hands as he greeted CSM Mansfield.

'Yes, great time, and no bother getting here; will be pleased to see our old CO.'

'Well, let's hope we can; first find the Essex Regiment headquarters, see if he survived the western front. I rather fear the worst, not hearing from him, but letters do go astray, especially to West Africa.'

Tomkins saw them coming.

'Blimey, talk about the long and short of it, 'arry, that one would 'ave to duck to git under the Marble Arch.'

'They're making for us, Bill, must 'ave 'eard wot yer said. Talk yer way out of that, ovverwise they'll slaughter us.'

But to their surprise the tall one stopped a few paces short and said, 'You must be from the Essex Regiment; tell me I'm right?'

'Yeah, we are,' Tomkins answered. 'Who wants to know?' Bravado taking over.

'You are speaking to an officer, Private,' CSM Mansfield barked out.

Tomkins came to attention. 'Sorry, sir, 'ow was I to know?'

'It's all right, of course you wouldn't have known; you can relax. We are both on leave from West Africa, that is CSM Mansfield and I, Captain Reid. The CSM spotted your badges; we only wanted to know if we are on the right road to the HQ of the Essex Regiment.'

119

'Yes, sir. Straight on until you come to Highbury fields, then turn left; our barracks are at the arse end – oh, sorry, sir, at the back – to separate us from the civvies.'

'Language, Private,' the CSM tutted.

Captain Reid laughed. 'I understand, at the rear end. Thanks. You wouldn't happen to know a Major Blankensy?'

The surprise registered on both Cooper's and Tomkins's faces. They looked at each other. *Two kids caught with jam on their fingers, guilty look on their faces.*

'Tell me; it's obvious by the expressions on your faces that you do. Did I make a *faux pas*, a clanger as you may well say? Let me explain. Major Blankensy was our OC. We served together in Africa, two bloody campaigns, Togoland and the Cameroons, at which we were victorious I may add. No finer soldier could one meet – and a friend indeed. He promised to write. I fear the worst, not receiving one letter. I know he arrived here, and was posted to take over a company of the Essex Regiment in France. I was told that by the movement officer at a holding company, Manchester, when the CSM and myself arrived there. So! Tell me. I must know.'

'Yes, sir, I was his batman; he wasn't killed,' Tomkins replied.

'Thank God – what a coincidence, meeting you. So, is he at HQ?'

'I fink it better if yer asks the adjutant there, sir.'

'I'm asking you. What's the problem? You say you were his batman; you must know. I don't want to go barging in at HQ if there is something I should know first.'

''e resigned, left the regiment; that's all I want to say, sir.'

'Resigned! No. Never. The major would never do that. The army was his life, a career man, never resign his commission. I can't believe it.'

'What's your name?' CSM Mansfield asked. 'Excuse me butting in, sir,' turning to the captain.

'Tomkins, sir.'

'Well, Tomkins, you was his batman, so where did he live when not at barracks? I'm talking about after the war had finished.'

'I wasn't his batman then. I told yer, 'e left; that's all I gotter say. Yer'll 'ave to ask at HQ.'

'All right – all right,' said Captain Reid. 'At least I know he is alive.'

'Blimey, that was a turn up for the book, Bill. Why didn't yer tell 'em?' Cooper asked after the captain and the CSM had left.

'Tell 'em wot? Why don't yer use yer loaf now and agin, 'arry? Tell 'em we want 'im dead? We would be the first suspects when Blanksy gits 'is rhubarb and custard, which 'e will; even if we don't do it, someone will. Those two would blabber to the cops if we had shouted the odds. Let them find out for themselves. They'll git the address, that's all; nobody at HQ is gonner give much away.'

A railwayman's creed is time. Live by the clock, always be on time, never late. As one well-known Irish RSM said when taking roll call, 'If you don't answer your name, you're not present.'

Ernie Betts wasn't present when the shift began, but was clocked in. On time.

His gang of platelayers that didn't lay plates were union men (had to be, or no job), stood shoulder to shoulder. They knew the ropes: Betts was taking the day off – it happened now and then – attending to union work for their benefit, of course. He would be in tomorrow on time. Nothing said.

They collected tools and paced the sleepers. No major incidents, mud slides blocking the rails, a bridge collapsing;

121

it was humdrum work, mundane. They had a refuge, brick built at the side of the track, used in inclement weather, to eat their bread and cheese, to make tea and, whilst the cat's away, to skive.

Clive Jones rolled off the sofa, folded the sheet that had covered his nakedness, placed it under a cushion. Slipped into his pants and trousers, went downstairs barefooted and barechested to the scullery, his father already at work in the bakery, having lit the oven fire two hours past, his mother cooking breakfast. He called out, 'Morning, Da; morning, Ma.' Filled a bucket with water, grabbed a towel, soap, his cut-throat, and moved to the backyard. Grace, at the marble-topped washstand in the shared bedroom, poured water from a jug to the basin, slipped her night-dress off. Gwyneth watched from her bed, waiting for her time to wash.

'Leave enough water for me. I filled the jug last.'

All, in all, a happy family, going about their usual routine, unaware of the events to follow.

The orderly room sergeant at the Essex headquarters examined the AB64 paybook belonging to CSM Mansfield to verify who he said he was. Took a 'gentleman and officer's' word, Captain Reid being such. He referred them to the adjutant, who gave them the address they wanted but would not discuss why Major Blankensy had resigned. He repeated what Tomkins had said: 'You will have to ask Blankensy yourself.' Omitting the rank of major.

'Your discharge papers are here, Roberts. You will be a civilian from tomorrow.'

The CSM was facing Roberts in the HQ office, having sent for him immediately after early morning parade

'Look at them.' He pointed to a pile on the desk in front. 'Damn nigh half of the company. Cooper and Tomkins are among them; at least Tony Kearns's boy is staying on. I'll do what I can to get him promoted. A chevron might ease the loss of his father.

'I sent for you so we could have a chat and to ask if you have anywhere to stay, give you time to think about it; not long now.'

'No, been trying to get my head around to it. I never thought the day would come when I would be getting my "ticket", let alone asking for it.'

'You can still sign on again, you know.'

'No. Not as a ranker, start again at the bottom. No. Thanks to that Blankensy.'

'Any idea as to what you might do?'

'Thought about it, applying for security guard with one of the big companies or a city bank, but a prison sentence on my records, that ain't so clever, is it? O'Leary is in the same boat. Wants me to go on some crazy hunt for buried treasure in West Africa, said his father soldiered there in 1900 – the last Ashanti war. Was told some lord had his head cut off and a cast made of pure gold of his skull, as a trophy of a previous battle, by the victorious warrior king of Ashanti at that time. It would be worth a fortune.'

'Irish, ain't he? Kissed the Blarney stone, I suppose; he'd believe anything. If you had been here earlier, you could have asked a Captain Reid. Believe it or not he is on leave from West Africa, him and his CSM. Came to see Blankensy, said they had soldiered with him in Africa, best of friends, would not believe Blankensy had resigned.'

'Did you tell him?'

'I didn't speak to him myself. The adjutant dealt with it. Gave him Blankensy's address, and told him to ask Blankensy himself. You gonner see him? Blankensy.'

'Oh, yes, I'm certainly going to have a word with him. Been biding my time, but now I'm a civvy, or will be tomorrow.'

'Don't do anything to land yourself in the shit, for God's sake.'

'I'll watch where I'm stepping.'

'All right. Listen, I need a forwarding address from you. You and Ireland can bed down here on the quiet for a couple more days, no longer; that's the best I can do. So let me have one in the morning when I dish out the "tickets".'

'I hear. I'll get one.'


'So that's it, Chas, we'll be free. See to that what's-his-name, Blankensy first, then seek our fortune,' Michael O'Leary remarked after Roberts had informed him that he would be a civilian as of tomorrow.

'Don't start that flimflam again, Michael, you know it's a no-goer. Even if we wanted to, how are we going to get to Africa: swim, or sneak aboard a trooper and end up in irons?'

'It's a yes-goer, Chas. I knew when my dad told me that one day it will happen, and as sure as pigs are pigs it will.'

'You've got that wrong; "if pigs can fly", you mean.'

'What?'

'Never mind, you're too big to argue with. I'm going to sort that Blankensy out now I'm a civvy, or will be tomorrow; won't have to worry about being put on a 252 then.'[7]

'Have you got the address?'

'Yes, but you don't have to come.'

'I'm coming, let's go.'


Outside they met Clive Jones on the way in.

'Just caught you,' Clive said. 'I thought it might be a good day for you to meet my parents, Chas, and you of

---

[7] A 252 is an army charge sheet.

course, Michael. You did promise, Chas, unless you have something else arranged.'

'As a matter of fact I have; I was on the way to sort this Blankensy out, the one that sent my platoon to hell.'

'I'll do that, Chas, I owe you, just tell me where he lives.'

'No you don't, Clive, it's down to me; what you can do is tell us the best way to get to Camden Town.'

'Camden Town! That's where I come from; my Da's shop is there. What's the name of the street?'

'Arlington Road. Do you know it?'

'Know it! It's just around the corner from the shop. I'll take you, not as escort this time, Chas.' He laughed.

'Better you stay out of this.'

'You've told me the address now; I'm in, like it or not, Chas.'

'No, Clive, no. Tell you what, show me the road and where your dad's shop is; I'll come there after. That's it, no argument.'

'Show *us* the road, Clive,' Michael butted in. 'I'm staying with Chas, and no argument. Let's go.'

They marched away in step.


'There you are, guv, Arlington Road. Wot number d'yer want?' the cab driver asked as he slowed, turning from the Parkway into the road.

'Number 86,' said Captain Reid. He and CSM Mansfield had caught the cab at Highbury Station. Thought it the best and easiest way to get there, not knowing London all that well.

The cab crawled along, the cabbie's eyes following the numbers of the houses, stopped outside 86. 'There you go, sir, that'll be two and six.' His arm stretched out and he opened the passenger door without leaving his seat.

They alighted; the captain gave him three shillings. 'Thanks, keep the change.' The metal flag clicked up indicating the cab was available as it drew away.

Captain Reid led the way down the stone steps to the basement.

'That's odd,' he exclaimed, seeing the door ajar and hearing humming coming from inside. He pushed the door inwards and went in, was greeted by a black cloud of flies rising and falling. A thousand wings beating the air, bluebottles incandescent – enraged, having been disturbed. He flayed the air with his arms to disperse them, which only angered them more, the humming reaching a crescendo. He moved forward, then he saw it, the body slumped in a chair, the head a mass of splintered bone, brain, blood and bloated bluebottles.

'Oh my God,' he cried. Stopped abruptly with shock.

CSM Mansfield, hard on his heels, almost knocked the captain over. 'What the hell's happened?' Peered over the captain's shoulder. 'Oh, Jesus, is that the major?'

Captain Reid removed a handkerchief from his pocket, held it over his mouth and nose, and stepped forward. He had seen many killed in battle, but this gruesome sight was a different kettle of fish; seeing his OC, half of his head missing, shook him to the core. He leant forward, grimaced as he brushed bluebottles from the dead face, stood with a jerk.

'Oh my sainted aunt,' he exclaimed.

'What's the matter?' said Mansfield.

'It's not the major, not our OC. I think I'm going mad, these bloody flies don't help...'

'Steady, sir. That's good, isn't it, not being our OC?'

'Yes, all right; bit of a shock, seeing what was our OC and then it wasn't.'

'Are we at the right address?'

126

'Yes, this was the number, and they told me at the Essex HQ that it was the basement.'

'Then who is this bloke, and where is the major?'

'Heaven knows.'

'We had better get out of here, sir. We could get pulled for this. The cab driver and those at the Essex know we came here. The police will nab anyone to get a conviction, won't believe we were friends; they'll say that we lied to get the address.'

'Wait a minute, check the other rooms.'

'A uniform hanging in a wardrobe, and some KD in the drawers.[8] So this is the right address; must have belonged to the major, wearing them when he left WA like we all do, changed on board when nearing the UK. Who else would have KD?' Mansfield said when he came back.

The captain was staring at the body. The right arm hung straight down on the outside of the chair; a revolver lay where it had fallen from nerveless fingers, helped by gravity. He stooped to pick it up.

'No, no. Don't touch,' shouted Mansfield.

Too late; the captain had it in hand and examined it.

'This could be the major's. Service issue, .38 Webley. A nick on the butt. The major joked about it, "like the cowboys, a notch for a kill"; it wasn't true, of course. I could check the stamped number on records when we get back to the regiment to confirm that.'

'Do you think he killed this bloke, the major?'

'Why would he want to do that? Don't make sense.'

'An intruder, a burglar, was threatened, shot him, panicked and gone off somewhere, back to WA maybe.'

'No, I don't buy it. The major never panicked, you know that. He was an honourable man, would have reported it. No I think it was suicide, this chappie killed himself.'

---

[8] Khaki Drill, army issue for tropical wear.

'How come, then? If you think it was the major's revolver?'

'Good question. I don't know the answer; it's a mystery. Let's get away from here, discuss this outside, somewhere to sit, a café, decide what to do.'

'Wipe that revolver, don't leave any prints.'

'I'm taking it with me, give it back to the major when we find him.'

'Is that wise? It is evidence. If you get caught with it, there'll be no way out for you; it will be the gallows.'

'If I leave it, the police will check whose it was, will know it's an army issue, nab the major. I'm taking it; get a cloth, duster, something to wrap it in, and we leave.'

They left the door ajar as they had found it. Mansfield, halfway up the stone basement steps, peeped through the railings. Called over his shoulder.

'All clear, no one about.'

On the pavement they turned right, took the first turning on the left.

'This will do fine,' said Reid, seeing the pastries in the window, the chairs and table at the counter, 'Jones the Baker's' on the sign. 'Better than talking outside; get a cup of tea and decide the next action.'

Back at 86, the flies settled for a second helping.

Clara and Alice, spinsters both, shared rooms at number 85. Which was almost directly opposite number 86 Arlington Road.

Stone steps from the pavement to the main entrance bridged the basement area, the 'ground floor' being higher than ground level, which gave them a clear view of the street from their window, unimpeded by the railings that guarded the basement.

128

*Better to have loved and lost then never loved at all.* One adage quoted. Debatable. Many war widows would agree. No consolation to those who never did have the chance to love.

The father of Alice and Clara left a leg and a half in the Crimea. Considered himself fortunate: a dutiful wife and two daughters to care for him. In due time a wooden 'peg leg' was strapped to the stump below the knee of the half and he was given two crutches. Clara at that time was two years older than Alice's ten years. Three years later their mother died. *Hard work never killed anyone,* so it is said. Four mouths to feed – drudgery – poverty – hunger. 'Heart failure', the doctor wrote on the death certificate. Clara became the breadwinner, got a job at the haberdashery, Alice the drudgery. No time to love.

Haberdashers dealt with farthings. *'That will be elevenpencethreefarthings, please – thank you.'* *'Oneandelevenpencethreefarthings, please.'* Never 'one shilling' or 'two shillings'. Some customers, the richer clients, buying silk ribbon perhaps, never bothered to pick up the farthing change. Clara pocketed that. At the end of a good day, as many as four. At the end of the week, between 20 and 24. That went into a post office savings account. £5 a year with interest. Clara was learning fast. Alice took in washing and ironing from those that could afford it.

Clara gradually took over the running of the shop, the elderly couple who owned it becoming infirm. She attended to their wants. It paid off. The shop and contents were left to her on their demise.

The years passed.

*'Old soldiers never die; they just fade away.'* So it is said. Their father did eventually fade away. Too late for Alice and Clara to find love. The Great War came and went. The shop was sold, rooms rented in what was a respectable area. Alice and Clara, no need to want, hoped to live

happily ever after. They took turns to make the first cup of tea in the morning and take it back to bed. No need to rush. A wash – a leisurely breakfast – a table and two chairs at the bay window, to play patience and watch the world go by.

'Arlington Road is the first turning on the left off the Parkway, there,' said Clive, pointing. The three of them were standing outside the Old Mother Red Cap at the junction of Camden High Street. 'Delancey Street is the first turning also on the left off Arlington Road, the way you will be going; that's where my da's shop is. You can't miss it. You sure you don't want me to come with you, Chas?'

'No, you go on, we'll meet you there. First left, first left, got it.'

Clive watched them go, turned and made his way along Camden High Street.

Captain Reid had decided it would be best for the two of them to return to their respective 'leave' addresses, and meet at the Manchester Depot in two days' time when due to report for returning to West Africa.

'We never saw our OC. Knocked at the address given, but no answer after trying twice and gave up, understand, Sergeant Major?' said Reid.

'Absolutely, sir, we never saw him.'

'Don't mention it unless you have to, either at Manchester or back at our unit. Any questions, I'll do the talking.'

They were enjoying a buttered scone with their 'cuppa' when Clive walked in. He nodded to them, ducked under the flap of the counter and was greeted by Grace.

'Are they coming, Clive?'

'Yes, won't be long, half hour maybe.'

'I thought it was arranged for this afternoon.'

'Change of plan, I met them at the barracks as they were leaving on the way to somewhere near here; have to see someone, so might as well come on here after. Doesn't make any difference when they come, does it? Oh, I see, you want to dress up a bit. Hope you're not disappointed; they're an ugly pair of so--' Checked himself. 'So-and-sos.'

Grace blushed. Gave him a hug.

'Very nice,' murmured Mansfield.

Clive heard. Said, 'My sister.'

'No offence,' Mansfield responded, 'but you must agree, your sister most certainly is. Or is it to be pistols at dawn?'

Clive laughed. Grace blushed again.

Alice reached and lowered the top half of the sash window, pushed the bottom half up, leaving a gap top and bottom.

'That's better, let the air circulate.' She sat down in her usual chair. 'Sevens this morning, I think, Clara.' Shuffled the cards, glanced out of the window.

Roberts and O'Leary at that moment halted outside number 86.

'I'll come in with you, Chas,' Michael said.

'No, I'll do this on my own.'

'You gonner kill the sod?'

'Six months ago, I wouldn't have hesitated. Had time to think about it since; is it worth it? He would have the last laugh: I would swing for it; it wouldn't take the police long to pin it on me. Revenge the motive. Then you would have to find that gold skull yourself.' He laughed. 'I'll see what he has to say.'

'Guess you're right, Chas. Give him a good kicking where it hurts, break an arm or two, make him suffer, same as you and Cooper did.' He wiped the sweat from his brow. 'This sun's a killer; I'll wait on the other side of the road.'

'Watch where yer going, yer daft sod,' said the cyclist as he swerved, narrowing missing O'Leary as he stepped off the kerb.

'Sorry, sun in my eyes,' O'Leary murmured. Crossed and sat on the steps to number 85.

Hardly two minutes had passed before Roberts appeared on the pavement again, gesturing, pointing to his right, and began walking in that direction. O'Leary crossed and joined him, pacing alongside.

'What's wrong? You was out of there a bit smartly.'

'Don't stop, keep moving. He's dead. Been shot.'

'What! Did you see the gun, touch anything?'

'No, the door wasn't locked, ajar, I walked in and saw him, slumped in a chair. Never stopped, came straight out.'

'Got his deserts, that's for sure. How long ago, you reckon?'

'Not long, the flies at it.'

'We'll have to tell Clive; he's expecting us. Not in front of his family, get him to one side.'

'Of course, act normal, don't stay too long if we can help it.'

'Then what?'

'Back to barracks, keep mum.'


'Can't tell yer much, I wasn't there when it 'appened,' the French polisher said. 'Didn't tell Cooper that he had done a bunk.'

'When wot 'appened? Yer said it 'ad been closed since it 'appened.' Cooper pressed the point home. He and Tomkins were in Bayham Street once again. The French polisher was a bit friendlier than the ironmonger had been last time they were there.

Cooper was doing the questioning, had told Tomkins, 'You're like a bull in a china shop; I'll do the talking.'

'All I knows is the rioters – bloody madmen – smashed the front winder in; as I said, I wasn't there at the time.'

'Why?'

'Because they were German, or used to be, been 'ere years. The muvver and son running the place since the father died. Nice people, the son 'ad gone to school 'ere. It was just after the war 'ad started.'

'Wot 'appened to 'em?'

'Wot d'yer want to know for? It was wartime, I was called up soon after. Ask the council if they know if yer can rent it. It would please me if yer did, it's an eyesore.'

'Wot's the matter wiv yer?' Tomkins butted in. Couldn't contain himself any longer. 'Why all the mystery? Yer like the bloke next door, clammed up, tight as a fish's arse'ole. Yer must know what 'appened. Told to keep yer trap shut, is that it?'

'That's it, git yer mate out of 'ere, or I'll call a copper.'

'All right – all right, we'll go. Come on, Bill.' Cooper took Tomkins's arm, led him away.

'I told yer to keep quiet, didn't I?' Cooper remonstrated with Tomkins when they were outside the shop. 'I was jest getting somewhere, now yer've blown it'

The door opened as they were walking away; the French polisher called out, his hand cupped over the corner of his mouth, 'Ask at the Islington Gazette, the young reporter'

'We've opened a can of worms, Bill,' said Cooper. ''is conscience is troubling 'im.'

'I didn't do much good in there, did I? Blurting out,' said Tomkins.

'No yer bloody didn't, but yer triggered 'im off. Can't let it go now we've been told where to start. Wot d'yer fink?'

'Nuffink better to do, so yeah. Never know, might git a good story to tell that publisher's agent bloke, git a ghost writer to write it up into a book, make some dough.'

'Wot agent? And wot's a ghost writer?'

'Never mind, 'ave yer got enuff for a cuppa at that sapper's dad's baker's shop?'

'Wot sapper?'

'Yer asked before, Christ almighty. Wot sapper – wot agent – wake up, 'arry, I'll show yer.'

Captain Reid and CSM Mansfield were just leaving as Roberts and O'Leary arrived at Jones the baker's shop.

'Recommend the scones,' said Mansfield. 'Don't get saucy with the lass behind the counter, her big brother's there.'

Roberts wasn't in the mood for chit-chat, kept quiet, but O'Leary, eyeing Mansfield up, said, 'We know that.'

'You must be careful what you say at times, Mansfield; that one who spoke, and eyed you up the way he did – Irish, if I'm not mistaken, and as big as they come – could have had you for breakfast. You never know, he may be the lass's beau. I might have been calling for a stretcher for you.' Captain Reid gave Mansfield a bit of ticking off as they walked away.

'That was quick,' said Clive from behind the counter as they entered.

Roberts put forefinger to lips with a slight shake of the head.

Grace never saw that. Her eyes were taking in Michael, and Irish eyes were smiling, holding her gaze. Paralysing her faculties.

'Grace,' Clive called to her; the spell broke. 'Run and tell the others they are here.'

He then cleared the top of the counter flap, hooked it back, went and closed the front shop door, locked it, turned the notice hanging there so the 'Closed' faced outwards.

'What happened?' he asked *sotto voce* as Grace left.

'Blankensy. Dead, shot in the head, found him like that,' Roberts told him. 'Talk to you later.' Hearing footsteps coming downstairs.

Gwyneth was the first in, closely followed by her parents; Grace a few minutes after, taking time to remove her overall and pat hair in place.

Clive introduced them. 'Sergeant Roberts, the one who saved my life – Chas, short for Charles – and Michael O'Leary – Michael or Mike, never Mick.'

Mrs Jones hugged Chas, with tears in her eyes. 'I can't thank you enough. God bless you.' Went to Michael, shook hands with him. 'You are his friend. You will look after him, please.' She stretched to look into his eyes. 'You know what I mean.' Said almost in a whisper, as for his ears only.

'Yes, I do, and I will.'

It was Mr Jones's turn next to shake their hands. 'Anything I can do, just ask, don't hesitate.'

Gwyneth leant forward and lightly kissed Chas on the cheek. Blushed. Said, 'Thank you, thank you.' Then shook hands with Michael, no kiss, seeing Grace watching.

Grace never hesitated, shook hands with Chas and thanked him, and then to Michael. Took his hand and held it to her cheek, never spoke, it wasn't necessary, they both knew. Destiny decided.

Mrs Jones noticed, raised her eyebrows, smiled, said, 'We weren't expecting you until late afternoon for a meal.'

'Sorry if we have upset your arrangements,' said Chas. 'Something cropped up.'

'No you haven't, don't say that please; you are welcome anytime, night or day. So can you stay awhile, have something to drink and eat?'

'How about the famous Welsh rarebit?' Michael got a word in. 'And make another time to call after working hours.'

'Good idea,' said Mrs Jones. 'I can do better than that, rustle something else to go with it. Take the girls for a walk in the park; they will show you where. It is a beautiful day. Clive can visit the off licence so you can quench your thirst when you get back, say an hour?'

'Can't argue with that, Mrs Jones,' replied Michael. 'We can spare that time, Chas. Right?' Nodding. Chas nodded back. Michael felt his hand squeezed. Smiled.

So it was agreed.


'That's odd,' said Alice, glancing out of the window.

'What is?' came from Clara, without a glance up from the cards spread in four lines on the table.

'Two couples on the other side of the road: the two men I saw earlier, and it looks like the Jones girls with them. It is, they're crossing over, I can see them clearly.'

'So what's odd about that? This is the sunny side; they're seeking shade.'

'I don't mean crossing the road; one of the men went into the basement flat opposite, and came out in a hurry. The only time I've seen anyone go there was a young lad, and he never went in, knocked then left.'

'Who lives there, do you know?'

'No, never seen him or her, whoever it is.'

'They go in at midnight dressed all in black. It's a vampire that stays there, can't go out in daylight, sucks their blood.'

'Clara!'

'Alice! Look at that, the four of spades, got it, I can run out. First time in a week it's come out.'


'Well, I'll be blowed,' Tomkins exclaimed. 'There's Lanky over there wiv 'is sidekick.'

He and Cooper were standing at the kerb of Camden High Street, waiting for a gap in the traffic to cross.

136

'There's those two from the Essex Regiment,' Captain Reid said almost at the same time. They in turn were standing opposite wondering which way to go. 'We can ask them, they're Londoners.' They waited.

Tomkins and Cooper crossed, dodging between horse carts, tramcars and other means of transport.

'Did yer see yer mate Blanksy?' Tomkins asked when they were safely across.

'Sir,' said CSM Mansfield. 'And it's Major Blankensy.'

'Yeah, of course,' said Tomkins. 'Major Blankensy. Sorry, practising 'ow to speak as a civvy, now that we are.'

'You are still in uniform.'

'Can't walk about in our undies, can we? – Sir.'

'All right, if you must know, we didn't see him; we knocked, but no answer,' the captain lied. 'Perhaps you could tell us where we can catch a main line train; we've had no luck trying to find a cab.'

'Yer'd be lucky to catch one 'ere, unless one's on the way back after dropping orf a fare. But it's easy peasy: cross over t'ovver side, catch a tram going that way. It don't go any furver than the end of Hampstead Road, end of the line. That'll be Euston Road. Turn left, do a Felix. Not far to Euston – St Pancras – King's Cross Stations. Three to choose from.'

'Thank you; wish you well in your new lives, both of you.'

'What did he mean, "do a Felix", Mansfield?' the captain asked as they walked away.

'Keep walking. Like Felix the cat.'

'Not a bad bloke after all, the captain,' said Cooper.

'No, seems wiv it. Now yer sure yer all right to make it to the Gazette office, 'arry? Yer look a bit seedy.'

'Yeah, can't give up now, git a cuppa tea. I'll be fine.'

'Can't keep away, can yer?' the bookie's runner greeted them at the corner of Delancey Street. 'Who yer after this time?'

'Come to see Clive, 'ave a cuppa at 'is dad's baker's shop,' said Tomkins.

'Yer know 'im, then?'

'Sort of, I know 'e's wiv the ginger beers.'[9]

''e's jest gone out, and 'is sisters wiv two blokes; one of 'em's from your mob.'

''ow d'yer know that? One from my mob?'

''ow d'yer fink? 'is cap badge, same as yours.'

'Is the ovver one big?'

'Yeah, yer can say that agin, and Grace is holding on to 'im like grim death.'

'Well, strike a light. I didn't know 'e 'ad any sisters, and I'm dead sure that O'Leary didn't. Trust the Irish to git a foot under the table. It must be 'im with Roberts; wait until I see 'em. Grace, yer say; yer know the family then?'

'Know 'em? Yeah. See 'em nearly every day. Go in for a break, git a bite to eat and a drink. Lovely folks. So yer know these two blokes?'

'Yeah, Roberts saved my life, and Clive's,' Cooper butted in.

'Oh, that's good to hear somefink like that. Yer going in?'

'No, we'll leave it now, make it anovver time.'

'There's a caf the ovver side of the junction in Chalk Farm Road.'

'Ta.'

---

[9] Slang for 'engineers'.

'Blimey, yer better stay outside, 'arry, it'll kill yer in 'ere,' Tomkins said after opening the street door to the premises. He screwed his eyes against the smoke-laden atmosphere to see four desks, with hardly enough room to pass between, each with a new-fangled pedestal telephone, a typewriter and sheaves of papers. Two were occupied by men in shirtsleeves, tie and collar loosened at the neck, coat hanging on the back of the chair, cigarette in mouth, tapping away on the keys, overflowing waste baskets underneath. An office at the rear with an interior window and glass-panelled door.

He approached the nearest desk; a thumb jerked, pointed him to behind. He moved to the next desk and waited, watched, fascinated by the typewriter carriage travelling back and forth, a *ting* sounding at each change, fingers dancing on the keys. A twirl of finger and thumb, the sheet of paper freed and now being read. He waited.

'What?' The voice sounded annoyed, the cigarette stuck to the bottom lip.

'I was told to ask for the young reporter that was here in 1915.'

'Who told you?'

'The French polisher.'

'You taking the piss? Shove off.'

'No, I'm not; sounds funny, I know, but it was a French polisher. 'e's not French, just wot they're called; I don't know why, but yer'll know that.'

The 'voice' looked at Tomkins's Pip, Squeak and Wilfred medal ribbons on his breast, said, 'I don't actually.' The cigarette came out and was stubbed by a shoe on the floor, and half a chuckle was heard. 'Look, I haven't time to listen to some cock and bull story. I was here in 1915, until called up. Be quick. What do you want, and why a young reporter?'

'Do yer know Bayham Street?'

'No.'

'I'm on to a good story, believe me, but I must speak to the young reporter who reported wot 'appened there in '15. 'as to be 'im. That's why.'

'You could look up back copies to find out, downstairs in the library; ask "Inky", give him a drink, he might do it for you. Roughly 1,825 of them, if my maths are right.'

'No, not bloody likely, and it might not be in one of 'em, because I fink it could 'ave been hushed up.'

'Whoa, steady on there, careful what you are implying.'

'Steady nuffink. Yer can always ask this young reporter after we've 'ad a word wiv 'im if yer tell us who it would be.'

'Hmm, sounds interesting; probably Jack "smart arse" Barnett. He was a cub reporter in the crime section at that time. Editor's favourite now, the one that got the first news about this Flint bloke cheating the gallows: got a mate in the prison service, leaked it to him before it was announced as "an act of God". Made the front page with his name as the reporter. Beat the Fleet Street Press to it. You must have read it.'

'Yeah. Got up your nose, did it, a young cub beating an old wolf?'

'Yeah, I suppose you could say that. He was lucky, was at the prison gates at the time of the hanging. Waiting for the bell to ring, like other morbid sods, to say it was done – although it was his job, had followed the murder trial – when a prison officer came and removed the public notice giving the time of hanging. It was Jack's mate, whispered to Jack. The trap door failed. Made Jack top reporter.'

'Where can I find him?'

'You tell me; will-o'-the-wisp is our Jack.'

'Give me a clue.'

'He drinks at the King's Head most lunch times; d'you know it?'

'I'll find it. 'ow would I know 'im?'

'Big ears.'

'Ta.'

Cooper was sitting on the steps leading to a house on the opposite side of the street, the shady side, when Tomkins came out.

'Yer *sure* yer all right, 'arry?' Tomkins asked as he crossed over.

'Yer, jest taking it easy. Did yer 'ave any joy in there?'

'Got a name, Jack Barnett, drinks in the King's Head; we can only try. Yer up to it?'

'Got no money for booze, Bill.'

'Don't worry, use our loaves.'

Tomkins shoved the saloon door of the King's Head open with his shoulder, struggled in supporting Cooper.

'Gis an 'and, someone, me mate's collapsed,' said Tomkins. A chair was brought and Cooper lowered into it. ''e ain't been out of 'ospital all that long,' Tomkins continued. 'Can 'e 'ave a glass of water, barman?'

The water was brought; Cooper took a sip and spat it out.

'Yer trying to kill me, Bill? Rot me guts, and I ain't got much of 'em left as it is.'

Jack Barnett, sitting listening to a nark, watched the act. Smiled, said, 'Trying it on, the pair of them.'

'I 'eard that,' Cooper said. Undid his tunic buttons and drew up his shirt. 'Wot's this then, Scotch mist?'

'Bloody 'ell,' the barman remarked, seeing the wound and surgical scars, the stitching showing like a double row of eyelet holes, angry red against the pallor of white skin across the abdomen. 'I'll get yer a brandy.'

'I'll pay for that,' Barnett called out. 'Sorry, mate,' to Cooper. 'I thought the pair of you was taking us for a ride, you know, for a free drink.'

'You Jack Barnett from the Gazette?' Tomkins asked.

'Yes. That's right, how did you know?'

'One of yer college mates at the Gazette told me how and where yer might be.'

'Did he now? Naughty of him, and it's "colleague", not "college".'

'Colliwotever, and we *was* taking yer on. But jest the same, as yer can see, me mate was in the war real proper, and that's part of wot we wants to 'ave a word wiv yer about: tell yer 'ow 'e got shot up like that, and ovver fings, on the QT, so 'e can sling 'is 'ook.' Pointing to the nark. 'But first yer can buy that drink. A Guinness is better for me mate's guts; come to that, me as well.'

'Well, I take my hat off to you for the subterfuge, but what makes you think I would want to talk or listen to you?'

'Do you know Bayham Street?'

'Bayham Street?' Jack Barnett frowned, pursed his lips.

'Yeah, *that* Bayham Street. Early 1915. Yer was there, pup reporter.'

'Two bottles of Guinness barman shove off Bert see you later.' It came out in one breath from Barnett as he beckoned Tomkins and Cooper over.

Cooper eased himself out of the chair, buttoned his tunic, left the collar clips undone and followed Tomkins. Two chairs were pulled close to the other side of the table, and the two sat facing Barnett. The Guinness arrived and was placed on the table, the two glasses raised. 'Cheers.' Replaced half empty – or half full, depending on how one thought.

Thirst half quenched.

'The only way to drink Guinness. Down 'alf in one go, then take it easy, right, 'arry?'

Harry nodded.

'Well,' said Barnett. 'What's all this about? Bayham Street?'

'You tell us, then we'll tell you.' Tomkins spoke for the both of them.

Barnett hesitated. 'Yes, I was a pup reporter then; I suppose this colleague told you that at the Gazette. Rioters smashed a shop window, the police were called to the scene, fighting broke out, a constable was injured, I think an arm broken. A man was arrested and charged. It made a couple of lines at the bottom of an inside page.'

'That's it? Come orf it, there's more to it than that, you wouldn't be buying drinks ovverwise.'

'They were Germans who had the shop.'

'Yeah, we know that, the French polisher told us.'

'French polisher?'

'Don't come the innocent lark, yer know who we mean. It might be four years ago, 'e's still there, in the shop next door to where it 'appened.'

'A lot of water has passed under London Bridge since then. Yes, I remember: I spoke to him, and the other shopkeeper, the ironmonger. The French polisher said he wasn't there, had locked up and gone home, didn't want to get involved, have his shop window smashed if he tried to intervene when he saw the mob coming. The ironmonger wouldn't talk. But what has this got to do with you two?'

''cos there's more in it than a smashed winder and a copper being assaulted. As I said before, it's tied up wiv wot we 'as to tell yer, and 'ow my mate 'arry 'ere got all shot up for sod all. But I'll tell yer this much fer nuffink: we did try to 'ave a chat wiv the ironmonger, and as yer just rightly said, 'e wouldn't talk. 'e'd been freatened, told to

143

keep 'is mouf shut, and even after all these years 'e's still in a funk, and if I'm not mistaken, yer've been told the same.'

'The press told to keep its mouth shut? No way. It was a case of let sleeping dogs lie. Yes, I was a young reporter; it was wartime, hundreds being slaughtered in the trenches, feeling running high against the Hun. The police would not respond to any questions. Didn't know who was the ringleader, or who smashed the window; none of the rioters arrested, they all kept mum, dispersed quickly, other than the one arrested for the assault on the constable. You can interpret that as you think fit.'

'So yer didn't try to awaken the dog?'

'No, not that type of dog.'

'Well, I don't savvy any foreign lingo to interpret, but a penny to a pinch of salt, that ironmonger knows somefink we don't.'

'You could be right, but I'm intrigued as to why the two of you have become involved in this.'

'Yer can git us anovver bottle of Guinness each to wet the tonsils and I'll tell yer.'

'You're pushing your luck; it had better be good.'

'Well, if yer don't fink so, there's the book publisher's agent in Arlington Road that would be interested.'

Tomkins waited. Barnett nodded to the bartender. The Guinness arrived and was duly sipped.

Tomkins leant back in his chair and began, related how he was batman to a Major Blankensy.


'Barmy 'e was, ordered a platoon of 'is company to attack and take a German redoubt, this the late evening before the armistice, knowing that it 'ad been agreed and would be signed within a few hours, actually 0500 hrs in the morning to come in force at 1100 hrs. The officer in charge of the platoon queried the order to no avail. The rest of the company watched 'em go their death. It was pointless, 'adn't a snowballs chance in 'ell, all wiped out except two – a Sergeant Roberts and me mate 'arry Cooper – in a matter of minutes, and they were seriously wounded. There wasn't one in the regiment that wouldn't 'ave strangled Blankensy wiv their bare 'ands at that time. When Roberts was finally discharged from 'ospital and arrived back, 'e marched straight into Blankensy's office and whacked 'im. Was court martialled, stripped to the ranks, and got six months in the glass'ouse.' Tomkins paused, took a mouthful of Guinness. Said, 'Yer can carry on fer a bit, 'arry.'

'I fought I was a gonner. Would 'ave bled to death in dead man's land,' Cooper said, 'if it wasn't fer the sergeant: saved my life, and got shot for it, all 'cos of the bastard Blankensy. First fing I wanted to do when I was discharged from 'ospital was to kill 'im.'

'I didn't hear that,' Barnett butted in.

'And I didn't say it.' Cooper carried on, 'So I got Blanksy's address.'

'Wait a moment, I'm not with you,' Barnett butted in again. 'Blankensy's address: wasn't he in barracks?'

'We're trying to tell yer 'ow we got involved, ain't we? That's anovver story; yer better tell 'im, Bill.'

Bill Tomkins took a swig of Guinness, wiped his lips and took over.

'Seeing as I was a batman at the time, I 'eard fings ovvers don't. Sergeant Roberts's court martial was convened by a Lt Colonel Stoney from the ginger beers, it being better to 'ave an officer from a different regiment, as not to be prejoo... prejoo...'

'Prejudiced,' Barnett prompted him.

'Yeah, whatever, like reading the accused's crime sheet before telling 'im 'e's fer the 'igh jump or not. Well, as I was saying before yer put yer spoke in, the sapper colonel could not let Roberts orf scot free 'cos 'e 'ad 'it an officer, a serious offence. It should 'ave been 12 months; the colonel reduced it to six months 'cos of the sergeant's records, holder of the MM and exemplary military conduct. Yer see, Blanksy 'ad blotted 'is copy book during the trial, accusing Roberts of turning 'is back on the enemy—'

'That was 'cos of me, 'e bent over to lift me up, I was bleeding to death,' Cooper broke in, cutting Tomkins short.

'All right, 'arry, leave it.' Tomkins said, and carried on. 'Yer could see the colonel wasn't 'aving that, said the sergeant was being charged for striking an officer, that's all; 'e knew Blanksy 'ad sent men to an untimely death. To cut a long story short, after the court martial 'ad finished, the colonel asked for a meeting wiv our brigadier. The CO, prosecuting officer, defending officer and company captain to attend. Like I said, I 'eard fings, like snatches of conversation in the officers' mess, and put two and two together. The RSM was told to say nothing. "There was no meeting." But I knew there was.

'A week later Blanksy resigned 'is commission. Resigned me arse; 'e was slung out, 'ad to find somewhere to live. Yer get it, Mr Barnett?'

'I think so: the major is no longer in the army.'

'So I got 'is address.' Cooper picked up where Tomkins had left off. 'I wanted to put tabs on 'im, find out the best way to do it: shoot 'im, push 'im under a train, or jest cut 'is knackers orf.'

'For Chissake don't tell me that,' said Barnett.

'Well, yer wanted to know 'ow we was tied up wiv it. Anyways, we – I say "we" 'cos Bill insisted 'e wanted to be wiv me, only fer the ride, yer understand.'

'That could be construed as aiding and abetting. You know that, I suppose?' Barnett added.

'Well, screw you too.'

'Listen, I'm doing you two a favour, so keep the smart retorts to yourselves. So get on with what you have to tell me.'

'I will if yer don't keep interrupting. We watched 'is flat – I'll skip a bit, 'e came out, we followed. Guess wot?'

'I guess you're going to tell me.'

''e went to Bayham Street. The French polisher's shop was closed. 'e went into the ironmonger's shop. After 'e left, we 'ad a chat wiv the ironmonger, or tried to. Made out we was interested in renting the boarded up shop. 'e clammed up, told us to eff orf. The next time we goes, the French polisher is there. We fought 'e might put a light on the scene, seeing 'e was a polisher – 'e didn't. Told us to go to the Islington Gazette, speak to you. So? What d'yer make of it?'

'Nothing. You've wasting my time and money. An officer sent a platoon of men to their death. Generals sent thousands to their death in one day; it was war. I grant you it was bad judgement on Blankensy's part, seeing it was only a few hours to the armistice being signed. He got his deserts, was "slung out" as you put it. The smashing of a window by rioters is old news. Blankensy could have wanted to buy or rent that empty shop seeing as he was now a civilian, the same as you made a pretence of doing when prying.'

'Last orders,' the bartender called out

'That's it, last orders, lads; sling the towel in, and no more shouting the odds about – you know – what I never heard and you never said.'

'Yer gonner leave it at that? I fought reporters 'ad a nose for a good story,' Tomkins said. 'You're missing out, yer know. There's more to this than meets the eye; yer'll be sorry yer didn't cotton on to it. It'll come out in the end, yer mark my words. Yer 'ave narks, like 'im.' Tomkins pointed. 'Sitting over there wiv 'is ears flapping, and I guess ovvers that gives yer the tip orf for a pint or two. Yer mate in the Gazette said yer got the word from a prison guard that the trap door didn't work fer that bloke Flint. Made yer top reporter. So I reckon yer must know a rozzer or two, seeing 'ow yer a crime reporter. Be 'andy if there 'ad been one there when the rioters smashed the winder, if yer gits my meaning? Sometimes it's not wot yer knows, but who yer knows.'

'I know you are overstepping the mark, Tomkins, and I can understand why you became a batman: look after number one, eh?'

'Too bloody right, mister. I 'ad to fight to survive when I wos a kid, eat ovver's leftovers, scrounge around the markets to forage fer wot costermongers 'ad slung away under their stalls to fill me belly. I joined the army so I could get fed and watered and a pair of boots to wear. No 'ero, never volunteered fer anyfing stupid like trying to win a medal, went over the top when ordered, ovver times kept me 'ead down. Yeah, rotten sod, eh? But I ain't got anyone's deaf on me conscience like Blankensy.'

'I'm closing now.' The bartender's voice interrupted the conversation. 'All out, if yer don't mind.' Tea cloths hung over the pump handles. 'Open again at six.'

Barnett stood, looked at Tomkins. Saw a face old before its time, eyes that were alive, defiant, facing the world, a cockney sparrow if ever there was one.

'I shouldn't have said that, Tomkins, I apologise. I have to go now, we all do; tell you what, I'll keep it in mind, catch up with you if needs be.'

The following day was a Friday. Pay day. Nobody goes sick on a pay day, unless they have one foot in the grave. So it was a surprise and cause of some consternation among the platelayers when they arrived at the railway works depot at King's Cross, most especially with Peter Fry, who had booked ganger Ernie Betts in yesterday, that he had not turned up again, and it pay day.

148

''e must be proper ill. Yer gonner let on that 'e never turned up yesterday, Pete?'

'I can't, can I? I'll git the sack. 'e was 'ere if anyone asks. Leave it at that.'

Half past five at the pay table

'Anyone know what's the matter with Betts?' the paymaster called out. 'No? Somebody find out, let me know, and when he will be in. Meantime you act as ganger, Fry.'

# PART TWO

Detective Inspector Bill Gordon. Detective Sergeant Jos Bancroft. Detective Constable Tom Fowler. DI. DS. DC.

All in plain clothes were celebrating the end of a case, drinks on the inspector. The venue, the private bar of the Brunswick Arms, tucked away in the back streets of Islington, North London, seeking privacy. A clerk left holding the fort in the local offices of the CID situated two floors above the Clerkenwell Police Station. Two plain clothes CID foot soldiers kept him company; one sat in the inspector's chair, feet up on the desk in front, the door wide open. 'He won't like that,' said the clerk. 'He won't bloody know, will he?' the squatter said.

It was a Saturday, 11.30 a.m. They had the bar to themselves; it was too early for those who drank in secret, didn't want it known, too early for those using the spit and sawdust bar who called in for a pint after finishing work for the weekend.

'Cheers,' the inspector called, as he raised his glass. 'Thank Christ it ended satisfactorily. I was going to say "happy ever after" but that would be for a fairy tale; this was fact, not fiction. What a case! A bizarre case if there ever was one. A son of a black princess of Ashanti found with his neck broken in Lord Hethrington's estate in Hertfordshire, Bert Craig garrotted in South London. Two

150

Mancini brothers, one killed, the other hung, "Herald-hark-the-angels-sing" Flint sent to the gallows and saved by an act of God. I give you full marks, Jos, you was the only one convinced Flint was innocent; all the evidence pointed to him, he was tried and found guilty by a jury, but what got up my nose was the mystery of the golden stool that had gone missing. Taken from the princess's son's neck, a miniature artefact – whatever – on a chain, and all the fuss and bother to find it, so much that Richard, Lord Hethrington's son, came to London wanting to offer a reward, more money than what it was worth to whoever stole it. I ask you, for a bloody trinket. What with the brass at the top on my back, I had nightmares.' He downed the ale in the glass in one go, placed it back on the table. 'Sod the golden stool; drink up, lads. What's the joke, Jos?' Seeing the DS smiling.

'Nothing much, guv; you getting het up over this so-called "trinket" gold miniature, I suppose. I guess its value is not what it is worth, it's what it stands for. The golden stool of the Ashanti. The real stool. I was curious; with nothing much to do after all the dust had settled, I made enquiries. Richard Hethrington questioned that Salvation Army lass, Barbara Evans, the friend of Bert Craig who was killed, so I thought I would. She had left the "Sally". I spoke to her friend; she told me she was going to Africa and was away training to be a missionary. Strange that this Richard and the Sally lass both upped sticks and left at that time. He knew where she was going.'

'Don't start me off again, Jos; drink up, take it easy.'

The desk sergeant at Albany Street police station looked up as the postman came rushing in out of breath, burst out, panting, 'You'd better get over there, or send a constable to Arlington Road, there's a dead body there.'

'Whoa, steady, take it easy. Did you say a dead body?'

151

'Yeah, the flies, thousands of 'em covering the head, not moving.'

'You sure? Whereabouts in Arlington Road?'

'Number 86, the basement, the door was open, I saw it.'

The sergeant called out for the duty constable to come up from the floor below where the cells were. Told him to go out, find the nearest constable on the beat, go to Arlington Road, 86, the basement, the door should be open, see if there is in fact a dead body there, don't touch anything, leave the door ajar so we can get in again, station the constable on guard at street level. Come back to report, confirm or otherwise on the double, don't want any kids poking their noses down there.

He turned to the postman. 'You all right? I'll get you a glass of water.'

'Yeah, a bit of a turn, but all right now. I've seen dead 'uns before, but listen, Sarge, this may seem crazy, but I think there may be another one at Landsdown Buildings. When I delivered the mail at number three, there was a mass of flies crawling around the letterbox flap, and as I pushed the letters through I could hear a hum, and the smell, blimey, what a pong. I thought Ernie had left some fish or meat uncovered. I knocked, got no answer; it wasn't until I got to Arlington Road and saw the body and the bloody flies made me think about it.'

'You know the bloke that lives there, then; you said Ernie?'

'Yes, Ernie Betts, works for the LNER out of King's Cross.'

'What about the one that lives at Arlington Road, do you know him?'

'No, never seen him; today has been the first letter I've had to deliver there. Can't tell you his name even, didn't register, only the number.'

'You got it, the letter?'

'Oh, Christ, I must have dropped it.'

'Understandable, must have given you a shock. Not to worry, we'll find it. You sit tight, I'll go and tell the inspector.'

The postman watched the sergeant disappear up the stairs, finished the last of the water. *Thought I'd get a brandy at least.*


'This is going to spoil someone's weekend,' the inspector remarked after listening to what the sergeant related to him. 'I guess, as he is a postman, we must give him credit. Better get it checked before I notify the CID.'

'I've seen to it, sir. Waiting for the constable to return, after he has posted a guard and checked at Arlington Road; shouldn't be long. What do you want me to do with respect to Landsdown Buildings? I'll need to bring one off the beat, and shall we break in?'

'No, wait until we get it confirmed there is a dead body at Arlington, then I'll let them know at Clerkenwell; that's what they get paid for. They can deal with the Landsdown problem as well.'


Back at the Brunswick Arms, glasses had been replenished, the ale sipped rather than gulped; as the DI had said, 'Take it easy, we've till two o'clock before we're slung out, then it will be heads down. Yours alongside Charlotte who's been cooking Sunday dinners for you, Tom?'

'Turn it in, Chief.' Jos chuckled.

The inspector was wrong, at least in the first place. They had barely finished the second pint before the door opened and a foot soldier poked his head in.

'Am I glad to see you, guv, must have damn nigh looked in every pub in Islington.'

'Well, you had better look in the ones you haven't. We're not here.'

'Understood, guv, but thought you ought to know, looks as if we've a couple of murders on our hands.'

'Oh, for Chrissake, no, and at the weekend, just when we thought we could relax after the Flint balls-up.'

'Do you want me to keeping looking for you, guv, or do you want to know?'

'Yeah, all right, Barcham, you've found us, so spill the beans.'

Barcham looked at the drinks on the table. 'No need to rush, it's in hand. Albany Street nick have plods on the scene, at least one of them, on guard. Not touching anything, leaving it for us. At the other one the door is shut; they're not sure whether to break in, as they don't know if a murder has been committed, only what a postman has told them. He was the one that found the first body, and thinks there is another one, so time to finish your drinks.'

'You finished duty at noon, didn't you, Barcham?'

'Would have done if this hadn't cropped up.'

'Thirsty work looking in half the pubs in Islington?'

'Didn't have one, if that's what you're thinking, guv.'

'Don't be so bloody daft, Barcham. Get yourself a pint at the bar, on me – you're off duty now, like we were before we were called back – then I'll have to call you back as on overtime. You can then sit down and tell us what you know.'

Barcham sank half the glass of ale in one go, then sat down, licking his lips, his tongue flicking out and in collecting the froth left behind.

'You're not getting another one; get on with it, we're waiting,' said the DI.

'The postman found the dead 'un at Arlington Road number 86, the basement: the door was ajar, called out, no answer, went in, saw the body, head covered with flies, rushed round to the nearest nick – Albany Street, told the desk sergeant. As for Landsdown Buildings, he – the postman – recalled the amount of flies and the smell when delivering mail to number 3 on the ground floor after his greeting with the dead 'un at Arlington Road. As I said before, Albany Street nick have a plod at each site. That's about all we have at the moment, guv.'

'Is it known who lives at 3 The Buildings?'

'Yes. Ernest Betts. Works for the LNER.'

'What about the other one at Arlington Road?'

'Nothing known as yet.'

'Right, well, you are officially back on duty; we'll call it overtime. Call a cab, a motor one that can take all four of us. Don't argue with the driver, it's police duty, commandeer it if necessary. You take charge at Arlington Road, Jos; take Barcham with you. We'll drop you off. You come with me, Tom. I don't have to tell you proceedings, Jos; make sure you get it all down on paper, don't rely on memory. When you have finished send for the morgue blokes to do what they have to, then they can take the body. Look for a door key; there must be one there, probably in the dead 'un's pocket. Lock the door, in any case leave a plod on duty. Meet me back at my office; we can compare notes, see if there is any connection between both cases, assuming there is a body at The Buildings.'

### *Arlington Road*

Alice did not take much notice at first; it was the usual morning. The postman's first delivery, but when he went to the basement at number 86 opposite he came out in a hurry, went back the way he had come, not carrying on with his usual round, the mail bag flapping on his back as he broke into a run. That was unusual, more so when two constables arrived. One entered the basement flat, the other remained at the railing gate. Not many minutes passed before the first one came out of the basement, spoke to the constable at the gate and left, the 'gatekeeper' staying with feet planted firmly on the pavement, his back to the railings. A sentinel in blue.

'This is getting interesting,' Alice remarked.

'What is?' Clara asked as she joined Alice at the window and sat down.

'First the postman goes down to the basement opposite at number 86, I assume to deliver mail; that's the first time I've seen him do that. He rushes out and scuttles away like a scolded cat, then police arrive.'

'Come for that vampire I told you lived there. The postman must have seen it,' Clara said with a laugh. 'Have they brought a mallet and stake, the police?'

'Clara!'


Young Jimmy was late for dinner. He knew he was late, as he had asked someone who was lucky or rich enough to have a watch. He had stayed too late in the park playing with his school mates. It was Saturday. On a Saturday, his dad knocked off from work as a labourer on a building site at half past twelve, stopped for a pint with a mate, and expected his dinner ready when he got home just after one o'clock.

'Just gone one o'clock,' Jimmy had been told, so he was in a hurry. Sausages and mash, fried onions if he was lucky. He could visualise the sausages sizzling and spitting in the pan; his mouth watered. He hurried his steps. Turned into Arlington Road from the Parkway and stopped dead in his tracks. A policeman was standing with his back to the railings at number 86.

*Crikey, that's where the two soldiers gave me a penny to knock to see if anyone was in.*

*A spy, I reckon. Looks as if the rozzers 'ave caught up wiv 'im.*

He carried on, not wanting to be late for dinner. His dad was strict, army discipline, but he knew he was lucky to have a dad; only two other boys in the class had one. His dad was lucky, he said; served in what he called 'Mespot', not in the trenches in France.

Jimmy stopped level with the constable; curiosity got the better of him. 'Caught 'im, did yer?'

'Shove off,' the constable said.

''e was a spy, 'im that lives 'ere.'

'Do you want a clip in the ear? I said shove off.'

'I knows it was, 'cos two soldiers was after 'im. They paid me to 'elp.'

The constable frowned, looked down. 'What did you say?'

'I told yer. Can't stop, me dinner'll be on the table.'

'Do you know who lives here?' Careful to put the question in the present tense.

'No, 'e wouldn't answer the door when I knocked, but I knew 'e was there, 'e 'id behind the curtains.'

*What's the kid going on about?* 'Listen, son, what's your name and where do you live?'

Jimmy realised there was more to this than met the eye; he had been blabbing too much, showing off. *Them two soldiers paid me twice, said they would call on me again if they wanted help, took my address; I might be able to make a penny or two.* 'I ain't saying any more, gotter go.'

'You have to tell me, you understand, otherwise I will arrest you.'

'It's Jimmy, Jimmy Wilde, 10 Osnaburgh Street.'

'That was easy, wasn't it? You should have shoved off when I first told you; our sergeant may want to talk to you. You can shove off now, get your dinner.'

'Yer late,' his dad greeted him. 'Wash yer 'ands.'

Jimmy bolted his dinner down, stood up to leave. 'Can I go out?' he asked.

'What's the 'urry, and where yer off to?' his dad asked.

'Arlington Road, somefink going on there, number 86.'

'Yer ain't been up to mischief, 'ave yer?'

'No, just nosy, Dad, that's all.'


The cab juddered to a halt outside number 86. DS Jos Bancroft and Barcham alighted. The cab drew away, gears crashing, black smoke issuing from the exhaust. The sentinel in blue, the constable on guard, saluted.

'The door locked, constable?'

'Yes, sir; the key was on the table inside.' He felt in his pocket and handed it to Jos. 'The flies are something horrible in there; cover your nose and mouth, sirs, if I may be so bold as to suggest.'

'You may. What's your name, constable?' Jos asked, taking the key.

'Lacy, sir.'

'Right, Lacy, we'll take a look-see.' Jos descended the stone steps, inserted the key, heard the hum, opened the door as far as it would go, and viewed the room. The hum increased in volume as a black cloud rose, the bluebottles angry at being disturbed. Jos saw the body slumped in a chair facing the door as if waiting for someone to arrive, the right arm straight down, the fingers open pointing to the floor. He caught a glimpse of the bloodied head, one side shattered, before the cloud descended and became a shimmering balaclava. His eyes searched the floor: no sign of weapon, the room sparsely furnished, a table, couple of chairs, a fireside armchair and bookshelves.

'Jesus, the flies,' exclaimed Barcham, looking over Jos's shoulder.

'Yeah, this hot weather brings them out, looking for blood. See if you can find something to cover our heads, and a sheet to cover this poor sod,' said Jos, taking a handkerchief from his pocket to cover his nose and mouth.

Barcham followed suit, looked where he placed his feet as he made for the other rooms. He returned with a towel draped over his head, another he passed to Jos with a sheet; Jos lashed out at the flies and managed to get the body covered and the towel over his own head. The flies, frustrated, attacked the invaders. Jos ordered, 'Retreat'; Barcham didn't want a second telling, made for the door, Jos on his heels.

'What now?' Barcham asked as they stood outside the door left ajar.

'We are not going to get rid of these flies; for every one we swat, others come to the funeral. The sooner we get the body to the morgue, the better. Why are they called bluebottles, Barch?'

'Dunno, got blue arses or noses, I've never looked that close.'

'Well, whatever. You have a look in the other rooms, see what comes to light, if there are any letters to give us a clue to his identity. I'll have a word with the plod up top, see if I can arrange for the body to be collected. Don't touch anything in this room; wait until I'm with you.'

Barcham covered his head and made his way back to the other rooms again as Jos climbed the stone steps to the pavement.

'I want you to do something for me, Lacy. You were right about the flies; we'll never get rid of them whilst the body is here, so I want it collected and taken to the morgue as soon as possible. I need you to have a word with your desk sergeant, with my compliments, if he can arrange that. He may want to speak to your inspector first. The thing is, my DI and a DC are investigating a report of a murder at Landsdown Road, so we are a bit stretched on the ground if you see what I mean.'

'Yes, sir, I understand. I can do that.'

'By the way, where is this Landsdown Road?'

'Not far, sir, it runs parallel to and on the other side of the high street.'

'Could you call there first, speak to my DI, see if there is a body there and if he wants it collected? If so, let your sergeant know; it might save two trips.'

'Got it, sir.'

'One more thing, a padlock and chain. When we are finished here and the body gone, the railing gate can be padlocked; save having a constable standing on guard fending off gawking nosy busybodies.'

'Like some cheeky lad that defied me when I told him to shove off, came out with some cock and bull story that a spy lived here. I didn't take much notice until he said he had called here. I questioned him then, was told he encountered two soldiers, one paid him to find out if the bloke was in, said he knocked, the bloke didn't answer the door, but he knew he was in, saw him peep from behind the curtains. Thought there might be something in what the lad said, so I took his name and address. Lives at Osnaburgh Street, not far from here.'

'You didn't mention this before; was you going to?'

'Well, yes, sir, that's why I took his address.'

'I'll take your word for that. I'll have a word with this lad later; you get off now.'

'Thank you, sir.'

Jos watched him go, glanced across the road to see a face at a window. *Have a word with whoever that is later.* He returned to the basement in time to see Barcham at the door. 'Any joy?'

'Not much. A major's uniform hanging in a wardrobe, Sam Browne, empty holster, five live cartridges in a pouch. Also some KD clothing, and an article that caught my eye: a short wooden-handled knife with curved blade coming to a sharp point. No idea what it's used for, was with the cutlery.'

'What d'you mean by KD?'

'Khaki drill. Army tropical wear. So this chap has served from somewhere where it's hot.'

'That might help. A major; shouldn't be too difficult to find out where from: the Middlesex HQ, yes? Was there a cap badge?'

'I'm not sure which regiment it belonged to.'

'They will know. We'll hold on to that knife and see what the major can tell us.' Nodding to the corpse. Jos folded back the sheet, endeavouring to brush away the persistent flies, felt in the pockets, produced a key, some loose change and a punched tram ticket, placed them on the table and quickly replaced the sheet.

'A tuppenny tram ticket, tidy bloke, didn't discard it on the pavement; the key looks new, check to see if it fits any of the doors here in a minute; let's see what we can find here.'

They searched every nook and cranny on their knees. One spent cartridge came to light and was placed on the table, no revolver.

'Fetch that knife, Barch, put it on the table with the other articles.'

Barcham did that, and Jos said, 'So what have we got? A knife – a key – a cartridge case – a tram ticket.'

'And a straw,' said Barcham, as he picked up a single straw that had been on the table. 'The one that broke the camel's back.' He laughed as he was about to throw it away.

'Hang on,' Jos called out. 'What's a straw doing here, and where would one come from in London? Not from Highbury Fields or Hackney Marshes, that's for sure.'

'A pigeon flew in with it, placed it on the table, I don't think so,' said Barcham. 'Could be from a costermonger's stall in the market, bananas are packed in them I think.'

'Keep it. Find out where the key fits, what the knife's used for, what journey the tram ticket was punched on, and we may be getting somewhere. We can check with the Middlesex Regiment if the major was on their strength. We wait for the body to be taken away by Burke and Hare. Meanwhile I'll have a word with the face I saw looking through a window opposite. You'd better stay here, pavement level, seeing as I've sent the constable away.'

'Can I have a word?' Jos called out, gazing at the face looking through the window.

Alice raised the lower half of the sash window and leaned over the sill, hand cupped over one ear.

Jos repeated it, added, 'I'm a police officer, I can show you my warrant.'

That made Alice's day. 'Much better than playing patience, Clara: a police officer in plain clothes, must be a detective, wants to speak to me. The front door isn't locked; come in, first door on the left. Ground floor,' she called out to Jos.

Jos took a couple of deep breaths of London air with mouth open and blew out. *Don't want them to smell my breath, think I've been drinking on duty.* Mounted the stone steps to the entrance hall, knocked on the door to the left and entered. The scent of lavender greeted him. A quick glance at the room: high ceiling with a plaster rosette in the centre and ornate cornice – marble fireplace with dark green velvet valance, gold tassels, hanging from the mantelpiece. A free-standing framed tapestry covered the grate, guarded by a brass fender with a seat at each corner. Wooden shutters folded back from the bay window, where two ladies sat, buttoned to the neck even in this hot weather. He smiled and nodded.

'I bid you good morning, ladies. I am Detective Sergeant Bancroft CID; my warrant card.' He held it so they could see it as he approached.

'May I hold it?' Alice asked. 'I've never seen one before, or met a detective.' Jos passed it to her. 'Look, Clara, it's akin to being in one of those murder novels.'

Clara, not so thrilled, nodded, said, 'How can we help you, Sergeant?'

Jos retrieved his warrant, pocketed it, thinking carefully over his words, not wanting to give too much away. 'Do you happen to know who occupies the basement rooms at 86 opposite?'

'Never seen him, a vampire only comes out after dark,' Clara answered.

'Clara! Don't joke with the detective, you'll get yourself arrested.' A rebuke came from Alice.

'Indeed so, a very serious offence,' said Jos, putting on a serious face, 'But, one never knows, could be Dracula himself.' Which brought a smile to their faces.

'Sorry, Sergeant, being frivolous,' Clara said. 'It must be serious to warrant a sergeant detective to enquire. Can I make amends by offering you tea? Will not take long, if you have time; my sister Alice could answer your questions whilst it brews, or would you prefer a glass of sarsaparilla, reasonably cool from the larder?'

'Sarsaparilla? I haven't had that for ages. There was a shop at the bottom of Holloway Road, near Highbury Corner, that sold it. I thought it a chemist, but could have been a herbalist. I was young, my first job before I joined the police. It was dispensed from a china tub with a tap at the bottom, from one end of the counter, three 'a'pence a glass, and worth it, delicious, nectar. I would love a glass.'

163

'Draw up a chair, Sergeant. Be seated, please,' Alice said after Clara had left the room. 'I, or we, I should say, do not know who lives there, to answer your question, and I must apologise for my sister's silly remark about vampires.'

'Perfectly all right. What would life be without a joke? Laugh and the world laughs with you, cry and you cry alone. I think a true adage. May I ask your surnames? It's a formality.'

'I understand; it's Barnard. But Alice is fine.'

'Thank you, Alice. Would you say you've noticed anything unusual with respect to number 86 recently?'

'Yes, as a matter of fact, three things; let me try and put them in sequence. Some days ago a young lad called there; that was the first time I had seen anyone call there since the new occupier. He entered the basement, was there for some minutes, ten perhaps, left and walked away. Then whoever lives there – a man – I saw his head appear looking through the railings; he waited until the lad had distanced himself, emerged and followed. I thought that strange.'

'Did the lad go inside?'

'No, as I could see his head at all times. I assume he knocked but got no answer.'

'Then, Alice?'

'Yesterday, two men called, one a soldier, the other a giant of a man; he waited at the railing gate, the soldier went down to the basement. After some minutes he came out in a hurry, and they both... I would say "hurried away", not running but very quick steps. Then, to my surprise, later, could have been an hour, they passed by arm in arm with the Jones girls.'

'The Jones girls?' Jos butted in.

'Yes, Jones the baker's daughters, Grace and Gwyneth.'

'You know them, then?'

'Yes, lovely family; their brother is a soldier. They have the baker's shop in Delancey Street, live on the premises.

They crossed the road to this side, the shady side; I would know them anywhere.'

'What time was it when the soldier went to the basement, would you remember? And if he went inside?'

'He did go inside, yes. I did not look at the time, but it was quite early, immediately after breakfast, which these fine days we eat early to catch the sun rising. I came to sit down at the window, as it was Clara's turn to wash up. That's when I saw the soldier go in, and thinking about it, there was no delay before he entered; the door must have opened at first knock. As though he was expected.'

At that moment Clara returned with the glass of sarsaparilla. Placed it on the table.

'There you are, Sergeant, see if that is as good as you remember the ones you had those years ago,' Clara said.

Jos took a sip. 'Absolutely: delicious, nectar.' He then took a swallow. 'Better. Do you make this yourself?'

'No, can't get the roots, but we know the herbalist, get a regular supply, ready made.'

'You will have to tell me the address. Now, Alice, anything else you can help me with?'

'Yes, the postman. This morning, first delivery, I saw him go down to the basement at 86; came out like a scalded cat, never finished on his round, went back the way he came, and ran when he reached the pavement. Something must have frightened him. And only that the lad I mentioned, he came along and spoke to your constable on duty at the gate, just before you arrived.'

'Yes, the constable told me. Thank you, you have been a great help. I drink to your health.' Jos finished the sarsaparilla. Rose to leave.

'Has there been foul play at 86, Sergeant, or can't you say?' Clara asked.

*Clara's the cute one of the pair; they are bound to see the body carried out, so...*

'The person living there is dead; we don't know who he is. That's all I can tell you.'

'I understand, Sergeant, wish you well with your enquiries.'

'Any luck?' Barcham asked after Jos reached him.

'Yeah, could be. One thing for sure, army personnel are involved. So first thing is to pay a visit to the Essex Regiment HQ and ask some questions, lots of them. Why two soldiers paid a kid to see if the bloke that lived here was in; did they want to burgle the place? And why did the bloke not answer, then follow the kid? Also who was the soldier who called and left in a hurry? Foremost, I suppose, is to identify the dead 'un and if he was an officer in the Essex Regiment.'

'Bloody strange, eh? Did you get all that from the face at the window?'

At that moment Constable Lacy arrived. Saved Jos having to explain.

'Your DI said for you to wait here, sir,' Lacy began. 'Said he would pick you up as he had retained the cab. There was a murder, the body will be picked up, the vehicle will call there first and then here, one journey. All arranged, sir.'

'You did well, Lacy; did you remember the padlock and key?'

'Yes sir, had to buy one, the station paid.'

Jimmy Wilde was on the way back to Arlington Road after wolfing his dinner down. His tongue probed the back of his teeth for scraps of fried onion that had taking up lodgings in the gaps; eventually he gave up and used a thumb nail. He turned the corner in time to see the covered body being carried out and the covered horse-drawn cart driven away, followed by a cab.

Constable Lacy saw him and called out, 'Hey, Jimmy.' Jimmy hesitated, not sure whether to run or wait. Curiosity got the better. He went to meet the constable coming.

'They got 'im then, the army?' Jimmy said as they met.

'What makes you say that?'

'Dunno, jest fought 'e was a spy when the soldiers asked me to see if he was in.'

'Don't let your imagination run away with you, Jimmy. You know the CID want to have a word with you? So when questioned just give facts, not fiction; you could get someone hung speaking out of turn. Don't hang around here, nothing to see, so off you go.'


### The Islington Gazette offices

'It's for you, Jack,' the clerk at the press desk called out, laying the telephone receiver on the desk. Jack Barnett stepped over and picked it up. It was well into the Saturday afternoon.

'Yeah, it's me. *What*? Hang on.' He reached for a pencil and pad. 'Yeah, you can, it's all right, carry on. Two, where, when?' He began scribbling. 'Not so fast, yeah, got it, and the other. Is that near the other? No, don't know it. Yeah, I know that, the big boozer on the corner. I won't, when you're off D. for sure.'

Jack hung the receiver back, tore the two top sheets off the pad and pocketed them. Knew all about indents left on the second sheet.

'On to something, Jack?' the clerk asked.

'You never know.'

Jack left in a hurry, hailed a passing cab. 'The morgue,' he told the cabbie.

'And yer in an 'urry to get *there*, seems like,' said the cabbie. 'They ain't going anywhere, those lying there.'

'Jest get going, will you?'


## The morgue

'Wait, cabbie,' Jack called over his back as he entered the morgue.

'Jesus, you're quick off the mark, Jack,' a white-coated attendant greeted him. 'They've only been brought in a couple of hours ago. How did you know? Don't tell me.'

'Only wanted it confirmed, Len, happened to be passing when the bodies were brought here.'

'Yeah, yeah, yeah, coincidental, eh? So why come again? Confirmed, my arse.'

'Fishing then, Len.'

'You'll get me hung, drawn and quartered one day, Jack. One throat cut, the other shot; that's what you came for.'

'Ta, Len, owe you.'

'Yeah, you do.'

'I won't forget.'

Jack hurried out, jumped in the cab. 'The Buildings, Landsdown Road, Camden Town: do you know it, cabbie?'

'Yeah.'

Jack sat back in the cab. *Those two squaddies were right, I should have given it more thought, could be a good story. They admitted they wanted to kill that Blankensy officer; I wonder, could they have? No, I don't think so, certainly not the one with the throat cut, and what's the connection with Bayham Street? This could make the front page. Think, Jack.*

'Yer talking to yerself back there? It's the first sign, yer know,' the cabbie said with a quick glance over his shoulder.

'It's the world we live in. You stick to sitting on your arse all day driving, don't get involved.'

'Mind me own business, guv, got it.'

'Number 3, ground floor.' Jack talking to himself again as he alighted outside 'The Buildings'. Another 'Wait' to the cabbie.

A police notice on the door. 'Do not enter.' The keyhole covered. Jack sniffed the air. *Phew, what a stink; fumigated?* He mounted the staircase, knocked at the door on the left, no answer, tried the one on the right of the landing, heard the footsteps, the door opened.

'Sorry to disturb you,' said Jack.

'No, yer not sorry.'

Jack put on his 'smile face'. 'Pleased to see you, and glad you opened the door. That better?'

'That's bullshit, wot d'yer want?'

'The name of the bloke at number 3 below.'

'Yer from the press?'

Jack nodded. 'The local, Gazette, do you read it?'

'After I've finished me fish and chips, if they've been wrapped in 'em. 'e's been carted away, the bloke.'

'Yeah, I know; can you tell me his name?'

'Five bob.'

'Half crown.'

A hand was thrust forward, the palm uppermost. Jack sorted through his pocket for change, placed a florin in the palm, held a sixpence between finger and thumb. 'And where he worked.'

'Ernie Betts, LNER out of the Cross.'

The tanner joined the two bob piece, the palm closed, the door slammed shut in Jack's face.

'And sod you too,' said Jack. He went down the steps two at a time. 'Arlington Road, number 86,' he told the cabbie as he climbed in and sat back in the seat.

The cab slowed to walking pace on Arlington Road, not much slower than when in top gear, the cabbie leaning out counting the numbers of the houses until he pulled up outside number 86.

'There yer are, guv, 86.'

Jack stepped down on to the pavement, disappointed as there was no constable on duty to wheedle any information from, saw the gate chained and padlocked, shrugged his shoulders. *Wasted journey.* He glanced around, noticed the open window opposite, hesitated, looked at the clock on the cab ticking away, thought *another time.* 'Back to the Gazette offices, cabbie.'

Sitting back in the cab he thought of headlines on a special edition, his name as top reporter, beating the national press on the streets as he had with the 'Flint, the man they could not hang' story.

'I wonder who that was?' Alice remarked on seeing the cab draw away.


## *CID offices, Clerkenwell*

'Couldn't say much in the cab, these cab drivers have ears like elephants, African ones,' said DI Bill Gordon, sitting behind his desk facing Jos Bancroft, Tom Fowler and Barcham, who sat opposite. 'Two murders. Start with you, Jos; what have you got?'

'Shot in the head, sitting in a chair facing the door,' Jos began. 'No weapon found. Clues: a spent cartridge case, .38. A key, a new one by the looks of it, loose change and a punched tram ticket from the pockets of the body. Uniform of a major of the Essex Regiment by the cap badge, no other identity. A knife with the cutlery I thought out of place: had a short wooden handle, curved blade coming to a sharp point. Curious as to its use, never seen one as that before, also a single straw.'

'A straw?' the DI queried.

170

'Used for bedding other than fodder, could have come from the killer's clothing, or a palliasse, the army use them on occasion.'

'What are you implying, Jos?'

'Well, I have a witness that saw a soldier enter and leave the premises early that morning. He could be a ripe suspect.'

'It's your case, Jos, I leave it to you; no doubt your first call will be to the HQ of the Essex Regiment. Keep me up to date.'

'Will do; what did you find at Landsdown Road?'

'Throat cut with a shard of glass, still embedded in the neck. This time we have a name: Ernie Betts, works for the LNER works depot, King's Cross. Tom will be taking charge of that one. Barcham can tag along with him. Liaise, the pair of you, see if any connection. I must say, seems unlikely: an officer and a bloke working laying railway lines. I suggest you find where that shard of glass came from, Tom, not that I want to interfere. See if we can get this under our belts a bit swiftly, then we can finish our celebration drinks that we were having before we got called to this.'


## HQ, the Essex Regiment

DS Jos Bancroft showed his warrant to the sergeant of the guard after the sentry had stopped him at the entry gate and directed him to the guardroom. It was Saturday evening; he had not wasted any time, had gone straight there after leaving the offices at Clerkenwell and having a quick bite.

'I wish to speak to the duty officer,' he said.

'I'll accompany you to the RSM's office, sir. He likes to know what's what, if you know what I mean, who comes and goes. You may be lucky, it being Saturday and this time

171

of the day, otherwise he'll be in his quarters, won't be happy.'

They were lucky, caught the RSM as he was about to leave.

'Sorry calling at this time, Sergeant Major, but it is important; I'll be as brief as I can. I need to know if you have an officer who has an address at 86 Arlington Road, Camden Town, on the strength of the regiment.'

'Did have.' The answer short and almost spat out. 'Why?'

'Excuse me, what do you mean by "did have"?' Jos was taken aback; did he know about the body there?

'Officially retired, unofficially persuaded to. So why do you want to know?'

'Because a body has been found at that address, no identity, but a major's uniform in a wardrobe, Essex Regiment badge.'

'You don't say?'

'You don't seem surprised, Sergeant Major.'

'Should I be? Let's start again. We did have an officer with us with that civvy address. A Major Blankensy, no longer with us.'

'Can I ask why he retired?'

'No, can't answer that, against regulations to divulge what is entered in an officer's records.'

'I'm investigating a murder, Sergeant Major. I have a witness who saw a soldier enter and leave the scene of the crime, also a witness who was given money by two of your soldiers to call at that address to see if the officer in question was actually inside, so I'm asking you again. Why did the officer resign?'

'Officially an officer's records are almost sacrament, but off the records, and I haven't told you if anyone asks. He blundered, shall we say – whether it was deliberate or not is debateable. It was an order that was incomprehensible, to

172

send a platoon on a suicidal mission a few hours before the armistice was signed, knowing the time had been agreed. Needless to say, the rest of the regiment watched that platoon walk to their death. Wiped out in minutes, did not stand a chance, only two survived, and both seriously wounded. It was utter madness to even think they could have achieved the task. Does that answer your question?'

'It may help. This order, I take it, would have been resented by the men, and those affected by the loss of a comrade or loved one might hold a grudge, seek revenge even?'

'You can say that again. Not some, but the whole regiment would. How would you feel, knowing that in a few hours it would all be over, no more worrying if the next shell, bullet or bayonet would be your end, and then ordered to a certain death because of a whim of a nut case of an officer? You know what he said to the sentry on the fire step that evening? "How say you? 'The Diehards go out in a blaze of glory.'" He even got that wrong. It's the Middlesex Regiment called the "Diehards". When overwhelmed ten to one by a German offensive, their officer called out, "Die hard, lads." They did, not one of them standing at the end.'

'I don't know what to say, Sergeant Major. I take my hat off to you blokes in the trenches; I can only try to imagine what it must have been like. The two that survived, are they still with the regiment, did they recover fully?'

'Spent weeks in hospital, touch and go with Cooper, waiting discharge, unfit for service. Roberts, who saved Cooper's life actually, seems to have done so, quite a tough character, been wounded before, won the MM at the Somme; he's not staying on. Was court martialled, stripped from sergeant to the ranks, and got six months in the glasshouse.'

'What? Why?'

'I've said enough, you're the detective, ask about.'

Jos made a mental note of the names: Cooper, Roberts. 'I will. You realise I will have to question some of your men?'

'No, the redcaps see to that.'

'Murder is a civil offence. You told me that Major Blankensy was no longer serving, so, if the body is indeed he, he is a civilian. The first thing is to get the body identified, someone who knew him.'

'I'll do it. When?'

'As soon as possible. I have a cab waiting, could do it now, take you there, bring you back; what say you?'

'You're pushing your luck; I was just finishing, off for a drink in the mess.'

'I'll make it up to you, the nearest local after you've done the good deed.'

'Fair enough, let's go.'

'It may seem a silly question, Sergeant Major: do the men sleep on palliasses in barracks?'

'No, biscuits.'

'Biscuits? Ask a silly question? Get a—'

The RSM laughed. 'That's what they are called, three squared thin mattresses. The beds are iron in two pieces, the bottom half is pushed back under the top half after reveille, all in line, the biscuits laid on top with blanket folded. More room in the barrack, to allow the floor to be bumped and polished; also the beds cannot be squatted on until made up at bedtime.'

'So would any palliasses be kept in store?'

'What is all this about? Might be used if the men were billeted out, but not in barracks.'

'Just curious, Sergeant Major, sorry.'

The RSM frowned. 'You blokes don't ask questions for nothing. Never mind, let's get to the morgue. You're making me thirsty; you can tell me then, after the first pint.'

'Yes, that's Blankensy.' The RSM confirmed it after the sheet had been pulled back to expose the face at the morgue. 'It's him all right. Shouldn't say it, don't speak ill of the dead, but he got his deserts. May have been a bit deranged, I think; blame the war. Who knows what he went through? Fought in Togoland and the Cameroons, you know.

'If I was you, I would not be overzealous looking for the one that put him out of his misery. Put it down to retribution. Now how about this drink you promised?'

Jos didn't comment, but would ponder on the RSM's words later. Did not tell him that another murder was being investigated.

Sunday the weather changed. Dark clouds rolled in from the Atlantic, drinking their fill on the way from the west, overladen, sunk lower and lightened the load passing Erin's shores, restoring green to parched earth, finally emptying bellies over Britain. Lightened, rose as fluffy white clouds and disappeared eastbound.

Gutters became awash, discarded matchboxes were carried along – barges on the Thames – stranded on the drain covers, as cigarette butts, matchsticks and other debris were swept over the precipice. Paving slabs acted as palettes for trodden dogs' turds. Those who had moaned of the heat now moaned as they gazed through rain-battered window panes.

Jos Bancroft woke with a headache. The so-called celebration drinks Saturday lunch time, which had been brought to a halt, and trying to keep up with the RSM's seemingly unquenchable thirst on top of visiting a murder scene and the morgue: this was the price to pay. *Must remember to put a chit in for cab fares, add a bit for witnesses' expenses.*

175

He became aware of rain battering at the window, adding to the knock-knocking of the hammer inside his head. Groaned with the effort to rise from the bed, padded downstairs to the scullery, held his head under the tap above the sink to let the cold water soothe his forehead.

'You're soaking the floor,' his mother exclaimed as she entered. 'Strip and have done with it, take a shower out in the yard.'

'It's bucketing down out there.'

'Well you wouldn't be able to take one if it wasn't. Take a bar of Lifebuoy with you, soft water gets a good lather. Your father did that in summer times. Help to get rid of that headache.'

'How d'you know I've got a headache?'

'I'm a tec's mum. Heard you come in, stagger up the stairs, woke me up.'

'Got a towel handy?'

'Heaven's sake, Jos, worried about your mother seeing you in the nude?'

'The neighbours.'

'Make the blokes jealous, give the girls a treat. Which reminds me, the Rose of Tralee called yesterday evening; you were supposed to call for her, take her out. She waited an hour, then came round to tear you off a strip. I calmed her down, told her it must have been something real urgent to have kept you.'

'It was murder, two of them. So, what with one thing and another, the morgue and ending up buying drinks for the RSM of the Essex trying to glean information from him, you could say I was a bit tied up, and I've told you before, Rose comes from Northern Ireland, not the south. Don't let her hear you say that.'

'Of course not; does it matter where she comes from? It's the song, beautiful, I like it.' She began singing, '*The pale moon was rising above the green mountain – the sun was—*'

'Turn it in, Mum.'

'All right; don't like my singing, eh? Get on with it, I'll get a towel and get breakfast ready, and you had better have a good excuse for yesterday evening, and being drunk won't do. Go and make your peace when you've finished breakfast, brave the rain, throw your hat in first. Bring Rose back for dinner, you can canoodle in the front room if it's still raining this afternoon, make a date for the wedding, it's about time, you've been engaged long enough.'

Washed by the heavens, fed and watered, Jos sat and waited for the aspirin he had swallowed to cushion the hammer blows in his head, collected his thoughts and pondered the RSM's words.

*Put it down to retribution. In other words, Blankensy was killed by someone seeking revenge. That someone has to be from the military. Top of the list of suspects with motive has to be Cooper and Roberts, the only two that survived from that doomed platoon. Next, relatives of those killed, friends, comrades, in the regiment. That narrows it down to about a thousand or more. I'm not going to get very far questioning them, bullying or threatening squaddies; the army stick together like shit to a blanket. Need to be diplomatic: softly softly catchee monkey.*

*'Ask about,' the RSM said. I will. Ask.*

*Who was the soldier that Alice saw enter and leave the scene of the crime, the same one walking with the girl from the baker's shop?*

*Why was Roberts court martialled?*

*Who were the two soldiers who paid the kid to find out if Blankensy was in?*

*A good place to start would be the baker's shop.*

177

'You gonner fetch Rose or not? Time's marching on, and I want to know to arrange dinner.'

His mother's voice ended his musing as her head peered around the door.

'Yes, I'll go now. Got a brolly?'

### Monday morning

The RSM of the Essex Regiment called at the CO's office before parade

'Thought you ought to know, sir, a detective inspector called late yesterday evening to report that a body had been found shot; he needed the body identified as an army uniform was discovered at the same address. Asked could it be one of ours. I identified the body as Mr Blankensy at the morgue. I did not want to disturb you as by that time it was past ten o'clock.'

A slight grimace showed on the OC's face. 'Thank you, Sergeant Major; I'll inform the officers.'

'Shall I make it known to the men, sir?'

'They'll be bound to know sooner or later. Yes, by word of mouth, if you know what I mean.'

'I understand, sir.'

The word spread like wildfire. 'Blanksy's been shot, a tec will come asking questions, lips to be sealed as tight as a fish's arse'ole.'

'Christ, someone's beat us to it, 'arry,' Bill Tomkins remarked to Cooper. 'I wonder who?'

Roberts and most of the regiment wondered also, looked at each other.

Jack Barnett grabbed the top copy from a bundle of the day's issue on the way to be distributed to shops and street vendors. He had talked the editor into printing a special edition, other than the weekly Friday one. Smiled as he read the headlines.

### _A killer loose in Islington_

**_Two bodies found murdered in Camden Town._**
**_A retired army officer and a railway worker._**

_First with the news, **Jack Barnett**, crime reporter._
_Further coverage inside pages as to why the officer retired._


_CID offices, Clerkenwell_

'You read this?' DI Bill Gordon shouted, spluttering and red in the face as he glared at Jos Bancroft and Tom Fowler. Slammed a fist on a copy of the Islington Gazette lying open on the desk between them. Jos and Tom took a pace back.

'Couldn't help seeing it,' Jos answered. 'Street vendors waving it under our nose and screaming "read all about it".'

'This bastard reporter Barnett knows more than I do; he's got names and details of Blankensy sending the platoon to their death. Did you know that?'

'I did, guv,' Jos said.

'_What?_'

The DI shouted so loud the desk sergeant on the ground floor looked up at the ceiling, blew through his lips. 'Someone will be walking the beat tomorrow by the sounds of it.'

179

'That's it,' the DI continued 'We'll all be back in uniform when the commissioner reads this.' He sat down. 'You'd better have an answer, Jos, so help me God, I'll—'

He never finished saying what he would do; Jos came right out with it.

'I got it from the RSM at the HQ Essex Regiment late Saturday evening. You told us to get at it, sew this case up quick. I went straight there after we had finished at Arlington Road, got the body identified at the morgue as Blankensy, cost me money and a headache, and found out how and why Blankensy retired. Didn't get home until almost midnight. How the hell should I know this reporter had got the tip off? He has narks in his pay, you can bet on that. Wouldn't have made any difference if I had known; the press was printing on the Sunday, ready for issue today.'

'All right, Jos. You did well. Get that sodding reporter here, frogmarch him if he won't come. I want to know who he got this information from.'

'He won't tell, guv, you know that, the power of the press. He'll have it on the front page the next day. "Police giving me the third degree for printing the truth."'

'Yeah, I guess so; he is the same one that got the stop press news on the Flint hanging case. Now who would know about the murders other than us?'

'That constable Lacy, he was there with us, and anyone from the Albany Street nick would know, but they would not know about Blankensy and the doomed patrol; only those in the Essex Regiment would have that.'

'Have you got anything else, Jos?'

'Not until I know for sure who the soldier was that entered Blankensy's basement and walked out with the girl from the baker's shop. Then I think we'll have the one that killed Blankensy.'

'Get to it, Jos; I need something to pacify the commissioner when he reads this.' Pointing to the Gazette on the desk. 'How about you, Tom: anything to go on yet?'

'No; being Sunday, Betts's gang could be anywhere. I'll catch them at the depot as soon as we have finished here. Question one at a time, see if anything comes to light. I know he was a union shop steward; perhaps he has upset someone.'

'Right, get at it, keep me informed. When I get the coroner's report I'll let you know; not as if it will make any difference to what we know. One shot, one throat cut.'

DC Tom Fowler pointed to the huge gates. The guardian of the portal-to-portal, watching from his hut the other side, shook his head. Tom held his warrant card high and beckoned only to see another shake of a head.

'Open a bloody gate,' Tom shouted, pointing with a finger to his warrant card.

The guard took his time leaving his hut to approach. 'Only authorised pers—'

Tom cut him short. 'I said open a bloody gate; I'm not talking through bars, otherwise you could end up behind another type of bars, obstructing a police officer in the course of duty.'

Tom held his warrant card so that it could be seen clearly. The guard squinted at it.

'Why ain't yer in uniform, then?'

'You gonner open a gate, or am I gonner get the Black Maria down here?'

The guard produced a large key, and one gate swung back.

Tom entered. 'That's better, now we can get on the right footing. I'm Detective Constable Tom Fowler CID and in plain clothes; that's how we operate. Who's in charge here?'

'Well, as far as who comes and goes, checks in deliveries and security, I am.'

'I want to speak to the men that work with Betts.'

'What's it about?'

'You read the Islington Gazette?'

'I don't buy one if that's what you mean, maybe glance at it if one's been left in the mess room.'

'Buy one today, you'll have your answer. Now where can I find the gangers?'

'You'll have to speak to Sizzle.'

'Sizzle?'

'Sizzle Fry, that's what the men call him. Get it? 'e's in charge as Betts is not here. I'll take you; we have to pass main lines, trains coming and going at all times, can't have you tripping over and ending up mincemeat under a locomotive. Don't try to cross a line until I say so, and keep close.'

'I will, not gonner argue with a train.'

The guard locked the gate behind them. They passed stacks of wooden sleepers, lengths of rail, heaps of stone chippings, rods and other equipment, finally arriving at a brick-built building alongside a siding, the platelayers' haven, mess room, rest room, refuge against inclement weather, to play cards and skive. Fry saw them coming, didn't like it one bit. 'Why didn't Betts turn up Friday? I'm gonner be for the 'igh jump booking 'im in Thursday,' he muttered to himself.

'This is a detective, come to arrest you, Peter,' the guard said as they entered.

Peter Fry nearly shat himself on the spot, turned a deathly white.

'What's the matter, Peter, a guilty conscience, been pinching rail lines? Only joking.' He laughed. 'The tec wants to speak to the gang, that's all.'

'I'll start with you first. Peter, is it? I'm not bothered if you pinched a train, just a few questions about Betts; did you buy the Islington Gazette this morning?

183

'No, never do. Well, I say never do; the only time I bought it was when that Flint trial started; it was the one with the first news of it. Why?'

'Never mind. How do you get on with him? Was you surprised when he didn't turn up for work on Friday?'

'On Friday, yes, as it's pay day.'

'What's this all about? The CID checking on Betts not turning up for work, what's 'e done?'

'Not what he's done, it's what someone else has done. We know he never clocked in Friday, and won't be clocking in any more, not here, maybe somewhere else high up if he has been a good boy during his lifetime.'

Fry's jaw dropped, showing a row of tobacco-stained teeth. He looked at the expression on the guard's face, and back again at the DC. Tom Fowler nodded.

'You've got it, it's all in the local Gazette. Betts's been murdered, and I'm gonner grill that sodding reporter to find who was the leak. So I'm asking again. Was you surprised when he didn't turn up on Friday?'

'Why ask me?'

'Let's say you've got his job, a bit more in the pay packet, didn't want him to turn up, ever, unless it was his toes in a coffin. You were a bit nervous and jumpy when the guard said I'd come to arrest you, also you looked like the boy caught with his finger in the jam pot; you're holding something back, so out with it, and I'll know if you are lying.'

Fry licked his dry lips, looked at the guard. 'Does 'e 'ave to be 'ere?'

'If you've something to say, Fry, say it.'

'Not while 'e's 'ere.'

Tom pursed his lips, blew out his cheeks. 'Give us a minute, will you, guard? Better still, I'll find my own way out if you don't want to wait, as I shall be some time interviewing the rest of the gang.'

'I should see you off the premises, but get one of the gang to see you to the gate when you have finished.' He looked daggers at Fry, and left with a bit of a huff.

Tom Fowler closed the door behind the guard. 'Don't waste any more of my time, Fry, out with it.'

'Off the record.'

'I'm warning you, Fry, I'm investigating a murder, so anything you say—'

'I clocked Betts in on Thursday.' Fry blurted it out, cutting Tom short.

'For Chrissake, is that all?'

'That all! I'd get the sack for that, and I didn't want the guard to know, 'e might nark on me. Yer don't get paid if yer don't turn up, did yer know that? Not like the likes of you blokes, get paid whether you turn in or not.'

'So Betts didn't turn up Thursday. You done this clocking in before?'

'I 'ad to. Betts 'as a day off now and again, told me to punch 'is card when 'e don't come in.'

'The rest of the gang know this?'

'Got to, ain't they? 'e's got 'em under 'is thumb. They do what they are told to do; 'e's shop steward, rules the roost.'

'So what did you do when Betts never turned up this morning? We know you didn't clock him on Friday.'

'Nuffink, thought 'e must be ill. I would only do it for one day, and that's dodgy, and now I can't tell the powers that be that I did on Thursday. Yer won't tell 'em, will yer?'

'Keep your fingers crossed – or the cheeks of your arse, in your case – that they don't ask. I'm not interested in the skiving and abetting. I now know Betts was not in Thursday, and you didn't know he wasn't coming in either. That right?'

'Yeah.'

'Where were you Wednesday night?'

'Wot! Yer don't fink I done 'im in?'

'I ask the questions, you give the answers.'

'I was at 'ome, never went out, yer can ask the missus.'

'I will, what's the address?'

'William Road number 8.'

'Give me a clue, where?'

'Off Hampstead Road, near Mornington Crescent.'

'Got it. Now listen, Fry. I have last week's "punching in card" of Betts's for evidence. If the coroner's report confirms what we the CID suspect, that Betts was killed between the hours of 8 pm Wednesday and 8 am Thursday, that puts you on the spot. You punched his card Thursday morning; you said you didn't know he wasn't coming in for work that day. That was a load of eyewash. Of course you did. You was trying to hide your tracks; instead, it was putting the noose around your own neck. You killed him, thinking we would be fooled that Betts was still alive on Thursday.'

'No,' Fry shouted. 'I told yer I was 'ome, never went out Wednesday night. The missus will tell yer.'

'Of course she would. Tell me, you walk to work?'

'Wot's that got to do wiv it?'

'I told you before, I ask the questions, you give the answers.'

'Yes I does, both ways.'

'So you leave home earlier on Thursday morning, ten minutes at the most to get to Betts's rooms, it's on the way. You knock, he opens the door, you push in, the job's done, you leave, close the door and walk away, carry on to work, clock Betts and yourself in.'

'No, no, yer got it all wrong. I know I told yer I punched 'is card in, that was off the record, I'll deny it.'

'You know the old saying, "Oh what a tangled web we weave when first we practise to deceive"? You are digging yourself deeper in a hole by lying. Don't kid yourself that one or more of the gang didn't see you punch Betts's card. You will accompany me to our station and make a statement. The inspector will then decide, on what you have to say or write, as to whether you will be charged with the murder of Betts. You understand?'

Fry's shoulders sagged; he began rambling desultorily, the words at times incoherent. 'Betts ran my life – Meeting tonight, Fry, door duty, check the brothers' cards, make sure they've paid their due to date – No yer can't, tell yer missus to sod off – I'll tell yer when yer can work overtime – now 'e's dead, and 'e's gonner get me hung.' He straightened, looked at Tom, said quite clearly, 'You've got the wrong man.'

Tom frowned, heard Bob Drummonds' voice.

*You've got the wrong man, I'm telling yer, yer got the wrong man, I know Flint never did it, 'cos I know who did, but I can't tell yer that. Yer sent 'im to the gallows. I prayed that night of the storm at Saint Paul's Cathedral, me who's only been to church once when I got married; the trap door didn't work, an act of God the official report proclaimed it. Flint walked free. The man they couldn't hang, the papers said.*

Tom shook his head. Looked at Fry, feeling compassionate. 'I have to take you in, sorry and all that.'

'I'll get the sack if I leave now, I'm in charge, can it wait until after work?'

*He's worried about getting the sack with a charge of murder hanging over his head; what is it with this bloke?*

'I could say I want you to identify the body. No? All right, leave it until then; that'll be what time?'

'Half five.'

'Fair enough. I'll be having a word with the rest of the gang in the meantime.'

'I can't let yer wander alone on the rail tracks; I'll 'ave to bring the gang back here.'

'How many are there?'

'Seven besides myself and a flag man. 'e 'as to be there at all times when men are working on the lines, so if yer want to speak to 'im, they'll all 'ave to stop work.'

'In that case I'll speak to him first, then one at a time and then they can return to work, so off you go.'

After Fly had left, Tom looked around, summed the place up. A gas ring, a tap over a sink, tin mugs and a tea urn, a cupboard, a pot belly stove with flue disappearing through the roof, a form each side of a long wooden table and a well-worn upholstered armchair at the head. He imagined Betts sitting there, laying the law down. He tried it out, very comfy, closed his eyes, a few minutes passed, his head dropped and he dozed off.

*'I'm telling yer, yer got the wrong man.' Bob Drummond was glaring at him across the table. ''e didn't do it, Bert Craig did, didn't mean to, broke that Ansa's neck in a scuffle pulling 'im off me.' 'So you was there, you sod, you admit that and you'll swing the same as him. You'll have to make a statement, I'll get the sergeant to sit with you, put it down in writing that...' 'A mate of yours heard Craig confess to the killing, maudlin after too many beers, and he told you.' 'Wot's that mean?' 'Weeping in his beer.' 'Just get it down, and I didn't hear what you did say, understand?' 'I fink so.' 'Make the statement then, make the statement, the statement the statement—'*

Tom's eyes slowly opened. A sparrow was watching him across a table; he closed his eyes. *Where the hell am I?* He forced his eyes open. The sparrow was still there, cocked his head to one side. Tom's eyes swivelled clockwise, taking in the surroundings; he realised where he was. *That Flint case, dreaming again; will it ever go away? Got the wrong man – got the wrong man – All right, sod you Bob Drummond, won't happen again.*

The door banged against the outer wall. Tom sat up, startled; the sparrow fluttered to the floor, began pecking for crumbs. Fry entered, followed by the flag man and the rest of the gang. Being a detective, Tom deduced that, as he was carrying a flag.

'Wot's all this lark then? Yer sitting in Betts's chair, 'e won't be pleased, an' you can shove off, me old cock sparrow, we ain't 'ad our grub yet.'

The sparrow flew to the open window, left a calling card on the sill before departing.

'You didn't buy the Islington Gazette, then,' Tom said, now fully awake and in questioning mood.

'Wot? Why, it don't come out until Friday.'

'As I said to the gate watcher and to Fry, I am Detective Constable Tom Fowler. I ask the questions, you answer. The first being "where were you Wednesday night?", and no whats or whys.'

The flag man looked at Fry, who nodded.

''ome wiv the missus, yer can ask 'er.'

'I thought so. Are all the rest of the gang married, Fry?'

'All except young Fred.'

'So where was you, Fred?' Tom asked, looking to see who Fred was.

''aving a drink wiv me mates at the Movver Red Cap.'

An hour or more later, Tom had answers. Betts was a rotten sod, a good bloke, a Marxist, didn't believe in democracy, what he said went. A hero, got us this mess room, we only 'ad a wooden 'ut before to put our tools in.

Sparrows were gathering on the windowsill.

'It's midday,' said Fry. 'They know it's break time.' Nodding at the sparrows.

'They had better have it, then,' said Tom

Fred, the youngest of the gang, lit the gas ring, his job to make the tea; the men retrieved their lunches from the cupboard, grabbed their mugs and sat down, to read the paper the food had been wrapped in. Tom was given Betts's mug and half a beetroot sandwich from one who didn't think all coppers were bastards. The sparrows joined them, waiting for the crumbs to drop. No need to sweep the floor after, every grain was devoured.

'I've changed my mind,' said Tom.

Fry listened, not daring to ask what it was that had changed his mind. Waited.

The men had left, led by the flag man making sure they didn't march at more than 4 mph. Also, it had been 'fly away, robin' – no, not, robin – 'sparrow, come back another day'.

'I'm letting you off the leash, Peter – I'm gonner call you Peter as Fry makes me think of chocolate, and you are certainly not that – but you are not off the hook, so you won't do a runner. I'll have a word with my inspector, wait until we get the coroner's report and take it from there. Betts's last week's "punching in card" stays with me. If you are told to make a statement, write that you punched Betts's card under duress. You understand?'

'Yes, thanks.'

'Don't thank me, thank Bob Drummond for small mercies.'

'Wot?'

'Do you know him? He's a porter, here at the main line station.'

'Know of him, 'e was the one that gave evidence at the trial for Flint, got 'is name in the paper, didn't do any good, the jury found Flint guilty. Why?'

'Never mind. Now, the railway staff, are they all – or were they – under Betts's jurisdiction? I take it they were all union members.'

'Yeah, 'ad to be.'

'Any at loggerheads with Betts, d'you know?'

'Not really; one or two moaned 'aving to pay subs, if they did not want in the union, but 'cos they 'ad to, Betts was on their backs if they missed any union meeting.'

'I get the picture. One last thing before I leave you in peace. Any minor damage to a carriage, for instance a door window needing changing: would that be down to your mob?'

'No, not allowed to do that; our work is on the track, replacing lines, sleepers, the signal linkage, checking spacing between lines, and other manual work on the embankments. The carriage would be side-tracked, taken to the works station.'

'All right, that will be all for now. You had better lead me to the gate; don't want to end up at Crewe.'


## Bayham Street

'Yer seen this?'

The French polisher burst into the ironmonger's shop brandishing a copy of the Islington Gazette.

'Yer gone mad? Can't yer see I'm serving a customer?'

'Blimey, I fought anovver war 'ad started,' the customer cried out. 'What's it all about?'

'Sorry. Sorry, I'll come back when you've finished serving your customer.' The French polisher scooted out as fast as he had come.

'Is he always like that?' the customer asked.

'At times; it's the methylated spirits he uses, sniffs it, has a sip now and then. That'll be fourpence 'a'penny; anything else I can get yer?'

The customer placed the right amount on the counter, picked up the bag of cut nails and left in a hurry. *Nuts, the pair of yer*, he mouthed as he reached the door.

The French polisher, watching from his own doorstep, came back as soon as he saw the customer leave.

'Someone's done Betts in,' he announced as he entered and placed the Gazette on the counter. The ironmonger read the headlines, turned the pages to read Barnett's report, folded the newspaper and looked up.

'So what? He's got what he deserved.'

'You know he was the same bloke that—?'

'Yeah, I know.' The ironmonger cut him short. 'Also that you shut shop and did a runner; that was four years ago, forget it.'

'Funny, two murders reported the same day; d'yer think the same bloke did both of 'em?'

'How the hell do I know? Nothing to do with me, or you, so leave it, take yer paper, cut it up for arse paper, I don't want to know, shove off.'

When the polisher had left, the ironmonger thought for a moment, felt on the shelf for the spare key and the old lock, grabbed his tool bag, went outside. The street was empty. He hurriedly removed the new lock of the empty shop, replaced it with the old one, forced the door closed, nailed the top and bottom corners of the door fast, covered the heads with grime. Then went back to his own shop placed the 'closed' sign in the door window, locked up, climbed the stairs to his rooms above. *I'm gonner get sloshed and sleep sound for the first time in four years.*

DS Jos Bancroft and Detective Barcham sat on a slatted bench seat watching two young boys, water up to their knees in the pond, trawling for tiddlers with what looked like half of an old potato sack. Two pairs of plimsolls and a jam jar rested on the edge; the jam jar had string wound around the neck, leaving a loop by which to be carried.

Jos and Barcham had arrived early, two hours before the kids had. The weather fine and dry after Sunday's deluge, a few fluffy white clouds of cotton wool high in the heavens played hide and seek with the sun. A sudden gust of wind sent a discarded spent paper bag into a dervish dance, caught up in the vortex; a leaf fluttered to the ground.

'A touch of autumn on the way,' Barcham remarked.

'They won't survive, you know,' Jos said.

'What? Who?' Barcham frowned, grimaced.

'The tiddlers; by the time the kids get home, they'll be floating on the top, bottoms up. Shades of childhood days.'

Barcham tried to imagine the DS in short trousers catching tiddlers; it wouldn't come. Instead, he asked, his patience running out, 'Why are we here, sir?'

'To ponder, meditate, observe, far from the madding crowd, Barcham, Any complaints? And you can cut the "sir" out while you're with me on this case.'

'No sir, I mean yes sir, Sarge.'

'That road meandering its way alongside the fields feeds the HQ of the Essex Regiment; did you know that, Barcham?'

'Not for sure, I knew it was near here.'

'Revenge is mine, said the Lord. I don't know how many men there are in the Essex Regiment, but I think one of them has taken over His Lordship's role. We have two witnesses, Barcham: Alice, who saw a soldier enter Blankensy's rooms, and young Jimmy Wilde, who said two soldiers paid him to knock on Blankensy's entrance door, God knows what for. It points to one of them; how say you, Barcham?'

'Retribution by a squaddie, yeah. But I can't believe it is coincidental, that the other murder is not linked in some way, that's what's been on my mind: one shot, the other throat cut, different method, don't add up, and where did the piece of glass come from the killer used to cut Betts's throat? It's a puzzle.'

'I'm with you. Tom Fowler and I discussed this with the inspector. Betts's murder could have been on the spur of the moment, but that's Tom's case; we need to concentrate on our job, we can liaise with Tom later. Now, any idea how we can identify the three prime suspects?'

'Identity parade, get Alice and Jimmy to point them out.'

'Oh yeah, and pigs will fly. Do you think the army would allow that? The press would have a field day; even if we applied to the War Office, the paperwork would fill the Albert Hall, and we would be retired by then. No, it's got to be *softly softly catchee monkey*, but we have one thing going for us. Alice told me a "giant of a man", her words, was with the soldier who went into Blankensy's rooms the morning before the postman discovered the body. He waited at pavement level and in civvy clothes, then later the two of them walked past with the two girls from the baker's shop in Delancey Street whose brother is a soldier. So there is a connection there. I'm banking the "big 'un", I'll refer to him as such, is a mate of the soldier, and they will come out together. The attraction the girls from the baker's shop; the big 'un unbeknowing is our clue. You with me, Barcham?'

'Yeah.'

'Good, so this is what I want you to do, if and when they come out, and I'm sure they will. You walk towards them, taking it at leisure as if out for a stroll, see if our suspect is wearing the MM ribbon, could be the first of a row of

194

others, and this is a long shot: pass as close as you can, see if you can discern that a sergeant's chevrons have been removed from his sleeve, maybe a different colour of the khaki. If you have 20/20 vision, you may notice where stitches have been.'

'What makes you think he's a sergeant or has been, and awarded the MM?'

'Cooper and Roberts were the two survivors of that doomed platoon, prime suspects. Roberts the sergeant had the MM, was stripped of rank, The CSM of the Essex told me that in between sinking pint after pint at my expense Sunday evening. So if this soldier is wearing the MM it has to be Roberts, if not we have to think again.'

'What if they are suspicious, and shout "Who you staring at?" and this big bloke grabs me?'

'Don't stare, just glance as you pass. I'd do it myself but I don't want them to see me yet.'

'All right, I'll have a shot.'

It was another two hours before Barcham could have his shot. The kids had left with two tiddlers in the jam jar. Soldiers had passed, two by two, most wearing campaign ribbons, none with the MM or with a 'big 'un', but there was no mistaking the 'big 'un' when finally two appeared breasting the rise; he was huge.

'Off you go, Barch, use your loaf,' said Jos.

Jos watched from a distance as Chas Roberts and Michael O'Leary wended their way down the slope in step on the road. Barcham crossed the field diagonally – a nobody out for a leisurely stroll – made his way to the road. He stopped, stooped to pick up a discarded cigarette packet, looked around. Inclined his head at a waste bin at the edge of the road that he had already had in mind, walked to it and dropped the packet in. Timed it nicely to arrive as Roberts and O'Leary approached, nodded to them as they passed.

195

Jos smiled. *Clever, Barcham, clever.*

Barcham then walked up the slope, breasted the rise until out of sight, turned and retraced his steps. Jos had left the bench and followed Roberts and O'Leary; Barcham hurried his step to join him.

'Easy peasy,' Barcham said. 'He was wearing the MM ribbon, first in a row of others; couldn't see any evidence on his tunic that chevrons had been worn, but it seemed the tunic had been well scrubbed.'

'Never mind, you did well, Barch, but as sure as eggs are eggs that is Roberts, the one that Alice saw going into number 86 Arlington Road, and the big 'un with him, what she described as a giant of a man.'

'So what now?'

'We follow them, see where they go, and I bet odds I know where: the baker's shop in Delancey Street. Split up, Barch; you know the procedure: we play leap frog.'

'What if they take a tram?'

'We do the same, after they had boarded; if they go up top, we go inside, or the other way round, but they won't, it will mean taking two, one to Highgate and another to Camden Town. They'll walk.'

Jos was right; they walked, turned off Holloway Road and took the back doubles to Camden Road, turned left to Camden High Street. Jos and Barcham followed at a distance, alternately taking the lead – *leap-frogging*. On reaching Camden Town High Street, Jos crossed to the opposite side.

The bookie's lookout nodded at O'Leary and gave a mock salute to Roberts as they turned into Delancey Street, smiled. 'No bets where you're going,' he said, remembering seeing them once before. 'Good luck.' O'Leary wagged a huge finger at him and chuckled.

Jos was just in time to see Chas and Michael's backs disappear into the baker's as he reached the junction. He beckoned Barcham to join him.

'I was right,' he said. 'They have gone into the baker's.'

'So what do we do now?'

'No point in hanging about here. Now that we are in the area, you go and have a word with young Jimmy Wilde at 10 Osnaburgh Street, it's not far. See if you can glean any more information on those two squaddies that paid him to knock at Blankensy's flat, description, or if they used any names he may have heard. Don't be harsh, it won't work, he's a streetwise kid, be nice to his mum. Then come to 85 Arlington Road; if your face fits you may get a glass of sarsaparilla. The real McCoy made from the root, nectar.'

'What?'

'Don't tell me you've never tasted it.'

The bookie's lookout, eyes always on the alert for the law, watched Barcham cross the road and converse with Jos, their heads together amidst the throng of window gazers and passers-by.

*Wot those two buggers up to? Plain clothes dicks by the look of 'em; ain't come to nick a bookie taking tanner bets, that's for sure. They're looking over 'ere; something's going on, wot wiv squaddies turning up a couple of times, one following another who's following a civvy; they're looking over 'ere. Got it, they've been tagging the one wiv the big 'un that's gone into Clive's the baker's.*

'That geezer on the corner of Delancey Street is watching us,' said Barcham.

'Yeah, I know, a bookie's runner, eyes everywhere, summing us up. You shove off now, I'll go via the Parkway to Arlington Road. Put the wind up him, walk over as though intent on nicking him, see what he does.'

The runner saw Barcham coming towards him, put two fingers in his mouth and blew a shrill whistle. The bookie at the other end of the street heard it and walked away, turning the corner into Arlington Road. Barcham called out.

'You needn't have bothered, I'm not bothered about your mate taking tuppenny bets, was gonner ask you where Osnaburgh Street is.'

'Take any turning on the right off 'ampstead Road past Mornington Crescent'll lead yer into it, but yer know that, 'cos yer a tec.'

'Clever sod, ain't you?'

'If yer sez so.'


After Barcham and Jos had left, the bookie's runner went into the baker's shop. Clive Jones behind the counter greeted him with, 'Tea, Bert?'

'Later, Clive, just popped in to let yer know' – nodding at Chas and Michael sitting chatting to Colin Jones – 'that two plain clothes tecs have been tailing yer.'

'Thanks,' said Michael. 'Forewarned, forearmed. Are they still waiting outside?'

'No, split up, one's gone to Osnaburgh Street, so 'e sez, the ovver one's gone the way 'e came, back along the 'igh street. Can't stay, gotta keep me eyes skinned, anovver two races to run, back for tea then, Clive.'

'What was all that about?' Clive asked after the runner had left.

'I guess they suspect me of killing Blankensy, but before you ask, Colin, I didn't; thought about it, as he deserved it.'

'So what are you going to do?'

'Nothing, I'm innocent. Get some civvies when my back pay comes through, not much as they dock the time I was in the glasshouse, look for a job.'

'Don't you worry about money, Chas, anything I have is yours; you saved my son's life, so please let me help in some way.'

Chas glanced at Michael, who inclined his head.

'Call it a loan, then.'

'That's settled, then,' said Clive.

'What's settled?' Grace queried as she entered from the rear room behind the counter after descending the stairs from the flat above.

'A picnic.' It came spontaneously from her father. 'The four of you, make the most of the fine weather while you have the chance. When they get back, Clive, take Chas to Kemps, get some civvies'

'Good idea, Da; I need a couple of things myself, get them the same time.'

'Brilliant, Da,' said Grace as she ducked under the counter flap. Michael stood and offered his chair; Grace sat, placed an arm over her shoulder to reach for his hand.

'Gwyneth will be down in a moment. She knows you are here, Chas; she is pinching her cheeks.'


_Arlington Road_

Jos was greeted by Alice and Clara from the window with 'Come up, Sergeant.'

'Is this a social call or official, Sergeant?' Alice asked as Jos entered their flat.

'I would like to say social, but regret I am on duty; compromise and say both, and I have a request for you, Alice.'

'How can I help, Sergeant?'

'It is quite probable that the soldier you saw enter number 86 last Friday will pass by this morning. If you could keep an eye open and confirm it is the same one you saw before, it would help with my enquiries.'

'You think this soldier is responsible for the...' Alice left it unsaid

'I can't say. I like to be sure of facts before I willy-nilly question anyone.'

'But surely you can just ask him?'

'And if he denies it?'

'I see your point. What makes you think he may pass by soon?'

'Not quite a shot in the dark, Alice, as at this moment the soldier and his big companion are at the baker's shop in Delancey Street. The attraction the sisters, I would assume. You told me they walked out with them previously, so they may do so again.'

'You traced them there?'

'Alice, an officer has been murdered; it is my duty to find the killer. If I know for sure this soldier entered number 86 not long before the postman discovered the body, he is suspect and needs to answer some serious questioning.'

Alice hesitated before asking, 'Does that mean if it was the same soldier, you would arrest him?'

'Certainly I would question him, depends on the answers he gives as to an arrest.'

'Oh dear, I don't know if I can do this; this young man walked past here arm in arm with Gwyneth, who I know, chatting and laughing, the four of them as if without a care in the world. One word from me, it would be shattered. It doesn't feel right, that he could have—'

'Murdered someone?' Jos finished the sentence for her. 'He is a soldier, Alice. Seen the slaughter in the trenches, no doubt killed as he was trained to do. Seen his platoon wiped out by the whim of this officer – court martialled – reduced to the ranks, spent six months in prison, his army career finished, all down to that same officer. I would say that is a good reason to be a suspect, more so entering that officer's flat at a crucial time. It is up to you, Alice, to decide. I promise I will not question him whilst he is with the Jones girl.'

'All right, Sergeant, I will.'

'Thank you, Alice; do you mind if I wait?'

'I'd rather you did.'

'I'll make some tea in that case,' said Clara.

Jos was disappointed, *no sarsaparilla*, said, 'Thank you, Clara.'

They didn't have long to wait; the foursome came into sight not much more than half an hour after Jos had sipped tea from a delicate bone china teacup. He watched Alice's eyes follow Roberts as he came closer; she nodded.

'Yes.' It came out in a whisper. 'It is the same man, and the large man with him. Dear God, I hope I have done the right thing.'

Barcham, on his way back from Osnaburgh Street, was greeted by the bookie's runner.

'Find it, did yer, Osnaburgh Street?'

'Yeah.'

'Those two yer were tailing 'ave gone.'

'So what?'

'So what yer doing back 'ere?'

'Nosy sod, aren't you?'

'Yeah, that's me, lookout, all nose and eyes, smell and see who comes and goes, like spotting you and yer mate, not 'ard to do, as yer stuck out like sore fumbs. The bookie pays me to keep an eye out for the rozzers, one in particular who's being trying to nab 'im for ages, but I'm one step a'ead; ovvers don't bovver, one's a regular punter. I can give yer a good tip if yer wants to lay odds.'

'I've heard that before; a certain winner, eh?'

'Please yerself, but I can tip yer off on somefing else; I know yous blokes pay for information.'

'What are you talking about?'

'Yer know wot I mean, sniffing around 'ere; yer on that Arlington Road murder case, I reckon, trailing that squaddie wiv the big 'un. It's to do wiv the army, ain't it?'

'How do you think you know?'

'I read the papers , the Islington Gazette, and as I said I see who comes and goes.'

'You can read, then.'

'Who's being a clever sod now? Yeah, I can read.'

'If you have anything to say, spit it out.'

'Look, I'm not a nark, but murder is different, and I've got a living to make, so 'ow about a fiver as a sweetener? Wot I 'as to tell yer could git yer promotion wivout yer getting a brown nose.'

'You watch your mouth, sunshine, you might get a fist in it, and if you think I run around with fivers in my pocket, you're sadly mistaken. I could run you in if I thought you were holding back information as to a murder.'

'All right, 'ave it your way, I don't know nuffink.'

'That means you do.'

'Wot?'

'Two negatives – never mind.'

'It's about the army.' The runner blurted it out. 'Two squaddies ring a bell?'

Barcham's ears pricked up. *I've just come back from talking to Jimmy Wilde, who said two squaddies had paid him to knock at the officer's door.* 'If you're taking me on, you'll be looking out through iron bars, not looking out here.'

'I'm not, guv, 'onest.'

'Give me an inkling and I'll see what it's worth; it would count towards a reward if it leads to an arrest.'

''ow much the reward?'

'That's down to the police commissioner, if he decides to offer one.'

'That's a bit iffy, ain't it?'

'Take it or leave it.'

'Gis us 'alf a quid, then.'

'The inkling first.'

'Christ, yer'd git blood out of a stone. All right. As I said, two squaddies. The first time I saw 'em, one asked the way to Arlington Road, the second one asked the same, said he was tailing the first one but didn't want be seen. I told 'im to go back along the 'igh street to Parkway and 'e could get into Arlington Road from there. The second time, a couple of days later, the first one that had come before turned up, said 'e was looking for a postman.'

'A postman? Why a postman?'

'Yer a tec, work it out.'

'An address. He wanted an address, of course. But he had asked for Arlington Road, had a name. I get it, no number and so many houses been made into flats, wasn't sure which. Ah, yes, must be the one that asked Jimmy Wilde to knock at the door, to make sure it was the right one.'

'Give yer top marks, not bad for a tec. Yer 'ad yer inkling, I take the ten bob now.' Held out his hand.

'Anything else to impart?'

'Yeah. Oh, yeah. To tell yer, if that's what yer mean.' He raised an empty palm. A ten shilling note was passed and pocketed.

'So what else?' Barcham asked.

'The one that asked for a postman was back again, he was following a civvy who turned into Arlington Road, and guess wot, anovver squaddie was following, I fink as a back up. Now yer've 'ad yer 'alf quid's worf, and I've still got more up me sleeve, but me lips are drying up.'

'I'm not a travelling bank, only have loose change with me now you've taken my last note. Come with me to Clerkenwell, see the inspector, see what he has to say.'

'Not ruddy likely, me in a cop shop, no way.'

'Look, I promise I'll do what I can to get you a few quid if what you tell me is on the up and up. I can also be naughty, tell the Albany Street nick to make your life a misery; your mate at the other end of the street will be lucky if he takes another bet.'

'Ain't got much choice, 'ave I?'

'Looks that way.'

'All right. Friday an officer and a warrant officer comes out of Arlington Road, early it was, I'd 'ad a bit of breakfast at the baker's, not on lookout at that time. They went into the baker's, and not long after the big 'un and medal, they turned up and went in. Soon after the officer and the WO came out and walked to the 'igh street, blow me down if they don't meet the two squaddies that had followed the civvy before, coming across the 'igh street. They spoke to each ovver, seemed as if the officer was asking the way, as one of the squaddies pointed south to 'ampstead Road then the tram stop for the one to catch for Euston Road. I fink they was going to a railway station, as they were both carrying luggage. The two squaddies then went into the baker's. Now that's worf somefing, ain't it?'

'Well, certainly something to think on; anything else?'

'The big 'un and medal came out wiv the two girls, Grace was 'anging on to the big 'un's arm as though she'd never let go. The squaddies came out and left together.'

'Notice anything special about the officer and WO?'

'They are not of the Essex lot. The cap badge looked like one of those tall palm trees.'

'Never heard of that badge, can't be an English regiment. You say they were carrying luggage. The WO not a pack or kitbag?'

'No. Hand luggage.'

'If that's all, I'll be off, pick my sergeant up who is sitting talking to Alice at 85. Do you know her?'

'Everyone knows Alice and her sister Clara. By the way, the big 'un and medal left just before you came back.'

## *Essex Regiment Barracks*

'The CSM wants to see you two.' (So the sentry at the gate informed Chas and Michael on their return, the two having enjoyed the picnic and a late afternoon tea at the baker's and left the girls with 'See you tomorrow'.) 'And good luck, Sarge.'

Chas brought his elbows forward, glanced down at where the chevrons had been removed. 'Can't see any stripes, Tom, and what's the good luck for?'

'In civvy street; you're leaving us. Never thought I'd see the day when Sergeant Roberts would be a civvy.'

'Thanks.'

'Come in,' Chas and Michael heard after knocking; they entered and stood to attention in the CSM's office.

'That's enough of that; now you are civilians, so you can dress as such, Chas. I'll call you that from now on. Have you got any?'

'Bought some today.' Chas held the carrier up for the CSM to see.

'Improperly dressed, carrying that in uniform.'

'Michael carried it,' Chas said.

The CSM laughed. 'Of course. Now, have you an address, I asked you before, where you will be staying?'

'Tony Kearns's widow is going to take both of us in as lodgers, help with rent.'

'That's settled then. Now, I have your pay up to today.'
He opened a drawer, removed an envelope and passed it to
Chas, who undid the flap to see a batch of banknotes
contained in a rubber band.

'Before you ask, everyone in the regiment contributed –
a day's pay from all the men, the officers various amounts,
some very generous. They knew you lost six months' pay
whilst in the glasshouse. I think you'll find £50 there.'

'I don't know what to say.'

'No need to say anything, you deserved it for whacking
Blankensy. Perhaps God may bless his soul for what he did.
I think he was a bit deranged; could have been due to
fighting those "Fuzzy Heads" in Togo-Togo land wherever.'

'I think they're in the Sudan, Sergeant Major,' Michael
butted in. 'The Fuzzy Wuzzies.'

'Michael, stop thinking.'

'Yes, sir.'

'Now, that's about it. This will be your last night here;
got an intake arriving, with a bit of luck get the regiment
back to full strength.' He stood and shook hands with both
of them. 'Good luck. Keep an eye on him, Michael.'

'I'll do that, sir. Thanks for letting me have a cot space
here.'

'Did you stay here? I didn't know that.' He laughed.
'Bloody Fuzzy Wuzzies.'

## CID offices, Clerkenwell

DS Jos Bancroft and DC Tom Fowler sat facing DI Bill
Gordon across his desk. Barcham sat back to one side.

'I'll start the ball rolling,' the inspector said. 'First the
report from the coroner's office and the lab boys. The shard
of glass embedded in Betts's neck did not kill him; he was
killed with a sharp blade, the time of death difficult to

ascertain accurately due to the warm weather. No maggots from larvae of the bluebottles on either body, points to both deaths occurring within an hour or two of each other, the early hours of the morning the postman discovered the body of the officer. At a guess the officer was killed after the other one. Before any comments, let's have your reports. You first, Tom.'

The DC began. 'Dead end, guv. Betts a bit of a Red, union official, knows his job, work to rule type, bit of a bully. His gang had nothing to say against him. No grudges, he got them better working conditions. The station staff, porters, cleaners and clerks in the same union; couple of them moaned about the way he lorded over them, chased 'em if they missed a union meeting. Nothing really.'

'Well, keep at it, see if any of the neighbours have anything to say. How about you, Jos, a glimmer in the tunnel?'

'Could be. I had it confirmed by the witness that the soldier she saw enter Blankensy's flat prior to the postman – the one who discovered the body – was Roberts. As you know, Roberts, a prime suspect, had all the motives, being the sergeant whose platoon got wiped out. Was stripped of rank and spent six months in clink for striking an officer – Major Blankensy, whom he blamed for the loss of his platoon. That's about all at present, except what Barcham has to say; I'll let him make his report.'

Barcham leant forward in his chair and began. Related what had occurred between him and a bookie's runner. Added, 'I also questioned Jimmy Wilde at his home. He told me that one of the soldiers who paid him to knock at Blankensy's door "had one foot in the grave" – his words – and the other one called him 'arry. Those must be the same two soldiers that the bookie's runner saw. The lone soldier that nosed around there, God knows who he was. Cost me half a quid to squeeze that out of the runner, and the saucy sod asked if there was a reward.'

'Bloody hell,' said the inspector when Barcham had finished. 'This is turning into a pantomime. This bookie's runner: what is he, a genie plucking bodies out of the air? Two clowns wearing palm trees – palm trees, I ask you? – coming and disappearing. Sisters, are they the ugly ones? A giant; all we want now is Jack and his beanstalk. We have a straw, a kid knocking at doors, 'arry with one foot in the grave and for centre stage a baker's shop. Let's have any comments now'

'It has to be someone from the military, revenge, the killing of Blankensy,' said Jos. 'Roberts, a hero, nevertheless prime suspect. Then one of the other army wallahs that were spotted nosing round Arlington Road. I don't believe in coincidence. Two murders committed within an hour or so, no break-ins, nothing stolen? The killer known by the victims, let him in. Strange that you said Betts was killed by a blade; could that be the knife that was found among the cutlery at number 86? Is the killer laughing at us, giving us a clue? Killing Betts, then shooting Blankensy with his own revolver, then there is the straw; could that have been placed there? But why leave one door open and close the other one? How about you, Tom: anything to add?'

'Same as Jos, revenge killing of Blankensy. The murder of Betts a separate case. No leads as of yet, early days, need to dig more.'

'And you, Barcham, I know you was dragged into this, so you stay with it now, any objections?'

'No, suits me fine. I agree with the DS and the DC that it was a revenge killing, that of Blankensy. I think the two wearing the palm tree badges hold a clue. What were they doing in a backwater of Camden Town, and of all places Arlington Road? How did they get there? They didn't know the area, as they asked the way, so the runner said, he thought to a railway station. It shouldn't be difficult to find out which regiment wears the palm tree as a badge.'

'The War Ministry will know that; I'll see to that,' the inspector said. 'Now I've listened to what you have said, and I must say, if it hadn't been for that bookie's lookout, we wouldn't have known about the palm tree pair – no pun intended – or the squaddies nosing around Arlington Road. You did well, Barcham; I think the half quid was worth it, put a chit in. The point you made about the two with palm trees, how they got there: might be worth checking out cabbies in the area to find out if one took a fare to Arlington Road. One was an officer and if from overseas could well have taken a cab.' The inspector paused, glanced at each one in turn. 'I agree with you as to the killing of Blankensy that it was revenge, and Roberts prime suspect. First the time factor. Did you ask yourself why Blankensy wasn't killed before? When I say before, I mean why wait until months after he gave that fatal order that sent a platoon to certain death? Only two survived. Cooper and Roberts, both seriously wounded, ended up in hospital. Roberts was the first to be discharged, returned to barracks. The first thing he did was whack Blankensy, get put under close arrest, get court martialled and spend six months in clink. Not long after his release, Blankensy was killed. The time factor. Anyone in the Essex Regiment bent on revenge had those months to have carried it out. I bet odds on Cooper's Christian name being Harry – 'arry – the one with "one foot in the grave", not long out of hospital. He's the next suspect, but, and a big but: Roberts was the one spotted going into Blankensy's flat.' He paused, stroked his chin.

'I've made up my mind. I understand Roberts is waiting for his discharge papers, so tomorrow, Jos, you pull him in for questioning before he disappears into the civvy world, and, Jos, not anywhere near the barracks; I don't want the army turning out with bayonets fixed. You understand? He is a hero. If that big mate is with him, arrange to have a couple of plods with truncheons to hand from the nearest nick on standby; you may need them. You go with him, Barcham.'

'Shall I charge him?' Jos asked.

'Say "suspicion of committing an offence". Once inside, if he denies entering Blankensy's rooms, we change "offence" to "murder". Don't tell him we have a witness.'

The inspector leant back in his chair, took a deep breath. 'That will start the ball rolling. Now, not one bloody word about this to anyone; I don't want that sod Barnett spreading the news over the front page of that rag he works for. Tom.' He faced the DC. 'Back to the Betts case. See with whom he drinks, if he has any mates. Delve into his past background; did he serve in the war? I doubt it, being on the railway; when did he join the union? This wasn't any on the spot, spur of the moment killing; someone had it in for him, a grudge fermenting. It was planned. Coincidence or not, same as the other. Revenge. That's my conclusion. Off you go, keep me informed.'

## *Brompton Barracks RE Chatham*

Lt Colonel Stoney RE MC placed the copy of the Islington Gazette on the desk in front of him, leant back in his chair after reading the report by a Jack Barnett. Frowned. *Must be a coincidence, must be.*

The newspaper had been delivered to his quarters with his personal mail, rolled and wrapped with a London post mark franked on the outside. No note attached, but he knew it was one of three who had sent it. He crumpled it, walked to the fireplace, set light to it and watched it burn in the grate. *So mote it be.*

The RSM looked up from where he was sitting behind his desk as the door opened and Captain Reid walked in, closely followed by CSM Mansfield. He hurriedly shoved the novel he was reading in a drawer and stood.

It was late afternoon, the sun peeping from behind passing clouds as it slid towards its rendezvous with the horizon, shedding beams of delight that bounced off the office window.

The RSM greeted them. 'Afternoon, Captain, sir.' A nod to Mansfield. 'Sergeant Major. Was expecting you; I'll inform Captain Richards you have arrived.'

He knocked at an inner door, held it ajar. 'Captain Reid to see you, sir.' Turned to Captain Reid. 'Go right in, sir. Nodded again to Mansfield. 'You can wait with me, Sergeant Major, tell me what's happening in London these days.'

Captain Reid ducked instinctively as he entered due to his height; Captain Richards rose to greet him and offered a hand.

'Not so hot as it was last time you were here; did you enjoy your leave? See your old OC?'

'You remember, then?'

'Oh yes, Major Blankensy, your OC posted to the Essex Regiment. You enquired whether he had passed through here, concerned as you hadn't heard from him for some time. It just happened that an incident had occurred at that time: a body had been found alongside the main railway line, naked, no distinguishing marks. A Detective Sergeant Warren had called enquiring if anyone from here had gone missing. I checked for you; your Major Blankensy had

211

arrived at the Essex Regiment and been sent to France. So did you meet up with him, your old OC?'

'No, unfortunately, left it rather late. He wasn't there when we called.'

'Pity, perhaps now he may get reinstated back to his old unit.'

'We hope so. Did this Detective Sergeant Warren discover the identity of the body?'

'Don't know, never heard any more. Why d'you ask?'

'No reason, just curious.'

'Well now, about your passage back to WA: I'm afraid you may have to kick your heels for a while. First let me tell you, this set up here is closing. Reverting to the TA. A few that survived are filtering back, risen in rank and wanting to carry on service. Weekend soldiering, show off their medal ribbons, don't blame 'em, they deserve it. So it has been decided. The colonel has already left, the RSM and myself any week now. Any coming and going of you chaps from the WAFF will be dealt with by the crown agents; passage on ships of the Elder Dempster Line, which are few and far between.'

'How long?'

'Hard to say, doesn't matter, you have accommodation, come and go as you please, so what's the hurry?'

Reid thought quickly of a reason that would suffice. 'Others are waiting for leave, and cannot go until the CSM and I get back. Surely you can find berths for two of us. You know the ropes, the shipping agents.'

'There is a ship tied up in in Bristol, bound for Lagos, Nigeria, due out any day now. A trader, takes a few paying passengers. A slow voyage, calling at Gibraltar, no doubt for water and provisions, trades at Freetown, Bathurst, Accra on the way. I could see if any spare berths are going. I don't know who will pay, but not your worry, the agents will bill me here. I'll forward it to the crown agents. By the time it is passed from one department to another, I shall be far gone; as you know, I was called back from reserve when the war started, so well finished my time. You take pot luck as to the accommodation, yes?'

'Yes, thanks.'

'You may change your tune if it turns out to be a rusty old tub. Now let's get you settled in your quarters. The RSM will see to your CSM. Then, while you are kicking your heels waiting, you may as well venture forth and sip the delights that Manchester has to offer – ruby lips as red as wine.' He laughed. 'Steer clear of the ones that chalk on their soles.'

'What?'

'Never mind, you obviously don't know Manchester.'


'What's in the wind, sir?' CSM Mansfield asked Captain Reid the following morning on meeting outside the coy office.

'We will have to wait and see. Captain Richards is after berths for us on a ship tied up dockside in Bristol. I'm off to locate the CID offices in town, see if I can have a word with a certain Detective Sergeant Warren – I have the name now – the one who was investigating the body found alongside the railway line last year, the time our OC went on leave.'

'You think that could have been the major?'

'I don't know, but we owe it to him to try and clear his name. No way would he have sent that doomed patrol to their death, or resigned his commission. This detective may know something that we don't. I can only ask.'

'Is that wise, sir? He would be the one asking the questions – who are you, where you from, why do you want to know? And most important: where are you going? Could delay our departure. What are you going to tell him? We went to see our OC in London whilst on leave, found him

213

shot, but it wasn't our OC. Fled the murder scene, taking the murder weapon—'

'I took it, down to me, Sergeant Major.' Reid cut the CSM short.

'No, sir, down to both of us; I was with you, part of it, always will be alongside you, and I'll come with you to see this "tec" if you're bent on going. Be careful what you say; it'll be taken down and recorded. The police think everyone is guilty until proved innocent, it's their job.'

'I just can't let it go, there must be an explanation. Who was the one we found shot, and why?'

'You must realise that we are already in the mire; it won't take the tecs in Islington long to discover we went to 86 Arlington Road. Trace the cabbie that dropped us off there, also the two soldiers from the Essex Regiment we met at Camden Town, the ones we asked the way to a main line railway station. This Warren will contact them, put two and two together, make five out of it – that we killed this bloke, settling a score on whoever he was living as our OC.'

'But we just can't let it go. What else can we do to clear the OC's name?'

'Write a statement. That you – put your name and my name – will state on oath that the body found at 86 Arlington Road, London, was not that of Major Blankensy. That we have no idea who the body is. Sign it, and post to the CID offices, Islington, London, the day we are due to sail. That should clear the major's name, at least.'

'You think they will take our word?'

'They would have to do something, find someone other than us who may know the major, or someone who could identify the body.'

'I think you are right. I'll do it. Let's hope Captain Richards finds us berths a bit sharpish. Let's take a walk, go over it again.'

'Too familiar, that CSM with his captain,' the RSM remarked as he watched from the office window the two walk away. 'Don't like it.'

'Different army to us, Sergeant Major. A handful of whites with all black troops, no white privates, the lowest rank a sergeant. They live in each other's pockets in an African country, the whites.'

'Still don't like it, not right walking out together here.'

'Where to, sir, anywhere particular?' Mansfield asked.

'The city centre? When Captain Richards mentioned to me about visiting the city centre, he said, "Stay away from the ones that chalk their soles"; do you know what he meant?'

'The price, sir, on the soles of their shoes.'

'Sorry, still don't get it.'

'Best not to, sir.'

Two days later, they caught a train. The first leg on the journey to Bristol.

'That will be the last time I wake to hear that,' Roberts said, swinging his legs over the side of his bed as the last bugle note of reveille faded.

'You never know, Chas. I said that months ago, and have been hearing it for some days now,' Michael O'Leary said, flat on his back in bed with arms behind his head. 'And remove that strip of medal ribbons from your tunic before you hand it in.'

'Why?'

'Just take it off, don't want any Tom, Dick and Harry filching it and parading in it as his own, the MM.'

'Any more orders? No? Right. I'll tell Grace you were still in bed on your backside when I left, shall I?'

Roberts dodged the boot that sailed through the air as he fled to the ablutions.

'It's a sad day, Roberts, sorry to see you leave,' the CSM said. 'You're always welcome to call any time.' He shook hands.

Chas and Michael, dressed in civvy clothes, stood in the CSM's office after their last army breakfast prior to leaving.

'There is someone waiting to see you at the guard room. You hang on here for a moment, O'Leary; I want a word.'

Cooper and Tom Kearns stood to attention as Roberts approached.

216

'We've come to see you off, Sergeant.' Cooper spoke for the two of them.

'Turn it in, lads, I'm a bloody civilian now.'

'Yer will always be Sergeant Roberts to us, never forget yer.' Tom Kearns's turn to speak. 'Yer saved my life as well as 'arry's 'ere; if I'd gone wiv the platoon that night, I'd 'ave bought it sure as 'ell.'

'You can thank your father for that, Tommy; he pushed me in a corner, didn't want your mum to lose both of you. We had to hold you back.'

'He did? Oh God.' He turned away to hide the tears. 'Fanks for telling me.'

'Yeah, Tommy; your dad and I served in some tight spots together. You'll make sergeant one day, like him, make your mother proud, and thanks for arranging digs with your mother; no doubt Michael and I'll see you when you get leave.'

'Wot can I say? Fanks, Sarge,' Cooper carried on.

'Nothing, you'd have done the same for me. I see Tomkins back there, grinning like a Cheshire cat; waiting for you, is he?'

'Yeah, I 'as to look after 'im, 'e finks 'e is looking after me.' He beckoned him over. 'Come and say cheerio to the sarge, yer silly sod.'

'I was waiting me turn. All the best, Sarge,' said Tomkins as he came and halted with a one-one-two, his feet slapping the ground as if on parade to rigid attention. ''ad to stand to attention for the last time, didn't I?'

'Of course you did.' Roberts laughed. They shook hands.

'Christ, never fought I'd shake 'ands wiv a sergeant.'

'Talk about good luck. Never thought to see this day, those of us that survived.'

'That's the way the penny drops, Sarge.'

'Guess so. You two sticking together in civvy street?' Roberts asked.

'Yeah. Old soldiers never... yer know.'

'Yeah, I know, use your loafs.'

'We does that.'


Back at the company office the CSM was talking to Michael.

'I don't know where you popped up from, O'Leary; I stuck my neck out letting you stay here as a mate of Roberts. How and where did you two meet up?'

'Call it kismet, sir.'

'You Irish! You going to tag along with him?'

'Yes.'

'Right. Catch up with him at the gate.' He shook hands. 'And, O'Leary, watch his back.'

'I'll rightly do that.'


Cooper, Tomkins and Kearns stood and watched Roberts and O'Leary pass through the gate, the sentry calling out, 'Good luck, Sarge'.

'Yer didn't tell the sarge about Blanksy's visits to Bayham Street, 'arry, so wot we gonner do now?' Tomkins asked after Tom Kearns had returned to barracks.

''ave anovver word wiv that ironmonger. Now that Blanksy's dead, we can confront 'im.'

'That's a good word, 'arry, wot's it mean?'

'Yer know bloody well wot it means, we ain't gonner be put off this time, we wanner know what's going on. I'll tell 'im we'll go to the police that 'e knows Blanksy, if 'e don't let on. We want somefink out of this.'

'Wot about this Jack Barnett reporter bloke?'

'Sod 'im, I fink we would do better talking to that publishing agent I told yer about in Arlington Road. We'll see wot the ironmonger 'as to say first, then make up our minds.'

Detective Sergeant Jos Bancroft and Constable (acting detective) Barcham sat on the same bench as they had previously, waiting for Chas and Michael to appear; they didn't have to wait long.

'Here they come, sir,' said Barcham as Roberts and O'Leary breasted the rise in the field and came in view

'Yeah, I can see them, and Roberts in civvies, both carrying valises, doesn't look as if they are going back to barracks any more. Good, shan't have to get tangled with the army now.'

'You going to arrest him now?'

'No, not here. No back up, they might do a runner. I know where they are off to, like bees to honey, to the baker's shop in Delancey Street to see the Jones girls; I'll bet on it. You slope off now, Barch, keep tag; if they turn off when they reach Holloway Road, we'll know for sure. Then you get to Albany Street nick, borrow a couple of their biggest plods and station one in Camden High Street and one in Delancey Street.'

'Don't look round, Chas,' Michael said as they reached Highbury Corner. 'We're being followed; must be the same two that the bookie's runner warned us about last time we went to Delancey Street.'

'So what do we do?'

'Nothing; they must have a reason, so we wait and see what transpires.'

'It's me they are keeping tags on, I'm prime suspect for the killing of Blankensy.'

'Must be more than you being a suspect. They have something up their sleeves.'

219

'Charles Roberts.' Jos Bancroft held his warrant card up as he stepped in front of Roberts. 'I am Detective Sergeant Bancroft, and arresting you on suspicion of the unlawful killing of a Major Blankensy. I must warn you that anything you may say will be noted and held as evidence.'

'You took a chance, arresting me by yourself,' Chas remarked

'Not really; there's a detective and constable behind you, and another constable in Delancey Street, so don't think of doing a runner, it will only make matters worse. Also, you may not think so, but I didn't want to embarrass you. I know of your army record; the CSM told me. A holder of the MM, for which I salute, and you are held in high esteem by the whole of your regiment.'

'You must have a reason other than arresting me on suspicion?'

'Yes. I believe you entered Blankensy's premises the morning before the body was discovered.'

'Keep mum, Chas,' Michael called out.

'Very wise advice your friend offering,' said Jos. 'But you will need to answer when you are questioned, so be careful how you do. Now are you taking a walk alongside me to Albany Street quietly, or in handcuffs between two in blue, being gawked at?'

'I'll walk, no talk.'

'Good, let's go.'

'I'll take your grip and wallet, Chas, for safe keeping.' Michael nodded as he spoke.

'The desk sergeant at Albany Street will log that,' said Jos.

'What's wrong in me taking it? There is the MM and other medals in there, and I need the money; the rent has to be paid, and other expenses.'

Jos looked from one to the other. 'You two muck in together?'

'Yes, and I want Michael to have my gear.'

'All right, but I need to see the contents.'

The valise was opened and the DS, satisfied, passed it to Michael.

'I'll give the MM to Gwyneth to hold, Chas, and I'll see you. Two on and four off.' Michael looked straight into Roberts's eyes, gave a hardly perceptible nod as they shook hands.

Michael watched them go, and made a bee-line for the baker's shop. Gwyneth, dressed in a white overall with cuffed sleeves behind the counter, her eyes searching for Chas as Michael entered, immediately asked, 'Where is Chas?'

'I'll tell you later. Is Clive in?'

'Upstairs, but what has happened, where is—?'

Michael lifted the counter flap, and was halfway up the stairs before Gwyneth could finish.

'They've nabbed Chas, so we need to act fast,' Michael blurted out to a surprised Clive lounging on a sofa.

'What? Where, what for?'

'Killing Blankensy. Remember the morning we first came here, we told you that we had found Blankensy shot? Someone must have seen Chas going into Blankensy's flat and told the police. Once the police have someone banged up, they'll push it all the way. Chas won't have anything going for him, already done six months in clink for whacking him. I'm gonner get him out before he's moved to a prison.'

'I can give him an alibi, swear he was with me at that time.'

'Won't work, Clive, you can bet they've a statement from the witness, they wouldn't have arrested him otherwise, and you'd be charged with perjury. I've a plan, had it in mind for some time.'

Clive frowned. 'Had a plan? Sorry, don't understand.'

'Never mind that now, haven't time to explain. I'm gonner get Chas out. Now, you know London. Where do I catch a train to Bristol?'

'Bristol?'

'Yeah, we are gonner get out of the country, the only way to save Chas. So where do we get a train to Bristol? I know where the ships sail to from there.'

'It'll be the GWR Praed Street Paddington, I guess.'

'Can you find out the time of trains leaving to Bristol early tomorrow morning?'

'Get a timetable or ask at the station, it's not too far from here.'

'Right, do that, Clive; I'll explain to your parents and the girls.'

'I'll be with you on this, whatever. I owe my life to Chas.'

'No, Clive, you have family ties. I'll free Chas, that won't be much of a problem, it's only a police station. You get the time of trains leaving; time is the factor.'


## Albany Street police station

The desk sergeant dipped pen in ink and laboriously logged the prisoner in while Jos patiently waited. Name, date of birth, time and date of entry.

'Nothing in hand?' he asked. Chas spread his fingers.

'Empty your pockets.'

'They're empty.'

'Empty them just the same.'

'He hasn't anything with him,' Jos butted in. 'I've checked.'

'Regulations, sir.'

'Turn your pockets inside out, Roberts, for Chrissake, to please me,' said Jos.

That done, the sergeant, satisfied, leant over the counter to look down at Chas's boots.

'Bootlaces, take your bootlaces off,' he ordered.

They were duly entered under Contents in the log-book, the laces placed in a drawer.

'Is that it, we finished now?' asked Jos.

'Not quite yet, sir. If you follow me to the cells below and confirm the prisoner is securely confined, sign the day book with the date, that will do it.'

The constable on cell duty rose from a chair as the sergeant, Roberts and Jos reached the last of the stone steps to basement level.

'One more for you to keep an eye on,' said the sergeant. 'Open up an empty cell; I want this one on his own. Name of Roberts.'

The jailor reached for a bunch of keys, selected one and opened a cell, stepped back to let Roberts enter. Slammed the door shut with a clang, locked it and returned the bunch of keys to the hook.

'Satisfied?' the sergeant asked Jos.

'Yes; make sure he gets something to eat and drink. I'll arrange a Black Maria to transfer him to Clerkenwell tomorrow.'

'As per regulations, sir, it will be, the meal.'

'Thanks for the courtesy back in Delancey Street, Sergeant,' Chas called out as Jos was leaving. 'I didn't kill Blankensy. Remember that.'

Jos was standing under the blue lamp outside when Barcham arrived.

'You all right, sir? You seem to be deep in thought.'

'Thinking what Roberts said as I was leaving.'

'What would that be, sir?'

'"Remember that". That he didn't kill Blankensy. As though it would come back to haunt me. Never mind. He is off my hands now. Where are the two plods?'

'Told them to keep an eye on the baker's shop, see what that mate of Roberts gets up to.'

'Oh, you did, did you? In charge of the investigation now, are you, Barcham? They will stand out like two sore thumbs. Get back there, tell them to report back to normal duty. You can stay for your trouble, keep out of sight. I'll see you back at Clerkenwell if you have anything to report. Don't be all day; I want to knock off early.'

Back at the baker's, Michael had explained to the Joneses how everything had come about, ending with the arrest of Chas.

'How can we help?' asked Colin Jones. 'We have some money saved, get a lawyer.'

'No, Mr Jones, as I told your son, I'll get Chas out. Not taking any chances. The police will persecute – prosercute – charge Chas, throw the book at him now they have him in custody. What defence will he have? Only to deny he did it, and that won't wash as you know; most of those in prison say they didn't do it.'

'How about yourself, Michael? If you're caught, you'll be charged with aiding and abetting.'

'No, they won't catch us, we'll be gone far away before they know.'

Grace came and held Michael's hand. 'When will you leave, Michael?'

'After night falls.'

'So we have some hours left; will you stay with me, please?'

Michael nodded. 'I will certainly do that.'

'And will I be able to see Chas, Michael?' Gwyneth pleaded.

'It will have to be brief; that's all I can promise.'


## CID offices, Clerkenwell

'It's done; Roberts is in custody at Albany Street nick,' DS Jos Bancroft told the inspector.

'You charged him?'

'Yes. On suspicion of the unlawful killing of a Major Blankensy.'

'Did he deny entering Blankensy's premises?'

'I never asked him, thought you would want to do the questioning. The Black Maria will collect and bring him here tomorrow, but I'm not a happy one, guv.'

'For Chrissake, Jos, he hasn't a leg to stand on.'

'It's what he said: "I didn't do it, remember that."'

'That's what they all say, "I didn't do it." It's a perpetual echo in the law courts.'

'Not the way he said it.'

'We are going ahead with this, Jos, that's it. Have you lost Barcham?'

'Left him at Delancey Street, keeping an eye on the baker's shop, see what that big mate of Roberts's does. He'll be along shortly.'

'Right, put it in writing, then get a bite to eat, take the rest of the day off.'


It was late afternoon when Barcham decided he had had enough hanging about; there had been no sign of Roberts's mate, so he wended his way back to Clerkenwell. No sign of the DS, so he knocked on the inspector's door and entered.

'Oh, it's you, Barcham; anything to report?'

'No, sir. Clive Jones the son came out, returned after an hour, one of the sisters also came out, went to the local chemist's. The big 'un didn't put in an appearance.'

'The DS has taken the rest of the day off, what's left of it, so you may as well shove off now. Report here tomorrow, I'll find you something to do. Don't be late.'

## *Bayham Street, Camden Town*

'Don't lose yer temper this time, Bill,' said Harry Cooper to Tomkins.

They were standing, looking at the ironmonger's shop from the opposite side of the street. Half an hour after wishing Roberts good luck at Essex HQ they had left the barracks themselves, now civilians. Tomkins had said, *' 'arry, yer come and stay wiv me at me mum's 'ouse, she'll be pleased to see anovver face and yer can do the washing up, no argument, but first a visit to that ironmonger, see if we can solve the mystery of Blanksy's visits, a story to tell that publishers agent in Arlington Road, make some lolly.'*

'I'll try not to, 'arry, so let's see wot 'e 'as to say.'

'Remember us?' Bill asked as they entered the shop.

'Yeah, I remember, so what d'yer want this time?'

'Yer read the newspapers? Major Blankensy shot.'

'Yeah, so what's that got to do with me?'

'That's wot we wants to know.'

'I don't know any Major Blankensy.'

'Oh yes yer does, 'e came 'ere, and we wants to know wot for.'

'I tell yer I don't know any Blankensy, so shove off.'

226

'Now listen, mister bloody ironmonger, we knows yer do; we followed 'im 'ere, saw you talking to 'im, and now 'e's been murdered. The police would like to know that, so come clean. Wot's all the mystery about? It's to do wiv the empty shop next door, ain't it?'

'I keep telling yer, I don't know him, and why was yer following him?'

'We wanted to see wot 'e was up to, but that's anovver story.'

'The only bloke that has come to see about the shop, other than you two, was the bloke that lived and worked there before the war with his parents.'

'Wot? Are yer saying it's the same bloke, changed 'is name, joined the army and became a major?'

'Shouldn't think so, he was German, likewise his parents were. He went to school here, the son; his father died; he carried on with his mother, leather workers.'

'Hang on a mo,' Tomkins said. 'The penny jest dropped. The French polisher in the ovver shop told us 'is mum was killed, and that sneaky bastard reporter Jack Barnett said it had been hushed up.'

'So yer know then, got nothing to do with your major.'

'But 'e came to see yer?'

'So you say; so what? Lots do, buy things, nails, not like the one you have loose in yer head, so shove, tell it to the marines, or better still the police.'

'Can we jest calm down?' Cooper intervened between the slanging match. 'All we wanted to know was wot Blankensy was up to. Yer know wot 'e did: 'e sent a platoon to certain death. A sergeant and me was the only ones left, and we ended up in 'ospital, lucky to survive. We're not batty, and I don't fink you are, so wot was this bloke like, yer say who lived 'ere?'

'Nice chap, got on with everyone, repaired boots, made leather bags and purses.'

'So why was his shop smashed up?'

'It was beginning of 1915, so many of our soldiers being killed, feelings running against the Hun. Some hothead found out he was German or of German descent, with others decided to take the law into their own hands. I suppose he should have been interred, I don't know. His mother was at the front window in the shop displaying goods for sale when the plate glass window was smashed with a brick.' The ironmonger spread his arms. 'I don't think this mob wanted to kill anybody, but it happened. I don't know whether she fell on the broken glass, but a chunk of it cut the side of her neck, the jugular vein, she bled to death there on the spot. The son went berserk, fought with the mob, the police arrived, a constable ended up with a broken arm, the son was arrested, taken away. I never saw him again until he turned up here the other day.'

'Was any of the rioters arrested?'

'No, not to my knowledge.'

'And you saw all this?'

'Yeah, so now you know,'

''ow the 'ell did this bloke end up in the army? I was 'is batman,' said Tomkins. 'I always thought there was somefink not right in the 'ead wiv 'im. Always on about tea at four, must be four o'clock.'

'That's Hans all right; he once asked me why the English have to have tea at four o'clock.'

'Is that 'is name, Hans?'

'Yeah. Hans Muller.'

They were quiet for a while. 'Wot yer finking of, 'arry? Tomkins asked, seeing Harry with his eyes shut.

'Finking of the captain wiv 'is CSM who asked us the way to our HQ and if we knew a Major Blankensy, also at Delancey Street they asked the way to a main line railway station. They were from Africa, so they must have known

Blanksy out there. We can't ask 'em now, they've gone, and we can't ask Blanksy, 'e's dead.'

'We ain't getting anywhere, are we, 'arry?' Tomkins said. Turned to the ironmonger. 'Yer told us 'e was a good bloke, this Hans?'

'Yeah. Mended boots, said "pay what you can, when you can" to anyone that was hard up. Made a special boot for a chap with a club foot, for nix. The chap himself told me that. Yeah, he was a good bloke.'

'Makes yer fink, don't it, 'arry, and we wanted to – never mind, someone did. I guess we'll never know.'

*Nightfall*. Last orders had been called, teacloths hung over pump 'skittle' handles on bar counters; the last of the stragglers wended their way home; randy moggies with night vision, emerald eyes, began their nightly prowl on garden walls and through alleys.

Inside the baker's shop in Delancey Street all was quiet. Grace and Michael, with her head resting on his shoulder, shared the sofa. Gwyneth and Clive sat with legs outstretched on the carpet, each with their backs against an armchair occupied by their parents. They had eaten, nervous, the sword of Damocles suspended above, waiting for hours to pass.

'How long does it take to walk to Paddington Station, Clive?' Michael broke the silence.

'Not much more than an hour, why?'

'Working out the time. I'll leave here about four o'clock.'

'I'm scared,' said Gwyneth. 'Will I see Chas?'

'Yes. I promise, I'll be back within the hour, then we shall have to leave in time to catch the 7.10 train. That's the time it leaves, you said, Clive, yes?'

'Yes; you sure you can do this, Michael?'

'Yeah, don't worry.'

'Then I'll come with you to Paddington, lead the way so you don't get lost in London's maze.'

'Right, but that's all, then you come back here.'

*Four o'clock*. Michael eased gently away from Grace; she woke with a start.

'Oh, Michael, is it time? I must have fallen asleep.'

'Hush, don't wake your parents.'

'With Chas, Michael, you will come back with Chas?' Gwyneth, fully awake, asked.

'Yes, I promised; there will not be much time before we have to leave again, you understand.'

The traditional blue lantern above the entrance to Albany Street police station gave a guiding if not a welcome glow to Michael, forging ahead through the murky darkness of a moonless night. He stayed his pace, and stood thinking of Grace.

The first time they had met, she had taken his hand in hers, no hesitation, it was to be, kismet, his life set on course. He knew and accepted it, had submitted to it from the time his father had told him that one day he would seek the golden skull. It was happening, the glasshouse, meeting Roberts, and Clive Jones, whose life Roberts had saved and who had escorted Roberts to the glasshouse, wanting to meet Roberts again to thank him, the baker's shop, and Grace. Grace: the warmth emanating from her made them one as they shared the sofa, her cheek against his breast, the fragrance of her, to be left behind to go and find – *to find – a place – that is known to God alone? What will be will be.*

He took the cork out of the neck of the whiskey bottle he had brought with him, took a mouthful of the whiskey, never swallowed it, gargled with it and let it dribble down his chin, repeated this, then sprinkled some on the collar of his shirt. *God forgive me for wasting good Irish whiskey.*

He stepped off and in a stagger began singing with slurred voice.

'*They're hanging thousands in the street for the wearing of the green…*'

231

The duty sergeant behind the desk in the police station pricked up his ears.

'*If on England's cruel red...*'

The words came faintly to his ears, then a crash and the sound of breaking glass.

*What the hell?* He rushed to the entrance, opened the door to see Michael swaying on his feet at the bottom of the stone steps, amidst broken glass and whiskey bottle. He looked up at the smashed lantern, the broken mantle, heard the hiss of gas escaping.

''s all gone, 's all gone,' Michael called out, and he fell across the steps.

'You bloody stupid, Mick? Look what you've done, get up.'

Michael got to his knees, lurched forward and grabbed hold of the sergeant. They both hit the floor inside the entrance.

'Get off me, you drunken sod,' said the sergeant, struggling to get free. 'You stink. Williams, get up here on the double,' he shouted to the constable below.

Michael lay prone as Williams arrived.

'Get up,' the sergeant ordered, finally on his feet. 'I'm arresting you for striking a police officer, damaging government property, and being drunk and disorderly; now get up.' He kicked Michael in the ribs. Michael never moved.

'Help me get him to the cells, Williams.'

Between the two of them, and with a little help from Michael, they got him to the head of the steps leading to the basement and promptly pushed him down. Michael landed in the area between the cells and lay still. They followed down.

'Open one of the cells, Williams.' The sergeant gave the order.

232

'Don't put 'im in 'ere wiv me, don't want him pissing and spewing all over the floor,' an occupant of one of the cells cried out.

'Shut your mouth, Briggs,' Williams told him

Michael, one eye open, eased his hands flat on the floor each side, ready to make a move.

'Open an empty cell, Williams,' said the sergeant.

Williams turned the key, the barred door swung back, Michael leapt up, grabbed the sergeant, one heave and the sergeant landed inside the cell, a shove in the back and Williams followed. The bars clanged as the door closed, the key turned. All happened in less than a minute.

'What kept you, Michael?' Chas, smiling, asked.

'*Tete a tete*. On the sofa.' Michael grinned.

'You won't get away with this, it'll only make things worse for Roberts, and you'll end up inside,' the sergeant called out.

'Then I'll have to complain about the kick you gave me,' Michael answered whilst he fumbled with bunch of keys, sorting for the right one to release Chas.

Briggs called out, 'Yer gonner let me out, ain't yer?'

'Can't do that. I'm a law abiding citizen,' said Michael. 'Let's go, Chas. Sorry to have to leave you sharing a cell with a sergeant, Williams.'

*Outside*. Michael locked the entrance door, having taken the key from the lock inside. Dropped the key with the cell bunch down the nearest drain.

Darkness enfolded them as they walked away.

Gwyneth was the first down the stairs on hearing the knock on the shop door, could not control herself on opening it, wrapping her arms around Chas, all demureness abandoned as she hugged him tight.

'I promised Gwyneth I would bring you back; I hope you like the hug, Chas.'

'Thank you, Michael, thank you, you kept your promise. I knew you would,' said Gwyneth, blushing.

'Where are we off to, Michael?' Chas asked.

'You'll know all in good time, but first to catch a train at 7.10.'


Grace, waiting at the head of the stairs, took Michael's hand in hers and led him to the sofa.

'My heart is beating again; it stopped while you were away.' She placed his hand under her breast. 'You understand, Michael.'

'Yes, I understand, Grace.'

'Will you come and sit with me while we have time?'

No need for an answer as they made their way to the sofa.


Clive Jones shook hands with Roberts. 'Glad to see you back in one piece, Chas.' Aside, asked, 'Did Michael – you know – the police?'

Roberts laughed. 'No, just locked them in a cell.'

Clive chuckled, shook his head. 'That's Michael. It could be the police will put a watch at railway stations.'

'We shall be far gone by then.'

'Nevertheless, it is a long journey, and you have to exit, best to leave separately then.'

'I'll talk it over with Michael. He's taken charge; seems I have to go along with what he has planned. He did get me out of clink.'


Mrs Jones fussed over Chas like a mother. 'I'll get you some breakfast, Chas; I don't suppose they gave you anything at the police station.'

'Gave me a cuppa tea.'

234

'That's no good, you want something inside you, won't take long, eggs and bacon and crusty bread, sit with Gwyneth meanwhile.'

*Time to leave*. Grips were packed. Sandwiches, towels and soap. 'You have to eat and wash,' Mrs Jones remarked as she added these to the other contents in the two grips. The articles Grace had purchased at the chemist's went into Michael's grip. Mr Colin Jones pushed an envelope into Roberts's pocket, saying, 'It's the least we can do,' brushing away Chas's objection. A final hug from Gwyneth and Grace, fighting to hold back the tears.

'You will come back, Michael, please,' Grace said as she let go of Michael's hand.

'It's in the laps of the gods.'

'Then I will pray, and they will listen.'

# PART THREE

*Bristol Harbour*

The stony eyes of Cabot faced the open sea across the harbour, immobile, standing firm on a plinth. Seagulls swooped and dived low over the harbour waters, seeking any morsel that could be devoured from the waste that had been jettisoned from a ship's galley. One alighted on Cabot's head, left its calling card before taking off, leaving the white shampoo to be rinsed by the rain.

Charlie 'Chalkie' White, arms resting on the taffrail of the starboard deck, peered over the side; his eyes followed the whirlpools of scum-laden debris as they lapped against the rusting hull of the *Dorina* tied up alongside the dock.

'A right bloody rust bucket,' he murmured. A visit to a shipping agent had secured him a cheap ticket and a berth. 'One way; I ain't coming back.' He strolled to the port side.

Barbara Evans stood alone watching the activity on the dockside, goods being swung aboard and lowered through open hatches.

'No one to wave yer goodbye?'

She heard the voice, turned to see Chalkie approaching.

'No, the journey, too far.'

'From London, eh?'

Barbara nodded. 'Yes, and you?'

'Yeah, yer can tell, can't yer? Charlie White, Chalkie to me mates.'

'Barbara Evans. Nice to know someone on board I can understand.'

'Where yer dropping off, Barbara, Gib? D'yer mind me calling yer Barbara?'

'No, of course not. Gib?'

'Gibraltar.'

'Oh, of course, Gibraltar. No. The Gold Coast. West Africa.'

'Wot, on yer tod?'

'Yes.'

'That's a bit dodgy, ain't it? Don't tell me Kumasi Ashanti?'

'Yes, the mission school, on probation, see how I make out.'

'Well, strike a light, I can't believe it. Rose Ayerling, Grace her daughter, yer'll love 'em.'

'You've been there before, then; know them?'

'Yeah, 1914, start of the war, with the Rifle Brigade, or part of 'em, attached to the WAFF, the West African Frontier Force. Fought wiv 'em. Togoland and the Cameroons. Stationed at the fort in Kumasi at one time, that's 'ow I got to know Rose and young Grace.'

'What a coincidence.'

'My old OC – you know, my commanding officer – Major Richard Hethrington used to say, "No such thing as coincidence; it's kismet. Destiny."'

'Hethrington? I seem to know that name. He's a lord's son, had to give evidence at a murder trial...' She turned away, took a handkerchief from a pocket, held it to her eyes. Her shoulders began shaking.

Chalkie couldn't believe it; Barbara was sobbing.

'Did I say somefink wrong, Barbara? I'm sorry.'

237

Barbara took a grip upon herself, dabbed her eyes, turned to face Chalkie. 'No, you didn't say anything wrong, Chalkie, sorry, not your fault. It was the name Hethrington, brought back memories of a murder. It's a long story. I'll be all right now.'

Captain Reid and Sergeant Major Mansfield came to a halt after passing through the gates to the harbour dockside.

'That must be the ship we're booked on,' said the captain, nodding at the *Dorina*. 'And what joker gave it that name?'

'Seems a like nice senorita's name to me,' Mansfield remarked.

'You obviously don't know, never been up the Niger; there, it's the name for a bloody hippo. We shall be wallowing all the way to the coast at about 5 knots. Take a month of Sundays. God knows what we have let ourselves in for. Looks like an old slave trader; we'll be sleeping on shelves below deck.'

'Can't be any worse than those "funk holes" in the Cameroons and Togoland we slept in.'

'No, you're right, we said we would never grumble again if we survived, and we are still here to tell the tale, so we are going on a pleasure cruise, right?'

'Right, sir.'

'Looks as if we have company,' Chalkie White remarked as he spotted Reid and Mansfield approaching. 'Talk about kismet, they're military. Ten to one they're WAFF and going to the coast; could be the fort at Kumasi.'

DS Jos Bancroft couldn't stop laughing; it was infectious. DC Tom Fowler caught the bug, couldn't contain himself, joined in.

'Turn it in, you two.' Inspector Bill Gordon got the words out between chuckles. 'You haven't heard the rest of it yet. When the night plods turned up to clock off at the end of their shift and found themselves locked out, they went home. Not one of them volunteered to call at their inspector's home that early in the morning to tell him the news. Can you imagine when he turned up to see the day shift sitting on the station's steps?' He burst out laughing. 'Now you've got me at it.'

It was midday, all sitting in the inspector's office. The Black Maria that had been sent to Albany Street police station to bring Roberts to Clerkenwell for questioning had been turned away. No explanation other that 'not wanted'.

At Albany Street, a locksmith had finally managed to get the station door open and release the sergeant and constable from the cell. No need to tell them to keep mum; they would be the laughing stock of the police force.

The inspector at Albany Street had finally come clean and informed Inspector Bill Gordon that the prisoner had escaped. And Bill Gordon was relating the tale to Jos Bancroft and Tom Fowler.

'So this mate of Roberts just walked in, locked the duty sergeant and the jailor in a cell, walked away with Roberts and the keys after locking the front door?' Bancroft asked between guffaws. 'Ruddy good job we didn't have Roberts locked up here, we're in the clear. So what's going to happen now, guv?'

'Dunno, they've closed the book on it, hoping to capture Roberts I guess. I can't see them doing that. Roberts and his mate will be far gone; they know how to look after themselves. If the press get hold of this, there will be hell to play.'

'So I never arrested Roberts, then? There never was a prisoner?' Jos asked. 'If we go along with this cover up, and it all comes out, we shall either be walking the beat or in civvies. Is that it?'

'Buggered if I know, Jos; the ball's in their court. It's stopped you laughing, thinking about it '

'We'll have to wait and see, sleep on it, guv; something might turn up.'

'A bloody miracle, you mean; meanwhile we still have Betts's murder on our plate. Anything new turned up, Fowler? Another bod we can give to Albany Street to lose?'

'Dead end, guv.'

'What about the knife? We now know it wasn't a shard of glass that cut his throat.'

'No joy on that, searched every inch of the premises and surrounding area; whoever did it took it with him. I've been thinking of that knife found among Blankensy's cutlery, but you did say that Roberts couldn't have killed Betts as well due to the time factor.'

'Yes, but say Roberts didn't kill Blankensy,' Jos butted in.

'Don't start that again, Jos,' the inspector shouted angrily. 'Roberts did it.'

'All right – all right, guv. But now that Roberts has done a bunk, are we to find another Roberts to pin it on?'

'You're overstepping the mark, Jos. I said leave it. Roberts did it. You can both shove off now. I'll see you in my office 0900 hrs tomorrow; perhaps by then the chief at Albany Street will admit he has lost a prisoner, or that something of a miracle you suggested may turn up and solve the mystery. Jesus, what a bloody vortex we've got sucked into.'

Captain Reid and CSM Mansfield entered the bowels of the *Dorina* via the gangplank from the dockside and were met by one whose skin was the colour and texture of mahogany, who introduced himself as the second mate.

'I've a cabin for the officer, but you will have to share one with four bunks. Sergeant Major, is it?' Looking at Mansfield, who nodded. 'One is occupied by a civilian but to me looks like an old squaddie, so you'll have company. All mess together, no segregation on board.'

'I could share her cabin, the skirt I saw on deck,' said Mansfield.

'You're one of those long white stem pipe smokers, are you? In your dreams, soldier.'

## *HQ Essex Regiment*

It was the day after Roberts's escape that Mrs Kearns presented herself at the entrance gate.

'I can't let yer in, Mrs Kearns,' the sentry told her.

'You know me then?'

'Of course, sorry about Tony.'

'Yeah, I know. I've finished wiv tears, like thousands of others, 'ave to lump it.'

'So what d'yer want, Mrs Kearns?'

'If I could see my Tommy.'

'I'll 'ave to check, 'ang on a mo.' He shouted at the guard room. 'Turn out one of yer.'

The sergeant of the guard came out. 'What's all the shouting about... oh, 'ullo, Mrs Kearns,' seeing her standing outside the gate. 'Yer ain't setting about my sentry, are yer? Making 'im cry?'

241

'No, 'e's a good boy. I want to know if I can see Tommy.'

'Is it important? I know we are a family, the regiment, but...'

'It's about Sergeant Roberts and 'is mate. Tommy arranged for 'em to 'ave diggings at 'ome, 'elp pay the rent now Tony 'as gone as yer know. I got the room ready, but they never turned up yesterday, and still no sign of 'em.'

'That's strange. I'll 'ave a word wiv the sergeant major, you wait. I'll get a chair brought out; you must have had a long walk to get here.'

'Me pins are all right, I ain't that old.'

Nevertheless she sank thankfully into the chair that was brought.

'Bring her in here,' the CSM said after the sergeant of the guard had reported and related what Mrs Kearns had told him.

'Will that be—'

'You deaf, Sergeant?' the CSM shouted. 'She wasn't here if you are worried about regulations. Bring her here, then find young Kearns, tell him to report here.'

'Any clues as to why Roberts and his mate didn't turn up, Kearns?' the CSM asked. Tom Kearns was standing to attention, a chevron newly stitched to each tunic arm, his mother sitting in a chair listening.

'No, sir.'

'Something bloody funny going on. You can stand at ease, Kearns. Roberts would not up stakes and move on elsewhere; he would have had to let me know a different address in that case. Don't make sense, unless the two of them went on a God Almighty binge, it being the first day as a civvy for Roberts, and ended up in a cell. No, I don't buy that. You sure you haven't an inkling, Kearns?'

242

'No, sir. Sergeant Roberts thanked me for arranging digs wiv me mum. 'e was very pleased.'

'Someone must have seen which way they were heading when they left here. I bet it's to do with Blankensy's killing.'

'Camden Town, sir,' Kearns blurted out.

'Camden Town? Why Camden Town?'

'Dunno, sir, jest came into me 'ead. That's where Blankensy went to live. I saw Tomkins there.'

'What was you and Tomkins doing there? Not thinking of... no, don't answer that. I remember him and Cooper sneaking out, and getting back late to barracks with some cock and bull story about falling asleep in the park there. That must have been the same day. So what happened then?'

'Tomkins told me to shove off back to barracks, 'im and Cooper would do what wanted doing.'

'I get it. Say no more. Did you see Roberts there?'

'No, sir.'

'Where did Tomkins and Cooper go, did you see?'

'Arlington Road, sir.'

'Did they, the sods.' His eyebrows raised, he stroked his chin, then frowned. Kearns waited, listened to the wall clock ticking. Finally the CSM spoke.

'Take your mother home, Kearns, then I want you to go to Tomkins's address.' He opened a register, read, 'Eight Matthias Road, Stoke Newington. Do you know it?'

'No, sir.'

The CSM wrote the address on a sheet of paper, passed it to Kearns and gave him a shilling. 'That will cover the fare, a tram to Dalston Junction, ask there for Matthias Road. Tell Tomkins I want to see him; if he is not in, leave a message with his mother – a friendly visit, no trouble. Cooper is staying with him, so you might see him. Don't

243

mention Roberts, or tell anyone else, at least not yet. Understand?'

'Yes, sir, but I am on duty.'

'I'll see to that. Off you go.' He stood and faced Mrs Kearns. 'Thanks for coming, Mrs Kearns. I'm sure there is a reason Roberts didn't turn up; I'll look into it, and we'll make a sergeant of your son one day. Who knows, he may even sit in my chair.'


## CID offices, Clerkenwell

'He beat you to it, the chief.' The desk sergeant raised his eyes to the ceiling. 'Not in a good mood methinks,' he greeted them as they entered.

Tom looked at his watch. 'It's only just nine o'clock. You go in first, Jos,' he said as they climbed the stairs.

'Thanks for nothing,' Jos said. 'Don't say a word when we go in, let the chief speak first.'

They knocked and entered. Inspector Bill Gordon sat with both elbows on his desk, chin cupped in hands. He eyed them up. Leant back and folded his arms across his chest. 'Sit down the pair of you, you're gonner like this.' And burst out laughing.

Two chairs were dragged forward and they both sat. The inspector passed a letter across to Jos.

'That something that you said might turn up, Jos, has.'

Eyebrows raised, eyes open wide as Jos read. 'Well, I'll be a monkey's fart,' he said. Shook his head and chuckled as he passed it to Tom.

'Is this a joke?' Tom asked as he took it.

'Read it, you'll see.'

'I'll go back on the beat, guv, I think, get my sanity back,' Tom said when he had finished reading it twice. 'Otherwise we'll all end up in the nut house.'

'We couldn't have charged Roberts with the murder of Blankensy if this letter had arrived earlier; it would have had to be of an unknown person. That's if you believe it,' Jos said.

'We have to believe it. Signed by an officer and a warrant officer. But doesn't alter the fact that, as far as Roberts was concerned, that was the man that ordered his platoon on a "forlorn hope"; I believe that is the expression the army use,' the inspector pointed out. 'You arrested him, Jos. But he's gone with the wind, and I don't think for one moment he and that big mate of his will be caught; they know how to look after themselves.'

'On your orders, guv,' Jos hit back.

'Everything pointed to him. Revenge the motive, a witness saw him enter the scene of the crime, now breaking out of a cell at Albany Street. That's not the action of an innocent person.'

'He was feeling the noose tightening around his neck, guv, knew the evidence was against him and that quite a few had met John Ellis on less evidence.'

'You were right on the Flint case, I'll give you that, but you'll have to come up with more than instincts to convince me that Roberts is innocent on this one.'

'You gonner show the letter to the chief at Albany Street nick?'

'No, I'll have a chat with him. The answer, if it gets leaked to the press, will be Roberts was taken into custody for questioning – new evidence came to light – he was released – end of story. You got it, Jos, and you, Fowler?'

They both nodded.

'You gonner tell the army that Blankensy wasn't Blankensy?' Jos asked.

'Sod the army, they were the cause of all of this in the first place. Now, what clever sod of a spider spun this web? Where do the threads link to? Both murders? Betts and the other body both snared. Who is he? The one shot? Where did he spring from and where is the right Blankensy? I think the killer cut Betts's throat, then shot the unknown bod, but the killer knew him, must have done. Whoever it is, he's laughing at us, leaving clues. So, let's get back on the right track; we were led astray. All right, I was. Led by the nose' Seeing Jos with a finger to his nose. 'So let's go over the clues again. First the key – new – someone made or supplied it, also a lock to go with it. Then the knife, assume it is the one that the killer used to kill Betts as it doesn't fit with cutlery in the flat, has to be a tool. Do we agree so far?'

Tom Fowler nodded.

'You, Jos?' the inspector asked, seeing Jos hesitating.

'That the two murders are linked, yes, but I don't think the same person killed both. You haven't mentioned the straw and the shard of glass; they are part of this, fit in somewhere.'

'The glass? I dunno, beats me, but the straw: you're not musing on a "someone drawing the short straw" tale, are you?'

Jos didn't answer.

'Well, at least we agree the murders are linked in some way. So, Tom, you work with Jos on this as one case; use Barcham to do any leg work. Visit tool shops, ironmongers, locksmiths, every one in London if necessary; find out who supplied them. Keep me informed.'


## Bristol Docks

The second mate at the head of the gangplank watched as the two approached. *I wouldn't want to mix it with those two; the big 'un looks as if he could take on Jack Johnson with one hand tied behind his back.*

'We could be in luck, Chas; that rusty old tub tied up alongside looks as if it plies trade along the coast where we want to be,' said Michael as the two of them strode towards the *Dorina*.

'And where would that be?' Chas asked.

'The Gold Coast of course, like I told you in the glasshouse. Our destiny, Chas, destiny to find the golden skull.'

Michael had flourished the travel warrants under the nose of the ticket inspector at the barrier gate leading to the platform (travel warrants from Michael's collection franked by the orderly room sergeant at the Essex barracks after a little persuasion, then signed and filled in by Michael). The inspector wasn't going to argue with a soldier going on leave who was six feet between the eyes. No trouble at the Bristol end of the journey, the two calmly strode through the barrier.

'Can we come aboard?' Michael called out to the figure at the opening to the bowels of the ship.

The second mate didn't answer, came down to meet them, dockside. 'What d'you want?' he asked.

'Depends on where you're bound for; a space on deck to lay our heads if it is where I think it is.'

'And where would that be?'

'White man's graveyard. We could work our passage.'

'You been there before?'

'No, but my dad did, 1900, the Ashanti wars.'

'What you done?'

'What d'you mean, what've we done?'

'You're on the run, I guess, travelling light, no baggage. All right, you don't have to answer. Old sweats, the trenches, yes?'

'You can say that again, four years of it.'

247

'We sail with the tide tomorrow, calling in at ports on way to Nigeria. Any money?'

'Some. The rust could do with a lick of paint; we are dab hands with a paint brush, whitewashing coal buckets when recruits. Army training, you know.'

'All right, I'm the second mate. There's two spare berths below, share with two others, cabin for four. One's a warrant officer, the other a Cockney civvy, but I'm sure he's an ex-squaddie. There is a woman on board and an officer. You can have hammocks under the awning on deck when we clear Biscay, then we'll see if you can handle a brush in a bosun's chair hanging over the side. Do enough to earn your keep. The captain will decide how much you're to pay. You're in luck, he's Irish.'


## Essex Regiment HQ

'Yer gonner tell 'im, Bill?' Cooper asked.

He and Tomkins were outside the company office after banter at the guard room.

*Yer civvies now, can't let yer in, not allowed. Yeah, well up yours too, tell the sergeant major we're 'ere, and the sentry 'as 'is 'and at the piling swivel, that's standing easy fer Chrissake, peace time soldiers I've shit 'em. Oh yeah, and 'ow'd yer like 'is baynet up yer arse?*

'Tell 'im wot, 'arry?'

'That Blanksy's not Blanksy.'

'Keep that to ourselves, we might want that as a trump card. Let's see wot he wants first.'

Tomkins knocked and entered. 'Yer wanted to see me, Sergeant Major?'

'What's he doing here – Cooper? I didn't send for him,' said the CSM, seeing Cooper standing at the open door. 'He your shadow?'

'Me *aide-de-camp*, Sergeant Major.'

'Batman to general now, eh? Always the comic, Tomkins; in that case you'd better let him in.' He laughed. 'And you can shut the door and sit down, both of you.'

'Fanks, Sergeant Major.'

'So, how does it go, civvy life?'

'Getting under me mum's feet, and Cooper does the washing up, but gotter get a job, can't live on fresh air. So, am I on a 252, Sergeant Major?'[10]

'No. No jankers this time. It's about Roberts. He seems to have disappeared, and Ireland, that big mate of his. They should have turned up at Kearns's address, digs had been arranged there, no sign of them. Mrs Kearns came to tell me. I thought that strange. Something underfoot going on, and I'd like to know what. I promised Mrs Kearns I would look into it. I sent for her son, he told me he saw you two at Camden Town, that day you were late back to barracks, remember?' Tomkins nodded. The CSM carried on, 'That's where Blankensy lived, enough said. You don't have to commit yourselves; this is between these walls. Did you see Roberts there? I'm trying to find a link as to why he has gone without a word. Have you a clue?'

Tomkins thought for a moment. 'The baker's shop in Delancey Street. The son is a sapper; he may have gone to see him. Yeah, he went in there, the same day we saw those two from Africa, a captain and 'is WO, asked us the way to a railway station.'

'Well, that's a start; perhaps Roberts did know that sapper. So can you get down there, sniff about a bit?'

'Of course, Sergeant Major, do anyfink if it's 'elping our old sergeant. I'll take Cooper wiv me. Get a cuppa char and a wad in the bakers, use me loaf, after all it is a baker's, ain't it?' He laughed. 'There's a bookie's runner 'angs out

---

[10] AF252 army charge sheet.

there on the lookout, got eyes in 'is arse, I'll 'ave a word wiv 'im as well.'

'Good lads. Here.' The CSM passed a couple of bob over. 'That'll cover the feast and fare. Let me know either way.'

'Not agin, who yer after this time?'

They were greeted by the bookie's runner as they entered Delancey Street from Camden High Street.

A nod and a wink from Tomkins. 'We're looking for our old sergeant. 'e's gone AWOL though, 'e's a civvy now. Fought the baker's son might know – wot's 'is name – 'e's a sapper. I fink Roberts came to see 'im. Yer keep yer eyes peeled; 'e was wiv a big Irish bloke.'

'Yeah, I saw 'em. More likely came to see Clive's sisters; they took 'em for a walk a couple of times.'

'Clive? That's 'is name, ta. I'll see if 'e's about, could do wiv a cuppa.'

'So wot's 'e done, your sergeant?'

'We'll know when we find 'im.'

Grace was behind the counter when the two of them walked in.

'Two teas please, miss.' Tomkins as usual did the talking. They sat down at the small table alongside the counter, and the teas were passed over. Tomkins looked around, at the pastries on the counter. 'Fancy one of 'em fancy cakes or a cheese roll, 'arry?'

'Cheese roll, I fink.'

Tomkins stood. 'Could we 'ave two crusty cheese rolls, please, and is Clive in?'

Grace frowned. 'Do you know Clive, then?' (The cheese rolls forgotten.)

'No, miss, but we are from the Essex Regiment. Sergeant Roberts was our platoon sergeant. We'd like to speak to Clive; it is important. We fought together. We won't be any bovver,' he added, seeing Grace hesitate.

'Just a minute,' Grace said. Opened the door at the rear and called out, 'Clive, two from the Essex to see you.'

A short interval and Clive appeared, looked at Tomkins still standing, asked, 'Do I know you?'

'No, I guess not. I'm Tomkins, me mate sitting down is Cooper. Sergeant Roberts saved 'is life. We jest want to speak wiv yer.'

Clive ducked under the counter flap, came and stood by the table, looked at Cooper. 'Are you the one that...?'

'Yeah, that's me,' Cooper said. 'And I'd do anyfing for the sergeant, anyfing, yer understand?'

'And me,' Tomkins joined in. 'So, can we 'ave a chat?'

Clive pulled up a chair and sat; Tomkins resumed his seat.

'Sergeant Roberts saved my life at the Somme, so that makes two of us.' Nodding at Cooper. 'So what is it that you want?'

Grace, listening from the other side of the counter, a little perturbed, called, 'Clive.'

'It's all right, Grace, I think these two ought to know.' He carried on. 'He's safe, Chas, he's with Michael, probably on the high seas by now.'

'Wot, why?' both Tomkins and Cooper questioned.

'He was arrested for the murder of Blankensy. Michael got him out of the cell he was being held in at Albany Street police station. Said he wasn't taking any chance of Chas being found guilty, although innocent.'

'Bloody 'ell. Michael did that? That's put the cat among the pigeons,' said Tomkins. 'I need this.' And he drank the tea in one go. 'Drink yer tea, 'arry, we need to 'ave a fink on this.'

'What d'you say that for?' Clive asked.

'It's got a bit complicated. Now that we are passing secrets, I guess it's all right to tell yer wot we knows. D'yer know Bayham Street?'

'Bayham Street!' Clive almost shouted it. He suddenly stood; his knee caught the underside of the small table, sent the cups flying. 'Hans, of course, I've been trying to puzzle out who it was ever since I bumped into him some days ago. It was my fault, I was in a hurry, he never stopped, well I'll be blowed. You saying Bayham Street jogged my memory. What you looking at me like that for?' Seeing Cooper and Tomkins sitting with mouths agape.

'Did yer say Hans?'

'Yes, why?'

'Yer know 'im, then?'

'Yeah, he had a shop in Bayham Street, mended our shoes before the war; you remember him, Grace?' Turning to his sister.

Grace nodded 'Of course.'

'Well, that's anovver cat in among the pigeons, it 'as to be the same bloke.'

'What you on about, for Chrissake?'

'We was gonner tell yer until yer upset the apple cart. Blanksy is not Blanksy, or wasn't now 'e's been killed.'

'Am I going bonkers, or are you two?'

'Yer not gonner like this. Blanksy was your Hans.'

'I don't get it, you're talking in riddles.'

'I fink we'll 'ave anovver cuppa tea, and the cheese rolls, The CSM is paying for it, and I'll explain.'

Grace was in tears by the time Tomkins had finished.

'I don't believe Hans would do anything like you said.'

''e was nuts – sorry, miss – out of 'is mind, deranged, yeah, deranged. Fink about it. Everyfink 'unky dory, then flash bang wallop, 'is world turned upside down. 'is shop smashed up by some mindless sods, 'is muvver killed, 'e's locked up – interned – for four years, enough to send anyone round the bend. 'is mind festering like a sore that won't 'eal, wanting revenge. Yeah, and we wanted to kill 'im for wot 'e 'ad done. Now I feel sorry for 'im.'

There was silence for some moments. Then Clive asked, 'How did you find out it was Hans?'

'Found out where Blanksy lived after 'e was forced to resign, followed 'im waiting for the right time to – never mind – to Bayham Street, saw 'im talk to the ironmonger, finally got it out of the ironmonger after threatening we would tell the police.'

'Proper pair of sleuths, aren't you? So how did Hans become Blankensy?'

'Dunno, your guess is as good as mine. Escaped from prison, wherever that was, knew they would be looking for him, saw the opportunity – what better disguise than an officer in uniform? Either 'e killed Blanksy or someone else did – stripped the body and the papers, took over the identity. Coincidental the officer was posted to the Essex HQ, London, where Hans wanted to go. Remember the war was still on; if 'e ditched the uniform and went as a civvy and got pulled in on an identity check, 'e would 'ave been nabbed, so 'e carried on wiv the subterfuge, got posted to France. Yer know the rest.'

'You gonner tell the police?'

'Wot d'yer fink, tell 'em we was stalking Blanksy? Not bloody likely. The cuffs would be on Cooper's wrists before yer could say Jack Robinson, 'im being top of the list of suspects, and me, for aiding and abetting. I'll tell the sergeant major about Roberts, 'e'll tell Mrs Kearns one way or anovver why Roberts and Ireland can't take up digs wiv 'er.'

'That's it?' said Clive.

'Yep, that's it. Lovely cheese rolls; 'ow much do we owe yer?'

'On the house. Come again some time, may get some news to pass on.'

'Ta.' *Forget about the sergeant major paying.*

'That's a turn up for the book,' Cooper said when they were outside. 'I wonder where in the 'ell Roberts and Ireland are orf to; nuffink in the papers about 'is arrest and the breakout. I would 'ave fought that smart arse of a reporter Jack Barnett would 'ave cottoned on to that, 'e 'as narks in the force.'

'Yeah, and they'll be looking for someone else to clobber now they've lost Roberts.'

'D'yer fink them two from Africa could have done it when they found out it wasn't Blanksy? They were 'ere at Camden Town, we saw 'em, and we know they asked for 'is address.'

'Gawd knows, finking of something else. Gonner see that agent in Arlington Road while we are 'ere.'

'Wot agent?'

'Don't start that "wot" agin, I told yer before about 'im. Yer coming?'

'I remember you,' the agent said, looking up as Tomkins closely followed by Cooper entered the basement office. 'But who is he?' Nodding at Cooper.

''e's part of it. Wot I 'as to tell yer. Yer told me yer could git a ghost writer to make a book about our memoirs.'

'Yeah, I remember, but it had better be good.'

'Yer won't know unless yer 'ear it. Yer got time?'

'You're pushing your luck.' He looked at the wall clock. 'Sit down, I'll make notes. If I nod off, you buzz off. You understand?'

'Yeah, got it.'

He didn't nod off. Was quiet for a while after Tomkins had finished (with interruptions from Cooper). They waited expectantly for the agent's comments

'Nothing in the papers about Roberts's arrest and escape. You've only the word of the son in the baker's shop.'

They were both surprised by the agent's statement. Nothing about whether it was any good or not, what he had been told. So Tomkins answered.

'Yeah, that's wot Cooper said. Nuffink in the papers. It's been hushed up, gotter be, and if the police wanner deny it, they'll 'ave to stand up in court and swear on the Bible. Roberts and Ireland are missing, that's a fact, and Clive is not lying.'

'All right, I'll give way on that. Now what you have related. Intrigue – mystery – three murders. But so far it is how you have got involved, which can only be a small part in the whole story, not enough to make a book. What about other characters, there must be some, and the police and their parts? Evidence, clues. Must have been some for them to arrest Roberts. Questions? Where was Blankensy killed, who found the body, any witnesses? The same police handling the three murders? If this is a revenge story, a whodunit? And most of all: who killed the Hans bloke? Readers would want to know. Do you know?

'No.'

'There, you've said it, and Roberts and his Irish mate can't just be left walking away in the sunset like a fairy story. So sorry, lads, come back with some answers and you may have the makings.'

'How we gonner find that out?'

'That's your problem.'

'Let's go, 'arry, looks like coloured chalks and finding a clean pavement for us.'

'Let's have it.'

Inspector Bill Gordon spat the words out. It was two days after the last meeting. DS Jos Bancroft, DC Tom Fowler and PC Barcham sat facing the music.

'The knife.' Jos answered for the other two. 'It's a cobbler's knife, used for cutting leather and trimming and repairing boots, many used by the man in the street for repairing their own other than by cobblers.'

'So we are at a dead end again?'

'Not quite, guv, worn a lot of leather checking, good job they are an issue, boots to our plods.'

'Get on with it, Jos. Any joy, that's what I want to know.'

'Yes, the mystery deepens.'

'I'll slay you, Jos, so help me God, if you don't get on.'

'All right, let me finish. We checked shops over a wide area that sell those knives, locks and keys – all right,' seeing the inspector's face turning red. 'We found a shop, or rather Barcham did, an ironmonger's, next to a shop that was boarded up, a leather workers and boot repairers, in a back road of Camden Town nor far from Arlington Road where Blankensy had a flat. The key we have didn't fit the lock, but looking through the chinks of the boarding, we could see the plate glass window was smashed. The ironmonger did sell locks and the keys, hadn't sold one from way back, his words. He didn't know who owns the shop, been boarded up since 1915.'

'Wait a minute, Jos, plate glass you said?'

'Yes, I thought that would interest you.'

'Let me think for a minute.' A pause. 'You any good at jigsaws, Jos?'

'I know what you are thinking, guv, that shard of glass.'

'Yes. Sod who owns it, we are investigating murders. Get a team down there, make an entry, force the door open, whatever, collect all the broken pieces, careful, don't crush any with your size tens, bring them back here, spread them out on a level surface to see if that shard dug out of Betts's neck fits. Ten to one it does. Then bring that ironmonger in to see where he fits in. Now anything else before you go?'

'Yes, guv. That letter from Captain Reid. It fits. I checked with Alice, the witness that saw Roberts enter Blankensy's flat; she didn't see anyone go in before Roberts that morning because she doesn't sit at the window until after nine o'clock. Also we found the cabbie that dropped him and his CSM off; the time was before Roberts was seen going in, so Roberts could not have done it. But, and a big but, Reid and his CSM could have done so, when they discovered it wasn't their OC.'

'All right, Jos, you've made your point. I'll give you that. Roberts is in the clear, but I don't go for Reid or his sidekick killing Blankensy, or whoever it is. They wouldn't have admitted they went there.'

'No, because they know we would have found out eventually they had.'

'Leave it at that for now, Jos; concentrate on if that shard of glass fits, and while at that shop, see if there is a cobbler's knife there. If not, I bet the one we have is the one that killed Betts, and the same bloke killed this unknown chap and left the knife there. Get to it, I want it done now.'

The ironmonger sat on a stool outside the entrance to his shop, as was his wont when the weather was fine and he had no customers (which were few and far between these days, the country broke after the war; those who had survived were scrimping and scraping for a living).

He saw them coming, recognised Barcham as the one who had interviewed him previously, leading two in plain clothes, followed by two constables, one carrying a large cardboard box, the other with a jemmy in hand. *What now? Trouble brewing.*

'You take charge, Tom,' said Jos, as they halted facing the boarded up shop. 'You know what to do. I'll have a word with the ironmonger. You come with me, Barcham; let's see what he has to say.'

'Prise the door open,' DC Tom Fowler ordered the constable with the jemmy. 'Go steady, don't smash it, we have to leave the shop secure when we've finished.'

'Let's go inside.' Jos nodded to the ironmonger.

'I'm DS Bancroft; you have already met PC Barcham. Now, what have you to tell me about next door?' Jos asked when they were seated inside 'You told Barcham it was boarded up in 1915.'

'You ought to know.'

'What d'you mean, I ought to know?'

'Well, you're the police.'

'CID actually, so stop pussyfooting about, or would you prefer sitting in a cell instead of here? Believe you me, my inspector has a very short fuse if it gets to him having to ask, and you don't answer what he wants to know, you'll be on bread and water in solitary. Now I'll ask again, you talk or walk, understand?'

The ironmonger wet his lips with his tongue. 'Can I get a glass of water, please?'

Jos could see he was scared. 'Barcham will get it.' Nodded to Barcham, who rose and headed for the back room.

'Is he from the local nick?' the ironmonger asked when Barcham was out of sight. 'If so, can I speak to you alone?'

'Why, so you can deny what you have said, your word against mine?'

'No. You will understand when I tell you.'

'All right, but I'm warning you, no beating about the bush wasting my time.'

'Go and give the others a hand, Barcham, I'm gonner have a cosy with this chap, understand?' Jos told him when he had returned with the water. 'I'll call you if I want you.'

Barcham wasn't quite sure if he did understand; he only knew that he was disappointed at being left out of the act.

The ironmonger drank the water greedily, while Jos watched.

'I'm waiting,' said Jos. 'This had better be good.'

The ironmonger placed the glass down. 'I was told to keep my mouth shut.'

'By whom, and why? I'm listening.'

'The police. That's why I asked if he was with the local police, your PC. Also that bullying sod Betts. Threatened me that my shop would be smashed like next door was.'

'Betts, you said: the one that was found murdered?'

'Yes, the one that started it all, January 1915. I'll tell you all I know now Betts is dead. I saw it happen.' The ironmonger began. 'Betts, leading his gang...'

Jos leant back in his chair when the ironmonger had finished.

'So this chap Hans Muller turned up out of the blue after four years. Where had he been all this time, do you know?'

'Locked up I suppose, Gawd knows where.'

'You changed the lock next door and left a key for him so he could get in. Why didn't you do it while he waited? Oh, I get it, didn't want to be seen, did it when no one was about. Why didn't you inform the police?'

'You kidding, tell the police after having to keep my mouth shut for four years? In any case, why should I? It was his place, entitled to go in, lost the key, or most likely had it taken away from him.'

259

'But you told Barcham you didn't know who owned it, the shop, when he questioned you.'

'Hans might not have been the owner, could have been his mother.'

'All right, I'll let you get away with that. Did you see him again?'

'No.'

'Why did you change the lock, fit the old one back?'

The ironmonger hesitated, finally blurted out – 'Look, this Hans was a good man, and his father before him was well liked. They killed his mother. Betts was responsible. When the police arrived, Hans was fighting mad, gone berserk, a copper got his arm broken. They took Hans away in a straitjacket, his mother to a pauper's grave. None of the mob arrested, Betts got away with it. All hushed up. I was told to keep my mouth buttoned up. The Mullers were German, served 'em right, eh, we were at war, yeah, yeah.'

'All right, you told me that, now answer the question: why did you change the lock back again?'

'What d'yer think? They cost seven and sixpence.'

'No, no, no, I'm not having that; you was protecting Hans, didn't want it known he was back.'

'All right. When I heard Betts had been killed, I...' He paused, grimaced.

'Go on, you thought what? I'll say it for you. You thought Hans had killed Betts. Revenge, eh? You were covering up for him.'

'I'm saying I kept the new lock, I had the spare key, so I could sell it. You can think what you like.'

'And I can charge you for withholding evidence.'

'Not if I give it to you.'

Jos smiled. 'Clever, eh? Hand it over, then, and the spare key. Tell me, where was this Hans staying after he had turned up?'

'I dunno, I told you I only saw him that once. You ain't gonner charge me, are you? I don't want to get involved again, a fly in a spider's web.'

'You sure there is nothing else you can tell me?'

'As a matter of fact there is. You asking where Hans stayed jogged my memory. Two squaddies from the Essex came a couple of times, asking questions; finally they admitted they had followed Hans here, so they must have known where he lived. So why don't you pull them in?'

'Followed *Hans* here, did they? How the hell did they know him? Do you know their names?'

''arry and Bill. That's what they called each other.'

'Harry Cooper. The one whose life the RSM told me Roberts had saved. One of only two that survived that fated platoon. Must have been him and his mate the batman Tomkins,' Jos murmured.

'You know 'em, then?' the ironmonger asked, catching the faint murmuring.

'They will bloody well know me when I catch up with them. I now know where your Hans stayed and who killed Betts.'

'Now I've told you all I know, can I have my lock and key back?'

The words fell on deaf ears as the door slammed shut behind Jos.

'I'm off to the Essex HQ; I'll see you back at the office, Tom,' Jos called out to Tom next door, 'You get started on the jigsaw when you have finished here.'

'Off where, why?' Tom queried, poking his head round the now-opened boarded shop door, only to see the back of Jos hurrying away.

*Essex HQ*

'I need to see the RSM.' Jos presented himself to the sergeant of the guard. 'DC Bancroft, I've been here before, I know where his office is. You may remember me.'

'Yeah, I do, but I'll have to escort you. Regs, you know.'

'Morning, Sergeant Major.' Jos gave a salute when shown in. 'Last time I was here I was left with a hammer inside my head knocking to get out the next morning.'

'You civvies, can't take a couple of pints.'

'More like a couple of gallons, I seem to remember.'

'It won't happen this time; I'm on duty. I take it this isn't a social call?'

'Afraid not. Something has cropped up regarding the murder of Blankensy. I need to question Cooper and Tomkins.'

'They're civvies now, what have they been up to?'

'Following Blankensy.'

'You're not thinking they killed him?'

'They had every intention of doing so. Tell me, when they were waiting for their discharge papers, were they free to come and go as they pleased?'

'More or less, but one day I had them over the coals, as they had left without asking and never got back until after midnight.'

'Could they have got to Camden Town, say, before seven o'clock in the morning?'

'No, they still had to parade before letting loose. Am I allowed to know what's going on? You still think they could have killed Blankensy?

'No, they didn't, but I still want to talk to them. Have you seen them since they were discharged?'

'Yes. Roberts and his mate seemed to have disappeared. They never turned up at the digs that had been arranged, so I asked Tomkins to nose around, see if he could find out where they were.'

'Oh!' Jos feigned surprise. *As if he didn't know.* 'And did they find out where?'

'They haven't reported back as yet.'

'I shouldn't worry about Roberts and his mate the sergeant major, no doubt they'll turn up. So, can I have Cooper's and Tomkins's addresses?'

'Cooper is staying with Tomkins, his mother's place.' He wrote it down and passed it to Jos. 'Do you know who killed Blankensy?'

'No.'

'Heads up, 'arry, trouble coming,' Tomkins said. 'Turn around and walk away.'

He and Cooper were crossing Highbury Fields on the way to the barracks to see the RSM.

Too late. Jos Bancroft spotted them. Called out.

'Hang on, you two, I want to have a word with you,' he said as he drew near. 'Lucky me, saves me traipsing to Stoke Newington, and we've got somewhere to sit away from the madding crowd and have a cosy chat.' Indicating a lone bench.

'Wot's all this about?' Tomkins, as usual doing the talking, asked as they sat down.

'I'll tell you what's it all about, and one porkie, so help me God, you'll see the inside of a cell. Bayham Street, that's what. I know all about your wanderings and the chat you had with the ironmonger there. You found out that Blankensy was a Hans Muller. Am I right?'

They nodded.

'Don't nod, you have tongues, use them.'

'Yes,' they both answered.

'Why didn't you inform the police?'

'It's down to me,' said Tomkins. 'I fought we could make some money, get a book written. I 'ad a word wiv a publisher's agent.'

'You bloody idiot. You realise what you have done? He could sell that to the press. You haven't, have you?'

'Was finking about it, to that Jack Barnett reporter.'

'For Chrissake, I could arrest you now for withholding information as to two murders, not just one. Now one other thing: what did you find out about Roberts and his mate disappearing as the RSM asked you to investigate?'

Tomkins told Jos.

'This is unbelievable. So, all the Jones the baker's family know? Tell me, Tomkins, do you stand in dogs' shit every morning?'

'They won't say anyfink, could be arrested for aiding and abetting.'

'And you, don't you want to help Roberts?'

'Of course.'

'Well, not a word. The police at Albany Street have egg all over their faces, are keeping mum. Roberts was never arrested, is innocent. You understand?'

'Yes.'

'So what are you going to tell your old RSM?'

'Nuffink, couldn't find where Roberts has gone, not a clue.'

'Right, and Muller?'

'Never heard of 'im.'

'Right again.'

'I wanted to kill Blankensy,' Cooper butted in. 'But when I found out 'e was Muller, I felt sorry for 'im; wot they had done to 'im sent 'im off 'is 'ead.'

'But you don't know a Muller, do you, Cooper?'

'No, of course not, sir, as Tomkins said, never heard of 'im.'

'Both of you, thank your lucky stars, and dogs' shit, that I don't run you in. So shove off and tell the RSM what you don't know.'

In the backyard of the CID at Clerkenwell, DC Tom Fowler stood to straighten his back.

'It fits, it bloody well fits,' he yelled.

He and Barcham had spent hours fitting the broken pieces of glass together.

'Come on, Barcham, I'll buy you a pint, leave the jigsaw for the DI to have a dekho to confirm the shard fits; we've solved it, yeah.'

The following morning, DS Jos Bancroft and DC Tom Fowler sat facing Inspector Bill Gordon across his desk.

'So that's it,' the inspector said. 'This Hans Muller killed Blankensy, took his identity then killed Betts. This means we have to check with every police force in the country for a murder taking place in 1918, and the body unidentified.'

'A right cock-a-doodle-do,' said Tom Fowler. 'Betts got his rhubarb and custard, so close the book on it, guv.'

'I'm the one that takes the can if questions are asked,' the inspector pointed out.

'Muller was a civilian when we investigated the murders. Proved he killed Betts. End of story.'

'No it isn't,' said the inspector. 'Who killed Muller?'

## The good companions

The *Dorina* wallowed, caught by the ground swell passing Lundy Island, rose, rolled and dipped. A prescription for *mal de mer* if ever there was one. Captain Reid stood on the starboard deck, legs apart, both hands on the taffrail, at arm's length. Eyes on the horizon as the sea swallowed the sun. *Evening's drawing in, soon be sunset at six o'clock.*

He had been pleasantly surprised (after the cramped quarters his cabin had offered) by the accommodation for passengers. A saloon, also comfortable chairs, a small bar and dining room adjoining. One of the crew, suitably attired in a brass-buttoned tunic, acted as mess steward, also attended the bar. All in all, not bad for an old converted slave trader.

He had met the other passengers at yesterday's evening meal, where introductions had taken place, and had been taken aback on coming face to face with Chas and Michael (no mistaking the big fellow); they had met in the baker's at Camden Town.

'Chop ready in 15 minutes. You up to it, sir?'

He heard Mansfield's voice and turned.

'Yes, a bit squeamish. This old tub rolling from starboard to port is getting to me. The others on parade?'

'Not the woman, the others yes.'

'I feel sorry for her if she is seasick, and forget all this "sir" while we are onboard as I feel the odd one out; we have a long voyage ahead, and living in each other's

266

pockets, the six of us, can be embarrassing, you understand?'

'Yes, sure.'

'Right, that's settled. How are you getting on with your cabin companions?'

'Fine. The Cockney White – "call me Chalkie" – has the bunk above me. Likes to chat, was in the Rifle Brigade. Surprise, surprise is going to Kumasi, knows our fort, been there during the war, and the mission to light a penny candle from the stars.'

'What's that supposed to mean?'

'I don't know; it'll come out in due time, no doubt, over a drink or two.'

'The other two mention seeing us in Camden Town?'

'Roberts did.'

'That all, not where they were heading?'

'No, and I wasn't going to ask, not yet, not the type to question, maybe later when we get to know each other better.'

'I know what you mean. How about Barbara Evans? No doubt you made a point of chatting to her.'

'Yes, ex Salvation Army, and she is bound for Kumasi, the mission school.'

'Well, I'll be a Dutchman, be strange if the other two are heading there. Makes you wonder what they are doing on this old tub.'

Below decks Chas was asking Michael the same.

'What are those two from West Africa doing on this old tub? Not on a trooper, very unusual for an officer – come to that, any military – to be on a private run ship. Strange, them being at the baker's shop in Camden Town, and Arlington Road just around the corner where Blankensy was killed that same morning. Came from the same mob as them, and they were there before we arrived.'

'What are you thinking, that they killed him? Why would they do that?'

'Dunno, grudge perhaps. They did us a favour if they did. Why don't you ask them?'

'Yeah. I might well do that.'

'It's time for grub, let's have that first.'

The meal finished, Captain Reid placed a bottle of brandy on the table.

'I'd be pleased if you fellow companions would take a noggin with me, and perhaps Mr White – Chalkie, if you don't mind me calling you as such.'

'Everyone else does.'

'Thank you – Chalkie, if you could induce Miss Barbara to partake of brandy also. You seem to be the closest to her. Medicinal, of course; it might not cure her sea sickness, but will help her to sleep. Tell her to lie on her side, knees bent, and try to eat something, dry bread, not nice being sick on an empty tummy.'

'I'll do that.'

'Thanks, Chalkie, bring the bottle back.'

Chas gazed at the untouched brandy in the glass, turned to Reid.

'Before I drink to your health, Captain, and now there are only four of us present, can I ask you something?' Chas asked after Chalkie had left.

*I knew this was coming.* 'Yes, go ahead.'

'Did you know a Major Blankensy? He was from West Africa same as you, posted to the Essex Regiment, resigned in disgrace and took rooms in Arlington Road, around the corner from the baker's shop where we met.'

'A question and a statement, Sergeant. Yes, he was my OC before the posting.'

'You know what he did, sent a platoon on a suicidal mission. I was the platoon sergeant and—'

'Before you go on, Sergeant, he didn't.' Reid raised a hand as Chas began to rise. 'Please sit, let me finish. This was much of a shock to me when your RSM told me. I could not believe our OC would do such a thing, and I was right; it wasn't the major. I know what you wanted to ask: did we visit him at Arlington Road? Yes we did, it was our intention to do so whilst on leave, CSM Mansfield and myself. We left it to the last minute, you could say, got the address from the Essex HQ; that's when the RSM told me. It was not our OC, believe you me, not Major Blankensy who had been shot.'

'What?' Chas shouted. 'It was, I saw him covered in flies, and that must have been after you had called there, as you were at the baker's shop before Mike and I got there. I was arrested and charged with his murder, that after I had done six months in the glasshouse for striking him.'

'It wasn't the major. We ought to know; we served with him since 1914.'

'Who was it, then?'

'I don't know, never seen the man before.'

'This don't make sense, what was you doing at the baker's shop?'

'We just happened to come across it, finding our way to a railway station, wanted to sit and have a cup of tea, think what to do.'

'There was no need to think what to do, should have called the police.'

'Yes, I know, but I did a silly thing; without thinking I picked the revolver up. To my surprise it was the major's .38, I recognised it, he had joked about a nick on it. Now it had my fingerprints on it, that would make me a suspect – motive, killing someone who had killed our OC. Thought about wiping it clean, but it wouldn't take long for the

269

police to find out we had been there – check taxis, we had taken one there, the cabbie would remember – so I held on to it, still have it. We left the door open as we had found it and, as I said, found the baker's shop. We only had two days' leave left, decided to report to the movement depot and leave the country, get a boat as soon as possible; that's why we are on this tub, the first one we could catch.'

'You left me in the shit. The police nabbed me for it, had a witness who saw me go in Blankensy's rooms that morning, and they weren't going to let go. I would have been for the hangman's noose.'

'No, no, Sergeant, you are in the clear, trust me. We made a written statement, signed it and forwarded it to the CID. Stated that we had found the body, it wasn't Major Blankensy, we don't know who it was, prepared to swear on oath in court if necessary.'

Chas swallowed the brandy in one go. 'It's unbelievable; what do you think, Michael?'

'Kismet, Chas, that's what it is, kismet, it had to be so. I'll drink to that.' And, as Chas had, swallowed the brandy in one go.

At that moment Chalkie returned.

'Barbara leave any for us, Chalkie?' Reid asked with a smile.

'I gave her a noggin, 'ad one meself, 'ad to, she wouldn't take it ovverwise. Choked on it, but got it down; she'll be fine, closed her eyes, nodded off.'

'We'll believe you, Chalkie; we'll finish the rest, celebrating – skeletons put to rest – and as such I'll supply the after dinner brandy whilst we are aboard, taken with water of course. I don't have to pay mess fees, it'll be cheaper. You join us, Chalkie.'

'I'll drink to that.'

'One thing that puzzles me,' said Reid, turning to Chas. 'You were arrested, how come you're on this tub?'

'The luck of the Irish,' Michael butted in. 'Leave it at that.'

'You look puzzled, Chalkie,' Reid said. 'Don't ask.'

'Wasn't gonner.'

'So, now you are in the clear, Chas, you going to get off at the next call of port and return home?'

'No.' Michael answered for him. 'We are going all the way to the Gold Coast.'

'Was that decided when Chas skipped jail?'

'No, it was enacted when I met Chas in the glasshouse.'

'Why the Gold Coast?'

'My father was there in the army – 1900 – told me about how Sir MacCarthy was beaten in battle and had his head cut off and a cast of gold made of his skull, paraded at a festival every year on a war drum by the chief of the Ashanti warriors. We are going to find it, must be worth a small fortune, or a big reward from his descendants.'

Reid laughed outright. 'Sorry, blokes, couldn't help myself. That happened nearly a hundred years ago.'

'Yes, I know that,' said Michael. 'Then, in 1874, Kumasi was razed to the ground by British forces led by Sir Garnet Wolsely seeking the golden stool of the Ashanti. It had been spirited away and buried with other treasure; the golden skull must have been with it; never found, so must be still there. Someone must know where, passed from one mouth only to another in secret, any other involved in the burial killed to silence them.'

'The history of the golden stool and the skull are known as your dad told you, I'll give you that, but you are on a wild goose chase. Don't you think it would have come to light, this treasure?'

'How come buried treasure didn't come to light in Britain after the Romans had left until hundreds of years later, and probably more still there?'

'And you think the luck of the Irish will find this one?'

'Why not? Stranger things have happened.'

'I think you'd be better off panning for gold, backbreaking, but with your Irish luck you could find some nuggets; better still drop at Sierra Leone, plenty of diamonds there, pick them up so I believe.'

'I'll do what my father told me to do, he was "*fey*"; right, Chas?'

'If you say so, Michael; we've nothing to lose.'

'You've been listening to this, Chalkie. You know the CSM and I are going to the fort at Kumasi, back to peacetime bullshit, Chas and Michael to seek the gold skull, so you gonner tell us the reason for your visit? I believe you told the CSM – "Manny", now we are companions – "to light a penny candle from the stars". What's that supposed to mean?'

'Michael here can answer that better than I can.'

'It is what the English couldn't do when they came and tried to teach us their way.' Michael gave the answer.

'Is that right, Chalkie?' Reid queried.

'Yeah, that's what Mike sang.'

'Mike? Pour the brandy, Manny,' Reid said. 'Chalkie will need his tonsils lubricated to tell us who Mike is.'

Chalkie wet his tonsils, cleared his throat and began.

'Michael O'Farrell, Mike to 'is mates. Irish and as big as you, Michael; the best shot in the Rifle Brigade, or was until Billie Martin turned up. Called up in 1916. 'e'd served wiv the rifles in 1900, the last of the Ashanti wars as a 17-year-old; it was eiver that or prison for 'im and 'is brovver caught nicking. Turned out the finest marksman the rifles 'ad ever known. Tom, a year older, was killed out there where we are going, Ashanti.

'Back to July 1914. The Rifle Brigade stationed at Colchester. One company, wiv spit and polish, was ordered to northern Nigeria under the command of Major Argyle.

272

The RSM came along to add a bit of pomp and colour to show off 'is medals, and that we used the S and P. All this to escort a Captain Hethrington acting as envoy. It seems the Germans were stirring up trouble, spreading propaganda against the British. They 'ad Togoland and the Cameroons, and wanted Nigeria. The mission to arrange a meeting for the district officer there wiv the Emir of Kano to cement friendly relations, or words to that effect. Mike, Arty Wivers, Greenie and me were in that company.

'We finally got there, no shanks, boat and train till a place called Bukuru, then we slogged it, and bloody 'ot too. Quartered or rather camped wiv the 9$^{th}$ Nigeria Regiment, that supplied us wiv camp beds and mosquito nets, fed and watered us.

'The mission going well, all 'unky dory so far, Captain Hethrington met wiv the Emir and his young son Ahmid. Then the spit and polish lark. We put on a display for the Emir, toy soldiers on parade, rifle drill. Mike showed 'is skill as a marksman, 'it a gourd at 800 yards. Then the usual ritual, "Would the Emir do us the honour to inspect the company?" Of course 'e would, and young Ahmid wanted to meet the soldiers, so sealed Mike's fate yer could say. It's quite a story, take a while to tell yer.'

'We've plenty of time, if not now there are other evenings, but carry on, we'll tell you when to stop,' Reid answered for the others.

Chalkie poured some water into his glass, took a sip, said, 'Make it last longer.'

'Good idea, Chalkie, take the brackish taste from the water. Help yourself to another brandy when you're ready, same for you Chas, Michael; no need to tell you, Manny.'

'Ta, Cap'n.' Chalkie added a nip of brandy to his glass and carried on with his tale.

'So it was "open order march" two paces between ranks. The Emir and young Ahmid followed by the RSM,

273

moustache waxed to rapier points, a chest full of medals daring any one of us to blink, walked the front rank, then wheeled to take them to the next rank. Talk about out of the mouths of babes, yer'd fink a young boy would be nervous, but not young Ahmid; 'e stopped in front of Mike, looked up, and without any more ado said in perfect English, "You are the one that hit the gourd at 800 yards, may I shake your hand sir?" Yer could 'ave 'eard a pin drop. Mike never moved a muscle, stood rigid to attention. The RSM 18 years in the army, and for the first time didn't know wot to say or do. The Emir, a man of wisdom no doubt, saved the day, said, "I think my son has forestalled me, Sergeant Major, but I think on this occasion he can act on my behalf; I'll chastise him later." The RSM recovered 'is aplomb, discipline taking over, said yes sir. Shouted, "You 'eard, O'Farrell."

'Mike bent down and took the boy's hand in 'is own. I was standing next to Mike, I 'eard wot 'e said, 'e spoke softly: "No one 'as ever called me sir before, so I'll be thanking you kindly, sir."'

Chalkie paused, took a sip from the glass.

'Yer know wot? I swear Mike grew two inches taller that day. No one dared take the piss out of 'im shaking 'ands wiv the kid. I'll never forget that day, it was the fourth of August, we never knew until later it was the day that war was declared against Germany. Everybody was pleased wiv themselves; the Emir must 'ave been as 'e laid on a feast, invited as all. Mike 'ad an idea, give the locals some entertainment, a tug o' war competition. Made up four teams, 'e borrowed a rope from the 9NR stores, and we marched to Kano. We stuffed ourselves wiv lamb rice, plantains and yams, ate wiv one 'and only, as the locals did. There must 'ave been 'alf of Kano there. I'm rambling on a bit, but yer git the gist of it, I 'opes.'

'I think that'll be all for today, Chalkie; you've done well so far, kept us in suspense as to how it was that Ahmid sealed Mike's fate. What do you say, Chas, Michael? Take another drink, yes?'

They both nodded.

The following morning Barbara joined the men for breakfast, wan but composed. Captain Reid drew a chair and guided it into position for her to sit.

'Thank you, Captain.'

'Please, Tim, short for Timothy. Can't have two captains aboard, can we? Did you manage to sleep last night?'

'After a fashion, thank you; the brandy helped.'

'Good. You must keep us company after dinner, partake of Chalkie's prescription, a nip in water, take away the brackish taste of the water, and listen to Chalkie, the story teller in vogue.'

'Depends on how the boat behaves.'

The gods were kind. The sea calm across the Bay of Biscay under a blue sky. Barbara found her sea legs, a comfortable chair under an awning stretched above deck, the 'good book' at hand.

That evening after dinner, Barbara, a colour to her checks, no sign of *mal de mer*, joined the others in the small bar. A nod from Reid to the barman, and a bottle of brandy and a jug of water were placed on the table.

'Would you like a drink, Barbara?' Reid asked. 'I take it you are staying to listen to Chalkie's saga?'

'Just water, Tim, thank you.'

'Two tear drops to take the taste of water away, and the germs,' said Chalkie. 'Friars thrive on it, give it a try; yer don't 'ave to drink it if it upsets yer.'

Barbara nodded. 'If you say so, Chalkie.'

275

The others helped themselves on Reid's bidding, and settled down to listen to Chalkie.

'So, where did I git up to? Oh yeah, the tug o' war, at the feast. The crowd drew back as Mike laid the rope down in a long straight line, tied a white rag in the middle, marked the centre line on the ground and the others four paces apart. The crowd looking on in silence, wondering if Mike was going to perform some magic, the Indian rope trick, a boy disappearing at the top, not having seen a tug o' war before. Mike then picked two teams who lined up alongside the rope, making a ceremony of it. Chairs were placed for the Emir to sit with young Amid on 'is right, and a factotum alongside to do the Emir's bidding. The district officer on the Emir's left, with Captain Hethrington, the envoy next.

'Next, to everyone's surprise, Mike marched to where they were sitting, saluted, faced the DO and asked, "Sir, would the Emir permit Ahmid to act as umpire, sir?"

'Before anyone could answer, Ahmid clapped 'is 'ands, called out, "Can I, Father?"

'"Silence is golden, remember," the Emir rebuked 'is son. Then spoke to Mike. "O'Farrell the marksman, yes. In that case, Ahmid has my permission. You will need to tell him the rules."

'"Thank you, sir, I'll do that." And Mike saluted again.

'Ahmid slid off 'is chair. "Thank you, Father." Took Mike's hand. That put another link in the chain, as they walked to where the rope lay. Yer wiv me? No, then I'll carry on, but first a nip. Cheers, Cap'n.'

Chalkie took a drink, and licked his lips.

'Lovely stuff. To carry on, Mike told the boy wot to do and to give the orders. Ahmid in 'is element.

'"Pick up the rope" the first order. The teams picked the rope up, and Mike held the rope steady with the white rag over the centre line, nodded to Ahmid who gave the order, "Take the strain." Then "Pull".

'The crowd now got the picture and cheered like mad as the teams heaved and tugged, Ahmid watching until 'e finally pointed to the winning team as the ovver one was pulled over the line. But the game wasn't over yet. Mike 'ad other ideas. Whispered to Ahmid to pick two teams from the locals, let them 'ave a go. Not against the British, as it would be obvious they couldn't win, and 'e didn't want to upset the applecart. It wouldn't matter who won pulling against their own creed. It was a bit of a shambles, ending wiv both teams on the ground, but all good fun, then to end it and make it right, Ahmid to pick a team of boys, let them win, make everyone 'appy. Ahmid picked 16, Mike said too many, eight in a team. Ahmid pointed to the difference in size to that of the British team. They compromised. Twelve, and Ahmid to lead the team. The youngsters could hardly hold the thick rope in their small hands; they won, of course, the crowd cheering them on as our team allowed themselves to be pulled over the line, collapsing, feigning exhaustion.

'Then Mike did a silly thing, 'e picked Ahmid up and sat 'im across 'is shoulders, the kid wiv 'is 'ands on Mike's 'ead. The Emir began to rise from 'is chair, the crowd went quiet. The district officer saved the day again, stood and called to the Emir, "It's tradition, sir, Ahmid is quite safe, the victor being paraded." Captain Hethrington then stood and began clapping, the RSM followed suit, and the British team. Ahmid waved to the crowd, who cheered and stamped their feet. The Emir sank back in 'is chair. Panic over. Mike approached the Emir, gently lowered the boy to the ground and saluted as Ahmid was embraced by 'is dad. The Brits in favour, the German propaganda forgotten, or so we thought.'

Chalkie paused, took a drink.

'Yer wondering where this is all leading to, why it sealed Mike's fate. All 'is life 'e 'ad been ordered about, told wot to do, wot not to do. 'e was a soldier, 'is dad was a soldier, spent 'is boyhood in army camps. Then 'e was called sir, 'ad 'is 'and 'eld by a boy, 'eld the boy close to 'imself, formed a bond.'

Chalkie shook his head, took another drink. Looked around.

'The next morning after the feast, Ahmid was missing from first prayer. 'is bed had been slept in, but 'e couldn't be found. The word went out. The Emir's son is missing. All of Kano to search. 'is body was found in a ditch, 'e 'ad been raped and strangled.'

'Oh God no,' exclaimed Barbara. And without thinking she drank from her glass.

'Sorry, Barbara, if I shocked yer.'

'I've still not figured out how this sealed Mike's fate,' said Chas. 'How did he react to the news?'

'Never said a word, walked out into the bush. Best to leave 'im alone when 'e was like that. I found 'im, sitting wiv 'is back to a tree. I sat and waited for 'im to say somefink.

'Finally 'e did. Very slowly said, "I WILL KILL THE BASTARD THAT DID THIS, SO HELP ME GOD."'

'Did he?' Chas asked.

'Yer want to know? I told yer, it's a long story.'

'You can't leave us high and dry. No pun intended,' said Chas, looking at the glasses.

'Drink up and fill up,' said Reid. 'What about you, Barbara? I see you tried Chalkie's prescription; can I top your glass up?'

'One glass is enough, thank you, Tim, although I must admit it does taste better.' Barbara smiled.

'Say if you change your mind, meanwhile we'll ask Chalkie to carry on.'

'Remember,' said Chalkie as he picked up where he'd left off, 'my company were of the Rifle Brigade, came to wave the flag, white troops, unlike the WAFF, but wot 'appened next, we became part of it. I'll try to tell yer the sequence of events the best I can, so bear wiv me if I go a bit 'aywire. The next news we got really knocked us for a six. A piece of torn cloth with a button attached was found in Ahmid's clenched fist. No mistaking where it 'ad come from. A mess tunic of a WO or sergeant of the WAFF. One of two issued to each. One in the wash, one in use. The button the give-away. Brown leather, embossed wiv a palm tree and lettering WAFF. The button – a metal loop at the back wiv a slip ring as to allow it to be removed for the washing and starching of the tunic.

'The inspector of the police was on to this like a shot. Accompanied wiv the district officer and Captain Hethrington as witness, not being an officer of the WAFF, visited each of the WOs' and sergeants' gidas – their huts – to inspect both tunics. A tunic from Sergeant Wilkinson's uniform case 'ad been repaired, the section matched that of the torn piece. 'e was formally charged and confined to 'is 'ut, two sergeants to be wiv 'im at all times in shifts, meals brought to 'is 'ut, awaiting court martial.

'The word spread like wildfire. A white sergeant killed the Emir's son. Rioting broke out. Crowds stormed the troops' lines, overran the sentry post, burned the huts.'

Chalkie looked at Captain Reid. 'No disrespect to your troops, Cap'n, but we were white rifles, the best, could outshoot any army. The RSM of the 9NR issued us wiv ammo, and our RSM, a veteran, took charge. We lined up, and on order fired over the crowds 'eads, then at their feet. We advanced wiv fixed bayonets, and they got the picture and backed off. Then, in the lull, Mike went AWOL. The RSM asked me where Mike 'ad gone as I was 'is mate. I didn't know, until later of course. 'e 'ad gone to Wilkie's 'ut, brushed aside the two sergeants like flies, picked Wilkie up in a strangle'old, looked in 'is eyes, said, "One word and I will know if you're lying. Did you kill Ahmid?" Wilkie said no, Mike said "I believe you", let 'im down and walked away.

'Then the craziest of all things, 'e takes Wilkie's boy Ali to speak the lingo for 'im, and wiv 'is rifle walks into Kano and, it's 'ard to believe, to see the Emir. Only a mad Irishman would do that. Sorry, Michael, but that's wot 'e did. 'e was met by an 'ostile crowd. Said, "Tell 'em, Ali, that they know me, I've come in peace to see the Emir, if you want to kill me go ahead, but who wants to be the first to die?" and aimed 'is rifle at the crowd. They drew back, Mike gave the rifle to Ali, which wasn't loaded anyway, and they let them pass.

'At the gate to the palace or wotever, Mike palavered wiv the factotum, told 'im the Emir would want to see 'im, and 'e would be in trouble if 'e didn't let 'em meet. Mike got 'is way. Told the Emir that Wilkie did not kill 'is son, but evidence was against 'im, and if found guilty 'e would face a firing squad, but 'e, Mike, would still find and kill the one that did kill the Emir's son. 'ow did Mike know that Wilkie was innocent, the Emir asked. Because I asked 'im and I would know if 'e lied, Mike told 'im, but meanwhile many would be killed if the rioting carried on; would the Emir order it to be stopped and let the court martial go ahead, and if Wilkie was found guilty so be it. The Emir said, you are Irish, yet you fight for the English. I fight 'em and I fight for 'em, Mike said.'

'This is hard to believe, Chalkie; you're not making this up?' Barbara queried.

'No, Barbara, this is no fairy tale, yer'll see.'

'So, did the Emir agree?'

'Yeah, 'e did. D'yer want me to carry on?'

'There is still brandy in the bottle, so yes, carry on, Chalkie, wet your throat,' Reid butted in.

Chalkie didn't want telling twice, emptied his glass and replenished it before carrying on.

'The button, that's wot saved Wilkie,' Chalkie began.

'The button?' Barbara asked.

'Yeah, so yer still interested, Barbara? The killer made a mistake, didn't know. It all came out at the court martial when Wilkie's boy Ali was questioned. 'e 'ad washed the mess uniform as usual and left it to dry in the sun; when 'e came back to starch and iron it, found a piece 'ad been torn from the front of the tunic. Frightened that 'e would be blamed, took it to a tailor and 'ad it repaired, changed it for the other spare one in Wilkie's uniform case. When shown the repaired tunic and asked if that was the one, 'e said yes. Then shown the torn piece with button attached to compare it with the repaired section on the tunic. 'e shook 'is 'ead, said, "It be wrong, sir." The defending officer leant forward, asked Ali, "Tell me, Ali, what be wrong?" Ali whispered to the DO, who smiled, stood and asked the court's permission to 'ave a mess tunic brought to court, and a full set of buttons. The prosecuting officer wanted to know why, and wot 'ad Ali said. All in good time, said the DO. The tunic and buttons were brought, and Ali was asked to fit the buttons to the tunic, which 'e did. It was then passed to the PO and the top ranking presiding officers at the table where the sword lay, and they were asked to examine the tunic to see that all the buttons had been fitted. Then the torn piece with the button still attached was passed round. The DO stood, said, "If you look closely, you will see what Ali saw, and know what he told me."

'It took a second look before the RSM who was in attendance called out, "It is a cuff button on the torn piece."

'"Thank you, Sergeant Major, and no doubt you will agree with me that neither Sergeant Wilkinson nor any WAFF WO or sergeant would wear a tunic with a cuff button on the front; it is smaller, and would pull through the button hole. Whoever fitted that on the torn piece didn't know, and must have been the assassin who killed the Emir's son. I therefore ask the court to return a verdict of not guilty."' Chalkie smiled. 'As I told yer, the button saved Wilkie's life.'

'You asked Manny and me if we could fathom it out; we could have done if we had seen the torn piece and button, so that wasn't fair,' said Reid.

'No, yer right there, I was being, wot d'yer say, a bit dramatic.

'So did the court concur on the not guilty verdict?' Reid asked.

'Yeah. Gawd knows what would 'ave 'appened if 'e 'ad been found guilty, 'e would 'ave faced a firing squad, but that would not 'ave satisfied the Muslim population, the rioting would 'ave started agin, the killing beginning. Yer could say a button not only saved Wilkie, but us and part of the British Empire.'

'We still don't know how this sealed Mike's fate,' Reid butted in.

'I'm getting there. Captain Hethrington made a statement. Said, "I came here to further relations, they hit rock bottom when this court martial was convened, now I hope to be back on good footings. The point I wish to make: who would want to destroy this relationship, the reason of my visit? Those who were spreading propaganda, the Germans, who we are now at war with, and I think I know the man. One that I bumped into on the train at Lagos; he muttered in German, and we also met on the road to Kano;

the vehicle he was travelling with had broken down, he asked if he could march with us. Although not in uniform I could tell he was a soldier or ex-soldier, the way he acted and marched in step."

'The Emir then rose and stated, "I want them, the Germans, out of my territory, but first the man that violated and killed my son. The man that captures or kills him can have all I have."

'Yeah, the prosecuting officer withdrew, Wilkie walked free. The police inspector came to see the colonel of the 9NR regiment, asked if the army would help in the search for this assassin. The colonel told 'im "we are now on war footing, I'm waiting for dispatches to arrive from brigade 'eadquarters, meanwhile all Germans 'ere will be arrested and detained for questioning".' Chalkie paused. 'Fings 'ad begun to move all right, no rest for us; we didn't know it, but bloody wars to come.'

'You are going astray, Chalkie,' Reid said.

'Yeah, sorry, but first fings first, I'm getting lost a bit. Oh yeah. All the "boys" in the camp were questioned; they all swore they would never sell or give a master's button away, were getting scarce. Perhaps a bariki boy, one boy added, said one 'ad gone missing. It didn't take long to round up all the Germans. Troops of the 9NR were on the warpath, their Emir's son 'ad been murdered, no pussyfooting, they went wiv fixed bayonets. Captain who could speak German and French fluently went wiv em. One trader was only too willing to talk. 'e told our captain that a compatriot 'ad turned up out of the blue one day at 'is 'ouse, dressed as a trader, said 'e was a sergeant Swartz from an askari regiment based in Togoland. If the trader didn't do what 'e was told to do and keep 'is mouf shut, 'e threatened to rape the trader's daughter and kill 'is wife, said it was for the Fatherland. 'e made the gardener, who was a Hausa boy, spread the propaganda to the locals that 'e 'ad instilled in 'im; beat the trader up, broke 'is nose and cracked a couple of ribs when 'e tried to object. 'e got this boy to sneak into camp, bring a tunic, any one that was laid out to dry, a usual occurrence, tore a piece off and told 'im replace it. Wot 'e didn't know was that the buttons were removed for washing, and 'e wanted it to be sure that the tunic belonged to a British soldier; 'e bribed a bariki boy to steal a button, then killed 'im so there was no witness.' Chalkie paused. 'Yer wondering 'ow I got to know this. Well, Sergeant Wilkie was wiv the 9NR, as yer know; 'e was there wiv is nose to the ground all the time. 'ad a gentle word wiv the trader's boys, and from wot the trader 'ad said and putting two and two together fathomed it out. This, Mike gleaned from 'im. Captain Hethrington got the description of this Swartz bloke, which tallied wiv the one 'e had bumped into, and who marched wiv us, unbelievable, 'e 'ad some nerve this one, give 'im that. So now the 'unt was on for this Swartz. But 'e 'ad gone, knew the game was up, back across the country to rejoin 'is unit. The bariki boy's body was discovered later.

'Yer wiv me so far? Better call it a day. Jest one fing: it was the third week in August. Seven 'undred and sixty-eight German men, 33 women and eight children 'ad been arrested and deported to England; us the Rifles were seconded to the WAFF but retained our own identity. The Emir of Kano pledged £10 000 a year towards the expense of the war. The order came for the WAFF, which included those based in Sierra Leone, Gambia, the Gold Coast and of course Nigeria, to invade Togoland. Mike couldn't get there quick enough, said if Swartz was there, 'e'd kill 'im. We marched away, leaving the walls of Kano behind, the Emir there to see us off, a slight raise of an 'and as Mike turned to 'im and nodded.

'All this water wiv the brandy, I'll be off to the 'ead.[11] Could do wiv someone to 'old me 'and, it's dark out there now.'

The next morning the *Dorina* docked at Gibraltar. Captain Reid asked Chas if he was going ashore, pointing out that if he wanted to change his mind and go back to England, this would be a good jumping off place. Chas said he would carry on with Michael's plan, and yes both of them would be going ashore to act as stevedores, loading stores, had to earn their keep, but would write to friends back home and post the letter from here.

'So be it,' said Reid. 'Manny and I are gonner stretch our land legs to the nearest bar; join us when you've finished your labours and I'll treat you to a beer or two.'

Chalkie took Barbara to see the Barbary apes. She didn't like them.

Back on board after dinner, Reid asked Chalkie, 'Are you gonner finish this saga of yours?'

'Yes, if I can remember where I left off.'

'Togoland.'

'Oh yeah, Togoland. We – when I say we, I mean our Rifle Company and the WAFF, the troops from Kano and us – slogged it to Bukuru, trained it to Lagos, then boat to the Gold Coast and linked up wiv troops there. News travels fast out there, war drums, bongo bongo, yer know. They knew we were coming, and proclaimed Togoland neutral, wanted to save the radio station at Kamina. We 'ad orders to invade, and that's wot we were gonner do, neutral or not. Three days later we crossed the border and headed for Kamina, very 'andy to 'ave a radio station already made to

---

[11] The head, a platform on the side of the ship with a hole in for the crew to relieve themselves.

use. It was jungle warfare at first, 'ad to move in columns, ambushed time after time, trying to stop our advance until we reached Nuaga, then it was open country, which suited us riflemen, skirmishing. I'll make this short. We finally reached the outskirts of Kamina and deployed. It appeared deserted. We could see the radio station and outbuildings of different sizes and the huts; our information was that the garrison there consisted of 300 white officers and NCOs wiv 1300 askaris, or thereabouts. Where were they? We soon found out; they'd dug themselves just north of the encampment knowing they would be trapped in the buildings, but they made a mistake, as we found out: they didn't sap the trenches, dug 'em in straight lines, three of 'em one behind the ovver. The order came to take the radio station. Sergeant Wilkie's platoon got the job to probe, us rifles gave 'em covering fire, aiming at the windows and doors, nobody poked an 'ead out. Wilkie and 'is men got there all right, crouched down along the outside, Wilkie tossed a grenade frough a window, and then the building blew up, the tower came crashing down. The enemy 'ad laid a charge and blew it, denying us the station, and taking some of us wiv it. 'ard luck, Wilkie, after all you 'ad gone frough.

'Now we guessed the ovver building would be booby-trapped, we could 'ave done wiv some sappers wiv us, but sod the buildings, go for the trenches. The gunners assembled the two mountain guns that 'ad been carried on 'eads behind us, the Gold Coast boys took up positions on the flanks. The gunners used the shells they 'ad, then the fun began. The Gold Coast boys moved in and couldn't miss the sitting ducks, pouring withering fire straight down the straight lines of trenches. The 9th Nigeria Regiment straining at the leash waiting for the order to go, us riflemen moved forward to take up position to give covering fire, when suddenly a white rag on the tip of a bayonet appeared over the top of the leading trench parapet. An order rang out, "Cease fire." All went quiet as a German officer stood on the parapet holding the rifle, scrambled down and began walking towards us holding the rifle high so we could all see the white rag. Then a shot rang out, the officer fell forward shot in the back and lay still. A figure appeared on the parapet and shouted out and pointed to someone in the trenches. Our RSM called out to Captain Hethrington, "What's he say, sir?"

"'He said, 'I'll kill anyone that surrenders, and you will be the first,' and I think he means whoever he is pointing to." The captain peered frough 'is field glasses that 'ad been 'anging around 'is neck. "It's him, Swartz," the captain shouted, dropped 'is glasses and reached for 'is rifle. "You sure, sir?" the RSM asked; the captain wasn't wasting time answering, was aiming, but too late, Swartz 'ad jumped down in the trench. Then the captain shouted again, "That was Swartz, the man who killed your emir's son." 9NR never waited for any order when they 'eard the captain, they were up and running shouting blue murder, and Mike was up wiv em as they passed us, couldn't stop 'im, so we upped and went too. Then it was bayonet to bayonet, close quarters, the Gold Coast boys closed in, and Mother Earth sucked blood.' Chalkie paused, wet his lips before continuing.

'It was slaughter, they'd no chance to stop us. A lot of the askaris dropped their weapons and 'eld up their 'ands. The white Germans put up a show, but their 'earts weren't in it, they 'ad wanted to surrender in the first place. I could see Mike's 'ead above the heaving bodies as 'e forced 'is way to the front. Swartz saw 'im coming; 'ampered by the bodies fallen at 'is feet, Mike twisted and leapt across the trench behind 'im, turned wiv rifle aimed, but it never fired, out of ammo I suppose. Swartz laughed, shouted, "You shoot me, Englander." Mike said, "Irish," laid 'is rifle down, raised both 'ands, fists clenched, made as snapping a twig. Swartz then laid 'is rifle down, taking up the challenge, shouted, 'Is good you come, ja,' and clenched 'is fists. Mike leapt across the trench. 'is nose shattered, spurting blood from a 'ead butt from Swartz's close cropped bullet 'ead as 'e landed, followed by a chopping blow with the edge of an 'and to the side of Mike's neck, and Mike went down, Swartz's boot driving into Mike's ribs. I was finking, Gawd Almighty, Mike's finished, this bloke can kill wiv 'is bare 'ands, but Mike wasn't finished. 'e rolled clear and grabbed the boot coming in for anovver kick and yanked it up. Swartz went back, twisted one leg over the ovver, both arms outstretched in front, crouched wiv knees bent all in one movement and both 'ands landed flat on the ground as 'e sprang and landed like a cat, kicked back wiv one leg, catching Mike in the ribs again as 'e was getting to 'is feet. Mike fell back, still holding the boot in one 'and, pulled Swartz towards 'im, dragging 'is face along the ground. I knew Mike was in for one 'ell of a fight, this Swartz was like a wild cat, 'is limbs loose, a panther against a bull. Mike fell back, Swartz was on 'is feet like lightning, one foot bare. Mike regained 'is feet, and they faced each other. Mike threw the boot, but this time waited for Swartz to come to 'im. A huge fist on the end of an arm solid and rigid and 'ard as old oak thrust out, and Swartz ran into it. Swartz's nose burst. Yer could say tit for tat, but this was no laughing matter. Two gladiators fighting to death. Mike's ovver fist sunk into Swartz's solar plexus, forcing all air from Swartz's lungs, quickly followed by a crashing blow to the jaw. This was Mike's fight, wiv fists. Swartz went down as though pole-axed and lay still. Friend and foe watched as Mike bent down, one arm under Swartz's right armpit, the ovver the inside of a thigh as 'e lifted Swartz above 'is 'ead and brought the body crashing down, the back across 'is knee, screaming, "That's for Ahmid." All was quiet as Mike stood, gasping for breath, looked down at Swartz, lying on 'is back, one arm across 'is guts, the ovver behind 'is neck, 'is eyes closed as if 'e was taking a nap.'

Chalkie paused. 'I 'ope yer got the picture, as there was more in the fight, but I did the best I could.'

'Yeah, I could imagine it,' said Michael. 'I've met hard sods like that Swartz bloke. Well, carry on, Chalkie.'

'Right. A few of our riflemen and some from 9NR 'ad gathered around. Artie Wivvers said, "I see yer did for the bastard then, Mike, we won't 'ave to kill the rest of 'em. All good pals and jolly good company now." Then somefink funny: before we could stop 'im, an askari crawled between our legs and kissed Mike's boots. Sergeant Williams of 9NR grabbed 'im by the froat. The askari then tried to tell us in broken pidgin English, "'e be bad man, 'e done jig jig my yaro." Greenie then called out, "Leave 'im, 'e just wanted to thank Mike."'

Chalkie paused again. 'Let me tell yer about our mate Greenie. A martial artist, black belt, spoke Cockney like me, but under the veneer was an educated bloke, spoke perfect English when needs be, speaking to officers on their terms. Anyfink yer wanted to know, ask Greenie. Nobody knew where 'e came from, why 'e was in the army, and yer never asked, get me? 'e got the MM in the Cameroons, but got killed—'

'You're getting off track again, Chalkie,' Reid butted in.

'Oh yeah, sorry, can't 'elp it sometimes. Well, there we were standing, nobody knew wot to do. Then Swartz opened 'is eyes, a sardine smile on 'is face—'

'Sardonic, is that what you mean?' Reid asked, laughing.

'Yeah, that's wot I said, sardine. Swartz then mumbled somefink. As luck 'appened Captain Hethrington arrived, looked at Swartz, said, "You do this, O'Farrell?" Mike told 'im yes. Sergeant Williams saluted. "Swartz, sir, 'e's finished, can't last long, wants to say somefink." The captain knelt down at the side of Swartz and listened, nodded and stood. 'e wanted to know why the rioting 'ad stopped at Kano, and 'e 'ad failed in 'is mission, the captain said.

"'Yer told 'im, I suppose; that shook 'im; wot did 'e 'ave to say then?" Williams asked.

"'Yer asking a lot of questions, Sergeant," the captain said. "You are with 9NR, so I guess yer 'ave a right to know. I told 'im it was a button, the bariki boy never knew 'e 'ad saved a sergeant's life, and you not knowing it was a cuff button."

'The captain then turned to Mike, said, "'e wants to speak to you, O'Farrell." Mike told 'im 'e didn't speak German. "'e understands enough English," the captain said. Swartz beckoned to Mike wiv one finger raised. Mike bent over, then it 'appened. Gawd Almighty, the bastard 'ad a knife in a sheath strapped to 'is back just behind the neck. The askari that 'ad kissed Mike's boots shouted a warning, too late. Swartz's ovver arm went round Mike's neck and pulled 'im down as the knife slid between Mike's ribs.'

Chalkie stopped, lifted his glass and swallowed what remained. Reid poured a double neat brandy into it, and Chalkie gulped that down. Said, 'Ta, Cap'n, I wanted that. Memories, eh, so easy to remember, so 'ard to forget.'

Barbara, with fingers to lips, uttered, 'Oh heavens be.'

Chalkie said, 'No, Barbara. No heavens be. I cursed 'im up there as I cradled Mike's 'ead in my arms and Captain Hethrington shouted for the medics as 'e tried to staunch the bright red blood that poured from Mike to no avail. Mike, 'is face ashen, whispered to me, "Pick a trefoil for me, Chalkie, and light a penny candle from the stars." I looked up at the captain who could see I didn't know wot a trefoil was, said, "A shamrock, White, a shamrock." A pink froth on Mike's lips formed a bubble, 'e sighed, the bubble burst, Mike's head dropped.' Chalkie paused.

'Now yer know why when Ahmid took 'old of Mike's 'and at Kano it sealed Mike's fate. 'e did wot 'e said 'e would, and paid for it wiv 'is life.'

Nobody spoke for a minute. Then Captain Reid spoke.

'I think we should take a drink for Mike.'

He poured a noggin in the glasses, added water to Barbara's and nodded to Chalkie, who said, 'Yeah, 'e would 'ave appreciated that.'

And the good companions drank a toast to Mike.


'So what happened next, Chalkie?' Reid asked. 'I take it that Swartz got what he deserved?'

'Yeah, he got 'is afters, but I fink it better if Barbara don't 'ear.'

'Perhaps I'd be a better judge of that,' said Barbara. 'When I was a Salvation Army lass, I served tea and attended to soldiers back from the trenches, and became hardened to the tales they had to tell, so not so easily shocked now. So carry on, Chalkie.'

'As yer say, Barbara, but I don't fink yer'll want to know me when yer've 'eard wot we did.'

Chalkie took a sip from his glass and continued.

'The askari that 'ad kissed Mike's boots touched Greenie's sleeve. Why Greenie, I don't know, but I'd guess because 'e 'ad stood up for 'im. Then 'e pointed to Swartz and beckoned Greenie to follow 'im. When they came back Greenie said, "Give us a 'and," as they tried to lift Swartz. Artie Wivvers took a leg, and I mucked in. Swartz groaned as we lifted 'im. I asked, "Where we going?" "You'll see," said Greenie. The penny dropped as we laid 'im alongside of the latrine trench. No sardine smile on Swartz's face then, only fear as 'e knew wot we was gonner do. The askari drew a knife and plunged it into Swartz's neck, then we rolled Swartz in wiv the toe of our boots. The filthy stinking sewage gurgled as 'e slowly sank.'

'Holy mother,' Barbara murmured. Said, 'That's what war does to men.'

'Yer may well say that, but that's 'ow it was, Barbara. It wasn't the war, it was wot Swartz 'ad done. We found out after, as quite a few of the Germans could speak English, that Swartz was a sadist, a merciless bully, all went in fear of 'im. They knew of 'is night time visits to do the same to local boys as 'e 'ad done to Ahmid, killing any that might talk. The officers put up wiv 'im as 'e was a professional first class soldier. I did say it better that yer didn't listen, and I guess now that I've blotted my copy book.'

'You can always start with a clean one, Chalkie.'

'Fanks, Barbara, I fink I did that when I first saw the church at the mission in Kumasi, but I'll come to that later.'

'Anything more to add, Chalkie?' Reid asked.

'Not much. The German officers 'anded in their swords, we collected all arms and ammo. One building was used as an 'ospital, medics from both side attended to the wounded. The askaris put to work digging graves all in neat lines, the dead buried. Major Argyle was one of them; that left Captain Hethrington in charge of the company. Service read. The Germans taken to the coast and shipped to Blighty, interned, fed and watered, so 'ave it cushy for the rest of the war compared to the troops in the trenches. The askaris set free, told to go 'ome. Many of them put their thumb mark and joined the WAFF. I exchanged my rifle for Mike's, looked after it real proper, not ashamed to say I sat by Mike's grave polishing for hours until Greenie came and kicked my arse. Told me wot's wot. We went back to the Gold Coast, still attached to the WAFF quartered at the fort. That's when I ventured to the church at the mission. Rose, I didn't know 'er name then, was standing outside. I asked 'er if I could light a candle for a mate of mine who 'ad been killed. She said, "Yes, of course," and led me inside. I've never done that before, only been to church at a wedding or funeral, and compulsory church parade, wasn't sure wot to do, I 'adn't got a candle wiv me, then I saw candles there. Rose nodded. So that's when I lit a candle for Mike, not from the stars, only the Irish can do that. 's right, Michael?' Michael nodded 'At church parades we 'as to kneel, so I fought I ought to. Rose said, "Do yer want to say somefink?" "Will 'e 'ear?" I asked. Yes, she said. I said, "I'm sorry for cursing yer when Mike was killed, and will yer look after Mike proper up there?" Rose said, "That was very good, can I ask your name?" I told 'er Charlie White, but everyone calls me Chalkie. "In that case I'll do the same, if that's all right," Rose said.'

Chalkie paused, looked around.

'I suppose you fink I was a right Charlie, like me name, but I felt good. Rose didn't seem a stranger to me; never met a woman like that, the only ones I ever knew were tarts after wot they could fleece yer for. I asked if I could come again. Of course, any time, Rose said. So after duty next evening I walked to the mission.

'Rose was sitting on a bench outside the school, a young girl sitting by 'er side. I asked, "Is that an angel?" Rose laughed, said, "No, it's my daughter Grace, and believe me, she is no angel, can be naughty at times." She introduced me as Mr White. Grace stood and 'eld out an 'and. Said, "Pleased to meet you, Mr White." I looked at mine, not wot yer'd call clean, calloused with broken finger nails, and 'esitated. "She won't bite you," Rose called out. Then I knew 'ow Mike felt when that soft 'and 'eld mine. I was 'ooked line and sinker. Grace asked if I was an English soldier, and did I know London? I told 'er I was born there. "Oh," she cried, "yer must tell me all about London." "If yer call me Chalkie," I said, "none of this Mister business." "I see," Grace said, "it is a nickname as white chalk; well, yes, if that's wot yer want." "Yeah, that's right, better than being called blanco," I told 'er. She cottoned on, seeing as there were soldiers stationed at the fort.

'So when I could, I sat on the bench outside the school while Grace bombarded me wiv questions about London. 'ad I seen the King, why do they call a clock Big Ben, and so on. I told 'er the best parts. The theatres, Rotten Row, where people rode 'orses, and trams that ran on rails, 'ad stairs and could be driven from eiver end wiv seats that could face both ways. The big ships that sailed up the Thames and Tower Bridge that opened to let them pass. I never told 'er about the grime and poverty, prisons and the 'anging. Let 'er dream, not 'ave nightmares. When it was time for 'er to go to bed, I would sit and talk to Rose. She told me she taught in the school, 'ad taught the son of Princess Ayaa until the war 'ad finished and 'e could go to England to some posh school to finish 'is education. Those days were the best times of my life. 'ad to end when order came for us to invade the Cameroons. Our company still attached to the WAFF, so we went along wiv 'em. That was war, not like the easy peasy one in Togoland. But we finally won, and took over the Cameroons. Then back to Blighty and the trenches in France. The Somme, don't say it.'

Chalkie stopped, frowned. ''ang on a mo. The Somme. Chas. Yer said yer name was Roberts, right? Was yer a sergeant, got the MM? Am I right?'

Chas admitted he was. 'Don't shout it about, all that is finished now. Forget the bloody war.'

'Well, it is a small world, ain't it? MM. They don't come up wiv the rations, no need to 'ide yer light under a bushel, Chas.'

'Turn it in, Chalkie. Finish what you was telling us.'

'All right, where was I? The So— no, forget that. I survived. Got my discharge papers when it all ended and the boot, fanks for nuffink. Swam across to Ireland. Picked a shamrock for Mike, and, as yer know, on the way to see

294

Rose and young Grace, though she is grown up now, I guess. Light another candle for Mike, think wot I am gonner do, 'itch'ike to Togoland, plant that shamrock at Mike's grave, then it won't be the only place where it grows. That's me finished, give me mouf a rest, one of you can 'ave a go now.'

'That was some experience, Chalkie,' said Reid. 'We drank a toast to Mike; now that I think Chas's light has been exposed, we should do the same for him.'

Four days later the *Dorina* dropped anchor at Cape Point, off the Gold Coast. The sun was peeping above the horizon, gathering strength to soften the pitch between the seams of the decking. Chas and Michael had earned their keep at Freetown and Bathurst loading goods from the holds to bum boats to be rowed to shore, and were preparing to do the same here.

'I'll catch a bum boat to take me ashore,' said Captain Reid, dressed smartly as becoming an officer in the WAFF: KD shorts reaching to the knees above drill twilled linen puttees wound from highly polished brown boots to the space of four fingers' width below knee caps. 'No need for you to come, Sergeant Major,' speaking to Mansfield. 'I'll see the OC in charge of the detachment present on duty at Cape Castle, see if any transport leaving for Kumasi in the near future, and catch up on the latest news. Be back before sundown, don't want the mozzies beginning their evening stint having a go at my bare knees.'

'Yes, sir.' *That's it, leave over, uniform in fashion. Sergeant Major now, is it? Yes sir, yes sir, three bags full sir.*

'I waited until we were all together, to let you know what is happening, and the news I have gleaned from shore.' Captain Reid back on board, dressed again in casual garb

295

(to Mansfield's surprise), was addressing the good companions. 'The *Dorina* will up anchor after breakfast, after giving us time to be rowed ashore, so this will be our last night aboard, and I add: the voyage has been a pleasant one due to the company. Now two pieces of news: one affects the WAFF, which has always been referred to as the WAFF, and has now been honoured and granted royal status by HRH, I assume for our effort during the war, the taking of Togoland and the Cameroons, adding a bit more to the British Empire, and a bit more to look after. That's the cheerful one, the second is not so good: no transport leaving for Kumasi for another two or maybe three days, unless of course if you, Michael, Chas, Chalkie, take a chance with the so-called bus, which you are expected to push on breakdowns. But don't be downhearted. There is a mission here, Barbara, and you are welcome to stay there in the meantime. I took the liberty of calling on your behalf, if that's all right with you.'

'Thank you, Captain.'

'Please. Tim. Not Captain. We shall be seeing each other again, here and in Kumasi; good companions, yes? Right, to carry on, I've pulled a few strings with the officer in charge of the detachment here. As you are veterans, Chalkie, Chas and Michael, cots will be found, and you will be fed as guests of the sergeants' mess with the detachment, and as the lowest white rank in the WAFF is sergeant, you are all sergeants, understand? One thing: if you have an MM medal ribbon to hand, wear it, Chas, and any other decorations; that goes for you, Chalkie and Michael. Now forget about the bus. We will be travelling to Kumasi courtesy of the army. You as well, Barbara, in the front next to the driver, he will like that, us in the back. Let me explain. For you that don't know, the governor resides at Cape Castle, hence the detachment stationed here, changed at intervals from the regiments of the Gold Coast Brigade. The transport coming from Kumasi is bringing extra troops and returning empty; that's our good luck. The reason why? Security. King Prempeh of Ashanti is returning from exile after 20 years. Briefly he was enstooled in Kumasi in 1888 at the age of 16 as heir apparent, made guardian of the golden stool in 1894. At that time his armies were causing havoc on the coast, slaughtering and slave running. 1900, the British wanted to put a stop to this, once and for all. Prempeh was defeated by British troops under the command of Sir Francis Scott, sent to exile, together with the royal Ansa brothers, Their sister Princess Ayaa Ansa was allowed to stay. She is still in Kumasi, under the guidance of one Okomfo Anokye, who you will meet, Barbara. Let me tell you something of this man. Believe me, he is a sage, a prophet, soothsayer, Svengali all in one. No secrets from him, he will read you like a book, never ages. Responsible for the golden stool, spirited it away when the British came to steal it, the only one to know where it is, so it is said. Whatever you do, Barbara, don't cross swords with him; listen to him, he will advise you. But I digress. Those years before 1900 the Ashanti warriors slaughtered thousands of the Fante tribes living peacefully in the south of the Gold Coast, and even now some of them, although they fought alongside those from Ashanti during the last war and now serve in the WAFF, still remember the families and relatives that were slaughtered and hold a grudge, and, not too happy on hearing of Prempeh's return, might want to take a pot at him. The governor will have to greet him, some sort of ceremony I guess, hence the extra security. No doubt there will be celebrations galore in Ashanti, in Kumasi more so. We will have to wait to see what happens next. I hope I've put you all in the picture. We will meet again ashore, and also when in Kumasi. All good companions like we were on the voyage. Any questions? I will try to answer.'

'I would like to say something.' Barbara spoke up. 'Also ask advice. It seems more than a coincidence that we all met on this ship; I feel that I have been caught in a vortex, no, not a vortex, but swept along in a stream of events that I have no control over. I have bottled my feelings up too long, but since meeting you all on this ship, I feel among friends, and feel free to speak. When I first met Chalkie aboard here, he mentioned a Captain Hethrington; the name conjured memories of events I tried to bury, then you, Richard, mentioned the golden stool.' Barbara reached and undid the necklace from around her neck and placed it on the table. 'I want to show you this, Robert.'

Reid picked it up and studied it. Asked, 'Where did you get this, Barbara?'

'From a collection bag. It had been placed there without my knowledge.'

'A collection bag? Perhaps you had better start at the beginning, Barbara,' Reid said.

'Yes, I can do that now among friends. I was a Salvation Army lass. You soldiers know we venture into public houses to collect funds to fight the good fight. I took over a certain area from one, not quite, shall I say, a lass, had many years' service behind her, ready to retire, one such pub being the Elephant and Castle in South London. I was rather nervous entering the public bar the first time, and he saw me. He was sitting with his back to the wall behind a table; turns out he always sat in the same place, told me later it was force of habit when frequenting bars in foreign lands so he could see who entered, the golden rule, watch your back. He called out, "Heads up, lads, the Sally is here, dig deep." He then rose and came to meet me. "You're new, don't be nervous, I'll come with you if it's your first time in a bar." I said I was capable. Never the less he walked with me, and chided those that didn't put enough in the bag, opened the door for me when I left. I was touched by that as no one had ever done that before for me. The next time I called there, it was almost a repeat performance, except this time on leaving he asked me my name, and told me he was Bert, Bert Craig. "Barbara?" he said when I told him. "You'll be a major one day, a Major Barbara," he said. We stood talking for a while outside; he had opened the door and come out with me. Said "see you next time" as I left.

'The next time I admit I looked forward to seeing Bert. He sprang to his feet when I entered, asked me to sit and have a drink, a lemonade or squash. London was in the middle of a heat wave, I was hot and thirsty, that was my excuse, I succumbed. "I'll take the collection while you sit and sip your R White's," Bert said. No one dared raise an eyebrow as I sat and Bert did the collection. When I arrived back at my quarters above the local Salvation Army branch, I found the necklace. I was flummoxed, wasn't sure what to do. I guessed it must have been Bert that put it there; was it supposed to be a gift, or for the collection? I could see it was gold, the charm looked like a throne to me. I pocketed it and decided I would ask Bert next time.

'He looked different when I saw him, until I realised he was wearing a jacket; it had always been shirt sleeves. Nights becoming cooler, he said. The heatwave had ended in thunder and a downpour. Asked me to sit and take a drink. I noticed a button missing on his jacket, and a small tear.' Barbara paused. 'Strange that Chalkie mentioned a button that saved a sergeant's life, and now I am relating about a button that...' Barbara leant forward and covered her eyes with a hand.

'You all right, Barbara? Leave it, take a rest,' said Reid.

Barbara looked up, her eyes damp. She produced a handkerchief and dabbed them.

'I'll be all right.' She sipped some water. 'I'll finish now I've started. Yes, about the button, that could save or cost someone their life. I offered to see if I could find one to

299

match and stitch it on if he would come back to where I was staying. He said he didn't think that right, him coming home with me. I told him I shared rooms above the SA with another lass, and he agreed to come. I could not find a matching button, but one that would pass at a glance, did the repair and stitched the button in place, brushed some dried mud from the coat. Then I tackled him about the chain and charm. He admitted he had placed it in the collection. Thought it was the best thing to do. I asked him if it was his, did it belong to him. He said no, thought I – me.' Barbara pointed to herself. 'Would know what to do. I asked him, so you expect me to find the rightful owner, how am I supposed to do that? "Dunno," he said. "But something tells me you will." I gave up then, couldn't think straight, said I would think about it. I made some tea, we sat talking for a while, idle chit chat, then he stood to take his leave. I said, "You don't have to rush away." "Yeah, I do," he said. "Thanks for repairing the coat; will I see you again?" "Of course," I said. I never did.'

'Didn't you visit the pub again, then, Barbara?' Chalkie asked.

'I did. He wasn't there. I asked the barman if he had seen Bert. No, no sign of him since he left with you, he replied. I asked him if he knew Bert's address, thinking he might be ill; no, he didn't. I asked those in the bar. One gave me a number of a house in a nearby road, thought Bert had lodgings there. I still had the chain and charm or whatever it was, couldn't make up my mind what to do with it, determined to find Bert and question him more, couldn't believe he didn't want to see me after asking if he could. I went to the address given to me. The elderly couple that kept the house told me yes, Bert rented the rooms on the upper floor, that he came and went at all hours, a nice chap, had decorated the parlour for them and did other jobs, yes I could see his rooms, you're a Sally lass, can be trusted, the door's never locked, go right up, couldn't remember the last time they'd seen him. The rooms were spick and span, clothes in a wardrobe, bed made. I noticed a shaving mug and razor on the washstand beside the bowl and jug, so the mystery deepened; surely he wouldn't leave without his razor. I found a photograph of him in uniform, hesitated, felt guilty, but I took it. In a drawer there was a cigar box; I opened it to find medals. I knew one was the MM, the others campaign ones, I think. So he had proved himself at some time, made me proud sort of knowing him, silly I suppose. I closed the box, stood for a few moments seeing his face in that photo, so young. "Where are you?" I asked. Thanked the couple and left.'

Barbara paused, looked at the others. 'You may feel it strange that I should be trying to find someone that I had met by chance, but I had never met a man that I felt for, and I was sure he felt the same way about me.'

'I know the feeling.' Michael said. 'It's called love, Barbara; some know it, some don't. Did you find your man?'

'You could say found and lost. No, that's not quite right. There is no end to my story really. I'll explain what happened. We have time?'

'Yes, carry on, Barbara. We're all ears,' said Michael.

'Fate dealt a hand,' Barbara began again. 'The next evening at the same pub, my mind still in a whirl, I tripped over an outstretched leg, stumbled and nearly fell. I apologised, said sorry, not looking where I was going. "No, lass, don't say that, it was my fault," he said. "Always doing it, fing is, if I tucks it in and nods off I tumble over."

'I laughed, couldn't help it, then I realised he only had one leg. "Sorry," I said. "I shouldn't have—"

'"Laughed?" He said it for me. "Laugh and the world laughs wiv yer, cry and yer cry alone, but yer knows that, don't yer?"

301

'"Yes," I said; "sorry about the leg."

'He smiled. "Which one, the one you tripped over or the missing one?"

'"Now you're making me cry," I said.

'"Don't say that, lass. Only joking. The 'shantis took that, could have been me head."

'"Shanties?" I queried.

'"Yeah, one of them Shanti warriors, in the Ashanti war, 1900."

'"Never heard of it," I said.

'"No, not many has. I wish I never had," he said.

'"Can I ask your name?" I asked him.

'"Charlie, Charlie Farmer," he told me, "but I'm not a farmer, don't sell carrots or spuds, got a shop wiv Tishy in Walworth Road, buys and sells things, new antiques, if yer know what I mean."

'"I think so," I said, "but who is Tishy?"

'"Me mate, young soldiers together, he lost an arm in Ashanti, all because of that bloody stool. We could have been in this last war, got blown to smithereens, whereas we are still here; lucky, eh? What's an arm and a leg?"

'"What are you doing here, Charlie? You don't mind me calling you Charlie, do you?"

'"No, that's me name; looking for someone," he said. "We think he lives in this area and comes in for drink; we're looking in all the pubs on the off chance we may catch up with him."

'"Who's we?" I asked.

'"Tishy and the major, they're in the other bars," he told me.

'I thought it strange, a major, so I questioned that, asked, "A major?"

'"Yes, Major Hethrington," he said, "or was, retired now. I served with him in the Ashanti wars, but he wasn't an officer then, a rifleman, same as me and Tishy. A real

302

gent though, a lord's son; we didn't know it then. He got commissioned in the last war."'

'Hang on a mo,' said Chalkie. 'Major Hethrington, this bloke told you, and he was in the Ashanti wars. I served with Major Hethrington in this last war, and he was in the Ashanti wars, but he was killed at Hemel Heights in 1918, or at least we thought he had been, couldn't find his body. Must be the same major, can't be two of them. That's anovver mystery.'

'We're getting bogged down,' Reid butted in. 'Does it matter about Major Hethrington? Let Barbara get on.' He turned to Barbara. 'Did you find your man, Barbara?'

'No,' Barbara said. 'Well, yes and no. After what this Charlie Farmer had told me, I realised it was a stool, not a throne, the charm: a golden stool. A miniature, I mean. I visited the library a few times to look up the history of the Ashanti wars; there it was in black and white, the golden stool, the cause of all the fighting. On one occasion I happened to pick up a copy of the Islington Gazette lying there, saw the headline, "The man they couldn't hang". A follow-on report of the trial of this man Flint, charged with murder, found guilty and sentenced to hang, who had cheated the gallows; the trap door had failed to drop, and he had been freed. An act of God, it had been decreed.'

Barbara paused, took a sip of water.

'I thought it must have been terrifying for this poor man. Was any of you in London at that time? You must have read about it?'

'Yeah, I did,' said Chalkie, 'and there was two other murders.'

Michael looked at Chas, shook his head slightly, as if to say, keep quiet. Then asked Barbara, 'So what did you do then, Barbara?'

'I decided I would have to get to the Gold Coast one way or another. I had a word with the principal at St Joseph's

Mission about becoming a missionary. He said he would help; I would have to have some training, but being a Salvation Army lass, that would help. Then it happened, so bizarre, unbelievable.'

Barbara paused again. Chalkie came and stood behind her, laid a hand on her shoulder. 'This is upsetting you, Barbara; just leave it. Yer don't 'ave to carry on.'

Barbara reached up for Chalkie's hand, placed her hand over his, felt the nearness of him, pressed her fingers into his knuckles. Said, 'Thanks, Chalkie. I want to finish; I shall feel better then. Can't keep it bottled up.'

Chalkie gently withdrew his hand and returned to his seat. Michael looked at Chalkie, gave a slight nod of the head and a smile.

Barbara carried on where she had left off.

'It was at the Salvation Army depot, where I shared quarters above the hall with Mary, where I had sewn the button on Bert's coat. It was soup kitchen day. The repast, bread, a cauldron of soup carried out to the trestle table at the entrance to the hall. I was on duty with ladle in hand. The main doors were opened and the queue shuffled in, the poor feeding the poor. The "Sally" with coppers collected from spit and sawdust bars and wherever to feed mostly ex-servicemen, now the dregs of society, thankful to have survived the most horrendous war history had known, which had brought a nation to its knees by the slaughter of its manhood. Now home to a 'land fit for heroes', so they were told. What a laugh. I have to stem the tears when I recall those men. Some with crutches like that Charlie Farmer, others like his mate, minus limbs. One hand to take a chunk of bread, the other, if they have one, to take a bowl and hold it to be filled.'

Barbara took a break, took a deep breath.

'You must forgive me; all of you served and suffered, perhaps hardened to the killing, put it behind you. I try to, so hard to forget, but we must remember, and generations to come must.'

'I – we – understand what you mean, Barbara.' Captain Reid spoke up. 'But there are some do not want to remember. The horror. But, as you said, remember the fallen, the sacrifices. One day, perhaps, a memorial, their names carved in stone. Whatever you are going to tell us, I feel you will master your feelings. I take you for a brave lass, taking this journey alone. I speak for the rest of us, I'm sure: it has been a pleasure knowing you, and will also be in the future.'

'Thank you, Captain. It has been for me also, and will be so at Kumasi. Now I'll continue. Back at the soup kitchen. I saw the button, it was level with my eyes, the one that I had sewn on Bert's coat, and the rent I had repaired. My mind could not accept it that it could be Bert. I looked up, it wasn't Bert, the ladle dropped from my clasp, it bounced off the cauldron and clattered on the floor. The last I heard was the voice saying, "You've dropped it, lady, I'll pick it up for you."

'When I came to, I was sitting on a chair in the hall and Mary was holding a bottle of smelling salts under my nose, I brushed it away. "What happened?" she asked. "You look as if you have seen a ghost."

'"I thought I had," I said. "That man was wearing Bert's coat."

'"What man?" Mary asked.

'"The one I was serving," I said. "Has he gone? I must speak to him."

'"No," Mary said, "you've had a shock." Pushing me back in the chair as I tried to get up. "I'll tell the principal, he'll call a policeman, let the police deal with it."

'A policeman came. A Detective Sergeant Bancroft, he told me. I thought it strange, a detective to investigate a reported stolen coat. The police must think it important.

Bizarre, in fact; I'm serving soup to a man I've never seen before who is wearing Bert's coat and a detective turns up. He asked me my name, and what had happened. Was I sure it was the coat I repaired; what was the name of the owner of the coat? I told him I was sure it was the coat, I recognised the button, and that it belonged to a Bert Craig, an acquaintance of mine. Where can I find this acquaintance? he asked.'

Barbara paused, took a sip of water.

'No need to repeat. I told him what I have already told you. "More than an acquaintance, this Bert Craig; close to him, were you?" the detective insinuated. "Have you the photograph with you, the one you took, and did you take anything else?" That annoyed me, and he knew it. No, I didn't, I told him. Sorry, he said, shouldn't have said that. He studied the photo, was quiet, didn't speak, frowned as though in thought, rubbed his chin. The queue had already departed; clearing up began. He looked around. Said, "Any chance of a cup of tea, and somewhere the two of us can sit and have a quiet chat?"

'"The courtyard," I told him. "I'll make the tea, you grab a couple of chairs."

'We sat and sipped tea. I had this feeling of dread that I was going to be told something I didn't want to hear.

'"Fond of this Bert Craig, Barbara? You don't mind me calling you Barbara, do you?" he asked. Caught me unawares. I admitted I was. He then asked if I read the newspapers. I told him I don't buy any, but at times, yes, if one is left in the hall, and I had when in the library; why? Did I read about the man they couldn't hang? Yes, it was headline news, the trap door failed. "That's right," he said. "That man was Flint, the man you say was wearing your man's coat; what I am going to tell you may be upsetting, but bear with me."'

Barbara paused again, took a sip of water. Said, 'This is what he told me. I quote.

'"We make mistakes, the police, we are only human, and at times it is because the right hand doesn't know what the left hand is doing. A body had been found with a broken neck in a country estate. I was in charge of the investigation. Don't ask the whys and what-fors of the Met being called in, but we were, and I was saddled with it. I won't bother you with details, but I was sure as could be that it had been an attempt of burglary at the manor, the victim had surprised the perpetrator or perpetrators, a struggle had taken place. A button with a piece of cloth was found at the scene of the crime, also footprints. A cast was made of the prints. The locals were questioned; they were loyal to the lord of the manor and the family, swore no one would have done such a thing. I had in mind a person or persons from London. I put the word around with the plods in town to keep an eye open for suspects, burglars, petty thieves, more so on the off chance that one had a coat with a button missing.

'Some time later a body was discovered late evening by a prostitute in a back alley on our patch in London. He had been garrotted. No identity on the body. Another detective was put in charge of that investigation. The morning following the discovery of that body, a vagrant drunk sleeping it off in a shop doorway, on being questioned, assaulted the constable, was arrested and placed in a cell. His boots and jacket removed, the usual practice. The desk sergeant noticed one button on the jacket was different to the others, also the boots were polished, almost new, not what anyone would expect a down and out to be wearing. He was asked if the coat and boots were his; all he kept saying was, "They're mine, they're mine." The sergeant notified me. I checked the boots with the casts, and the buttons on the jacket with the one found at the scene of the

307

crime. They matched. He was asked again if they were his. The same answer. "They're mine." I wasn't too happy, something didn't add up in my mind, he was simple-minded, and where did he get the whisky from to get drunk on? Just gave a silly grin when asked. "Found it," he said. He was charged with the murder, found guilty by a jury, sentenced to be hanged. You read what happened. He had been baptised, his Christian name Herald. The angels must have sung for him. An inspector from the PWD inspected the trap door and the apparatus the day after it had failed, tested it with the correct weight, and it worked. Act of God, it was referred to as. He was freed. The same man you saw wearing your man's coat.'

Barbara paused again. Looked at the others. Said, 'I dreaded what Detective Sergeant Bancroft was going to say next. My mind was in a turmoil, fearing that the body in the morgue was almost sure that of Bert by the photo I had shown him, and the coat in question belonged to him, and that put Bert at the scene of the crime committed at the country estate in Hertfordshire. I asked the inspector, if Flint was innocent, why did he say the coat and boots were his? He replied that it was because he didn't want them taken away from him, or to admit he had stolen them, and he had no idea he would be charged with murder. The inspector told me I had solved the mystery of where Flint got the coat and boots; he'd taken them from Bert Craig's body. I then asked Bancroft if he was implying Flint killed Bert for his boots and coat. He said Flint didn't, bearing in mind another detective was investigating the murder of the unidentified body in the morgue and it could have been one of the many discharged soldiers living rough. He also said that the other detective didn't know any more than he did at the time, that Flint had in fact exchanged the good boots and coat on the body for his worn out ones. That he had had Flint locked up and charged with the murder that had taken place miles away, the right hand not knowing what the left hand was doing. The fact being that Flint, insisting the coat and boots were his, had condemned himself. So I asked Bancroft who killed Bert and he said it was a long story and I had better ask Detective Fowler, as he was the one who had solved that. He said it was nobody I would know, Mancini, a revenge killing. Caught because he smoked Abdulla cigarettes. The inspector laughed as he told me that. "You won't believe how one small item could solve a crime." He then added, "We have two more murders on our hands, both on our home patch this time." Why he told me that I don't know.'

'Two murders?' Chas asked in surprise. Looked at Michael, who shook his head.

'Yes, that's what he said,' Barbara carried on. 'So I then asked Bancroft what happened next. I would have two choices, he told me: I could identify the body in the morgue as Bert Craig, and swear the coat that I had seen Flint wearing did belong to Craig – that would put him at the scene of the crime and prime suspect – or do nothing, so I could keep the photo and the memory of Bert Craig as I knew him, his name unsullied. Flint is a happy man, a bit of a celebrity in fact. Bancroft also warned me that some time had passed and as no one had claimed the body at the morgue it may well have been disposed of, so it was down to me to decide.'

Barbara leant back in her chair and sighed. Took another sip of water.

'I don't know why I'm relating all this to you; it started with me showing the gold chain with the charm, I guess, after meeting on this boat, all bound for the same destination.'

'It's down to destiny, Barbara,' Chalkie said. 'Yer don't 'ave to tell us wot yer decided on, but I know wot I'd 'ave done, let it drop, no sense in bringing it up, wasn't gonner do any good.'

'Chalkie's right,' said Captain Reid. 'I agree.'

'Me too,' Chas butted in. 'That Bancroft tec was right when he told you they make mistakes, the bast— so and sos, sorry Barbara, slip of the tongue.'

'Seems as if yer 'ad an up and downer wiv 'em, Chas.' Chalkie chuckled as he spoke.

'You can say that again, and you're right when you said it was destiny meeting on the boat, for me meeting Captain Reid, but I'm not going into that. Maybe another time,' said Chas. 'Let Barbara tell us – if she wants to – what she decided.'

'Thanks for your support.' Barbara picked up where she had left off. 'I did ask Bancroft if I could be charged for withholding evidence. No, he replied; if Bert Craig was alive, he wouldn't have been giving me any choice, so no point in bringing it up now. I'll keep the photo and the memory, I told him. So that's how I came to be on this boat, starting a new life.'

'Well done, Barbara,' said Reid. 'And as it is our last night aboard, we have to finish the bottle, so will you take a nip with your water, Barbara?'

'I will this time, thank you.'

'Let me look at that chain,' said Chalkie.

Barbara passed it to him.

'I thought so,' Chalkie said. 'I didn't want to interrupt before, but I'm sure Captain Hethrington wore that at one time. He was very friendly with Princess Ayaa when we were in Kumasi.'

'For heaven's sake, Chalkie. Don't muddy the waters any more.'

'I'll keep mum, then.'

310

After an early breakfast, the good companions were ferried ashore. Chalkie, an eye on Barbara and a hand to her arm, supported her on the hazardous (for one wearing a skirt) transfer from the ship to a bum boat alongside, rising and falling with the ground swell, then sat holding her close as they rode the surf to the shore. This did not come amiss to Michael, who smiled to himself.

Five days later, after a wait at Cape Point, they entered Kumasi to be greeted by gaily coloured ribbons hung from trees alongside the road.

'Not for us,' said Captain Reid. 'A welcome to ex-king Prempeh, must be due any day now.'

Okomfo Anokye (known by the Ashanti as the one who materialised the 'golden stool' as the seat of power for the Ashanti Kingdom when acting as factotum to King Osei Tutu; reincarnated at the death of all kings since, to remain as everlasting guardian of the golden stool) watched as the truck approached, pulled up outside the fort in a cloud of dust, steam erupting from the bonnet; the huge doors of the fort opened, the truck was driven in and the doors closed.

He walked to the palace grounds where Princess Ayaa Ansa sat on a bench in the shade of a baobab tree. He addressed her without any formality. 'They have arrived, little one. A woman will bring the necklace to you. Do not question her.'

'You knew, Okomfo, your doing,' the princess responded.

'Yes, it had to be so. Your father and brothers will return soon; it has been two decades; welcome them and be thankful.'

He turned and walked away as abruptly as he had come.

Back at the fort, Sergeant Ellis held Barbara's arm as she stepped down from the truck.

'It's been a pleasure driving with you alongside,' he said. 'I'll come and see you at the mission when you have settled in, if that's all right with you.'

'I'm sure that will be,' Barbara replied. Thinking, *What have I let myself in for?*

The fort's RSM came forward and saluted Captain Reid. 'Glad to see you back, sir, hope you enjoyed your leave, and you, Mansfield. Any news of Major Blankensy, Captain?'

'Later, Sergeant Major. I'll report to the colonel; he will decide what to announce; it's a bit tricky, shall we say. Meanwhile, let me introduce you to the newcomers. Miss Barbara Evans, who will be joining the mission. Sergeants Roberts MM, O'Leary and White. All veterans of the Somme. White served here before with the Rifle Brigade. You may remember them, attached to us for a while in Togoland and the Cameroons. He also will be staying at the mission. No doubt, Sergeant Major, you could arrange for Roberts and O'Leary to stay as guests of the sergeants' mess for a few days until they get equipped. Can't have Brits from the old country living in the trees, can we?'

'No problem, sir, I'll see to that.'

'Good. That's settled. So I think refreshments are in order now. I'll accompany Miss Evans to the officers' mess. I'll leave the rest to you.'

'Of course, sir.'

Later, after refreshments had been partaken of, Chalkie found himself feeling a little bit out of his depth in a sergeants' mess, but thankful for Captain Reid's – tongue in the cheek – inclusion of him as a sergeant. Thought it was time for him to leave, but was concerned about Barbara's need to be walked to the mission. Decided to ask CSM Mansfield.

'I shouldn't worry, Chalkie,' Mansfield said. 'The officers won't let Barbara leave in a hurry. A white woman here is an advent, any one of them would be pleased to escort her, she will be quite safe, but I guess Captain Reid will do the honour. You shove off when you're ready, I'll tell her, and I'll see you off and on while you are in Kumasi.'

Grace Ayerling (born in Kumasi those 12 years ago of Swiss parents, both doctors of medicine who had founded the mission just before the turn of the century; her father had died when she was six years of age), sitting on the verandah in the shade of the thatched overhang of the roof, became conscious that someone was watching her.

She looked up from the book she was reading; it was quiet, the heat oppressive, not a leaf rustled. It was late afternoon, two hours to sundown, no mad dogs or Englishmen astir. She stood, leant forward, brushed her blonde hair back, screwed up her eyes against the glare of the sun to discern a figure standing, blending with the shadow of a tree on the perimeter of the open play area. Blinked a couple of times, her mouth opened with surprise, she leapt down the steps from the verandah and ran.

Chalkie dropped his backpack, came to meet her. Grace embraced him, her arms around his waist, cried out, 'Chalkie, oh Chalkie, I knew you would come, I knew it.'

'Yer remember me then, it's been three years, and my, my, how you've grown.'

'Of course, look, the bracelet you gave me.' She held her arm up to show him. 'And I remember all about the London trams you told me about, how the front can be the back, and the back can be the front, so they can be driven from either end, and they have stairs with seats on top. I heard the army truck arrive earlier, you must have come on that, yes?

'Yes, I'll tell yer about it later.' Chalkie hesitated. 'Is yer mother all right, is she well?'

'Yes, she is fine, resting; come, Chalkie, let's surprise her.'

Chalkie hurriedly brushed across his eyelids with a knuckle, picked up his pack, slung it over one shoulder, felt slim fingers slide into a palm of one hand, and dutifully let himself be led away with a song in his heart.

They stopped at the foot of the steps to the verandah.

'I'll wait here,' Chalkie said.

'No, no, come in, Chalkie.'

'Please, Grace, just tell yer mum there is someone wants to light a candle.'

'Oh.' Grace's face showed disappointment. 'You came all this way to light a candle; I thought you had—'

'No, no, Grace, I came to see both of you, but I also promised I would light a candle for a fallen friend. I brought something for yer, so there, yer must believe me.'

'You did? Can I see?'

'Later, Grace. Please just tell yer mum what I said; she will understand.'

Grace smiled. 'I believe you, Chalkie.'


Five minutes later, Rose Ayerling appeared on the verandah.

'Chalkie, it is so good to see you again,' Rose exclaimed. 'I knew it was you when Grace told me someone wanted to light a candle. We prayed for you.'

'I reckoned yer must 'ave done, Rose, as I survived; been to 'ell and back, but no talk of that.'

Rose stepped down from the verandah, came forward with arms outstretched.

'No black fingernails this time, Rose,' Chalkie said as Rose took both of his hands in hers.

'No more soldiering then, Chalkie; come, let's go inside, you can light a candle whenever.'

'Later, Rose, let's have a chat first, I want to take my time, 'ave a chat wiv 'im up above at the same time.'

'Are yer expecting a lass from England, Rose?' Chalkie asked after they were seated comfortably inside.

'Yes we are, but no actual date when she may get here.'

'Well, she is at the fort; we travelled here together wiv two soldiers back from leave, and another two ex-soldiers. We were given some refreshments, the officers have the lass cornered in their mess, yer know what I mean, a fresh white woman from England, quite an advent, making a fuss of her. One of them will escort her here sooner than later. I left as soon as I could, couldn't wait to set eyes on yer both.'

'Bless you, Chalkie. So we will have quite a community here. I see you have a pack with you, so before you ask, you are welcome to stay here.'

'Ta, Rose, I was hoping so. I can kip anywhere, yer know that, make one of those... bashas, gidas, huts, whatever yer call them out back, plenty of room, no trouble.'

'You seemed to have worked it all out, Chalkie.' Rose smiled. 'Meanwhile you can have the sick bay, it's empty, class you as a patient.'

Back at the fort, Chas and Michael, being fed and watered, were warned by Captain Reid, 'You don't know a Major Blankensy if anyone asks you.'

In the officers' mess Barbara, like Chalkie, was a little out of her depth; never in all her life had she had that much attention paid to her. She was concerned, aware of time passing; finally she asked the colonel to be excused. 'I really should let the mission know I have arrived.'

'Of course, young lady, Captain Reid will escort you.' Nodded at Reid. 'And I want a word with you when you get back.'

'Yes, sir.'

At the mission, Chalkie laid his pack on the table at which the three of them were sitting, opened it and fumbled with one hand in the contents.

'That's funny,' he said. 'I must 'ave left it on the boat, could 'ave dropped out when I was packing.' And he winked at Rose.

'I saw that,' said Grace.

'Saw what?'

'You winked.'

Chalkie chuckled. 'Can't hoodwink yer now yer grown up, eh?' He took a small parcel from the pack and handed it to Grace, who opened it to expose a bottle of ink.

'Oh! Ink, Chalkie,' Grace said, trying to hide her disappointment.

'It's the best, yer know. Stevens ink. But no good wivout this.' And Chalkie produced another slim wrapped parcel and passed it over. Grace's face lit up, and she tore the wrapping off, opened a narrow box and held the object up. Frowned.

'What is it, Chalkie? Never seen one like this; is it a pen?'

'Yeah, a fountain pen, no more inky fingers; yer fill it up and yer writes, don't 'ave to keep dipping a nib in the ink.'

'How does it work?'

'I'll show yer. See that lever at the side? Yer puts the nib in the ink, lift that lever—'

'Oh, can I do it, Chalkie?'

'Yeah, carry on, yer work it out, and yer name is inscribed on the lever; it's silver, yer know.'

316

'Oh, thank you, Chalkie.' Grace leant over and kissed Chalkie on the cheek.

'Yer musn't do that, Grace, not allowed.'

'Why not?'

''Cos I don't fink I could wash that cheek any more.'

They laughed.

'I've got somefing else, but that'll be for tomorrow.'

'Oh, Chalkie, please.'

'I fink yer mum should 'ave 'er present now, don't yer fink?'

'Of course, sorry, I was being selfish.'

'No, yer wasn't finking, that's all.'

Chalkie dived into his pack and brought out two books. Handed one to Rose. 'For you, Rose, as we are in Africa. PC Wren, *Cupid in Africa*. Just published, and as yer can't wait, Rudyard Kipling for you, Grace. That'll do for today.'

'Thanks, Chalkie, I must have read the books I have time after time.'

At that moment footsteps were heard on the verandah, and Captain Reid appeared in the doorway.

'Hullo, Rose, Grace. Nice to see you again; I see Chalkie has his feet under the table already. I have brought a newcomer; may I introduce Miss Barbara Evans? A welcome face to our community.' He held an arm out for Barbara to step forward. 'Barbara, Rose, and her daughter Grace.'

'Thank you, Captain,' Rose said as she embraced Barbara. 'We've been expecting you, but no time given.'

'Can't stay, more's the pity,' Captain Reid said. 'The colonel wants a word with me, and you know what that means.' He shook hands with Barbara. Nodded at Rose. 'I'll call again, Rose.' Saluted and left.

Barbara was pleased to see Chalkie's smiling face as she was made welcome.

317

'Sit down, please, Barbara, you must be tired after the journey from the coast and trying to contend with the heat. I'll make some tea, then I'll show you to your quarters, a single room I'm afraid. Tomorrow we can discuss the running of the mission and your role, Grace can show you Kumasi, meanwhile take it easy. We have plenty of time, no hustle and bustle here, and you can always lean on Chalkie; he's been here before.'

'Yer know that, Barbara,' Chalkie said. 'Yer in good 'ands 'ere. I'll leave you ladies to 'ave a chat, go and light a candle for Mike if that's all right, Rose?'

'Of course, Chalkie; do you want me to come with you?'

'I can do it myself this time, Rose, and I 'ave a shamrock; Mike asked me to pick one for him. I did, 'ad to go to Ireland, it's the only place they grow, yer knows. I 'as it wiv me.'

'Can I see?' Grace asked.

''Course,' Chalkie said. Took an envelope from his pocket to show her.

'There is more than one, Chalkie.'

'Yeah, fought I'd get spares.'

'I'll get a prayer book, Chalkie, press them between the leaves,' Rose said, looking over Chalkie's shoulder.

'Good idea, Rose.'

Rose did the best she could with the dried leaves, gave the prayer book to Chalkie, who left.


At the fort, Captain Reid with cap in hand made his way to report to the colonel, who had retired to his office after Barbara had left.

'You wanted to see me, sir,' Reid stated rather than asked, after he had knocked and entered.

'More than that, I want some answers,' the colonel growled. 'How come you took upon yourself to arrange board and lodgings for two civilians here in the fort?'

318

'It is only temporary, sir, and strictly speaking they are military, both regular sergeants, served their time, Roberts awarded the MM and on a month's leave before transfer to reserve.' Reid crossed his fingers as he spoke.

'So why have they come here of all places. The so-called "white man's graveyard"? It's no holiday resort.'

'It is quite some story, sir.'

'Fairy story?'

'No, sir. Hard to believe, but true. Mansfield and I were involved.'

'Not up to hanky-panky on leave?'

'No, sir, it happened.'

'You had better sit down and tell me how it happened, then, and it had better be good. Incidentally, I never heard from Major Blankensy. He promised to write; did you catch up with him, or find out if he was posted to France?'

'Never saw him, but...' Reid paused.

'But what, Reid, for Chrissake?'

'It is all in what I have to relate, sir.'

'Well, get on with it.'

Reid sat and began.

Chalkie, bareheaded, stood for a few moments before he stepped inside the small chapel.

A few empty rows of wooden forms waited each side of an aisle. He stopped and looked up at the ceiling; his lips formed words.

*I've come back, mister, like I said I would to light a candle for Mike. I hope yer looked after 'im as I asked yer to. 'e was a good bloke, went to mass when 'e could, not like me, but now I'm staying at the mission; yer can never tell.*

He went forward to where a candle stood – a sentinel – guarding a cross mounted on a black polished wooden table, the wick curled, beckoning to be lit.

*Is that for me? No, light a penny candle from the stars, yer said, Mike. I've brought one, cost a penny, could 'ave got one for 'a'pence, but yer said a penny one. I'll 'ave to light it wiv a Lucifer, yer knows that, I'm not Irish, and I picked a shamrock wot yer asked for, got it pressed between the leaves of a prayer book that Rose 'ere at the mission gave me, yeah, me of all people, who'd 'ave fought that? I fought I'd let yer know that bas— Gawd, I nearly swore, not allowed in 'ere – Swartz, 'im that did it to yer, got 'is rhubarb and custard, we rolled 'im in the crap trench wiv a knife in 'is gizzard. 'e gurgled. I met a lass on the boat from the smoke like me, so we talk the same lingo, she's gonner work at the mission, and I'm staying there, so can pop in and 'ave a chat.*

Chalkie took a candle from his pocket, struck a light and lit the wick, placed it firmly in a holder, moved back and sat on the foremost bench and watched the flame burn.

*Waited three years to do that.*

Inside the mission quarters, Barbara sipped the last of her tea. Beads of perspiration formed on her brow. Rose noticed that. Said, 'Shall we sit on the verandah? It may be a mite cooler. You can tell us how it came about, you joining us here, and a little of yourself. That's if you are not too tired.'

'That would be nice; it is rather hot. It was when we left England. A heatwave, we call it, the subject of most tongues back home the weather when meeting. "Is it going to rain?" "Looks like snow coming", or "It's a lovely day".'

'Here we know what the weather will be. Hot, and when the rains come.'

The three of them, Barbara, Rose and Grace moved to the verandah and sat. Shadows lengthened and disappeared as the sun bowed out, the stars taking over in an inky blue sky.

320

The sudden change surprised Barbara, who remarked on it.

'Much the same time every day,' Rose told her. 'Think six o'clock sundown. The sun does set in this part of the British Empire.'

'You asked me how I came to be here, Rose,' Barbara said. 'It was destiny, as Chalkie told me when I met him on the boat and he heard I was heading for Kumasi. But who decides one's destiny? A divine power? I was a Salvation Army lass, never heard of Ashanti until I met this old soldier with a wooden leg.' Barbara stood. 'Excuse me, I have something to show you; I'll fetch it; it may shed some light on the events that led me here.'

Barbara on her return handed the necklace of gold stool and chain to Rose. 'If Chalkie was right, my destiny was to return this to the rightful owner.'

'Good gracious,' exclaimed Rose. 'Where did you – how did you come by it?'

Barbara sat down. 'It was placed in a collection pouch, the one I used when a Salvation Lass.'

'This is the necklace that the princess wore. Did you know that?'

'Not at the time, later. Captain Reid told me when I showed it to him whilst aboard ship.'

'I know the princess gave it to her son to wear when he left for England to attend boarding school. So whoever placed it in the collection must have stolen it from Richard, that was his name, and killed for it. Did you know that?'

'I did not know it was a son of a princess, or that he was wearing the necklace. Nothing mentioned in the newspapers as to the name or the necklace.'

'Did you know who placed it in the collection?'

'Not at the time, I did discover who later.' Barbara paused, closed her eyes, blinked a couple of times, wiped her eyelashes with a finger.

'You all right, Barbara?' Rose asked.

'Yes, a little upsetting, the memory. It was someone I met; he helped with the collection at times. We became close friends. I guessed it must have been him, he admitted it after I had challenged him, told me that I would know what to do with it. Those were the last words he said to me. He was killed.'

'Oh my God.' Rose placed a hand on her lips. 'There is more to this than meets the eye; are you up to the telling?'

Barbara nodded.

Rose turned to Grace. 'Will you fetch some water, please, and squeeze a lime? I'm sure Barbara would like something to moisten her lips.'

'It was a remark made by that old soldier with the wooden leg,' Barbara began after taking a sip of the water Grace had brought. Rose leant back in her chair and listened intently as Barbara related how it had come about.

'Incredible,' Rose said when Barbara had finished. 'But it is said truth is stranger than fiction. You may think it strange, Barbara, if I tell you that I believe there is intrigue woven into the events you have related, by another hand that brought them about. The princess and I are good friends. I attended her ills, acted as midwife at the birth of her son, held him in my arms, was his tutor-mentor, watched him take his first steps. I know who the father is. A young white soldier, here with the British Army in 1900, saved the princess from being raped by a drunken soldier. She gave him the necklace that she wore, the one you brought. Told him to wear it during the war, that was the Ashanti war; it would protect him. It did, saved his life. He returned it to her when the war finished and he left for England. The princess was 17 at the time, madly in love with this man, wanted his child. Such is destiny. He came back in 1914, this time as a captain. They met again. He met the boy, did not know it was his son, she never told him. He served in the Togoland and Cameroon campaigns, then left when that ended. And as I mentioned, the princess gave the necklace to her son to wear when he left.' Rose paused, took a sip of water, dabbed her lips and carried on.

'How do I know who was the father, or I should say "is the father", you may be thinking. I am a woman; that's all I can tell you at present. Tomorrow I will take you to the princess; you will also meet Okomfo Anokye. A sage – seer – manipulator, a shadow in the background with power. His word is law with the Ashanti. A divine power, I will add.'

'D'yer mind if I join yer ladies?' A voice from the shadows and Chalkie came into view.

'Didn't hear you coming, Chalkie, engrossed in what Barbara was telling us,' Rose called out. 'Join us, please; you need to bring a chair from inside, the bench can't take four of us.'

'That will be one of the first jobs to do, make another bench,' Chalkie said after he had brought a chair and sat facing them. 'I take it Barbara has told you how it came about that she came here; some experience, eh?' He nodded to Barbara. 'That's good, get it off yer chest, put at the back of yer mind, look to a new life wiv good friends.'

'And you, Chalkie. Did you light a candle for Mike?'

'Yeah, said me piece 'ow yer told me to do last time I was 'ere, Rose, three years ago, just seems like yesterday.'

'That's fine, Chalkie, now would you like a drink of lime water?'

'Lime water! Eh – yeah, yeah. Ta.'

Back in the fort, the colonel leant back in his chair, shook his head in disbelief after listening to what Captain Reid had told him.

'You stumbled in on a murder scene and picked up the murder weapon? Is that what you are telling me? You must have been out of your mind. You should have gone to the police.'

'You may well say that, sir; it was too late, my fingerprints on the revolver. I know I made a mistake. It was quite a shock seeing that body covered with flies, then discovering it wasn't the major. The police would have had me banged up for murder. Even if I had wiped my prints off, it wouldn't have taken them long to find out we, Mansfield and I had been there – the taxi driver would know, for one thing, and we had got the address from the regiment that the major had been posted to. Bear in mind we did not know at that time that Roberts had been charged with murder. Right or wrong, I decided to take the revolver.'

'So later you decided to write to the police, tell them it wasn't Major Blankensy to clear his name from the charge of sending a platoon to their death. Also that let Roberts off the hook, or from the noose, should I say?'

'Yes, that's right, let the police puzzle it out.'

'So then you met Roberts and O'Leary on the ship, and it all came out. Why didn't they leave the ship at Gib, it being a British port, and return home?'

'You won't believe this. To make their fortune, find MacCarthy's golden skull.'

'What?' The colonel almost leapt out of his chair. 'Oh for Chrissake, I've heard it all now, bring me a straitjacket, no, two. Now we have two *mad* Englishmen out in the midday sun; why not a pot of gold at the end of a rainbow, or King Solomon's mine whilst they're at it?'

'One of them is Irish, sir.'

'Oh, so that makes it OK, does it?' The colonel shook his head, began to chuckle, couldn't contain himself and burst out laughing. 'Irish, didn't fancy digging for gold in the streets of London, decided to do so here. I guess it was his idea? How did he know the history of MacCarthy's golden skull?'

'His father told him, served here in 1900 at the siege of the fort, was part of the relieving force.'

'And he believed it, O'Leary?'

'Well, it did happen, although it was about a hundred years ago. We know the skull was paraded every year at the festival of the yams, passed on from king to king until Prempeh was defeated and exiled. His treasure was never discovered. Strange that O'Leary turns up here at the time when Prempeh is due any day. One never knows. The luck of the Irish? O'Leary might just find it.'

'Hung upside down by his heels to kiss the Blarney Stone – of course – and cajoled Roberts into joining him. Well, kiss my arse. Told you this aboard the ship, did he?'

'Not that he had kissed the Blarney Stone, sir.'

'Reid, you trying to be flippant?'

'Sorry, sir.'

'All right, I've heard enough of the Irish. This body you found on leave, did you know who it was?'

'No, sir.'

'So we don't know what happened to the major. I'll inform the regiment that Major Blankensy was killed in action on the western front. Leave it at that, you don't know any different if anyone asks. O'Leary came to see where his father fought, and Roberts came as a companion – mate – whatever, and tell them to keep their mouths shut about what happened in London. You understand?'

'Yes, sir.'

'They can stay for a week in the fort, no longer. Have a word with the QMS on the side to issue them with KD; you didn't hear that from me. I don't want them walking about improperly dressed.'

'Yes, sir.'

The subject of the colonel's merriment and sarcasm, O'Leary, was placing a number of bottles on the shelf of a locker. Both he and Roberts were unpacking their few belongings having been allocated quarters, issued with camp beds complete with mosquito nets and rods to support them. 'Have to share a room, best I can do,' the RSM had told them.

'What's in the bottles, Michael?' Chas asked. 'Did you bring them all the way from home?'

'Quinine. My dad told me, if you ever get to go to the Gold Coast, take quinine; it's worth its weight in gold. A life-saver against malaria. I asked Grace to buy it for me, she knew the local chemist in Camden Town. No problem.'

'You never said.'

'No need to, we had other things on our minds. You were banged up in Albany Street clink, I was making plans to get you out.'

'Talking of clink, I never thought in my wildest of dreams it would happen, what you told me when we were in the glasshouse. But we are here, in the fort where your father stood those 20 years ago.' Chas paused. 'Quinine, eh? Let's hope we don't get malaria. We have been lucky so far, getting a cheap passage, and now quarters here for a bit.' Chas paused again, stroked his chin, shook his head. 'We are not gonner find this golden skull, are we, Michael? So what are your plans?'

'Keep our eyes and ears to the ground; it's called the Gold Coast, got to be gold here. Don't want to have to go back empty handed.'


*Sunrise in Kumasi*

The first rays of sun filtered through a fine mesh, mounted on a wooden frame, that covered a vent cut in the outer mission wall above eye level. It shed the pattern of a mosquito net on the sleeper beneath.

Barbara 'came to' rather than waking fully, her senses dulled by the humidity and heat. She reached out and felt the mosquito net; realisation came. Chalkie joining the three women on the verandah, reminiscing on past escapades, retiring with 'make sure you tuck the mosquito net in, Barbara,' unable to sleep, perspiring in the lightest of night dresses until finally eyelids, heavy, registered sleep.

A knock on the door, a voice called out, 'You decent, Barbara? Can I come in? It's Rose,' brought her back to the present.

'Yes, yes, of course,' Barbara answered. Drew back the mosquito net, swung her legs over the edge of the bed and stood. 'Am I late?' she asked as Rose entered.

'No, not at all, I am an early riser, have a rest in the afternoon. Did you sleep all right?'

'Eventually, not accustomed to the heat.'

'This is the hottest time of the year; it will ease off a little after the rains, due in a couple of weeks' time. Milly, one of our helpers, will bring you some water; we have no running water here, ablutions rather primitive I'm afraid. After breakfast we go to meet the princess.'

'Does she know?'

'Okomfo Anokye will have told her.'

'But how does he know?'

'He knows, believe me.'

Chalkie White bedded down in the sick bay, woke to the faint sound of a bugle calling reveille at the fort.

*Blimey, I thought I was back in the barrack room for a moment. Reveille! Not for me ald cock it ain't.* Placed both hands behind his neck, lay back and closed his eyes.

Both Chas and Michael heard it, louder than Chalkie did. 'Hope they don't expect us to parade, Michael,' Chas said.

'Guess wot?' Chalkie announced over breakfast at the mission. 'When I unpacked last night this came to light, anovver one of them PC Wren books – *Beau Geste* – for you, Rose. Fancy me forgetting, eh?' He winked at her. 'But I couldn't forget a paint box, or could I? Right down at the bottom of me pack, 'as to be for you, Grace, I can't paint for toffees, it's got brushes as well, yer mix 'em wiv water, so expect some nice pictures to 'ang on the walls.'

'Oh, thanks, Chalkie.' Grace came and gave him a hug.

'That's not allowed, yer know, and I've got a pack of playing cards, teach yer 'ow to play patience, keep yer out of mischief.'

### *The palace courtyard*

Okomfo Anokye, sitting alongside Princess Ayaa Ansa, suddenly stood and raised an arm. 'Listen,' he said.

'What is it, Okomfo?'

'The drums. Prempeh has left Cape Point; he's on the way.'

'How long before he arrives?'

'Within three days.'

At the entrance to the palace courtyard, Rose stopped.

'I will wait here, Barbara, you go to the princess; that is Okomfo standing next to her. There is nothing to fear; you will become friends. Trust me.'

The princess saw Barbara coming; she rose and came to meet her. They met and the necklace with the golden stool came back to Kumasi.

## Jones the Baker's, Camden Town, London

London was bracing itself for a heatwave according to weather forecasts, similar to that of last summer.

Grace Jones, placing the newly fresh cooked pastries in the glass cabinet on the counter, suddenly stopped transfixed. Cried out 'Michael!' then whispered, 'Michael?' Her face lit up, and with no more ado, she ducked under the counter flap and was out of the door before one could say Jack Robinson.

'Don't stand gaping, Gwyneth,' Mrs Jones said. 'Go.'

Michael and Chas were a few steps into Delancey Street from Camden High Street when Grace came into sight, running, closely followed by Gwyneth.

'Wait for the onslaught, Chas,' Michael said. 'We are in for a beating or a hug. How did they know we were here?'

'Celtic' was the one word he could get out before the girls reached them.

Grace was the first. She moulded herself to Michael, her arms embraced him, her cheek against his chest. Gwyneth, a close second, embraced Chas.

The bookie's runner standing at the corner looked on with amazement.

*Crikey, the big 'un and 'is mate back. No odds on as to what will 'appen next; they're trapped, poor sods, the girls ain't gonner let go now. I should be so lucky. I'll get meself a cuppa in the shop later, see wot's in the wind.*

'A Detective Sergeant Bancroft came to see us after you had both left,' Grace said. 'Told us that the charge against you, Chas, had been dropped, and you had been released.'

They were sitting comfortably in the living room on the first floor, Grace snuggled up to Michael, taking up the sofa, Chas in an armchair, one hand on Gwyneth's shoulder. Gwyneth herself sat on the floor, a hand on Chas's, one arm across her breast. It was after the initial welcome, handshakes from Clive Jones and his father Colin, a hug from Mrs Jones, who had taken charge; being a woman, knowing what the girls would want, she had given the orders, '*Take the lads upstairs, girls. You have something left in the oven to see to, Colin, yes? You, Clive, can keep an eye on the shop while I'll rustle up a meal for the lads.*'

'He would, wouldn't he?' Chas said. 'Didn't want custard all over the CID faces. That must have been after he or whoever received the letter from Captain Reid. Didn't want to admit that Michael had sprung me from jail.'

'Captain Reid? Where did he come into the picture?' Grace asked.

Michael looked at Chas.

'You do the talking, Chas.'

So Chas related how it all had come about up until the time they had ended up in the fort at Kumasi.

'I can hardly believe this, it's like a tale from the Arabian Nights; you really didn't think you could find this golden skull, surely?' Gwyneth asked. 'But gold or no gold, we are over the moon to have you back. Right, Grace?'

'Absolutely. Nevertheless, there is more to add, I would think, so what happened next?'

'Your turn, Michael, you carry on as you were the one involved more than me,' Chas told him.

'Right or wrong,' Michael began, 'I got to see the fort, stay in it, and of course Chas did too – the one that my father had fought in for the relief of the siege in 1900. I did not know that Prempeh, who was the king at that time, had been exiled and was due back any day until we arrived on the coast to see all the banners and whatnot. That seemed to me an omen, him gonner be there the same time as us, might get a chance to have a word with him; if anyone, he would be the one to know where the gold skull was. A couple of weeks later he turns up, wearing a bowler hat; whether he thought he was an ex-guards officer in mufti or a butler that had worked for a lord of the manor is anyone's guess.

'Two weeks later, the rains came, torrential rain; every pool, the smallest of receptacles that could hold an inch of water was a breeding heaven for mosquitoes. I guess Prempeh, living in a malaria-free country for 20 years, came back at the wrong time, slept without a mosquito net. I don't know so, but he went down with malaria. *Male aria* – "bad air". For years it was thought bad air caused the fever, hence the name. Quinine was not available for the indigenes, but I had plenty; remember, Grace, I asked you to buy as much as you could as my father had told me to take some if I ever I went to the Gold Coast. The long and short of it was that I gave a bottle to Rose, the missionary who was treating Prempeh, enough for a dozen doses, one a day. It was touch and go for him, but he survived. Rose told him it was the quinine that I had given. He wanted to thank me, said I had saved his life. This was my opportunity to have a word with him. Took the bull by the horns, asked him outright if he knew where MacCarthy's skull was buried. He laughed. Said, "That was before my time, almost a hundred years ago when King Osei Bonsu cut off MacCarthy's head. I couldn't parade it like he did; it would have started another war; we'd had enough warring about the golden stool. No, it was melted down." Then he asked me if it was the gold cast I was after. I admitted it was. "I can give you some gold for saving my life," he told me, "and if you have any more quinine, more gold for that."'

Michael paused. 'Pure gold. You don't believe me, do you?'

'Sounds like another of those Arabian Nights tales,' Grace said. 'Enough for a wedding ring?'

'For two,' Gwyneth added.

Michael laughed. Looked at Chas, who nodded.

'Yes, twice,' Michael said. 'And plenty left over.'


## 85 Arlington Road, London

Alice sat by the bay window watching the world go by as was her ritual after breakfast. The bottom half of the sash window raised, fitting neatly behind the top half, allowing the slight breeze to enter. She blinked a couple of times, leant forward. Murmured, 'Déjà vu.' Called out, 'Clara, come and see.'

Clara came and looked over Alice's shoulder. 'See what?'

Alice pointed to the two couples, arm in arm, laughing and joking, passing by on the opposite side of the road.

'The two Jones girls with the same two men I saw last year. One that entered the flat where the murder took place whilst the big one waited outside.'

'So? They look happy, off to the park I should imagine. We never heard from your detective friend, the one that liked sarsaparilla, as to who it was that was killed and who did it.'

Lt Col Stoney MC CRE stood smiling at the assembly in the officers' mess.

'Thank you all for this turn out at my retirement, and for this parting gift.' He held a gold 'Hunter' and chain high. 'No need to listen for reveille; I shall look at this to know the time to rise, turn over and close my eyes again.'

Laughter from the assembly. A captain stood. Called out, 'Charge your glasses, gentlemen; a toast to the colonel.'

Glasses were raised. Voices called, 'To the colonel'; glasses were drained and banged down on the table.

The colonel sat, picked up the sealed envelope that had been weighed down by the wrapped present on the table, opened it to read the typewritten words.

*Sir. For peace of mind on retirement. I showed him the straw, he understood. I gave him a choice. He used his own revolver. I left the straw.*